the art of *Me*

s.j.blaze

THE ART OF ME

This book is a work of fiction. While reference might be made to actual historical events or existing locations, the names, characters, places and incidents are either the property of the author's imagination or are used fictitiously, and any resemblance to actual person, living or dead, business establishments, events, or locales are entirely coincidental.

Book Cover Design by Marisa Rose Shor of Cover Me Darlings
Art by Jacob Elbaz
Interior Design and Formatting by The Killion Group, Inc.
www.thekilliongroupinc.com
Edited by Keidi Keating of Your Book Angel
Proofread by Laura Floyd
Published by CreateSpace

Dedication

I'd like to dedicate this book to everyone with a forgotten dream.
Those of you bogged down with life, with family,
and with simply living that your
'Once Upon a Time' dreams become a distant fuzzy memory.
May all of your dreams find their way towards reality....
It is NEVER too late!

AND...

To Noah...
The biggest cheerleader I never knew I had.
To Gabriel...
Gifting me a new fairytale land to explore by your side.

Chapter 1

COCKY ASS!

An anatomical impossibility, yes...and yet, there he is. Staring.

Just staring at me. I'm doing my best to keep my face impassive. Aloof. I don't want him to know I've noticed him. He shifts in his chair placing his elbow on the conference table while rubbing his bottom lip, smirking and brazenly checking me out.

I shift my gaze to the man next to him, Greyson Collins, CEO of Collins Corp, also known as Cocky Ass' dad. Would that make him Cocky Ass Senior? Most likely, as he exudes the same degree of superiority. I bet he's even banging his secretary just because he can. Despite his age, probably in his late sixties, his salt and pepper hair meticulously styled and gelled into place along with those broad shoulders and his billions in the bank…I bet he has no problem warming his bed at night. He's so busy eating up Brantley's ass kissing, he doesn't notice his son's incongruous behavior.

Sitting next to me across from Cocky, Tom clears his throat. "Well, gentlemen, should we begin?"

Greyson claps his hands and agrees. "That's a great idea. Let's get started." He tilts his head to the side while shifting his eyes to me. Great…now I'm stuck in a double Collins showdown. The Asses versus me. "Since this is a rather sensitive agreement," Greyson continues, "I think only necessary personnel are required."

With that foreboding statement, a third of the table on the Collins Corp side stand and leave the room in silence. A gorgeous tall blonde woman with the tightest royal blue dress that stops about two inches below her crotch, bends over to address Greyson. She whispers in his ear while tucking a curly lock into place. She's flawless and probably spends hours working on her makeup and hair. I hate her! He keeps his eyes fixed on me while agreeing with whatever she says. Ah yes, I was right, he's definitely getting some at the office. She nods, smiles flirtatiously at Cocky then walks out of the room. That's interesting. Maybe two Collins for the price of one?

Olivia, Brantley's secretary, who's been standing to the side serving coffee, leaves just as quietly. You can hear a pin drop. Greyson clears his throat and raises his brows at me expectantly. Cocky leans forward and smiles. "Sweetheart, we're gonna need you to leave the room." He speaks the words slowly as if I'm an idiot, articulating every word. I continue staring impassively. Inside though, I'm stewing. Sadly, this isn't the first time I've been dismissed on my looks. My jet black straight hair is pulled into a crazy tight bun at the nape of my neck, while my glasses hide grey eyes that are sporting some light mascara today. My face is makeup free showcasing my freckles loud and clear while my lips are painted a nude gloss. My top is a pale pink fully buttoned top, hidden under the oversized navy blazer from my pant suit.

I'm certainly not flaunting any of my goods.

Brantley and Tom look at each other, confused. "Coen, but you specifically asked for her," Brantley says.

Greyson looks aghast. "We wanted Charlie Paz. He's the one we were told to usher us into this trillion-dollar deal. That's why we're here!" His face is flushed. Poor billionaire. "Not some teenage girl with pubescent feminine issues." I nearly chuckle.

Tom finally speaks up. "But this *is* Charlie!"

"NO!" Greyson spits. Cocky Coen furrows his brows and his bottom lip juts out a bit. He has nice full pink lips. They look soft. Wait…why am I noticing that?

"Charlie is a brilliant corporate lawyer straight out of Harvard's upper crust. I've heard from at least three of my cohorts that he's saved them hundreds of millions. Where's that guy? I want that guy! That's why we came to your firm."

I fight the urge to stand, cup my tits, and scream…*does this look like a guy to you, Cocky?* But alas, I do not.

Olivia peeks her head in. "Excuse me." She looks nervous as she shuffles over to me and drops a memo on the table. I casually look it over as I contemplate my next move. It's the Boys and Girls Club. I sometimes do pro bono work for them, mainly on the big cases, as I'm not really a trial lawyer. But let's face it, the public defender's office doesn't have loads of time to dedicate to some of these kids. And in Boston, we have all sorts of troubled youth in need of a hand out or a hand up.

Looks like I now have my exit strategy.

I start gathering my papers, while listening to the men argue about whether or not I'm the real 'Charlie.' As if the partners would trick the exalted Greyson. Feeling eyes on me, I glance up to see Coen is still studying me. Dismissing him with an unladylike eye roll, I stand and capture the room's attention.

"Well, this has been vacillating! However, it does appear I'm needed and wanted elsewhere." With my papers firmly clutched to my chest, I begin to walk towards the door. "Oh, I nearly forgot. Despite not having the proper documents from the Collins Corp legal team to review, I found out that your amended Certificate of Authority has been declined by the state, so that's going to put you behind your target date. Not to mention that the Consent Resolution is unachievable at this point. That is, if you'd like to avoid dissolution." I keep charging on. I knew it would come to this and I'd be dismissed. I had to be prepared. "I did discover that Prête Managerie, a subsidiary of Renault Matre, the company you're merging with, is preparing its partners for bankruptcy. That's a possibility of millions coming directly out of your pocket. Not to mention that despite what you've been told and are paying for, I have it on good authority that the revenue shares from this quarter have taken an abysmal nose dive. At least a double digit loss is predicted." I take a deep breath, relishing the confused twin looks from father and son Cocky.

"But it's obvious you don't *need me*. I'm sure your legal team is on this. I'm sure they have the critical experience in International Law and a full understanding of the French legal system that they can navigate their way through. You certainly don't need a, what did you call it again, a teenage girl with pubescent feminine issues and a Harvard law degree to step in your way. Good day, gentlemen."

I leave the gaping faces and exit the boardroom. I finally crack the smile that's been dying to come out for the last fifteen minutes. Relieved that I'd got out of there before I said something too offensive, I walk down the hall to my office, and despite my need to scream and slam my door, I do neither. Instead, I delicately close it and lean my head against it. The audacity of those arrogant pricks. I feel both smug and utterly disappointed at once. You'd think I'd be used to this by now. I bite my lip to muffle the groan that slips out. Shit, get it together. Walking to my desk, I throw the papers down and rip off my jacket. I'm burning up. The flush on my face is climbing down my neck. Why did Cocky keep looking at me? I roll up my sleeves, undo a few top buttons, and grab my purse from the desk drawer.

Walking out of my office and over to Olivia's desk, I'm about to let her know that I'll be out of the office for the remainder of the day when I notice the boardroom door swings open. Coen looks furious while jerking his head around. My instincts tell me to move, so I do. I give Olivia a slight wave and hustle towards the elevator. But it's too late. I can feel his eyes on me.

I wait nervously - pushing the button down over and over again as if that will speed the elevator along. I feel Coen creep closer. "Charlie..."

Oh, so now I'm Charlie. Where was he ten minutes ago?

The elevator doors finally open, and I slide in without responding. I turn to push the first floor when Coen climbs in. He leans back against the wall crossing his arms over his broad chest and crosses his feet at his ankles. I face forward while watching him in my periphery vision. His crisp grey suit is tailored to mold to his body perfectly. He's wearing a violet button up with a paisley tie in vivid purples, blues, and grays. All the while, those beautiful ice blue eyes are shooting in my direction. His dark blonde hair is short on top but longer on the sides as it curls slightly at his ears.

"It's unfortunate." His voice is smooth, serene, yet careful.

He's baiting me. He wants me to engage. Not today, Cocky. I remain still and wait for him to resume. I know he's dying to. He continues staring at me and sighs, having figured out that I won't respond. He's quicker than I originally gave him credit for.

"It's unfortunate that you think you got away today. Your little display has only sealed your fate."

To what is he referring? That I'm now locked into position on his legal team? Yes, I'm sure that's it.

Although the guy is cocky, I suppose he's earned that right. He's been linked to some of the most stunning women in the North-east, even models and a few actresses. I'm surprised they haven't given him his own show to pass out roses - he's so high in demand.

But that's just the shell.

The cover art.

It's just skin and shapely muscled bones drowning out what looms inside.

We're so busy gawking and drooling that we don't see what the beauty hides beneath. I know this all too well.

Shit, I perpetuate that theory.

That's where I live. That's where I hide.

Despite this tempting eye-gasm, I'm not interested. I have too much on my plate. I look up studying the numbers continually descend, and as the elevator reaches ground level, I finally speak up. "Yes. Have a good day, Mr. Collins."

It's like I'm agreeing to some unknown tragedy. It's unavoidable, though. The partners will demand I stay involved on this deal and my path will cross with Cocky et. al. I bite my tongue to stop any further conversing. I want this little chat over and done with. The doors finally open, offering a new sense of freedom that the enclosed space has denied me.

"It's Coen, love."

I nod once and walk out. I hear him chuckling softly behind me as I walk to the parking garage.

He's following me, but soon I feel his presence dissipate. He's gone. It's for the best.

Chapter 2

HIS HAND FIRMLY LOCKED ON my bare shoulder, I feel his thumb run small circles in the solitary place. Over and over. It's both soothing and semi-annoying. He leans over and kisses the other shoulder, his breath warm and his soft lips lingering. All the while he continues talking to the three elder gentlemen engrossed in the dissolutions that politics bring. My eyes are practically rolling in my head, I'm so bored. But my mind isn't needed tonight. Nope, I'm a show pony. A trophy on the arm of a powerful man.

I've been dating Andrew for about four months. You would think that amounts to a solid relationship, but with his constant travelling, we barely see each other. Congressman Andrew Carpenter is a very busy man indeed. The people of Boston adore him. His father, Governor William Carpenter of the great Commonwealth of Massachusetts, has high political aspirations for his son. The White House kind.

We met at a charity function, much like this one. He pursued me relentlessly until I finally gave in. He's not bad, though. His brown hair is tightly groomed to his nicely shaped head. Face clean. Strong features. He's probably just shy of six feet, on the thin side, but not disturbingly so. He's attractive, although not 'Stop the Presses' attractive. But he's sweet to me. And at times he makes me laugh.

He's tolerable and suits my needs. He's not the least bit threatening to me. He doesn't know me…not the real me. Only the art I display.

I look around the grandeur of the room. The Hotel Commonwealth is elegantly charming, perfect for this evening's endeavors and it's easy to get lost in its beauty.

Circle, circle, circle. I feel pleasantly warm in Andrew's arm, so when a chill descends my spine, my entire body locks up. Something's off... different. I attempt to casually take a sip of the champagne that's remained stagnant and forgotten in my grasp. It's warm now and genuinely unpleasant, but it's a distraction as I eye all of the attendees trying to find a set of eyes on me.

And there he is.

Staring. Just staring at me. Wait, not at me. At Andrew. He looks angry, though I can't imagine why. His beautiful icy eyes look even frostier now they're narrowed in on their new target. He looks just as handsome as he did yesterday, although he's exchanged his suit for a gallant black tux. Coen is perfection personified. He's ignoring the red head, too old to be a debutant but too young to be his mom, as she drones on and on. He looks like he's getting ready to cross the room my way. Not happening, Cocky. I have to defuse the situation before it begins. I don't want another eerie staring contest with the way he throws up those pheromones. Certainly not in front of Andrew.

"Andrew, darling." I interrupt his tête-à-tête, not caring if I disturb anyone. "Would you like to dance?"

He smiles tightly and nods to his audience, almost excusing my behavior as if I were a child.

"We were just discussing how combating the Super PAC's will secure the failing infrastructure, dearest. It's really not the time for dancing."

Despite my almost five inch Giuseppe Zanotti Open Toe Platform Evening Sandals, (yes, life is good), I have to arch up to reach Andrew's ear. "But darling, I'm desperately aching to have your body pressed against mine. Listening to you talk shop is doing all sorts of...." I take a deliberately slow breath out and shudder. "... things to me." I look away and blush then wait patiently to see if he bought my act.

The circles stop, and he gives my shoulder a firm squeeze. Dropping his arm from my shoulder, he brings it over to link with my hand, interlocking our fingers. Checkmate.

"Well friends, I'm afraid you'll have to excuse me. I hate to disappoint my dearest heart." He stages his charming smile and ushers me to the dance floor. Coen's eyes forgotten.

Taking my drink, he nearly throws it onto a nearby waiter's tray.

After finding the perfect spot, he kisses my knuckles lightly then wraps my hands around his neck. "Mmmmmm." He pleasantly sighs then rubs his nose in the crook of my neck while pulling me into him by my waist. "Have I told you how stunning you look tonight? Breathtaking!" He grinds his hips slightly, still mindful of where we are. "You've done beautifully tonight. Just having you in my arms makes all of this seem tolerable." He chuckles, as if he told me some inside joke. I smile, though he can't see me. He's easy. He's safe.

We dance for several minutes before I feel a presence and hear someone clear their throat. Again, I lock up. Andrew pulls back to see the intruder.

"Son, forgive my imposition. Charlie, you look lovely this evening." The elder Carpenter smiles warmly my way.

"Thank you, Governor Carpenter. You look dashing yourself."

"Please, I told you to call me William. Andrew, I hate to interrupt, but there are some friends of mine I'd like you to meet." He gives Andrew that look which says, *you're coming with me whether you like it or not.*

Andrew nods then leans down to kiss my cheek. "I'll be back. Wait for me." He winks and then he's swallowed in the crowd of black and white.

I'm about to step off the dance floor and find something to entertain myself with when someone grips my wrist. He pulls me towards him and beams. "Ah, we meet again, love." This man? This cocky man? Where the hell did he come from? He was clear on the other side of the room.

"Mr. Collins," I greet him, while trying to loosen his hold and back away. He pulls me even closer so my face is firmly in his chest. He's nearly a foot taller than me, even in these magical shoes and I can't help but breathe him in or I could willingly asphyxiate. Both seem like viable options in this moment. Nope, breathe him in I do. He smells delicious. Darn, I should have gone with the latter option. I take another deep breath of Coen, to make sure I didn't imagine that delicious smell. Snap, he's still good.

I feel the chuckle coming from his chest. "I believe I told you to call me Coen, love. How are we going to get to know one another if you insist on such formalities?" He smiles and looks directly into my eyes tilting his forehead closer to mine. His icy eyes have warmed slightly and almost appear to sparkle in this light. Black tux and icy eyes, such a beautiful contrast of color. I'm charmed and dumbstruck by his appearance. I need to get away from him.

As I'm contemplating my next move, I hear him say, "No!" All the warmth is gone, replaced by that icy chill. He tightens his hold and continues. "We've just begun." I shiver. His effect on me is alarming.

"You look exquisite, love. Without your glasses, I can see the storms brewing in your magnificent grey eyes." With that eerily strange sentiment he continues staring into them. Searching? Hunting? I have no idea.

The glasses he spoke of are fake. I only wear them at work. It's part of the image I attempt to propagate. Tonight I'm not hiding behind my clothing. Nope. My Oscar de la Renta strapless sweetheart gown in cream looks striking against my lightly bronzed skin. My dark hair is tied up in curls around my head, leaving my shoulders bare. My eyes are heavy with shadow and my lips are a strong mauve. Tonight, I feel beautiful and strong. Or at least I did until I got caught in Coen's fishing line.

He clears his throat, trying to garner my attention, and rubs his thumb over my brow. "You're thinking too much, love." He then wraps his hand around the back of my neck, extending his long fingers to encompass it entirely. His hand is smooth and although his hold is tight, it feels surprisingly comforting.

He lifts my left hand from his chest and begins kissing the fingertips. Then, he stops and pulls them back to take a look them. "Hmmm?" He looks confused as the sound comes out deep in his throat, reluctantly. I know what he notices, and I wait for the inevitable question. But he doesn't ask. Instead he kisses them once more and places my hand back where it was. He finds my eyes again and continues the hunt, this time with purpose. I'm a puzzle he's desperately trying to piece together. Good luck with that one, Cocky. I've been trying for the last twenty-one years with no luck.

The mood has intensified. I need an out and now. Plus, I don't want Andrew to see me in this strange Coen embrace. I give myself an internal pep talk and school my features. Purposely softening my face, I smile sweetly. "I'm afraid I've had too much champagne this evening. Would you excuse me while I visit the facilities, Coen?" I plead with my eyes while nearly fluttering my false eyelashes off my face.

His entire face lights up as he gives me the most dazzling smile I think I've ever seen. It's pure light, emanating from deep within, like his soul is the sun, barely contained. Its only release is with this majestic smile and maybe in those eyes. Damn those eyes. This guy is dangerous. That smile could melt my frozen heart that I've worked so hard to preserve. I can't have that.

Reluctantly, I pull away and walk out of the ballroom straight into the women's facilities. There's a seating area off to the side, away from the toilets, where a couch is waiting patiently for me. Thank goodness. I could use a moment off my feet. My head is spinning. I'm flashing images of Coen repeatedly, trying to connect this newest conundrum. It doesn't help that I have a photographic memory. I see everything. It's like watching TV and clicking through the channels at an insane pace. Image after image. All of Coen. Smiling. Thoughtful. I'm looking, searching, to no avail. What does he want with me? And better yet, why?

I'm interrupted from my deep Coen drowning when I overhear a conversation in the toilet area.

"I can't believe Andrew Carpenter is off the market. That guy had so much potential," a lady shrills, her Boston accent thick with alcohol.

"I know, Dena! I'm devastated. He was such a good lay, too. He told me he doesn't do the whole commitment thing. Just a regular fuck. I don't see what makes her so special? I have fantastic tits. He loved them!" she coughs out, her voice rough. Maybe she's a smoker or maybe older, I can't tell from here. Andrew is ten years older than me. Maybe he wanted a woman closer in age?

I'm having trouble following their conversation. How does our dating pull him off the market? I'm not even sure if we're officially exclusive. So, fuck away old lady!

"I don't know, sweetie. They haven't even been together that long. But you know what we heard. He said she's the one. He wouldn't tell his dad that unless it was serious. I wouldn't be surprised if he popped the question soon."

"Dammit! Could you imagine me on his arm in public? I bet he's gonna be President one day. I definitely see him in the Governor's seat at the very least. First lady of Mass. Or shit, of the free world. God, I missed the boat there! Fucking cunt! Let's go find that chick and trip her. She deserves a good face plant for taking my gig!" She sniggers and snorts. Such a lady.

"You're so bad, Dee!" She joins in her laughter as they make their way out of the room. I briefly see the back of them as they walk past.

I'm still sitting there dumbfounded. I don't view the old witches as a threat. It's the part about Andrew and marriage that has me shaking. He's the first guy I've really dated, and I use that word loosely. Yes, we've had a few dinners together. He has also swung by the office to bring me lunch. Sweet guy, right? A couple of weeks ago we even had lunch with his dad, as he was unexpectedly in town and Andrew wanted to catch up with him. I guess that sounds a bit suspicious now. At the time, I assumed he was being thoughtful. Sweet, thoughtful Andrew.

I'm too young to get married. And do I really want to spend the rest of my life in a shadow? He'd control everything. I wouldn't be me anymore. I'd be on the political trail nonstop, with people analyzing every bit, every blob, every bulb.

They'd dig up my past and that sure as shit can't happen. Air. I need air. I can't breathe.

My hands immediately go to my neck. Fuck, I might be at the start of a panic attack. I need to get out of here. I haven't had one in so long I'm not even sure what to do anymore.

Focus. Breathe. In, out. One, two, three.

I feel a trickle of sweat rolling down my spine. I finally move to the sink and rush my hands into the cool water. That's better. Looking at myself in the mirror, I shake my head. Breathe. You can do this. I'll end it with him. No big deal. Sure, he's sweet and I enjoy his company but he's just another guy. When I'm ready to give this dating thing another go, I'll find myself another man.

With a renewed purpose, I make my way towards the door and walk right into a wall.

"Whoa there, love. You okay?" the wall, also known as Coen, asks while steadying me. I guess I'm still not fully grounded. "You get lost in there? Hey..." He tilts my chin up with his thumb and forefinger. His eyes flicker back and forth between each of my eyes. He's searching. His other hand slithers around my neck locking me in this position.

"What happened? Talk to me." His touch is soothing, but my

emotions are still flailing.

I feel the flush spread along my face and downward. I'm probably all glistening, too, and not in a pretty look-how-sexy-I-am way. No, probably in the I-just-left-the-gym-and-I-need-a-shower way.

"Mr. Collins...I'm sorry. Didn't see you there. I'm…I'm fine. Yes. I'm fine." Geez, I sound like a moron. "I mean. What I meant, is that I need to go. Not feeling great…" Then I whisper conspiratorially, "Menstruation issues."

He makes some weird noise, almost like a smothered laugh, which slipped out. He smiles and bites the inside of his cheek. Jerk! I'm not liking you, Cocky!

He looks relaxed. Not like the Cocky from yesterday's boardroom fun. His eyes are a light crystal blue, not as icy as I've usually witnessed, and even they look like they're smiling at me.

His thumb moves slowly back and forth across my cheek. His other hand kneads the muscles in my neck. My breathing slowly regulates and my heart rate decreases. He's soothing me. Calming me. Bringing me back down to earth.

He puts his forehead onto mine and stares into my eyes, his smile lost. He runs his nose along the bridge of my nose and his breathing feathers along my lips. I can nearly taste him. Whisky or is it scotch? Should I ask? Would that be rude?

He abruptly closes his eyes and the pressure on my forehead increases.

"What are you doing to me, love?" he barely whispers.

"I…have to go," I whisper back, not wanting to burst this little bubble we've created, but desperate to be free of it at the same time. "Coen?"

"Right, love." He takes my hand and leads me away from the restrooms. We stop at the coat check and grab my cover. It's early March and the chilly air would knock my frozen ass over in my strapless getup. Never letting go of my hand, he directs me to a tall man standing just inside the doors. His posture alludes to military training. By his stance, I'm guessing Marines. He's got that vibe about him. A rule guy and probably armed. "Davis, would you please take Ms. Paz home. She's not feeling well." He says this last part while smiling at me. Clever.

"Love, this is my right hand man, Davis. He'll take care of you."

I look at him, somewhat saddened that he won't be joining me.

"Okay?" It's a question. I'm not sure if I should go with Davis or grab a taxi. Andrew had a limo commissioned this evening, so I don't have my car here. My options limited, I guess Davis looks like the best bet.

"I have to stay. I'm giving the opening remarks tonight, but Davis will get you home safely." He smiles, grabs the back of my neck, and kisses my temple. "I'll see you soon, love." He winks and lazily walks away, his hands in his pockets. I guess it's my turn to stare because that's exactly what I do…I stare at his retreating form wondering what in the hell am I doing?

Davis, now next to me, clears his throat. "Ms. Paz, the car is ready." He doesn't smile but I can tell it's his way. I follow him out of the door and to a waiting Town car. He opens the door and ushers me in. After I give him my address to head downtown and onto Portland Street, I text Andrew letting him know I came down with a stomach bug and had to leave early. I'm sure he's so caught up in his political swag he doesn't even know I'm gone. Maybe he gave the old witch another go.

Davis doesn't only drop me off at the curb, he walks me inside my building. Coen wasn't messing around when he said Davis would get me home safely.

There I'm greeted by my boy, Freddie. "Good evenin' sweet thang. You have yourself a pleasant night? Bring your boy a treat?"

Freddie's one of the door men at my building and I tend to spoil him. He's my favorite, after all.

"No goodies, I'm afraid. But I'm starved. You in the mood for some pizza?"

I'm not big on eating alone, so when I know my boy's standing watch, we sometimes spilt a pie.

Plus, I ducked out of the fundraiser before I got fed and I'm hungrrry!

"Hell yeah, girlie. Hook us up!" I smile and wave while heading for the elevator.

"You always have dinner with your doorman?" Davis asks once we've entered the elevator.

"Not always but he's fun to hang around with and I don't feel like eating solo tonight."

He nods. The elevator doors open and he ushers me to my condo. He waits patiently until I've unlocked and opened the door before wishing me a pleasant rest of my evening and heading back.

I wonder if he walked me to my door for safety reasons or so he could tell Coen exactly where I live. I'm guessing both. Quickly calling the order in, I then strip myself of the beautiful ensemble I've been paraded in all night and jump in the shower. Dressed in sweats, my hair up in a wet, messy bun, and my face clean, I head downstairs for the pizza that's calling me.

Downstairs, I'm laughing so hard with Freddie and stuffing my face with pizza, I don't even realize that a new face has joined our group. I guess I'm not sure how long I've been down here gabbing for but enough time must have lapsed for Coen to finish his time at tonight's event. Jacket off, sleeves rolled up, he looks relaxed.

"Save any for me, love?" He picks me off my chair, sits down, and places me on his lap, all while leaning over and biting my pizza. I can't help but laugh.

"Do you mind? I was eating that, Mr. Collins. Didn't they feed you at that fancy shindig of yours?"

"I never mind, love. And no, I wasn't fed. I was in too much of a hurry to see you. So now you're obliged to feed me."

"So that's how it works?"

"Yep, that's how it works."

He winks and eats more of my pizza. I reach over and grab him his own slice. I may be all about philanthropy, but not when it comes to my food, especially pizza.

Freddie, Coen, and I talk, laugh, and eat for another hour. I'm having so much fun I've completely forgotten how hideous I look. But I can't find it in me to care and Coen doesn't seem to mind. He catches me on my third yawn and tells me it's time for bed. Ordinarily, I hate being told what to do. Instinctively, I want to argue. But right now I don't think, I just follow, as he steers me to the elevators and to my condo.

"Sweet dreams, love. I'll see you soon." He kisses the top of my head, winks, and walks back to the elevator.

Plopping down on my bed I stare blankly at my ceiling. I only met this man yesterday. YESTERDAY. Why is he lingering in my thoughts? Why does he keep calling me 'love?' What's with that? Is he conditioning me? Love, kisses, see you soon?

Am I Pavlov's dog turned Coen's plaything?

I let him in too much tonight. Thanks to my internal meltdown over Andrew, I didn't stand a chance against his wit and charm. I need to be stronger. Tomorrow is Friday and I have a very long day ahead of me. Not to mention some much needed relief approaching. I need to stay focused and sharp, not be a mindless twit with Coen drool.

My last thoughts before drifting off to sleep, was that Andrew never checked in on me. But Coen did.

Chapter 3

MY HAIR IS IN TWO tight French braids down the crown of my head and tucked in. I've got my black face paint running a streak across my eyes and I'm sporting my tiny black boy shorts and my black sports razorback bra with pink piping. I just need my hands wrapped and I'm ready to go.

It's Friday night.

Fight night, baby.

And I'm on the docket tonight.

I'm pumped, so freaking pumped. I need this tonight. This week has been outlandish and I'm dying for release.

My legs are shaking relentlessly while I wait on this hard metal bench in the locker room. It smells in here; like fungus filled feet mixed with body odor and sweat. It would be nearly nauseating if I didn't love it. But I freaking love this shit! I love what it represents. I love what's waiting for me.

No, I'm not in some fancy ass auditorium with TV sport's anchors giving tonight's play by play.

No way. This isn't the UFC. This shit is unsanctioned. Back alley and through the busted door with a password type of unsanctioned. They'll be no weigh in. No press conference. And certainly no billboard with my face on it. And I wouldn't have it any other way.

I'm not here for the fame nor the notoriety. I'm not even here for the purse. But I am here!

I watch Tony pace back and forth. Back and forth. Even though he's agitated, I find his pacing hypnotic. He doesn't usually come to these things with me. That's usually Tank's job. Tank Remmington is my mentor, my trainer, and now he's the UFC's golden child, which blows for me. Because he's got to be squeaky clean and nowhere near here, where I need him.

That leaves me with Tony, Tank's right hand man and younger brother. Although Tony has no beef with the unsanctioned fights, he has a thing about female fighters. He's okay to train us, he's even okay to spar with us, but he can't stand to see us beat and bloody. I get it. Some people don't like watching female fighters. That's usually why we're the opening act and not the main event. I'll go on early and be out the door in no time.

I hear Tony's cell interrupt his pacing. "Y'llo? Yeah, yeah, she's good, man. I got her. Naw, she's fine…this aint her first time, bro. She's got this. She's wicked good. Yeah, ya know I'll keep my eye out. That's what I do. Naw…it's cool."

He pauses, walks over, and hands me the phone. "He wants a word."

"Tank. I miss you. It feels weird here without you." This is my first fight without him. I feel off, like I'm skipping some important warm up ritual.

"I'm with ya in spirit, baby. Ya know me. Ya got my heart. Ya okay? Tony being good to ya?"

"Yeah, Yeah." I play it off, as I don't want him worrying. But really Tony has done nothing to help me prep. No pointers. No pep talk. Nothing but pace back and forth. "It's all good. Tony and I are gonna rock this bitch. I'll see you later tonight, right?"

"Of course, baby. Wouldn't miss my victory smooches for the world. Remember, keep your hands up and use your feet. Don't let her take ya to the mat. No matter what. Ya hear me."

He tells me this nearly every time I go out there. I guess even Tank doesn't like the idea of me out in the cage. "I got you!" I huff out.

"Stay strong, baby girl. I believe in ya." With that, he hangs up. But he's already given me what I need. He believes in me. Sometimes, you only need one person to vocalize such a powerful sentiment. I don't care if I know this. I don't care if he's even told me this a million times. Right now, I need to hear it. And Tank is so fucking awesome that he knows it.

In no time at all, I'm at the locker door. Rage Against the Machine's *Killing in the Name Of* blares out indicating that it's time to walk, baby. It's on. With my flip flops clucking, I'm bouncing down the makeshift aisle passing the hundreds of people swarmed into this oversized gym. But I only have one thing in my sight. The Cage. Salvation.

I climb the steps as Zack starts softly singing, "*You did what they told ya.*" The chant gets louder and louder with each step until it erupts into a violent scream, *"Fuck you, I won't do what you tell me!"* Over and over I jump as the mantra moves me, invigorates me, reminds me that nobody can control me. Nobody, I am me. And tonight I own this Cage. I am the animal.

I play it up to the audience. Jumping, screaming, and even giving them the finger. Let them boo, let them cheer, I don't care. I'm here to fight. I'm here to win.

A new round of music begins, something rap. Its bass has the crowd thumping and I watch as my opponent climbs into my domain. She thinks she's got this. I don't know her name, don't know her face. She's got at least four to five inches on me. That I do notice. That means I need to stay out of her grasp. Her swing will reach me faster. I'll need to keep my distance.

Tony comes over, grips my shoulders, and looks me in the eye. "Stay outta her reach, ya hear me. Do this fast. Don't tire yourself out dodging her, ya strike and ya leave. First round." With that, he shoves my mouth guard in and walks out of the Cage.

They introduce my opponent, Paige Champion. Ha, Champion my ass, not tonight!

Then they begin on me; name and stats.

Tonight, I'm Lady DOA and I'm undefeated. No, I don't walk in here as Charlie. Not that I'm embarrassed. But I like to keep my extracurricular activities to myself. Charlie has her time and place and so does Lady. Does that mean I have a split personality? Some fucked up duality? Hell no! Everybody has some alter ego and right now, its Lady's turn.

It's Lady's night!

The Ref goes over the rules and asks us to bump fists. I smile big, revealing my black mouth guard with pink letters spelling out "Fuck You." Poor Paige looks pissed. Let the games begin.

The whistle blows and she comes charging at me. The animal released. I've never seen her fight so I haven't mapped out her moves. Yet. She jabs and crosses straight at my face. I twist narrowly avoiding her strikes. She takes advantage and lands one on my ribs.

Jab. Hook. I see the pattern. She tenses her shoulders just before the strike. Tense. Strike. Block. The pattern continues until she tires and throws her shoulder low into my gut. She slams me against the Cage wall, hard, the metal cutting into my back.

My arms throw up in front of my face, taking a defensive stance. Tense. Upper cut. Hit. Tense.

Cross. Hit. She's nailed me in the upper side of my right lip. No doubt, it's a deep laceration. The blood pooling and dripping down my mouth proves it. Another throbbing pinch indicates I've been hit on my left cheek. No wetness, though. My skin is still intact.

I snap out of my haze and move. So far I've just been coasting and mapping her out. It's time to show her why I'm the CHAMP. I hammerfist the side of head, one after the other, and then again and again. Next I add legs with multiple leg kicks, each landing near the knee area. I've pushed her back as she tries to avoid my blows. But it's time to end this.

I build up my momentum with each step gaining speed, and then I throw a spinning back kick straight to her face. She stumbles to the left and then she's down. It's a glorious site. TKO, baby.

Everything speeds up now. The Ref declares me the winner and I'm back in the locker getting patched up. Three stitches in my lip and a bag of ice on my cheek. Shit....at least my hands are good.

I shower and dress. Tonight, I'm going out. Black leather pants, low on my hips. White tank top with my black bra slipping through and my biker boots on. Heavy eye makeup, red lipstick covering most of my busted lip, and my jet black hair climbing down my back past my shoulder blades. I'm in full play mode.

Tony walks over as I'm throwing the last of my shit into my bag. "Where do ya want tonight's purse to go?"

"Boys and Girls Club. Southie."

"Anonymously?" he asks, although I know he knows the answer. It's always the same.

I nod and make my way out. By now, Malice has dropped off my ride and I don't want to be late.

I creep behind the drunken crowd as they cheer for the next victor. The sound is deafening. I'm nearly to the outer door when I feel his presence and then a tension pulls on my wrist. He's got me...again. How he's here, I have no idea. Coen and Cage fighting isn't exactly synonymous. He sticks out with his black button up shirt and khaki pants. This is more of a beer and nuts, tees and jeans kind of place.

I hold on tighter to my jacket and bag as I try to wiggle out of his grasp. He's not having it and grabs my neck with his other hand, his thumb under my chin pushing me to look him in the eyes. I find them darting frantically over my face. I've never seen his eyes so frosty. He looks more than mad. He looks, he looks, what? Confused? Hurt? I don't know, but it's chilling.

His other hand slips from my wrist and he rubs his thumb softly against my lip, his breath coming faster, harder. "Fuck," he mutters, repeatedly. He smoothes my hair from my cheek to see the swelling there. I can tell he's not happy with what he sees, as he closes his eyes and turns away, his jaw ticking and the veins in his neck pulsing.

Suddenly, a wash of guilt enflames me. Like I hurt him. I wronged him. Like I need to apologize.

But why? I won. I should be proud. If I was male, he'd be patting me on my back telling me what a killer job I did, and we'd rehash the look on my opponent's face when she went down. I'd be a hero.

But no. I'm standing here feeling like I've wronged him. Fuck that. I find myself desperate to flee, yet again. What does this guy do to me?

"I've gotta go, Mr. Collins."

His head snaps back toward me. Eyes angrier. "First, tell me what that was about?"

I don't have an answer and I don't owe him anything. So, I tell him exactly that.

"I just met you. I don't need to justify what I do. I don't owe you. I don't belong to you. But I do need to go."

He tightens his hold and looks directly into me. His touch isn't comforting this time. It's unnerving and I want to escape. "Charlie." He growls. Yep, growls. "I don't like this shit. I don't like seeing you injured. I don't like watching you get hurt and then you telling me there's not a fucking thing I can do to help."

He breathes in deeply, trying to calm himself. "And whether you know it or not, you do belong to me. You do owe me. Now, love, tell me where you're going."

The words fly out without bypassing my brain. My emergency filter forgotten.

"BedHead." Was that out loud? I didn't even think it. It slipped out as if the answer had come from somewhere inside of me and I had no way of stopping it.

He nods and smiles briefly, and then releases me. He pulls my jacket and bag out of my arm and holds the leather jacket out to me. "It's chilly tonight."

After dressing me he grabs my hand, and we start walking. The night air is a chilled warm. My body is still overheated from the fight and Coen's closeness. I point out my ride.

"That's me."

Coen looks around the lot, confused.

"The Harley."

"Of course," he mutters, probably more to himself. "What model is this?"

I beam. "She's a 2013 Dyna Fat Boy Lo. She's a Lo because she's closer to the ground, which is great for a vertically challenged individual such as myself. She's totally custom. See the matte black painting with the hot pink striping… that's all hand done. And so is the bucket black leather seat with the pink skull. And over here, the solid disc wheels are even coated in black. You see how the front tire is smaller than the back? It's actually 140 mm wide, and it helps mitigate feedback from the road for a smoother ride. And thanks to those chrome mufflers, my baby purrs. I even upgraded to the High Output Twin Cam 103B engine to give her more power. She's a fast little thing and since she's obviously female, I've dubbed my girl Flabby Abbey."

I'm such a dork. Coen patiently waits for me to finish my geekdom nodding like he understands when I'm sure he's clueless. Mind you, I've been pointing and throwing my hands around animatedly for the last few minutes. I never explain this part of myself. Why it all came out, I honestly don't know.

He chuckles softly. "It's a nice bike, love." Nice? It's a Harley. This bitch aint nowhere near nice.

I grab the bag off his shoulder and then shove it into my saddlebag. "Thanks." I pull out my helmet, which I had custom made when I got the bike. It has the same coloring and matches perfectly. It even has a pink skull in the back. I'm still a girl. A fashionista knows how to accessorize in all things.

I grab my long hair, pull it to the side, and start a loose braid, tying it off. My hair is so long that if it's not restrained it will fight me later. Dropping my helmet on my head, I'm about to clasp the straps when I feel Coen's hands go under my neck taking them from me. He stops my movements and pulls me forward. I throw my hands onto his chest to brace myself.

Again, he's staring. "Are you hurting?" I nod, while keeping my head tipped up because this beast of a man is so tall. I consider that I might as well be honest as he seems to get things out of me in one way or another.

"Are you okay on this thing?" I nod again. Don't insult my Abbey. Did he not hear my enthusiastic mini sermon on the perfection that is my girl?

"Are you gonna be safe tonight?" I shrug. You never know with me and the night is still young.

He tsks softly, his warm hands returning to my face. "No more injuries, love." He chuckles darkly. "I don't think I could handle it." Hhmm. Not sure how to respond, so I try to smile. Ouch. Forgot about those stitches. He sees my wince and his face hardens.

"Charlie, please." He says this softly and I feel his words go through me. He rarely says my name, so when it comes from his lips, it sounds reverent. But I don't mistake the desperation I hear for anything else. He's anxious over this. Over me. I'm not his normal. He doesn't know what to do with me. I guess that puts us on even ground.

He kisses my nose and secures my clasp. Stepping back, he's waiting to see me off.

I climb my ride, start her up, and give Coen a quick wave before heading out of the lot. In my rear view mirror, I see him with his chin resting low and his hands in his pockets. He's sauntering towards a black Town Car. Davis. How did I miss that? I have a feeling this isn't the last I've seen of Mr. Collins tonight.

Chapter 4

I PULL FLABBY ABBEY DIRECTLY ONTO the sidewalk in front of BedHead. The club sits on the outskirts of Bay Village and smack dab in the heart of nightlife central. There are clubs on every other block, the perfect location for a nonstop party.

A nice breeze is coming off the water tonight bringing in a slight chill, and with the full moon, I couldn't help but take my time riding over. I needed a view of the ocean. It's serenity. I needed the calm before the approaching storm.

Climbing off of Abbey, I undo my braid and remove my helmet. I see Malice waiting. He looks impetuous, not that I care, as I write the man's freaking check. He can wait.

Righting myself, I walk towards the front. A long line of people locked into place with black velvet rope snakes to the right of the building. They impatiently wait. Coming from the left, I catch the eyes of a few line connoisseurs and hear them calling to me. I attempt a smile and wave, but don't slow down until I hit my destination.

"Hello, gorgeous. Welcome back." Zeke, the head of security greets me. He's bald and as wide as a house, if that house was pure scary muscle. He's a dark African American with the most beautiful green eyes. I overhear the chatter coming from his earpiece when I lean in to kiss his cheek.

"Watch my girl tonight?" I ask nodding at my bike.

"I'll get Jonah on it. No worries, beauty. Play on," he states nodding his head towards the bouncer at the main door.

I wink and walk away with Malice by my side.

Malice is a hairy beast. He's six foot four on a bad day, and well over 250 pounds on a good one. I'm still not one-hundred percent sure where he got all of his training; maybe as a French spy or under the Direction Centrale du Renseignement Intérieur intelligence services. Either way, he's lethal and scary. I finally couldn't handle the secrecy and dug into his background, hacker style, and let's just say, he wasn't the only spy in the family. I can't imagine what that dinner table conversation was like. Dark hair coats his head and most of his face. His beard is trimmed matching the polished suits he insists on wearing. His eyes are not dark brown, but black. Age hasn't dimmed the intensity in them, although he's only in his late thirties. He's always anxious and always ready… for what, I don't know, but when it comes I know he'll have my back.

He fell into my world nearly two years ago. I think he was looking to get out of the life, which is why he moved to the States. That and his sexual orientation, which wasn't as widely accepted in that 'world.' He needed a fresh start and I needed him.

We just work.

"On dirait qu'il fait mal.Vous allez être ok ce soir?"

It looks like it hurts.You're going to be ok tonight?

I take off my coat and hand it to him with my helmet.

"Ça ira. Je l›ai connu pire et être mieux. Merci d›être passé hors Abbey. Pouvez-vous prendre soin d'elle ce soir? Je prévois de lâcher un peu."

I'll be fine. I've had worse and been better. Thanks for dropping Abbey off. Can you take care of her tonight? I plan on letting go a bit.

"Dois-je à craindre?"

Do I need to worry?

"Toujours."

Always. I smirk. It's playtime!

I can hear In This Moment's Maria Brink crooning out *Whore* through the speakers. It's darkened beat causing all the bodies in the club to pulse in a hypnotic wave. Its ebb and flow breathing like a singular organ.

"I am the dirt you created." Truer words.

Malice leads me through the crowd to the back and up the stairs. I nod to random people as we go, still partially hidden by the mammoth in front of me. Really, it's just a blur. Colors and sound and the back of Malice.

He pulls open the door and pushes me into the quiet.The pounding in my head slows and I hear the familiar laughter assaulting me.

Sitting on the two red leather couches and a few random chairs are four of my favorite people in the entire world. And a couple of chicks I couldn't give a shit about.

"'Bout time you showed up, baby girl. Who won?" I stick my tongue out at Gunner and grab a bottle of water off the table in the back of the room. I don't like it when they bring girls back here. This is our space, our time to do our thing, They can get their easy pussy anytime. The fake laughter and nasty auras they're perspiring is making me feel sick.

"Let me see the damage."Tank walks over and begins his perusal. I know he's spoken with Tony as he moves the hair covering my left side over to study the swelling, like he knew it was there. He makes some grumbling noises. "Got any headaches or blurry vision? And how's the ribs?" He cocks a brow like that's gonna do me in.

"I'm good, Tank. You know how this works." I sigh.

"I know. I know. Give me what I need and I'll get out of your hair." He opens his tan arms and I greedily take shelter there. I love Tank. He's the first person I bonded with nearly six years ago when I moved to Boston from Florida. I stumbled upon the gym he and his brother own, 'Tornadoes,' and it has been a whirlwind ever since.

He kisses the top of my head three times. One for each of my injuries. He's a big softy…well, at least on the inside.

"Dang Tank, have you gotten bigger? I swear you're all muscle now. Where's my pooch gut? I miss my poochy." I pout, mainly because I know he hates it and I know I can get away with it.

"Oh he'll be back, baby girl. He's on vacation for a bit. Along with beer, and cake, and fried chicken, and those delicious wrapped cookie things ya make me, and…" Poor guy. The UFC is a big bully.

He catches me rolling my eyes. "No, ya don't, baby girl." And then he tickles me. Hands all up in my tummy and laughing in my face tickle. Yes, it's a sad reality and one I scarcely admit, but I am indeed horribly ticklish.

Naturally, all eyes lock on the obscene behavior which is causing that horrifyingly piercing sound coming from my rather busted lips. I take no responsibility for this. It's all Tank. I'm screaming, and in my attempt to flee, I fall to the ground. He jumps down following me and continues his torture.

"Stop, stop. I give. Uncle or auntie or whomever will make this stop!"

Does he stop…no.

"Say it and I'll quit."

I shake my head back and forth as tears trail down my face. I can't even imagine how screwed up this looks. Tank with gargantuan colorfully tatted muscles protruding from every crevice hovering over my tiny writhing form. And does anyone from the couch abyss jump in and save me…or even the monster I pay to take care of me? Nope.

"Okay, okay…Tank is the absolute best at everything." I breathe in, quickly trying to fill my lungs, now that he has backed off.

"And…" His hands hover above me, wiggling, and taunting me.

"I'll never be as awesome as the master, Tank Remmington."

He smiles big and stands up. Reaching down he asks, "Was that so hard, baby girl?"

He over-pulls and I go flying up into him. Pulling back, my hand lands on my stomach and my voice weak. "Yes sir, it was, sir!" I mock salute him and practically run to the couch, jumping on Bullet. The fuzzy blonde next to him whines and murmurs something I couldn't care less about.

Tank strolls out with a backwards, "See ya." But I could have sworn I heard him mumble, *Pain in my ass*. Sounds about right.

"Hi Bully." I rub his bald tatted head. He's shirtless, like always, and I can't help but eye all of the colorful tattoos that cover his chest, arms, and neck. Just above his heart, he has a tattoo of a bullet sinking into the skin, and scratched into the base is the word "Shooter." I lean over and kiss his chest, and then rest my head there. I can feel him running his fingers through my hair.

"Hi, baby girl. You have fun over there?" He has the absolute deepest voice ever. It isn't smooth, though. It's all gravelly and broken and rough.

I look up and smile my painfully swollen smile. "Sure, if that's what you'd call it."

He eyes my lip and looks away quickly. He knows better than to say anything.

Gunner chimes in from the other couch he's sharing with Trigger. "How many stitches?"

"Three," I say, keeping my head on Bullet's chest.

"How's your hands?" I can hear the anger in his voice rising.

"Fine."

"Trig, can you do back up, tonight?"

"I can still do it. Fuck, Gun, I told you I had scheduled a fight when you booked us this. You can't get all fucking pissy," I pipe in, finally meeting his menacing stare. "I'm fine. What the hell. I'm not complaining. I didn't fucking ask for help!"

"Maybe you didn't, but your face sure as shit did!" He stands up and walks to the table of drinks and sparse amounts of food.

Steve-O, the club manager, walks in and lets us know it's time to go on. Great... a pissed off Gun at the ready.

We climb onto the stage and take our spots.

The curtains go up and the spotlight lands on me, or rather my hands.

My fingers glide up and down the neck of my Gretsch locking in the rhythm. Setting the mood and opening the song. Opening tonight's set.

I solo for maybe twenty seconds before the drums and bass kick in. Now we are picking up steam and the crowd is screaming with need. They want more. They demand satisfaction.

Gunner steps up to the mic. "BeddddHeadddd!" he screams and draws the word out like a referee. "Thank you for spending the night with us. Oh and some of you will. My name, in case you forgot, is Gunner." He pauses, the dork eating up the screams for marriage and baby making later. "Over on drums we have Bullet." More screaming. "On bass is Trigger." Pause. More screams. "On rhythm guitar, our lady of the night..." Wait, what the hell does that mean? Is he calling me a hooker? "Shooooooter." I give them a little smile and laugh at Gunner as he sticks his tongue out at me like he's Gene Simmons. "And we are..." He waits for everyone to scream our name. "LOADED GUN!"

Then Gun goes into sexy rocker mode and starts singing his crazy beautiful heart out. Nothing stops this guy from his music. He's such a rock star. He was born to do this. He's got that lean swimmer's body, with dark wavy hair that lands around his shoulders. Leather bracelets climb his arms, and he's wearing dirty, torn to shreds jeans, and a tight black t-shirt. He's even sporting rings. He has a couple of hoops in each ear and two in his right brow, plus a lip ring. He's all blinged out. The only bling on me, right now, is my Gretch Cadillac tailpiece on my guitar. Oh, and I put my navel ring back in, but that's mostly covered by my top. And, of course, Sussurro.

Forty-five minutes later and I'm a sweaty mess. My hair sticks to my face and my black eyeliner has probably melted under my eyes. My body is quickly catching up to me. My hips have been undulating away lost in the music and forgetting to acknowledge my bruised ribs. My voice is getting hoarse from the stress of the week and the backup vocals I'm producing. I look over and see the boys are about as spent as I am.

But no matter what, I love these nights. I love when we play for a crowd and they feed off our music, and in turn we feed off of their excitement and energy. My favorite part is when I connect with these three amazing men on stage. It's the only time we're completely harmonious. They're my best friends.

Lost in my head, I barely hear it when Gunner yells, "Good-night, BOSTON! We fucking love you!" The curtains come down and we climb off stage, the roar of the crowd still echoing through my ears.

I unplug and hand Malice my Black Penguin beauty then follow the sounds of glorious, sweet relief. Shots!

"Who wants in?" Gunner lines up eight shots of Patron. I grab my two and slam them back. One followed by the next. No lime needed. The skanks from earlier forgotten on the couch, I smile at my boys and say, "I love you, losers!"

An arm encircles my waist and Bull leans over. "Oh, we fucking know!" I elbow the jackass.

Gunner sniggers then plants a kiss on my forehead. "Another round?"

"Patron me, baby!"

"Uh, oh. Our girl is getting lit tonight. Malice, you on this?"

I roll my eyes, grab the shots, and down them.

"I'm out." I wave to the boys and hastily make my way down the stairs with Malice hot on my tail.

"Allez-vous attendre pour moi ou continue agir comme un enfant?"

You going to wait for me or continue acting like a child?

Decisions, decisions. I slow down and wait for him to catch up.

He stops before getting in front of me, in his preferred spot, and gives me the evil eye. Then he continues. As the lights pulses all around us and the bodies squeezed into the club rock us, bump us, and practically knock us over, I can feel the alcohol warming through my blood. I start to giggle. And sway. But I'm so happy.

I grab Malice's jacket and give it a few tugs. He stops and turns to me, confused.

"Je t'aime, Malice."

I love you, Malice.

He looks me over and shakes his head. Then he throws me over his shoulder. Yes, this position is definitely helping my predicament. That's funny.

"Je veux vos fesses."

I like your butt. I giggle while patting said body part. I'm full of funny tonight.

A second later, or maybe more, I'm upside down. Maybe time moves faster when you're upside down. I should look into that. I'm dropped onto an oversized plush chair in the VIP area, which is separate from the rest of the club.

Another second later a bottle of water is thrust into my hands.

"Boire."

Drink.

For a man who speaks six languages fluently, you'd think he'd use more words. I laugh again. At no one. To no one. Basically, with no one. But shit, I'm funny tonight. This is golden! Oscar worthy. Maybe not, but I'm cracking myself up.

Malice is gone again. Into the shadows. He likes to watch me from a distance. Because if I pass out on my face and break something, he'll have a nice distant shot of that.

I'm not alone for long because the goofball trio and their band of slutty mutts stroll in.

"Hey three amigos. Did you miss me?" I give my cheesy smile, the throbbing in my lip gone. Ohhhh, I love alcohol. May I have some more?

Since I know Malice is out there watching and monitoring my alcoholic intake, I go into incognito spy mode. "Psst. Bully, get me a shot."

He's got a beer in one hand and what looks like some DD fakeys in the other.

"Baby girl, I'm sort of busy. Why don't you get it?"

The VIP bar is only like fifteen feet away but Malice might as well be a grumpy grandpa with laser vision. He misses nothing and I know he won't let me get another shot. I have to play the sneak.

Next victim.

"Psst. Trig..."

"Nope!" Dammit. He's chatting with some butch looking dude, or it could be a chick. My eyesight isn't exactly 20/20.

I look at Gun…one more try.

He sees me and shakes his head, giving me a hard glare and then goes back to the brunette who's straddling him and licking his face. Her skirt is hiked up so high I can see her…well hello there.

Three strikes and you're out.

Time for another tactic. I start bopping to the music, letting it take more and more of me. I get up still keeping the same bopping thing flowing. I take a big chug of water. Water is so good. So refreshing. Totally not thinking about Patron right now. See Malice, I'm happy with bopping and water.

I move towards the railing, still bopping. I've added a sway. Now maybe some arms. Better put the bottle down, don't want to hurt anyone. Those wicked plastic bottles can be so dangerous.

I'm bopping and swaying and my arms are joining in. Now to move, step back, step back, and sway and sway and sway. Getting closer to the Patron promise land. Step back, step…

Warmth. I suddenly feel warmth against the length of my entire back. Strong warm bands wrap around my middle and the most beautiful voice says softly into my ear, "Hi, love." Sigh. What Patron?

I smile and do some weird owl neck thing to get a better look. "Hhhhiii."

Then I sense the pounding in the floor as Malice marches over.

"Qui est-ce? Pourquoi est-il vous touche ?"

Who is this? Why is he touching you?

As I'm about to answer, Coen pulls me rather quickly, hey ninja, behind him. Protector Coen equals all kinds of Sexy Coen. Me likey!

"Mon nom est Coen Collins et je suis Charlie. Et tu es?"

My name is Coen Collins and I am Charlie's. And you are?

Malice isn't used to people calling me by my first name, so he assumes I trust this guy, rather incorrectly, but I'll deal with that later.

"Je suis sa garde, Malice. Vous prenez soin d'elle ce soir?"

I am her guard, Malice. You're taking care of her tonight?

"Bien sûr, elle est à moi."

Of course, she's mine.

Malice looks over Coen's shoulder and gives me a questioning look. I respond with what I think to be the universal, 'I don't have a fucking clue' look, but apparently it came across as the 'yes, I'm gonna hump this guy' look, because he leaves. Leaves, leaves, or goes back to the shadow leaves...I don't know.

Coen turns around and rubs my arms. I say the first thing that pops in my drunken genius head, "Youuu speak Frenchhh."

Coen smiles. "Yeah, love. You got that all on your own, did you?" He cups my face and looks at my eyes. Only this time they're not probing. "How much did you drink tonight?"

I hold up four fingers, triumphantly.

"When was the last time you ate?"

Now he's hitting me with the hard questions. "Ummm. I think. Arowwnnnd. It was after…but wwway before…Oh, I know. I had a granola bar around two-firdy." Ha. I remember. Not drunk at all. Brain intact and working brilliantly. And the award for awesome rememberer is…

Chapter 5

I BREATHE IN AND STRETCH THE sleep out of my muscles. Yum. These sheets feel deliciously soft and silky, which is weird since my sheets don't feel like this. But apparently my brain and my eyes haven't fully woken, as they're still in sleep coma heaven. However, it would appear my bladder has. And so has the exceptional throbbing coming from a variety of places. My tongue glides across my outer top teeth. They feel gross and I wince with the movement. Ouch, memories are resurfacing from the fight. That would explain most of the throbbing.

Grudgingly, I get up and walk over to a cluster of doors. With one eye still partially closed, I push the one with the light seeping through and find a bathroom. Well, maybe that's an understatement as it's more like an in home spa. With no time to enjoy the whimsy this place brings, I hunt for the toilet...my one and only focus.

Locating a side door, I find blissful release.

Washing my hands, still in a daze, I find myself staring at my reflection. I know I should be freaking out right now. I'm not in my house and I'm not in one of my guy's houses. But I know Malice wouldn't have let me out of his sight without good reason, so I imagine I'm not in any harm's way. Plus, I trust my instincts. And right now, I don't feel any fear, but rather a strange calm.

What is a little frustrating is that I'm only in my bra and panties. I'll dig into that one later. Leaning forward to examine the day after bruising, I notice a bunch of men's aftershaves and other toiletries on the opposite sink. I walk over, grab the mouthwash and take a gurgle then grab the aftershave to take a sniff...yummy! I had an inkling, but now I know for sure. I'm at Coen's. I know that smell.

I wish I could remember more. The last I recall I was still at the club. Was Coen there? Honestly, I'm not that much of a drinker. But between my face hurting something fierce, the Andrew bomb, and Coen's peculiar presence throwing me off kilter, I deserved some! Hell, I deserved some Dom not tequila.

I gently push open the door and spy Coen still asleep on the bed in only a pair of red tight briefs. He's on his back with his right arm cocked over his face and his left on his abs. I know I should be thinking about the tightness in his stomach, which although no true six pack, is still quite a sight to behold. And the pale hair cascading downwards towards the unknown. I should think about the way his arms bulk slightly even in this relaxed mode. Or his thick thighs.

But I don't. What I do notice is his smooth skin with not one scratch, mole or freckle. Not one birthmark. And most definitely not a drop of ink, anywhere.

I have to physically look away, as it hurts so much to see him. I suddenly feel dirty and beneath him. I want to cry.

"Hey." His morning voice calls for me. He has moved both arms behind his neck watching me.

"You feeling better, love?"

Even though I have no clue what he's talking about, I want to leave.

"Absolutely! If you just point me to my stuff, I'll get out of your hair." The pounding behind my eyes grows. Now I'm really starting to feel sick. And for some ridiculous unknown reason, I cross my hands in front of myself in some vain attempt to hide. Doing some weird pretzel thing I only prove my awkwardness. He reaches over to the nightstand and walks over to me.

"Here. Take this, it'll help with that headache."

Wanting to move this along, I grab the three painkillers and swallow them with some water from the bottle he handed me. "Keep drinking, love."

Okay. I drink another few mouthfuls and put on a fake smile. "Sooooo. I'm here and I have no clothes on. Feel like sharing?"

With that, he smiles darkly, eyes all glittery-mini-disco-ball-esque, and he slowly gazes down my body. Eyes returning to mine, he smirks. "Things seem about right to me."

I look down eager to get away from all that sparkle when I notice his feet. Geez, even those are freaking pretty. Are guys supposed to be this pretty? They have no bunions and the nails are all trim. His toes are lined up perfectly in ranking order. I want to stomp on them and see if they'll go on attack. I crack a smile at that.

Then I feel his hand move to my waist. Warmth. The pad of his thumb brushing up and down from my ribs down and then up, the rest of his fingers spanning the full cross length of my back.

"I noticed your tattoo at the fight. What is it?"

He runs his thumb over the beautifully inked creation. On my left outer rib all the way down until about two inches below the left side of my bellybutton, sleeps a remarkable delineation of a phoenix. "It's a phoenix," I whisper, not meeting his eyes.

"Why is it all black? I can see the fire, the intricate feathers, but it's all in black? The shading is remarkable, but no color, love?"

I shake my head still staring at his feet. My answer too personal to share.

Suddenly his beautiful face pinches in alarm and he grips me almost painfully. His eyes narrow and look confused. Then he drops to his knees...a bang on your knees drop.

He's closely examining the phoenix, or rather what it hides. The jagged raised puckered line of skin, that's six inches long. If I didn't feel so fucking raw before, I certainly do now. And those damn painkillers haven't kicked in yet.

Instinctively, my stomach muscles tense, my fight or flight predisposition on the verge of kicking in. His grip is tight as his breath cascades across my belly causing all kinds of uncomfortable goosebumps. He presses his forehead firmly to the silent atrocity. "What happened?" he grinds out brokenly, head unmoved.

I shake my head, as I'm not about to tell him. Even if he doesn't see it, I know he can feel it, and he can probably hear it through my silence. Coen is too clever not to notice. Besides, it's hardly first date conversation, not that we've even been on a freaking date.

He falls back on his haunches, then slowly stands, his eyes remaining on the offending scar the entire time. "I asked you a fucking question. What the hell happened, Charlie?"

A curse word and my name. That's like a double negative. But this isn't one story he's getting. You're so smart, Cocky. You figure it out. "Where's my clothes, Mr. Collins?"

"No, don't you dare run. Why won't you tell me?"

You'd think that would be obvious. Maybe he's not as smart as I'm giving him credit for. "Where's my fucking clothes?" I scream at the top of my lungs. I'm shaking now. I don't know if I'm angry or hurt or who the fuck knows? I hate feeling this vulnerable.

I've pushed him away and am frantically looking around. I can't see my boots, my cell, anything. He comes after me, grabs my head, and pulls me into his chest when I notice that he's shaking, too. "I'm sorry, I'm sorry." He rocks us gently. "You don't have to tell me. Its fine, we're fine." He breathes in, shakily and continues. "I'm having your clothing laundered. You were sick on them last night. Please stay, love. Please. Take a shower, it's still early. Please!" His voice is shaky and everything feels odd.

I swallow and after some hesitating, nod. Realistically, what are my alternatives? I don't have any clothes, or a ride, and I don't know where I am. Plus, a shower in the whimsy spa of Chez Collins sounds about fantastic right now.

He squeezes me and kisses the top of my head over and over. "Thank you, thank you. I'll grab you some of my clothes. They'll be big, but at least you won't be walking around like that."

Rich billionaire sex god, says what? He tries again. "I mean, your body is perfect, love. You can walk around here naked." My head snaps up to glare at him.

Shaking his head and murmuring about what an idiot he is under his breath, he walks over to an oversized dark oak chest, rummages through some clothes, and hands them to me. "Here. You shower. I'll wait for you downstairs." He stops at the dresser, grabs some clothing for himself, and walks out of the room without looking back at me.

I'm standing in the middle of his room completely lost. This is worse than a rollercoaster. It's not just up and down, high and low. No, it's more like some cracked up tilt-a-whirl.

After showering and getting dressed in a long sleeved baggy Red Sox t-shirt and a pair of oversized sweats that I've rolled down the waist twice, I leave the bathroom. There's not a whole lot of improvements I can yield especially since I have no makeup to hide the bruising behind a painted face. Running my fingers through my long dripping wet hair in an attempt to untangle it, I notice Coen's cell on the far night table. Score.

I may or may not have done a random background check on Coen. I like to know who I'm working for, and as of Thursday morning, when the partners cornered me and told me exactly this, I took it upon myself to learn about my new employer.

Information is the real source of life. At least in my world.

It's locked…hmmm, time to utilize my newfound knowledge. His birth date? Too obvious and too narcissistic. Not Coen. Let's try the date his mother died? Nope, didn't work. Her birth date? Reversed? His graduation from Stanford? No. Shoot, I don't know the date he lost his virginity but would that really be his password? No, probably not, he's not that vain. Think, think.

Something momentous.

What do I know about Coen? What does he value? Piece it together. I flick through the images I have of him in my mind. Where is he? What's he doing? Who's he with?

A number pops out. Can't be. But I try anyway, plugging it in. 0 3 1 1

Wednesday's date.

Unlocked.

Without processing that implication, I quickly call Malice.

"Allo." His gruff voice sounds like he's just woken up.

"Pourquoi suis-je dans la maison de Coen Collins?"

Why am I in Coen Collins' house?

"Vous avez dit que vous vouliez aller avec lui."

You said you wanted to go with him.

"Eh bien, maintenant que je dis me chercher la baise."

Well, now I'm saying pick me the fuck up.

"Où es tu?"

Where are you?

"Je vous ai dit au Coen. Je ne possède pas d'adresse. Mais me trouver et venir me chercher !"

I told you, I'm at Coen's. I don't have an address. But find me and come get me!

"Je suis en route. Je vais le trouver. Ne rien faire."

I'm on my way. I will find it. Don't do anything. He hangs up.

I erase my call from the log and look towards the door. I might have a few more minutes. I decide to snoop around and notice a lengthy text between Coen and Davis yesterday.

6:33 DAVIS: SHE'S LEFT HER OFFICE AND HAS TAKEN A TAXI SOUTHBOUND. I'M FOLLOWING.

6:38 COEN: DON'T LOSE HER

6:58 COEN: WHERE IS SHE?

7:02 COEN: DAVIS....

7:06 DAVIS: THE TAXI DROPPED HER OFF AT AN OLD ABANDONED FIREHOUSE IN LYNN.

7:07 COEN: DID YOU FOLLOW HER INSIDE?

7:10 DAVIS: YES, IT APPEARS TO BE SOME UNDERGROUND FIGHTING RING. SHE'S ENTERED ONE OF THE FIGHTER'S LOCKER ROOMS.

7:11 COEN: WHAT? GET IN THERE!

7:12 DAVIS: I'M AT THE DOOR. I CAN'T GET IN.

7:14 COEN: I'M ABOUT TWENTY MINUTES OUT. DON'T TAKE YOUR EYES OFF THAT DOOR.

7:38 COEN: I'M HERE. WHERE ARE YOU? WHERE IS SHE?

I'm startled with a noise coming from the hall. Coen is on his way to the room. I quickly secure the phone in the same spot I found it and drop to the floor looking under the bed.

"Charlie, love, where'd you go?" he asks, walking into the room. He must have showered elsewhere because his hair looks damp and he's wearing jeans. Only jeans.

"Hey." I'm peeking my head over the bed, still kneeling. "Have you seen my phone? I can't find it."

"You left it downstairs. Come on, I've made breakfast." He ignores my flush, thinking it's 'can't find my phone' frustration, when really it's 'what the fucking hell, he had me followed' flush. He takes my hand and leads me downstairs into the kitchen. He has me sit on a stool then proudly hands me a plate of eggs, bacon, and toast. You sweet, creepy man.

"Oh, um, Coen, as delicious as this looks, I don't eat bacon," I say, pushing the plate away.

"Is it just bacon or do you not eat pork?" he asks looking truly interested.

"No all pork; bacon, pepperoni, sausage, and other piggie parts and pieces."

"That explains the pineapple cheese pizza the other night. Is there anything else you don't eat, love?"

"Yes." But I don't want to talk about this. I want to know why you had me followed.

"Please, tell me. I want to know all about you." He takes my hand looking exceedingly sincere and genuine. This is the first time anyone has said that to me. Not interview me. Not interrogate me. And certainly not dissect me. But want to actually *know* me.

Although he's asking for all of me, I only give him a bit of the surface. The glossy pages in the front of my story. I don't want him in too deep. Then he can hurt me. I can't allow that. I don't know him and I don't fully trust him.

I continue talking about my food likes and dislikes. It's a safe topic, friendly, yet personal. He smiles and laughs along. I think he likes my sharing. He seems pleased and for some unknown reason, I like that.

While he is busy declaring his love for the new restaurant he just found, the one with the best duck in town, I get lost watching him. Not just his lips and the way they pucker and stretch, but how his entire body speaks to me. Shirtless, I see how his deltoids rise faintly with each of his breaths. His hands, still seated on his legs, twirl with each thought extending the triceps and biceps. Everything bunches and moves. It's elegantly fluid. He's so graceful and beautiful.

And... he's stopped talking. I look up from my enamored perusal to meet his eyes. He's watching me watch him. He's the one who started this whole staring thing. I guess I just threw my hat in the ring.

His bottom lip is tucked between his teeth, his stare intense. I can only imagine my face is the same. Minus the lip part, I'm still sore where that's concerned. Plus, he has that delicious scruffy yummy look that men sport in the morning.

"Hi." He smirks, finally releasing that lip, though I can still see the indentions there. He must have been biting pretty hard. I bet he tastes good.

Chills. Everywhere. "H..h..hi-ye," I croak out. Was that a real word?

His frosty eyes light up even more landing all over me now. They aren't searching, they're taking all of me in. While I'm wearing this ridiculous shirt. I look down. Yep, it's still there.

He reaches over and cups my left cheek. His thumb rubs my bottom lip. "This mole…" Don't talk about my moles. Is this a skin screening? "This sexy as sin beauty mark, I want to lick it."

I've seen cartoons where the dog or rabbit or whatever animated character becomes speechless because their tongue drops out of their mouth and rolls about a mile on the ground. I think my tongue might very well be hanging out of my mouth. It might have even rolled up the stairs for all I know. Because, right now, I don't know. Everything is Coen. Even I am Coen.

He reads my silence. Then suddenly there's movement and I'm on his lap, straddling it. All I see is icy blue. I must feel icy blue because I can't stop shivering. I'm lost in the blizzard, possibly never to be found again. His gentle hands seal us together. One around my face, the other on my lower back. But I'm not moving; this moment has been branded into me. He's still watching me, his smirk gone. He leans forward, holding me frozen with those majestic eyes, and softly kisses the mole that resides under the left side of my lip.

It must have been some type of hormonal button because I find myself wrapping my arms around his neck, running my fingers through his honeyed curls.

His lips, never moving from their new found corner, bite my mole. Yep, bite it. I yelp and he chuckles, pulling back slightly. "May I taste you?"

"Yes, please," I whisper. Though I'm not sure if manners are required at this moment. These kind of occurrences don't happen often for me. Hence, the new found knowledge of the happy button mole. I wonder if it only works with Coen.

He licks his thick lips, the moisture giving them a beautiful shine. Then his nose starts a slow lazy trail from the bottom of my jaw. He's rubbing scruffy yummy all over. His nose leading the way from my jaw higher. More chills. He breathes out filling my senses with more Coen. Taste…please. I need taste but he's over my eyes. Kissing each one with gentle lips. His nose runs down mine, up and down. He's moving dreadfully slow. It's nearly painful. My body is wound tight anticipating the arrival of a Coen kiss.

Finally, he places his lips on mine, but rather than kiss me, he rests them there, breathing me like I've been breathing him. He moves them ever so slowly from side to side, maybe testing their firmness or their softness. Then he opens his lips marginally and kisssssssssses me. I pull him further into me, silently begging for more. He grants me another kiss. This one is sturdier perhaps more assured, his lips opening wider. Then another firmer touch, and this time his tongue licks my bottom lip enough to taste me. I part my lips begging for his entrance. He meets my needs, his tongue darting out a little inside waiting for mine to grant permission. I willingly consent and we are touching. We are tasting. We are breathing.

Lost in our heated frenzy, he bites my top lip and I wince and pull back. I'm woken from my Coen coma. "Shit," he whispers pulling me even closer, his head finding the crook of my neck.

"I forgot about your injury. I'm so sorry, love."

I've fallen down from the glittery rainbow and have landed in a puddle of muddy dirt. I nod and lay my forehead on his scruffy yummy chin. Closing my eyes, I try to ground myself. I'm tilted. My axis has been fully knocked over.

"I'm sorry," he whispers.

I nod against his chin again, attempting to comfort him and this fleeting moment. We're lost in our own heads for a while before we hear a banging at the door.

"I'm not expecting anyone. Stay here, I'll be right back." Putting me back on the stool next to him, he nods and placates a smile.

Then I hear yelling and a loud beastly voice.

Coen comes back with Malice hot on his heels.

"You called him?" he asks accusingly.

I nod. "I can't stay here, Coen. This isn't a surprise."

"I would have taken you home." His voices rises and he points at himself.

He's acting as if Malice has come to take his favorite toy away. Childish. I'm not his plaything. I'm not his...well, anything really. I mean, except his employee in a roundabout way.

Oh my goodness...I work for him.

Aren't I the one who purposely hides behind glasses and clothing so I won't be viewed in some demeaning sexist way? Because some chauvinistic ass hats believe that the bigger the chest, the smaller the IQ? No way! I want the corporate world to see me as a productive counterpart. As an equal. Not as the convenient whore that works so well *underneath* them. Because there are those that do. They believe a woman doesn't belong in the harsh realities of law. Somehow those confines are too structured for the weak minded, delicate female sphere. I've worked my ass off to get here. I'm not ready to walk away.

I can't have a physical relationship with Coen. This is wrong. Despite my skewed view of life, even I know this isn't right. Sure it isn't truly wrong either, but I can only focus on one thing at a time.

"Malice, vous attendez-moi dans la voiture."

Malice, will you wait for me in the car.

He nods and leaves after a grunt of affirmation. Who needs words?

Turning back to a frustrated Coen, I try to extinguish the slutty walk-of-shame chick I've turned into by channeling my inner lawyer. I can see by his stance that he's preparing for a verbal fight. He knows what's coming. Coen is incredibly perceptive and he reads me too well, which I'm unfamiliar with. I need to be more creative in my approach.

"Thank you fot taking care of me last night."

"Of course," he answers, still waiting on my move.

"I was hoping after the merger is complete, we could spend more time together." He looks confused and quirks a brow. "What do you mean?"

Tricky. "It wouldn't be prudent to be seen together while I'm under your employment. But there's an end date. I'd like to explore the possibilities of a friendship?"

He didn't like that. "Did that look like friendship, love?" he says pointing to the stools we've just vacated. "And you're *not* my employee."

"Semantics, Coen. Please don't be difficult."

"I'm difficult?" he says towards the ground, eyes latched onto his beautiful, yet strangely manly feet. I must be developing a fetish. "Maybe you're right?" His eyes harden and shoot me with disappointment. "Maybe this connection I feel, this crazy tethering, is too difficult. Maybe knowing you, cherishing you, aching for you is difficult. Yeah, that's it. *I'm* being difficult."

And that is how the lawyer crumbled, at least internally. My breath stalls somewhere in my lungs. My heart beats slam into stutter. My fingers twitch by my side. I can't find my words. I can't find my voice. I'm not even sure if I can find a thought. Everything random is splintering through me. Around me.

Bobbing my head, yes, no, I'm not sure. I spy my boots on a glass table in the living room. If that isn't a sign…

I clear my throat hoping some sound will emerge. "Well then." Deep breath. "Thank you for your time. I look forward to working with you, Mr. Collins. Have a lovely weekend."

I move over and grab my boots and cell phone that has been placed next to them.

As I make my way to the door, in my periphery vision I see Coen with both hands pulling at his hair, his body locked tight. Muscles tense. It's not until after I close the door that I hear him scream. Like a battle cry scream. It sounds both angry and hurt. I can't tell if he's prepping for war or succumbing to defeat.

Chapter 6

I'M LISTENING TO EDWARD GRIPE to the table. "It's just a commercial solution," he screeches exhaustedly.

Jordon joins in. "Darrien is being incomprehensible. His demands are unethical. He's forcing us to redraft this proposal without the additional addendums and proper corrections."

Usually, my head is fully submerged in the murky waters of corporate bureaucracy, but my focus has washed away. Out with the tide.

I've been sitting at this table since eight-thirty this morning trying to piece together what the Collins Corp or CC legal team has made an absolute debacle. Pages and pages of regurgitated drab.

The head of the CC legal team, Jordon, had food brought in twenty minutes ago, attempting to keep us here with this vacant bribe. I think he's hoping we'll stay and finish the work he seems to be so adequately inadequate to do.

Though the abject fear he emits is strangely intoxicating, I can't stay. There's an edginess in the air; a prickliness that my skin has absorbed. It fell upon me the second I walked into the Collins Corp building. It began harmlessly as goosebumps across my flesh. Then an accelerated heart beat joined the collaboration. Next, came the pounding in my temples, my lack of sleep the most likely culprit. Finally, the trepidation jumped in to harmonize. A full orchestra of idiomatic panic.

I know he's here. I can almost sense him. When watching those psycho fanatical killer movies everyone loves, every time the murderer/creeper/run-away-from-him-he's-totally-gonna-kill-you guy is near, there's this eerie chilling music that alerts the viewer something bad is coming. A warning. And I'm totally hearing it now.

Honestly, Coen hasn't even crossed my mind in the five days since I left his house. The man that was everywhere I turned has suddenly been swallowed back into the 'never knew he existed' pile. No cocky stares. No quirky smiles. And certainly no yummy fuzzy scruffy have made an appearance.

Instead, I've buried myself in the world of work and make believe. Not that the two go hand in hand, mind you, but it exists on this new Coen free plane I've created. I'll be the first to admit, not thinking about Coen Collins while working on the Collins contracts, is a little challenging but I've held my own.

I remove my glasses and squeeze the bridge of my nose. The pulsing behind my eyes is compounding at an alarming rate and I deem this a medical emergency. I need meds stat. Since this is our first face-to-face exchange, the CC team and I, and Lori, the legal aid I brought over, my fight night injuries work to my advantage. And I greedily take their sympathy if it gets me out of here.

"Excellent progress. I suggest that we welcome any advice from council on how to progress. Please refer to the addendum on CVR and connect with Darrien on how to proceed with the transaction bundle." I look over the table and see nods of agreement. "Now, if you'll excuse me, I've got to see a man about some stitches." I chuckle, so they think the story I told them about my clumsy fall off the curb when I went running last weekend, is legit, and that they're privy to some inside joke.

I ask Lori to stay in case anything is finalized during my absence and meander down the hall towards the elevator, when some curly blonde hair catches my eye. The sight of him alone is enough to freeze me to the spot, but it's the woman on his arm who captures my attention.

She's classically dressed in a short Valentino long sleeved dress in flower prints with matching boots. She's elegant and adorable. Her hair is an inverted chocolate bob with bangs that feature her blue eyes, not icy blue like the man next to her, but a darker deeper shade. She's scary thin, not at all curvy like I am. And she's tall. She has a tiny nose and thin straight lips that are garnished with an audacious red coating. The lipstick color is fitting for her, but on Coen, not so much.

It would appear that Mr. Collins has been doing more than

lunch in his office this afternoon.

We connect, my fucking ass.

Difficult.

That fucking cocky ass, made me hate that fucking word. Made me loath myself for being so reasonable.

I haven't slept since that Coen *difficult* montage started circling in my head on a continuous fucking loop.

And he's getting lunch?

Red fucking lipstick lunch?

In his office?

She's laughing and touching his chest. Her claw-like fingers with long painted nails in the same slut color digging into his heart. He smiles his quirky smile and rubs some of the smeared lipstick off. Letting his thumb, the one he kept wrapping around my neck, touching my cheek with, feel her pale completely un-sun kissed skin.

I bet he didn't tell her that she was being *difficult*.

God, I hate that fucking word!

I need to move. I can't stand here watching them be all canoodle-y. My stomach is churning.

Jesus, it has been so long since I've felt duped. Suckered. Tears are burning my eyes and I blink to try to encourage them to abort mission. My nose sniffles and that soft sound, out of every clatter and verbal white noise in the building, is heard.

By the wrong person.

His eyes widen and he immediately stops touching Bombshell Non-Boob Betty. He pales. Oh wonderful, now he and his slut partner match in coloring.

Gathering whatever cool points I have stored for a rainy day, I ever so casually finish walking down the hall and to the elevator. There aren't many escape routes on the thirty-fourth floor, so I thought this move seemed the most viable, although I did briefly consider jumping out of the window.

I pretend to have only just noticed him and his slut du joir. I press the down button and smile.

"Mr. Collins, it's LOVE-ly," yes, I'm using that word on purpose because he deserves the dig, "to see you again." I pull out every drop of charm I can muster. And I blink, like I'm thrilled to be in this Cocky son of a bitch's presence.

Then the shit hits the fan. Stick figure Betty smiles, leans down to 'my' height, and says, "Aren't you just the cutest?" She then turns to Coen. "What a wonderful company you have here to help these young individuals with those 'special needs' I keep hearing of." Then she kisses him in front of me.

And there's more. She's back to me. Again with the lean. "Oh honey, did you get a boo boo? I think I have some gum. Would you like some gum?"

Why is she trying to give me candy?

And it looks like I'll be taking the stairs.

Coen is a fucking statue. He looks so lost.

Yeah, well fuck you!

I nod once, my facial features tight and drawn. There are simply no words.

I push open the heavy metal door that's leading away from this debacle. I'd open the gates of hell if I had to, in order to get away from this fucked up shit. Besides, I need to burn this energy off before it gets the better of me. I'm a runner. I have an endless endurance and like to move. So speed and stairs become my two best friends. One floor down into my descent I hear that POS yelling my name.

Too late, Cocky. Too late.

Chapter 7

I WANDER AIMLESSLY AND NUMB. SOMEHOW, I make it to my appointment on time for the removal of my stitches, and since my brain is semi-operable, I decide it's better not to be home right now.

But I'm tired and drained.

I make my way across town to Gunner's. I've seen the black Town Car several times in the last week, and although I don't believe he's watching me now, I'm not risking a Coen encounter.

Gun opens the door looking like he's just woken up, even though it's nearly four in the afternoon. His black hair is sticking out in random places and sleep lines map out his pillow position. Though his piercings are still in place, he looks more human without all of the extra jewelry he wears on stage. Gunner *is* rock and roll. It isn't just something he does, it's who he is.

It defines him.

He's in charge of all our online merchandise and most local bookings, though we have a manager. Basically, he gets to do whatever the hell he wants, when he wants. The life of a rocker.

He pulls me in and kisses my head. "Baby girl. Whatcha doing here on a school day? You skipping?" His chuckle reverberates through his chest. It's so easy to love on some Gunner.

I squeeze him tighter and rub my face against his bare chest. My guys rarely wear clothes and I've seen every part of skin that God gave them, and the fairy inkers tatted.

After he gives me some clothes to change into, we spend the rest of the day on his couch, eating stale nachos and flat soda. He asks me about Coen, or the 'preppy shit' I was hanging out with Friday night. I tell him everything, even the ugly parts from Saturday morning. Gun is my best friend and I trust him with my life. For the most part he gives shit advice, but underneath it all, he's really smart and he loves me.

In the early evening hours Trig comes home with some random guy and a sweet, surprisingly shy girl with a pixie haircut featuring pink and blue in her blonde hair. Gunner and Trig live together while both Bull and I chose to live solo. Don't get me wrong, I love these guys, but when you live in a small bus together, touring for six straight weeks, you want space. I know more about these three guys than I should. Hacker or not, some shit is just foul. Oh to be naïve, again.

The random is geeking out about how our music has changed his life. He even has our emblem tatted on his arm. Crazy. But the good kind. Not the Non-Boob Betty kind. He and shy girl eventually go back to Trig's room. I guess it's playtime.

For me, this is the norm. Actually, it's better than the norm. Sometimes, they just whip pieces of themselves out and get to it, not caring if I or anyone else is in the room has to witness such human sexual constructs. Some things your eyes can't un-see, especially for someone with my memory.

Just as I hear the moaning building, Bullet comes waltzing through the living room and takes the spot next to me on the couch.

"Are you on babysitter duty?" I ask pouting. Does Gunner think he can pull a fast one on me?

Bull laughs. "I'm your entertainment, baby girl."

Gunner chuckles while standing, and rubs his now beer bloated gut. "I gotta date. Gotta head out."

"Why didn't you tell me? I would have gone home."

"No fucking way. You're always priority!" To prove his point, he leans down and smooches me flat on the lips. "Love you little pistol."

And he's off.

Bull pulls me practically on top of him, grabs the remote, and starts flipping through channels. "I got you, baby girl. Go to sleep. I'll beat the shit out of any bad dreams that come your way."

He rubs the spot where the stitches were removed then leans down and kisses it. "Love you, baby. Now sleep before I spank that sweet fucking ass of yours."

"You didn't have a date tonight?"

"Hell nah. I got my baby girl!" He scratches his nose. He's lying. He cancelled. "I love you, Bully."

He looks at me, softly caressing me with his soulful eyes while he leans down again and kisses me harder, square on the lips. And again, lightly.

I lay my head across his lap and drift off as his fingers brush through my hair. All wrapped up in a soft fleece blanket and in Bullet's arms.

Who needs Cocky, when I've got Bad Ass?

Chapter 8

FRIDAY MORNINGS AT THE OFFICE are mayhem. Of course, my day began that way. Sadly for me, chaos attracts like chaos. I woke up on top of Bullet. Not that I'm complaining as the man is gorgeous. But it's the way I awoke. I'm quite sure I was in the deep depths of sleep fully ensconced in his warmth, when that foreboding feeling of being watched woke me. Not the gentle wakening when each of your senses slowly connect with the world around you, and your brain finally catches up. Nope. This was a *fuck I'm up* type of wakening. One second dreams of color and light, and the next, eyes wide open, trained on the strange little creature staring at me. It was the shy chick from last night, Trigger's ummm… friend? She's only about ten inches from my face…too close for comfort.

"You awake?" she asks. I notice her makeup is smudged under her eyes and her cheeks are more hollowed than I noticed last night. She's also wearing only a bra and thong.

"Yeah, I believe you took care of that for me. What time is it?"

"Sixish, I think? Are you Shooter?"

"Sometimes," I reply, honestly. I can feel that Bullet has woken up. His hands that were placed around my back move up and down. But he appears to be staying out of whatever this little chit chat is about.

"Do you like girls?"

"Ummmm, I guess." Most of my friends are male. I find women to be catty and mostly untrustworthy. But I do have few female acquaintances.

She brushes some purple hair back, seemingly nervous.

"Do you like to date girls?" Oh, now I get it.

She reaches over and sweeps some hair off my face then touches my brows with her frail fingers. Not sure what to do, I shift lightly on Bullet. I'm not a huge fan of being touched, especially by strangers. She stands, unclips her bra, and lets it drop to the floor. Little boobs with pointy pink tips are staring at me.

"You're so pretty…we could…"

"I'm not really into all of that," I interrupt with seriousness filling in my tone. I'm more uncomfortable than frustrated and I want her to go back to wherever her clothes are.

"I could help. I, I mean, have you ever tried? I'd be willing to help, I mean, offer myself for whatever you need." Where's Trigger? Why doesn't she go back to him?

I feel Bullet underneath me freeze and then something else hardens wakening up and joining our conversation. Hello there, little Bullet. It's not really little. I mean, I don't have loads to compare it to, but it looks to be a good size, but with all of the metal in his piercings there, it's difficult to tell. He has a Jacob's ladder. I think there are at least four bars going through his…shaft climbing all the way up or down. But I'm usually too distracted to count.

His voice is raspy and even deeper filtered with morning sleep. "Yeah, Shooter. Maybe you should consider her offer. I could even supervise. Make sure she does the job properly."

She smiles, her straight perfect teeth on display. I'll admit that she's attractive. A little too thin, seriously, go get a Big Mac, but pretty nonetheless. Still.

I shake my head no.

"Please," she whispers, almost looking on the verge of tears. "I came here with Trigger and James so I could meet you. I'm your biggest fan! You have no idea how your music changed me. What you guys are all about just speaks to me…" She wipes under her eyes. "I've had the biggest crush on you for like ever." That's weird since the band has only been around for a few years.

"If maybe we could...ummm, I'd do anything. Anything. We could be friends if you want. I could get you coffee…or um, I could massage your feet? I could…I could…"

This desperation needs to end and my real day needs to kick start into gear.

"Thank you, I appreciate the offer and your love of our music. What's your name?" This tends to calm the usual over enthusiastic fan. They know I'm paying attention and that I'm interested, when in reality, I just want this torture to end.

"Peyton. My name's Peyton. If you want some breakfast, maybe I could make something for you?"

I appeased her with allowing her to feed me while Bullet looked too pleased with himself, probably hoping something will eventually go down and he'll have a front row seat.

A cereal-filled belly later, I ran home to dress for work, and a chilly feeling came over me. Though nothing looked to be missing, it felt as if someone had been there. Inside of my home. The air seemed off, I can't explain it. But I knew it. Always trusting my instincts, I began circling the condo looking for a clue. Picking through my memory, it appeared nothing had been touched. But that nagging feeling was there...

Changing quickly, I made it back to the office with only minutes to spare before the morning meeting commenced and I had to give an update on the Collins Corp negotiations.

A few hours later and I am chained to my desk, figuratively, of course, in the midst of a brief I am working on for the Boys and Girls Club case when I get an unwelcomed interruption.

"Charlie, there's someone here to see you," Olivia says pushing the cracked door further open.

"I'll greet him. Where is he?" I assume it's a male, because nine times out of ten, my visitors are.

"He's at the front desk. He's quite attractive, too." She winks at me.

"You should ask him out then." I stick my tongue out at her. She's always trying to set me up thinking I need a good guy in my life. Little does she know it's not the good ones I like. As she's one of the few people I like in our office, I take her verbal extortion.

Across the entry way I spot said undesirable.

"Davis, how can I help you?" I don't want him coming back to my office. Whatever he is about to say or do, is no doubt a directive from Cocky. And I want no part of that man.

"Ms. Paz, may I have a moment of your time?"

"No."

He's carrying what appears to be several white boxes stacked together with a long string wrapping them. It looks like food, maybe from a bakery? I take a deeper breath letting my sense of smell take the lead, and yes, it is food.

Holding it out as if the boxes were cumbersome, he gives me a pointed look and walks back to my office, as though he's been there twenty thousand times already. Dick.

He places the boxes on my office table and sits in the chair facing it.

I remain motionless standing in the door frame, hands crossed, and wait him out. Sometimes, silence says so much more than words ever could. After several minutes of neither of us budging, he finally engages.

Turning in his chair to face me, he sighs. "Ms. Paz, would you be so kind?" He points to the chair.

"No," I repeat. It feels as though I've used this word a lot today. I hope there's no limitations on daily usage allotments. I'd be doomed, the day not nearly half over.

He begrudgingly stands and walks towards me, stopping as his toes nearly connect with mine. He's too close.

"Ms. Paz?" He's trying to intimidate me. Does he really think he's the scariest thing I've ever dealt with? I eat men like him for breakfast with syrup and powdered sugar when I'm feeling saucy. He lives in his rules. I can see it. He is a trained Marine and most likely so institutionalized that he probably couldn't deviate from an order even if it killed him.

Although I like rules and guidelines and razor edged boxes, we aren't nearly cut from the same cloth. I make my own box, sharpening the corners and pushing the lines back, stretching and shaping to my will. It looks as though Davis' box was handed to him. I think it's cardboard.

"Mr. Collins has some gifts for you," he says arching one brow.

"Please thank Greyson for me." Strike one.

"It was Coen who sent the gifts."

"Then I recant my thanks." Booyah, strike two.

Oh, he is getting frustrated I can see the buildup brewing.

"Have a nice day, Mr. Fielding."

So, I may have checked up on him. I may have, accidentally, dug into his military training and background to find out what I was dealing with. I may know more about this jarhead than Coen.

And, I may really like that.

It would appear that he doesn't.

Strike three.

I move from the door and motion with my head that he should get the hell out. I've said and done my limit with this man. He represents ugly to me. Cocky ugly.

He clears his throat, places a long rectangular box on the table, and walks over to me. Toe to toe, yet again. His eyebrows furrow and his lips pinch to the side. Then he seems to make his mind up and leaves.

Of course, the second he's out the door I run to the box and open it, dying to see what's inside. I know by the shape it's a bracelet, but I had no idea it would be a *bracelet*. Damn, this thing is stunning. Cartier. It has four strands of yellow gold that synch into diamonds and black onyx, creating one perfect creation. It is both light and dark, and I have no doubt ridiculously expensive.

I wonder if he picked this out or had one of his harem members fetch it for him. Either way, I can't have it.

I grab the bracelet and box and run after Davis, hoping I can still catch him. He's just entered the elevator. I'm running and yelling, with as much professionalism and sophistication as I can muster. "Davis, take this back."

The doors close as I spy the smallest of smirks.

Oh, hell no! Time to recruit backup.

Chapter 9

I HAVE A TEMPER.

In general, I do my best to preempt any potential blowouts. I do breathing exercises. I write music. I run. I lift weights. And my personal favorite, I get to punch people or bags if nobody is willing.

Cocky tests my ability to preempt my hysterics with his shitty attitude and his annoyingly acute presence.

Earlier today, Malice swung by my office to collect Coen's unwelcomed offering. He claims that although he hit some roadblocks, mainly a nasty secretary, the bracelet was returned personally to Coen, along with my message.

Done.

End of story, right?

No way…not with Coen feasting on his usual breed of cocky.

I was having a quiet, relaxing dinner with Andrew at Ostra before catching a show at the Wilbur. Despite not checking in on me after the charity event, he eventually called on Saturday. He claimed he never got my text and things were rather chaotic with his father at the helm.

I'm not sure if I believe him. He's a politician after all, and lying is part of their nature, like a receding hairline. It's already in their genetic makeup, waiting to come out.

Since he was stuck in Washington all week, this is the first opportunity I've had to see him.

Then out of the corner of my eye, I see Davis. Dammit! I can only imagine what is coming next.

Ignoring this new impending obstacle, I check in to catch Andrew whine about what he plans to do in regards to his constituency's stance on Social Security funding and why they are wrong, why we are all wrong, when my mind takes a detour.

Toast. I'm staring at him thinking, toast.

I remember watching *My Big Fat Greek Wedding*, and the adorable dad kept crying about E-yan Miller's family being dry and boring; toast. Plain, dry toast.

I guess Andrew is my toast. Only not.

He's a graham cracker.

Although, tasty, nobody ever craves a dry, flavorless, graham cracker. Not even pregnant women.

Toast, though dry, is the first thing you eat after being sick all night. It's the baseline on the journey to rebuilding daily health after an empty stomach has rebelled. It's even part of the BRAT diet, almost like a necessary evil.

But a graham cracker is a different monster altogether.

By itself, it's easily forgettable. But crush it and use as a crust for pie…then it becomes an essential part of the dessert. You want that crust in each sweet bite.

Or get even louder with a smore. Two graham crackers, with a decadent piece of chocolate paired with a gooey melted marshmallow…and you have firecracker magic. No longer is the cracker deemed mundane, but rather masterful. Artistic while touching a genre of flavors and textures.

Andrew is a graham cracker.

Is that why we are together? Am I so chocolate, so loud, and so audacious, that I need dry graham crackers?

I'm completely lost in my world of toast and crackers that I neglect to notice a waiter appear adding a full place setting and a superfluous chair, which seemed to be immediately occupied.

Coen sits down and starts discussing his order with the waiter while another brings him a glass of Scotch. He unfolds his napkin, places it across his lap, and politely smiles at Andrew before his gaze returns to the waiter. "What are tonight's specials?" he asks.

As the waiter goes over his spiel and collects Coen's order, Andrew sends me a hard glare, his hazel eyes looking darker, greener, accusingly, like I had something to do with this.

"Andrew, did I mention how handsome you look tonight?" I ask trying to distract him. Andrew has a big ego that responds well to people feeding it, although he truly does look handsome. He's wearing a charcoal grey slimming suit, I think it might be a Hugo, with a collared buttonup in a soft teal. His tie black.

"Thank you, my dearest. You look quite spectacular yourself. The color is stunning on you. It reminds me of the ocean off the Agiofili Beach in Greece. Maybe we should vacation there soon. Take some time away from the city."

Tonight I opted for a more casual take on evening wear. A Tadashi Shoji cap sleeve gown in mystic blue with nude lace cut-outs. I have to confess; I love this color on me. It gives my grey eyes a bluish hue. It feels elegant, but feisty in a subdued way. My dark hair is curled into a forty's top reverse roll, at least that's what my stylist, Fernando, told me. It's curled softly and tucked in with a few diamond barrettes.

I wanted to make sure I left a lasting impression.

"Sounds wondrous. I think some time away from the city is exactly what I need." Andrew looks pleased with my answer, despite Coen's proximity.

The waiter returns. "Would you like more wine, ma'am?"

Hell yes, fill her up, my good man. I smile politely and nod. "Thank you."

"You look like quite the vixen, love." Coen smirks at me.

Andrew questions, "How do you know each other? And why the hell are you disturbing our dinner, Collins?"

"Did I neglect to tell you, Andrew? I've teamed up with Collins Corp on their next merger. Negotiations are currently underway with our estimated deadline in early May."

"Sounds trying, dear. Those Collins' men can be distressingly difficult."

"You have no idea." I snicker.

"Yes, Carpenter. We *can* be difficult, though I like to think of it more as persuasive," Coen adds, sticking his nose into our private conversation.

"Collins, when are you going to step up and let Greyson retire? He's getting up there in age and deserves to have a little fun," Andrew questions.

Coen and Andrew banter back and forth, mainly on which is more stressful, politics or running a multi-trillion dollar corporation. I fall reticent. My carefully orchestrated night derailed at the first crossing.

The food arrives and the boys silent their conversation in an effort to enjoy their meal. Somehow, the addition of Coen to our table is acceptable. The interruption forgotten.

"Excuse me, I hate to bother you while you're eating, but are you Shooter?" I hear from a gentleman behind me. I shift to see the inquirer. He looks to be in his mid-twenties and has a short goatee.

My lips quirk to the side and I try to look confused. "Shooter? Are you asking me if I've shot someone? I assure you, I don't have a weapon." On me right now.

He flushes in embarrassment. "No, of course not. She's a guitarist for my favorite band. You look so much like her. I apologize for the interruption."

I chuckle, like this little mishap is amusing. "It's quite alright. She must be quite good if you came over here hoping to find her. I'm sorry to disappoint."

Andrew chimes in. "My girlfriend gets that all of the time. She must be her doppelganger. Maybe I should look up this Shooter musician." Yeah, I bet you'd like her…darling.

Goatee smiles broadly. "She's seriously hot! And she totally shreds, man. Your girlfriend here, freaking looks just like her. You're one lucky man."

Coen decides to jump in and add an extra heaping of tension spice to the mix. "I think rock stars are incredibly sexy. If you find that Shooter, send her my way." He chuckles. He already knows exactly where Shooter is but he's figured out that Andrew doesn't and he thinks he's one upped-him.

"Really, Collins? I had no idea you were into such debauchery. I thought you were out hunting that perfect debutant, not some tattooed rocker. The rumor mill has placed you and Mandy Morninglane on the list of up and coming couples. She's quite the catch. You need to lock that down before another steals her away."

Mandy? Maybe she's Non-Boobs Betty? Please, please leave Coen. I hate you, I hate you, I hate you. I can feel the heat pooling in my cheeks as thoughts of yesterday bubble through my veins.

I interject quickly while smiling broadly at asshole-de-ville. "Yes, Mr. Collins. She sounds like a fetching catch."

Half a millisecond later, Coen grabs my hand in his, like we're long lost lovers united and smiles proudly at Andrew. "You must have heard wrong, Congressman. I have my sight on only one starlet and I do plan on locking her down sooner than later." He shifts triumphantly while turning to look at me. "Oh, love. I nearly forgot. In your haste to get to work on time this morning, you forgot your bracelet."

He gracefully pulls it out of his breast pocket, no box this time, and locks it on my wrist. Then brings my inner wrist to his lips and kisses it, his gaze returning to a perplexed looking Andrew.

"Charlie, darling, would you like to explain?" Andrew asks with raised brows.

This would be one of those times when my temper might flare up. Where I envision thirty-six ways to dismember Coen. Or thousands of explicatives that would make the entire restaurant blush.

I'm about to elucidate, when Coen feels the need to continue his ridiculous ruse.

"Carpenter, don't play dumb. It's unbecoming." He swirls the glass with the amber liquid in his other hand then takes a calculated sip. "You already know she's a catch and yet you've neglected her needs. I've simply stepped in to fill the void." He brings my hand, which has been nestled in his, to his lips again, smirking at Andrew.

I can't help but laugh. Coen is telling Andrew that he's neglecting *my* needs. What's with this guy? This pissing contest has gone stale.

Coen turns to look at me, confused by my amusement, then chuckles along like he's in on the joke. Only, I have no joke. I'm just dreadfully tired.

"It's funny, isn't it love? That Carpenter, here, thinks he can hold onto a woman like you while having fun with his kept women in DC. Did you know about the apartment he rents for two of his little toys? Or that he gives them a monthly stipend and pays their credit cards."

Andrew shifts nervously. "Ignore him, darling. He's obviously fabricated a fantastic story. I have eyes only for you. Surely by now you've figured out my feelings for you."

Pulling in vain to release my hand, I finally slip it through. Exasperated, I turn to Coen.

"Do you think me naïve?" I glare at Coen's furrowing brows. He thought he came here to change my stance on Andrew, thought he was dropping a detonated bomb on my lap. He thought he would push me away from Andrew.

"You've severely miscalculated the situation yet *again,* Mr. Collins." I turn my focus back on Andrew. "I believe he's referencing Shaylen Turner and Brittney Messing. Hardly a fabrication."

My voice is hollow.

Andrew makes a choking noise and pales. His shoulders sag and his lips tremble in confusion.

"Charlie," he whispers.

I dig into my purse and pull out the keycard I was planning on using later, but Cocky has forced my hand. I place the card on the table and slide it across the white linen cloth towards Andrew.

"Room 606 at the Boston Harbor Hotel. I took the liberty of using your credit card."

Andrew smiles menacingly, seemingly unconcerned with my usage of his card. Clueless. "Oh thank goodness. Yes, a hotel." He tries to capture our waiter's attention, using hand signals to let him know we're ready for the bill.

I'm saddened by the entire situation. I clear my throat and stand. Both men are looking a bit lost.

"I've already taken care of the bill." I then move to Andrew's side of the table and lean over. I run my fingers through his hair, enjoying the last time I will be able to touch this man. I press my lips softly to his. Then pull back and slowly stick my tongue out and lick up his mouth. Instantly, Andrew's eyes dilate and his breathing grows heavy. He moans.

He attempts to reach out to me but I pull back, tsking. "Darling," I purr. "I don't like to share." I continue running my fingers up and down, caressing his face.

"The hotel is for you and your DC strumpets. They've been eager for your arrival." I kiss his lips one last time. Despite this ending, I did enjoy his company. He was easy. Not at all like the tension and confusion I've felt when I'm with Coen.

I close my eyes savoring this last sweet moment. Then whisper into his mouth. "Goodbye, darling." With that, I straighten up and nod a silent farewell to the table. Coen pouts angrily, his arms tightly crossed. I'm guessing he didn't like seeing me kiss Andrew. I kind of know that feeling.

I take my path towards the front, where Malice has been keeping his eye on me. I usually wouldn't have him accompany me on a date, even in his shadows, as that would be unnerving. But he insisted. He wasn't sure how Andrew would handle things.

Neither of us, however, anticipated the monkey wrench that is Coen.

But I gladly leave them both behind me.

Chapter 10

THE LAST THREE WEEKS HAVE been uneventful. Both men are now background noise. They are no longer a compulsory part of my world, but their presence still exists, mainly in the form of texts and calls, and the daily gifts of flowers, or food, or jewelry. I've contacted a local charity that passes out flowers to the elderly and gifted the flowers to them. I returned the jewelry via Malice, and I eat or share the food goodies. Chocolate dipped strawberries, cakes confessing various forms of affection, fruit baskets, and sometimes full meals.

Olivia and Lori climb into my office every day at lunch time hunting for a piece of the daily spoils. As a result, they are much more pleasant around the office and all too willing to copy, file, or do anything to assist with my cases. Needless to say, I've had to hit the gym extra hard to keep up with all the sweets and fatty foods.

Tank doesn't seem to mind, though. During the week, when the weather permits, I would simply run around the area for my daily exercise. But with the spiking of caloric intake, I've had to add extra workout sessions at Tornadoes.

I can't gain an ounce right now. My older sister is getting married in two weeks and my bridesmaid dress has already been altered to my exact measurements. Mother has warned me that if I do anything, anything at all, to mess up this wedding, I'll be officially disowned. Sadly, I don't believe this to be an idle threat. She means it.

My sister, Joelle, is three years older and very much mother's mini-doppelganger while I remain the 'freak' of the family and the bane of mother's existence. I know she doesn't hate me; she just doesn't understand me, which complicates our relationship. My father has more patience and tolerance, but mother rules the roost.

I'm dreading going back to Orlando for this wedding. What's worse is that I can't even bring one of the guys with me for backup. Not even Malice. Mother would nearly die in her Prada heels if she saw me bring a tattooed menacing looking bad boy to the ceremony. So no Tank, no Mal, and no temptation trio. I'm blindly going into the world of Paz alone.

We are heading to BedHead tonight for some fun. I haven't been out in a while thanks to all of the work on the CC case and avoiding Cocky and the Congressman.

Tonight, I'm in full force Shooter mode. Black painted on ripped jeans hanging low on my hips, and a tight black long sleeved shirt with the entire back made of sheer netting. It stops just above my belly button. I'm on full display tonight and looking for fun.

Being the owner of one of the hottest clubs in town definitely has its benefits. I climb onto the center bar stationed along the backend of the main floor. The DJ turns off the music as the lights hover over me. One would think that with my history I'd be the shy introvert in the corner, afraid of attention. But I love to push myself.

I screech into my earpiece. "Hello fellow Head-anites. How the fuck are you?"

All eyes fall on me as people scream and wave while others pull out their cellphones to film or shoot pics. They crowd in closer to the bar.

"So, I have a very important question; has everyone gotten HEAD tonight?" They scream wildly encouraging my shenanigans. "Oh no…that doesn't sound right. I said…has everyone gotten some HEAD TONIGHT?" More screams crescendo.

I chuckle into the mic attached to the headset. "That's what I want to hear. Now, who wants to meet the sexiest mixologists in Boston?"

My six bartenders climb onto the bar. By now the bar is clear and people have grabbed their drinks. This is a pretty regular thing, at least in my bar. I wait as they line up, then begin the introductions.

"Starting with my right, we have the lusty Lola, next is the bombastic Babs, killer Cosmo girl Kelly, followed by Debbie does drinks, Sassy Sammy, and lastly sweet as sunshine, my girl Savvy."

The girls bow or wave as I go through each name and then jump off the bar.

"Who am I?" I wait as people scream my name. "That's right lovers. My name's Shooter. Welcome to my playground!" I open my arms widely as I grin haughtily.

"Hmmm," I pout while popping my finger on my lip. "I notice that my bar is looking a little dirty tonight. Who thinks it needs to be cleaned?" People scream and chant, "Clean it, clean it, clean it."

I walk to the end of the bar and hand my earpiece to Savvy then walk to the other end as the girls hold up a bottle in their right hand. Next, a towel that has been folded a few times sits on the bar. I run to build up momentum then drop to my knees on the towel as it goes flying across the bar.

Each girl is pouring their alcohol from the bottle to moisten the bar, and with my mouth wide open, I drink it while my front soaks it all up. My last bottle is the Patron and I pull it out of Savvy's hands and stand up and scream, "Hell yeah!" I'm handed my earpiece. "The bar is *clean*! Now go grab a guy, grab a girl, and get some *head*!" I can't help but laugh. I love hearing the crowd, and the alcohol has begun to warm me up.

"Make sure you find someone to tuck you into bed and have a fucking fabulous night! Oh and don't forget to take good care of my girls. Tip well and tip often." Then I end the way I do every single time and everyone joins in. "The bar is OPEN!!!!" With that the overhead spotlight goes off and the DJ picks up the music. I giggle shamelessly as I crawl down the front of the bar, everybody grabbing and wanting to talk to me. I even get a few lascivious offers. I love this place. Naturally, by this point, Malice is in full freak mode. He growls off any man in the vicinity and he and some of the club security have circled me as we walk to the VIP.

Reaching the seating area, I plop down when I see my guys. As per usual, they have women and men all over them. I squat on the armrest next to Bullet, most of the other spots are occupied since I'm the last to arrive.

Bullet leans over and licks my neck. "Yummy…Shooter and vodka. I think it's my new favorite flavor." I'm soaked. My hair is streaked with different liquors and my makeup must be a mess. But I'm happy. I haven't seen the guys in at least a week, and that's just not our norm.

He's smiling while focusing his attention on me but I guess the girl next to him doesn't like feeling neglected. She unbuttons his jeans and starts sucking his cock right there.

I feel my eyes nearly bulging out of my head. This isn't the first time I've seen this, but right in the VIP lounge while he's chatting me up?

"What the shit, Bull?" His eyes close and he starts moaning and biting his lip.

I don't need to see this shit. I begin to stand up and walk away when he grabs onto me.

"You're gonna stay. It's my birthday weekend and you aren't going anywhere. This won't take long." As he says that, he eyes my tits. I can't wear a bra with this shirt and with all the alcohol it is sticking to my rather chilled nipples. He licks his lips and whispers to my tits, "So fucking sexy."

Even over the music, I can hear the girl's slurping and sucking and I feel the bile creeping up my throat. I try to move again but his lock on my arm is intense. His veins moving under the sugar skull tat on his forearm make it look more menacing.

"Where's my birthday kiss, baby girl?" The slurper thinks he's talking to her so she starts to lift her head. "Not you…get back and suck me dry. Finish what you started."

I catch a quick glint off his piercings before he grabs my head. "About my birthday kiss…"

His fingers locked in my hair, he pulls me towards him and kisses me hard. His kisses turn more incessant as he trails to my neck, then buries himself there. Although it's wrong, I'm pretty sure I'm getting turned on. I usually try to have some control over my libido but even that seems to be slipping. I watch the girl bob up and down, her hands gripping and pulling him. I feel his breathing grow harder and harder against my neck and his hold on me tightens almost painfully. Then he bites my neck and murmurs my name as the slurping grows in crescendo and explodes.

Everything silences around us and I wait. Full of pride, the girl, who I now notice is a brunette smiles broadly and blinks her too-wide-for-her-face-and-it's-really-creepy eyes. She licks her lips and sighs happily as if his cum was ice cream or something. Bullet's cock is left hanging out, nearly forgotten, yet it remains in my sight. Bullet clears his throat and pulls away from my neck to look into my eyes. He studies me and then slips his view downward, stopping for an extra moment on my breasts and my tightly crossed legs. They were straddling the armrest earlier. I don't remember crossing them.

"Tricks," Bullet calls over his shoulder. "Go get me a Wilhelm Scream. They only serve it at the main bar." He pulls his wallet out and hands her a twenty-dollar bill. His cock still laying there. Yeah, I keep noticing that.

I guess the brunette bug-eyed chick is Tricks. Sounds about right. She whines, "But they won't let me back into VIP. I don't have a bracelet." She's right and Bullet knows this, yet he replies. "Nah babe, they'll remember you. Just say you're with me." He smiles assuredly at her. She nods, takes the money, and is gone.

He leans closer to me. "You wet?"

Uhmmm. How should I respond to that? I shrug. Bullet looks over my shoulder and I follow. Trig has a girl next to him with her hands down the front of his pants. Gunner has two girls around him. One next to him and the other straddling his legs, and by the noises and the positioning, they're definitely going at it. Again, this isn't a strange sight for me. They do this all the time.

Bullet grabs me off of the armrest and places me on his lap, straddling him. "When was the last time you had an orgasm?"

My face flames up and I lick my suddenly dry lips. "I think it might have been on T.. Tuesday night?"

He shakes his head looking incredibly sexy as he stares at my lips while licking his own. "No, with a partner, baby." His voice is laced with a raw edginess to it that I've never heard directed at me. It elicits all types of tremors to rip through my body.

Bullet knows my history, maybe not all of the specifics, but he knows; so his question throws me. I'm not sure if I should tell him the truth, so I sit there immobile. But the ache in my core isn't going away and with Bullet's warm breath cascading across my face, the smell of him so intoxicating, I can't focus.

I shake my head, no.

He gnaws on his lower lip while seemingly making his mind up about something. His hands move to my ass as he begins to slowly knead, making things worse for me. I feel his cock pulsing back to life between my legs. But it's the heat there that has me humming. I'm dying.

He checks over my shoulder once more then rips off the black shirt he's wearing placing it next to him and pulls out his leather jacket wrapping it over my shoulders, cloaking us from wondering eyes. His callused strong hand moves around my waist while his thumb slides under my wet shirt and begins a back and forth movement inching higher with each gradual procession. My breathing becomes laborious and that slow simmering ache intensifies into a raging inferno. My nipples grow painfully hard with these foreign ministrations and I whimper disconcertingly.

"SShhh…I got you, baby girl. I'll always take care of you," he murmurs and presses his lips against mine. His teeth dig deeply into my bottom lip, engraving this moment in sharp tingles. I whimper my need for more, and with the hand still on my ass, he obliges with sliding me back and forth on his unconfined cock. His hand tantalizing under my breast is maddening. I need him to touch it. Grab it. Twist it. Hurt it.

He continues his torture and my entire body feels combustible. Although my last heated moment was over a month ago with Coen, this feels different. I've had Bullet in my life for over three years and he is one of my best friends. This isn't some guy I just met. If I lost Bully, it would kill me. He's in way too deep.

The tightening in my core is rising and coiling at a steady pace. It's too late to return to the ground. The bungee cord will be pulled at any moment and I will freefall back to earth. Until then, I have no choice. My mind is lost to the man before me. And, assuredly, Bullet is all man.

His kisses turn demanding and more daring. His tongue moves in to clash with my teeth. This isn't gentle. It's rough and passionate. But right now I can't find the energy or rational to care.

"Shooter," he murmurs. "Let go, baby. Stop thinking and give me this, tonight."

I want to let go. I want to be free. Even if for only a moment, I want to completely connect and feel safe. I want to be lost. I don't want to be me.

The tightening intensifies and I'm barely hanging on. His warm hand encompasses my entire breast and he squeezes hard. He then jerks and pinches my nipple to a deliciously painful point.

I'm lost, spiraling out of control into the infinity of darkness and space. I'm weightless. My muscles lock into the orbits of my flight.

I think I may have touched the sun and then I'm swirling and twirling back down to earth.

He holds me close and whispers in my ear, "I got you, baby. Just breathe. I'll never let anything happen to you." He whispers my name in between tender kisses, and despite the reality setting in that this did indeed happen here in the middle of a nightclub, it relaxes me. With one hand in my hair, the other grabs the shirt and cleans up the mess on his stomach, then he finally tucks himself away. Darn. He looks at me shyly and smiles serenely. We are both lost in each other's stares, coming down from our highs, when an angry Gunner grabs a hold of Bullet.

Both of Gunner's hands wrap tightly around Bull's neck, which has his face reddening with a lack of oxygen. "We made a fucking pact, brother. None of us were to touch her. She means too much. You fucking know that. You stupid fucking shit." He screams into Bullet's face.

Although it takes a second, I freak out. "Get off of him, Gunner!" I scream scratching at the hands around Bullet's neck. My shirt is still bunched under my breasts, but I don't care. I don't understand what is happening and I want them to stop fighting.

Gunner finally releases his hold and sends me such an ugly look that I swear my heart stops. He shakes his head and without another word, storms away.

Bully fingers his neck while gasping for air. How could things have gone from such an unbelievable high to an unbearable low in less than a few minutes?

I stand and walk around the couch to better examine Bull when Trigger walks over. He points his finger in Bull's face. "You fucked up. You could have any pussy in the entire fucking world except hers." He shifts that pointing finger and glares at me. "And you…I thought you were better than this." He shakes his head as a guy walks over and rubs his back, then brings Trig back to their vacated spot on the couch.

In the corner, I see Malice. He, too, gives me a look of distain. I don't understand why everyone is agitated. I love Bullet. He made me happy tonight. I made him happy, I think, so why is everyone acting like it's the end of the world?

Bullet, Gunner, and Trigger are my lifeline. They ground me. I'm lost. Like all of the time, lost. Without them, I may as well be the wind. Wandering aimlessly with nothing to pull her in. Nothing to capture her or harness her energy. I need these guys, probably more than they need me.

"Bull, are you ok?" I whisper. The tears clog the back of my throat and force my words to come out hoarse.

He stands from the couch, still missing his shirt and throws his jacket on. "I'll be fine, Shooter. No worries, okay? I'll always have your back. No matter what, you feel me?"

"Yeah." I attempt a smile but he sees through it.

"I better go. Have Malice get you home safely. Love you." He leans over kissing me on the forehead then another to the top of my head and leaves.

I hate this. It feels like I've crossed a painted line and I'm now stuck at a crossroads. I'm not sure what to do. What to say. It feels like everything I do is wrong. I hate being wrong.

Chapter 11

THIS WEEKEND WAS AN EPIC fail. After Friday night, I didn't make contact with the guys. I wasn't sure who was in the right or who was in the wrong. And with all honesty, I didn't want to face them.

I guess my mood transpired into work since Lori and Olivia noticed. We were noshing on chocolate dipped fruit, when Olivia decided to break the ice. "You seem a bit off this week. Is everything okay? I noticed the flower arrangements have stopped and you're getting less messages. Is that what's getting you down?"

I no longer know what has me distressed, just that I am. "No. Lesson learned. I'm ready to get back out there and try again. I think?"

"Why don't we go out tonight? We could meet up at a bar and have a little evening fun. Just a Girl's Night Out. Gosh, I haven't had one in *forever*! Please say YES!" squeals Olivia.

And that's how I ended up in a bar on a Thursday night. I've decided to dress up a bit. I'm not in my usual jeans or leather pants. I traded it for a tight white long sleeve dress. The collar scoops around my neck and the body has a huge cutout of both the front and back of the right side of the dress. It curves low touching my hip and then across nearly revealing my belly button. My hair is pulled into a tight ponytail atop my head. My eyes are painted an alluring smoky shadow and soft pink colors my lips. I'm ready for whatever this Girl's Night Out brings.

Both girls walk right past me, as I stand by the bar. I guess they didn't see me. "Hey, don't I get any love?" I ask putting my arms around them.

"Holy shit," Olivia gasps. "I swear you almost look like a different person. Jesus, you look hot. We're gonna find you a sexy stud and you're gonna love every second of tonight!"

This is the most fun I've had with girls since law school. Being surrounded with my guys, I barely have time for any female friends, though they tend to be in short supply.

However, tonight I'm not a playmate prop, I'm not even Shooter. Instead I can try to find my rhythm as Charlie. A fun friend. I'm still learning the ropes but maybe I could get used to this.

After what happened in Gainesville, perhaps on some subconscious level, I've fallen out of touch with the female population. Maybe that's why I've kept them at arm's length.

The girls and I grab a booth to the side and order a round of Cosmos and potato skins, bacon on the side for the girls. Yummy, I think I'm digging being a chick.

I get lost in conversation about Brantley's son Taylor's ass, apparently it's something I should 'definitely' notice. We joke about Jim McIntry, our tech guy, and how he talks to your tits and never meets your eyes; when the song *F.E.A.R.* from Papa Roach comes on. Lori starts shaking and screams, "Oh my god, I love these guys. This song is epic...let's dance."

I shake my head. "No thanks, you guys go. I'll stand guard at our booth." I don't mind just chilling and jamming to the beat from afar.

"No way sexy, I wanna watch you work it!" Olivia sings pulling me out of the booth. Tantalized with the thought of dancing with the girls, I willingly follow them onto the dance floor.

Immediately, they start twerking and shaking and laughing and even screaming along with the lyrics. They look like they're having so much fun that I decide to let go a little more. It's time to let go of the past. Or to try to.

I jump in and scream and dance and laugh and laugh. The beat drives our movements and my hips rock on their own accord. My hands flail up in the air, Lori grabs one, and we do some weird twisting thing. With a hand behind my back, she dips me low and I nearly touch the floor.

Why not, right? We're having a blast. I'm lost in this moment, fully ensconced in the beat, the movement, the bodies grinding against us.

We continue dancing and writhing around each other. Laughing ourselves into hysterics and eating up song after song. After what feels like hours, but is probably closer to only one, I feel the effects on my feet and I'm dying for some liquid relief. I yell into Olivia's ear that I just received a desperate plea from my feet asking for a mini-break. By now, the music has shifted to a slower beat and they think we could all use some libations. I couldn't agree more.

As we make the painful hike back to our booth, Olivia's arm entwined with mine and Lori taking the lead with my hand in hers, I spy a familiar build in a back corner booth. Turning my head to get a better look, I see that it's Trigger with two females, and across from him is Bullet with that Tricks girl (strange since he doesn't like redo's), and another girl.

Damn it! Immediately, all of my happiness, the fun I am having, peels away leaving the resounding hurt and anger that constantly lives there.

I haven't heard a peep from any of the guys. Yet, apparently, they're still hanging out with each other. So, I'm being ostracized? I don't get it. They fuck around all of the time. I let loose for a nanosecond and now I'm the leper? The black sheep? I get enough of that shit from my family, I don't need it from these guys.

We make it to the booth. "You in for another round, Lee?" Lori calls over the table. She's officially dubbed me Lee, tonight, but I kind of like it. Or I did. But now my night has soured and I'm a ball of hurt.

"Hook a girl up!" I shout back. I look over to the bar to make sure Malice is still there, or maybe he's bailed on me, too. Apparently, it's real fucking easy to do. But he's watching me, and as attuned to me as he is, he's noticed my mood swing south. His eyes narrow, but I try to send him a reassuring smile. It's just another speed bump, I try to tell myself. I'll deal with any decisions when I return from Florida.

I'm trying to focus on the girls when Olivia freezes and I feel someone standing to my left. "Holy shit! Are you Trigger?" she asks in awe.

"Yeah, every day and twice on Sundays." He smiles and winks then throws his arm around my shoulder. "I need to speak with you." He looks serious and motions with his head, while flailing some of his Mohawk, for me to move.

No, thank you. I was available all week, but apparently, I wasn't important. "Wow. Trigger from Loaded Gun-AWESOME! But, NO! I'm hanging out with my girls. They're my NEW BESTIES!" I reply with near venom in my voice. I can't hide my hurt or anger and Trig should know me better.

"Lee, you know Trigger? That's crazy," Lori squeals while clapping her hands.

"Yeah, crazy LEE. Let's talk. Now!" Trig replies looking agitated.

"Nah, I'm good. But it was freaking fantastic running into you." I'm dismissive and cruel but I'm hurting too much to be anything else.

"Fuck," he grunts. "Take care of my girl," he says to the table and kisses me on the head before walking away.

"Lee, who the fuck are you? You look like the angel of sex tonight and you hang out with rockers? Day-am, I wanna be in your world," Olivia says.

Lori adds. "You know, you kind of resemble that rocker chick in their band. What's her name?" She looks at Olivia who adds. "Shooter."

"Right, right Shooter. Are you her?" Lori continues.

I squint my eyes. "Oh most definitely. I lawyer by day, and by night turn into a hardcore rocker chick." I laugh while stating it sarcastically. The best lies always have truth built in.

I'm all about truth…in lies.

They laugh with me, shaking their heads, because the notion is truly preposterous. That's why it's fantastic.

Suddenly, a pissed off Bull storms towards our table. He doesn't ask to speak with me. Fuck no. He simply leans into the booth and picks me up, throwing me over his shoulder. My ass hangs out as the thong I'm reluctantly wearing easily broadcasts my ass cheeks.

"Bullet Harrison, get me the fuck down now! My ass is showing! You big muscle head. Dumb, dummy!" Apparently, I can't think when my ass cheeks are escaping. He covers my ass with his big fat tatted hand to hide said cheeks and continues his trip down the hallway. I glance up to see Malice looking confused, still seated at the bar. "Intervene, dumb ass!" I scream. He shakes his head and smirks.

Finally, Bull throws me down against the wall by the back door. I immediately go into fight mode and start punching him in the chest, screaming. "Never ever touch me like that. I don't deserve this. You ignore me and hang out with your friends. I'm not worthy of you." I'm so livid as thoughts come at me from every which way.

He grabs my hands and throws them above my head with one hand, and then pushes his body hard against me, caging me in. His other hand goes over my mouth. "Shut the fuck up! You don't fucking hit me. You got me. Calm down…you need to calm the fuck down. Now." I'm still screaming and attempting to add my knee to his rather important man parts. I can get out of this, I know I can, but I can't stand the idea of hurting Bully. It hurts to fight him. To fight with him.

I shut down and stop all movements.

"You good, baby girl?" he asks, his hand releasing my mouth. "You gonna listen?"

But I don't nod. I'm breaking down, and I can feel myself crumbling. My bottom lip starts to tremble and I'm trying hard to keep it locked in. Lock it in. Just a speed bump. Breathe. One, two, three.

It's too late. A tear falls free and slides down my cheek. He spies it. "No, no baby girl. Please don't cry. I've got you. Everything is fine." He coos and hugs me so tightly that my feet no longer touch the ground. "Baby..."

I shake my head and pull away. He doesn't get it. I wipe away my foolish tear and try to pull air into my lead filled lungs. Everything feels heavy and like I'm slugging my way through.

"No, you're wrong. Six days, Bull. Not one word for six days. And if you didn't see me tonight, who knows when I'd have heard from any one of you." I start walking backwards, walking away.

"Charlie," he grinds. "That's not what's happening here."

But it's too late. I'm done with this conversation. He never called.

No correction, he never called *me*!

Dead girl walking.

Chapter 12

TODAY IS THURSDAY, APRIL 23, the day I've been dreading for the past nine months. That's right, my sister's wedding. Dum, dum, dum. Cue evil dark music and the sounds of women screaming in fear. That's what's circulating in my head right now as I wait to board my flight to Florida. I haven't been home in more than three years and would prefer to keep it that way, but my sister had other plans. She always does.

I scroll through my phone for one last time before boarding and shutting it down. After last Thursday Bull, Trig, and Gunner began operation "Annoy the shit out of Charlie." It always starts the same; we need to talk. I know we need to talk, I'm just afraid of what will come out of me when we do.

I wasn't an original member of the band. In fact, I thought they were terrible and I was their *biggest* critic.

There are three levels to BedHead; main level, upper level, which houses the VIP, and the basement. The basement is reserved for up and coming bands, or bands trying to get their foot in the door. When I created the club, about three and half years ago, Loaded Gun was determined to make it big and would hit every venue in the general Boston area and beyond.

In those days, I was more of a control freak. When investing a shit ton of money, it's advised to keep a solid watchful eye on it. BedHead was my first investment after I bought my condo. I would observe the various bands in the basement and determine if they could hit the main floor with Steve-O by my side as manager.

I was always drawn to the trio's band when they would play, but I never connected with their music. However, I did see the potential. They had the 'It' factor. They were gorgeous, had a unique sound, and they had the drive. For some crazy reason, I would find myself in their audience week after week, always trying to figure out what was missing.

Finally, one night, I grabbed a blank music sheet and started changing rhythms and adding riffs and chords. I followed the guys offstage and brought them into my office. I handed them the sheet and told them my recommendations and that they had tremendous potential, they just needed to harness it. But I may as well have been a punk teenage kid, the way they treated me. I was eighteen, after all, and they thought I was playing dress up in my daddy's suits as club manager.

After several attempts and having them finally look at my revisions, they took notice. They also applied my recommendations. I liked the change and so did the crowd. Their sound slowly evolved. Gunner was rhythm guitarist at the time, and one night after the show when I handed him my nightly observations and critiques, he asked for me to play. Picking up the guitar I played their songs with my modifications, never thinking twice. After a few more weeks of this, they would join in, playing with my adjustments. We had a nice flow. We ended up hanging out and eventually developed a surprising rapport.

They had been playing the main stage for a couple of weeks, when out of the blue, they called me up during the show. Not wanting to stop the show and upset my paying customers I joined them. It was an unforgettable moment that altered my world permanently. I became part of something more.

Looking back, I now see that I was just an addition. A new beat, which might easily be removed. We aren't an 'us.' Instead, it's the trio and then further down the line, me. I've been living in a music dreamland for the last three years and I've finally awoken. Reality is unpleasant but necessary.

Of course, this epiphany comes to light when I'm hours away from five days of pure, unrelenting torture. Yes, please pour acid on my ripped open heart…thank you ever so much.

The flight flies by too quickly and I'm in my rental car driving, when my cell rings. Mother was already frustrated with me about my delayed arrival. Apparently, when I told her that my plane arrived at 3:14, she thought it meant I'd be at a spa appointment across town and through Orlando traffic by four. How could

I have been so cruel as to upset her only days before her big event?

After being griped out during the forty-eight-minute ride from OIA to the Ritz-Carlton, I wasn't surprised to be attacked the minute I walked in the door. Mother was standing there ready to strike. First, came my tardiness. Next, my attire was ripped to shreds, verbally. Finally, my hair.

Mother had already taken the liberty to determine exactly what needed to be done to correct me. And she literally threw me to the wolves to do so.

The Paz family dynamic is horribly dysfunctional, to say the least. Mother, aka Delilah, is a Savannah Southern Belle by every sense of the word. She has blonde straight hair styled into a short bob, she's statuesque at five foot seven, and she still wears a perfect size four. Her eyes are a stunning emerald green and everything about her is proportionate. She was a model prior to meeting my father, mainly in print ads as she never evolved into runway.

My sister favors mother, though her hair is wavy and light brown, naturally anyway. She is five foot eight with a similar build but Jo's eyes are brown and prior to her rhinoplasty, she had my father's bulbous nose. Though three years older, I was always far ahead of her in school, which somehow crowned her as leader of the "Charlie is a freak" fan club. Needless to say, we never got along. My mind was fully engrossed in my books, while her pursuits were more superficial and trivial. We have never gotten over that hurdle. At least, I haven't.

During my senior year, when I was recruited by the University of Florida on a full scholarship, I jumped at the chance to escape. I couldn't get out of the house fast enough. Mother refused to allow me to go until certain measures were put in place by the University for my safekeeping. Since I was still a minor, I didn't have a say in that. I realize now that she had my best interest at heart, even if it didn't make a difference.

By the end of the day, nearly every hair on my body had been altered in some way. The hair on my head was threatened to be cut, as according to mother it is too long. I had to put my foot down on that, only to be persuaded to get a trim and add auburn highlights. Next the hair on my legs and underarm area were waxed, along with a more sensitive area. Why mother would be concerned about my bikini line, I don't even want to know. My brows were tweezed, my stache threaded, and any extra hair on my face plucked away.

Needless to say, that was the least relaxing spa day ever!

After a trying dinner with my parents, I attempted to shower, making sure the hot water didn't spray my sensitive now hairless parts, and then I finally climbed into bed. I'm in my old room turned guest room, messing with my cell when I get a text.

10:18 COEN: YOU LEFT BOSTON?

I'm not surprised Coen knows I've left town. I think he's still having Davis follow me. I know it was Davis who entered my apartment, though I have no idea what he was doing there. I've now taken some precautionary measures and installed a more responsive security system to at least slow him down.

Coen has texted me a couple of times a week since our peculiar dinner with Andrew six weeks ago, though I never respond. Andrew, however, has stopped contacting me entirely. In his last text, he called me a stuck-up, self-righteous cunt. That one kind of stung.

10:23 CHARLIE: I'M AT MY FOLKS…

10:24 COEN: IS EVERYONE OKAY?

10:26 CHARLIE: PROBABLY NOT. MY SISTER IS GETTING MARRIED.

10:27 COEN: SOUNDS SERIOUS, DO YOU NEED BACKUP?

10:28 CHARLIE: YOU'VE GOT NO IDEA HOW YOU JUST HIT THE NAIL ON THE HEAD.

10:29 COEN: I CAN BE THERE IN FIVE HOURS.

10:30 CHARLIE: MR. COLLINS….

10:30 COEN: PLEASE, CHARLIE.

10:31 COEN: BELIEVE IT OR NOT…I CAN'T STOP THINKING ABOUT YOU.

10:33 CHARLIE: IT DIDN'T LOOK THAT WAY WHEN I WAS LAST AT YOUR BUILDING.

10:34 COEN: I AM SO SORRY ABOUT THAT… PLEASE, CAN WE TALK?

10:34 CHARLIE: NO

10:35 COEN: PLEASE CHARLIE….

10:40 COEN: PLEASE, LOVE…

Like all men in my life, Coen has let me down. Saying one thing while meaning another. I turn my phone off and place it on the nightstand. Restless, I can't fall asleep. The gaping burning hole in my chest is expanding and slowly eating me entirely.

On Friday afternoon, we all move into the Ritz-Carlton for the weekend. Although the wedding is on Sunday, family members will be arriving any time. It is Orlando, after all. Home of tourist mania.

I spend time loving on my grandparents and catching up with other members of my family. The contrast between mother's family and my dad's is undeniable.

My father, Maurice, was born in Morocco. When he was a child, he and his family moved to Israel. He speaks four languages, the two he was raised with; French and Arabic, and then he learned Hebrew upon his move to Israel. After completing the IDF, he moved once again, this time to the US where he learned English. He's a brilliant man and works as an I-O Psychologist, which basically means he has his PhD. in Industrial-Organizational Psychology, for Darden Restaurants.

At five foot eleven with black wavy hair and almond-shaped

dark grey eyes, he was everything mother was looking for; tall, dark, handsome, and rich!

Despite my griping, even I notice that although they're in their early fifties, they still make quite a stunning pair. I'm envious. With my one failed attempt at a relationship, I recognize how challenging it can be.

The family Friday night dinner is relatively peaceful and I reach my room without attracting too much attention. Tonight was the first time I've met my sister's fiancé, Gene Mc Fadden. I can't place my finger on it, but he gives me the willies. His family seems off, too. But mother…she was in her element. Outside of her attacking my wardrobe choice, she was pleasant all evening.

People still look at me strangely. They all know my history. My father's family, more so than mother's, are the biggest gossips. They love to get their hands on juicy information, and my life has provided no shortage. And they don't even know the current craziness in my life.

After climbing into the quiet room I again scroll through my phone. I have two calls and one text from Bullet, making sure that mother hasn't eaten me, yet. And another call and text from Coen.

8:17 COEN: ARE YOU STILL ALIVE?

10:57 CHARLIE: BARELY…

10:58 COEN: HEY LOVE, YOU SEEM DOWN. DO YOU WANT TO TALK?

The sad thing is that I think I do wish to speak with him. I feel an inexplicable pull to him. And right now I feel as though I've been cast out in the middle of the ocean. It appears that Bullet has found a regular to entertain himself with, and whatever moment we shared, was fleeting. As for Gunner and Trigger, I can't get those looks out of my head. It felt like I had disappointed them. Betrayed them. I feel incredibly alone, and being surrounded by my family, I'm only reminded of how alone I am. Of how I don't quite fit. I'm the square trying to squeeze into the circular hole. I can't reshape myself, no matter how hard I've tried.

I need a friendly voice to tell me that everything is okay. I'd bug

Tank, but he's in Vegas prepping for his big UFC fight next month.

So, Charlie plays stupid and picks up the phone.

With the receiver nestled between my ear and the pillow, I hear it ring.

"Hello, Charlie?" he asks softly.

"Hi," I respond with a whisper in the darkened room.

"Hi. Love, tell me what's wrong. I'll do anything you need to fix it."

"I wish you could, Coen. I'm fine, though. I mean, I guess, shit, I hope I will be."

"Did something happen there?"

"Just the usual."

"Then what has your beautiful voice sounding this way? I know…you're missing me?" Cocky has reentered the building, ladies and gentlemen.

I can't help but snort. "Always so full of yourself, Mr. Collins."

"I got you to smile, love. That's all I want in this world."

"All you want?" Why am I being flirtatious with this man? It's like rolling around in raw meat then running through the tiger enclosure at the zoo.

"Mmmmhhmm. You may be right. I've had a desperate craving for a certain mole."

Sigh…now my head is back there. Visions of Coen's body pressed to mine. Visions of what happened after.

"Coen, can you do me a favor?"

"Anything!" he replies instantly.

"Can you…um...can you tell me that everything will be okay?" I ask, while fighting tears. I'm hurting so hard right now.

His voice becomes hard and serious. "What happened? Tell me. I'll kill anyone that's fucked with you!"

"No…it's…um…it's nothing like that. I swear. I'm just…I don't know. Never mind…it was silly." I lean over and grab my sleeping pills and a bottle of water. My head is a mess. The only way I'll get any sleep is with medical assistance. There's silence on the other end for about half a minute. I question if he's still there.

"Charlie, everything is going to be okay. Do you hear me, love?" He says this with such conviction that I nearly believe him. But he doesn't know me. I'll never be okay. The tears choke my throat and burn my eyes. I swallow hard to rid them.

Clearing my throat, I whisper to Coen. "Thank you. Sleep well, Coen. Sweet dreams."

He sighs. "They're only dreams when you're in my arms, love. Sleep well, Charlie. Please call me tomorrow."

I hang up and press the phone to my heart. My head nestled in the pillow, I can feel my body getting heavy, the pull of the medication. I know that when I blink next, tomorrow will be here.

Why can't they make living pills like this? You blink and it's a day...you blink and it's a year. I just want life to fast-forward.

Chapter 13

WAKING UP GROGGY IN THE morning, I decide that a dip in the pool would wake my senses and help me put a positive spin on the day. Tonight is Jo's bachelorette party and by default I have to go as one of her bridesmaids.

Mother had other plans. As soon as I was situated on the lounge chair, after a few laps to get the blood flowing, mother found me and asked, well demanded, that I pick up some family members from the airport, insisting that I take her Mercedes, as her SUV would be more accommodating than my rented compact.

Maybe it was an excuse to keep me out of her hair, but it kept my mind occupied for the most part. On one of my trips, I did get to pick up my Aunt Perla and her family. When I moved to Boston to go to Harvard, I lived with them in Swampscott instead of one of the dorms in Cambridge. My cousins are a few years younger than me, but I had a lot of fun with them. It was one of the few times I remember smiling in those early years there.

Now sitting in the hospitality room after dinner, I'm caught up in watching my father and his siblings make fun of each other. My father is one of twelve children and he falls in at number eight. Personally, I'd wear that number like the ballplayers do. *Hey, I'm number eight.* That would be so funny, but there are only two in my family and Joelle wants nothing to do with me.

My dad's older brother Maxim, has gone around the table asking each of us what we were before we were reincarnated. I laugh and say Cleopatra and my uncle goes into a five-minute discourse on why he thinks I feel that way. I should have thrown him off and said Mary Cartwright, a British mathematician in the early 1900's and the first to analyze a dynamical system with chaos. I guess I'm feeling a little chaotic right now. But I didn't think that's what he was going for, so I gave him something grander.

My father's peer pressuring has me on my second shot of Arak, its taste similar to Uzo. He tells me it will put hair on my chest, I wonder if he knows I'm female and we generally frown on that sort of thing. I think he wanted a boy, hence my name, but I don't mind doling it out with him and my uncle. It makes me happy to see my dad in this light. I'm laughing and shooting the shit, when my sister and her evergreen cheer squad hit the room.

"Charles, what the fuck are you wearing?" She yells from across the room, and she purposely kills my name. I look down noting my AG rollup skinny jeans and my black tank top. I mean yes, there are some rips in them but that was the eleven-year journey look that made it costly. I paired the outfit with super cute Tory Burch wedge leather sandals in black. I don't think I look so bad.

"I thought we were getting bachelorette party shirts. Did you want me to change?" Better not to poke the bear. I'm now standing before her, trying to make up the four-inch height difference by broadening my shoulders. Who am I kidding?

"Mother!" she screams at the top of her lungs. Calling for backup. I look over at my father and everyone else that have a front row seat of Jaded Joelle the Judgmental Jackass.

Mother appears out of nowhere. Maybe she's a genie or a vampire. I glance at the ornate mirror on the wall to see if she has a reflection. Damn it, it's there. "What's wrong, Elle?"

"Charlie isn't cooperating. Look what she's wearing. How am I supposed to be seen with her? This is my night, mother. She's already ruining it and we haven't left the hotel yet," my sister gripes, rather loudly, to mother and quite possibly the rest of the room.

"Oh Charlie, can't you be cooperative for one weekend? Honestly, what am I going to do with you? Please, don't test me. Go and change your clothes," Mother says giving me a dirty look. If she could see her forehead all scrunched up like that, I bet she wouldn't do it. Time for some more Botox.

Again, I look to my father for some backup. Hey, Jo got backup. Tit for tat, right?

"Father, are you going to step in and help me? I didn't even do anything," I ask in Hebrew.

"Please sweetie, just do what they want. It'll make things easier," he

replies.

Some help. My warm Arak buzz is now gone. "What would you like for me to change into?" I ask dejectedly, my eyes on the floor.

Mother smiles and pats Jo on the back. "See honey, she can be reasonable. Remember, you're supposed to have fun tonight. Relax." She gives me a pointed look and walks back to her host-ess-ing duties.

Joelle smiles triumphantly. "We're going to City Walk and will probably club hop there, so you need to look good. Not like this shit." She motions to her cheer guard who throws a Pepto-Bismal pink midriff showing tank at me. "Put this on, fix your hair, put on makeup, put on a skirt, and get some decent shoes. That's all I ask. Oh, and the limo will be here to pick us up in fifteen minutes, so you better be downstairs and ready to go!"

She sniffs and walks away with her little posse in toe. Oh, tonight will be fun. I turn to look at my dad, who immediately takes another shot.

"You...you're on the top of my shit list!" I nearly shout at him in Hebrew, hoping that most of the guests won't understand.

I know, that was rude. But if she gets to yell at me, then I feel it only fair to share the love.

After racing to my room and changing, I still manage to get to the limo on time. Though my sister guffawed anyway.

Up and down we trolled City Walk. I got two Hurricanes from Pat O'Brien's. Damn those things were good, and I figure it's the only way to survive the evening; to be highly intoxicated. We had shots at some Bob Marley place and then danced some reggae.

On Jo's shirt, it lists all of these crazy stunts she has to complete tonight, like kissing a bald guy on the head. I took great liberty to make sure each task was successfully achieved and since she was just as blitzo as I, she willingly agreed. I think it was the most fun we've ever had with each other. Guys were hitting on us left and right and I kept screaming to randoms that my sister was getting married. We didn't even have to pay for a single drink.

The Hurricanes had caught up with me, and the girls finally found me a toilet, but when I got out, they were gone. My vision had doubled by that point, so I wandered for about fifteen minutes hoping to find a familiar face.

They ditched me. I shouldn't be surprised. Jo isn't my number one fan, but even this seems a bit mean for her. Trying to keep myself together I find some stairs and crouch down. The hotel is at least twenty minutes away. Maybe I could call my dad to come get me. He might be sympathetic. Mother would no doubt blame me. I grab my cell out of my back pocket and call. He doesn't answer.

My mind is a complete blank as I stare at my shiny cell. Cell, do you have the answer? It's moving as it stares back at me. It looks like it's winking but it doesn't have a solution. I close one eye in the hopes of finding a local taxi number to pick me up. Everything is getting blurry and I'm getting panicky. I tilt my head one way, then the next, but the words aren't straightening up. Instead they look like they're moving on the screen. I start laughing loudly. I'm so screwed. I will probably black out soon. Maybe I need some food to soak up some of this alcohol.

I attempt to stand up but nearly topple over. Wow, I don't remember gravity being so strong. "Careful," some guy says walking over to me and putting his arms around me.

"Don't touch her!" comes a deep voice on the other side of me. It's strange because he totally sounds like Coen. And upon closer examination, he looks like him, too. A Coen look alike… this could be fun!

"Chill out, guy. She looked like she was gonna fall. Just wanted to help." He raises his hands and backs away.

Coen look alike comes over, picks me up, and carries me in his arms. Wow. Coen look alike is strong. I can't help but reach out and touch his face.

I giggle out. "Youuu look sooo much like Coennnn. Disguuu know thattt?" Look at that nose. That is such a pretty nose. I rub the bridge. It's so straight but wavy. I doubt it has ever been broken. Mine has been broken. But Coen is too perfect to ever be broken. "Yurr not brokkkin," I sigh aloud.

He keeps walking with a solemn look on his face. I think he's mad at me. Why not, everybody else is, right? "Yurrr mmmad." I pout.

"Don't worry about it, close your eyes. I'll get you back to the hotel," he says without meeting my questioning face. He *is* mad.

I don't want to be near him. I want to go away. Away from my family. Away from the trio, and away from Coen.

"Stop it! You're going to fall if you keep squirming, Charlie!"

He's so angry. I didn't even realize I was wiggling.

"Pooot me durnnn, COO-innn. I dunnnneed you. I wurrd ave binnn fine. Lemmme gooo!" The tears are clogging my throat and the alcohol is slurring my speech. I push at his chest but nothing happens. I'm too weak. I can barely see now and he knows this is a losing fight for me.

I must have passed out for a minute because I find myself being jostled into a car.

"It looks like you found Ms. Paz," someone states in the front seat while starting the car. Coen closes the door and moves behind the car to enter next to me. He gives me a strange look and then pulls my head onto his lap. Clinging to me. He's wearing a pink polo and khaki board shorts. How a guy can look so hot in pink, I don't know.

With my ear pressed to his upper thigh, I feel him running his fingers through my hair. I hear his breathing regulate and find it soothing.

His breaths. His fingers. His thigh.

Coen is here.

Chapter 14

SOMETHING HARD IS UNDERNEATH ME. I try to arch away from it but it only brings on more pain. It feels like there's a marching band in my head. Bang, bang, bang, step, march, march, march. Crash the cymbals. Drumline go; ticky tank, ticky tank, ticky tank, ticky tank, tank, tank.

I already know I'm not going to like what I see when I open my eyes, so I think I'll keep them shut a bit longer.

"I know you're awake." Is that the drum major? Somebody shut him up. "If you open your eyes, I'll give you something for that headache."

I throw my arm over my eyes, just in case they thump out with all the banging. "Nnnnoooo!"

He exhales and I feel his heat creep towards me. His breaths are even and soft and I can smell how minty it is. "I met your mom last night."

I jackhammer up. Shaking my head, I pray that he's lying. "You're joking, right? Please be joking."

He reaches over and tucks some of my mangled tresses behind one ear. His hand lingers there for a few seconds before moving it away. He puts the pills in my hand and a bottle of Gatorade in the other. He thinks twice, grabs the drink, opens the top, and replaces it in my hand. He waits with his brows raised. I swallow down everything and match his stare. "Well…."

"She caught me carrying you in last night. She demanded to know who I was."

"Sounds about right. So, what did you say?"

"I gave her my name."

"I know it wasn't that simple. Tell me the rest."

"Okay, she wasn't appreciative of your predicament. And, love, I had to agree with her."

"Those words should never, ever come from your mouth!"

"You could have been seriously hurt, Charlie. I do *not* condone you risking your life!"

I stand up, using the wall for guidance. I don't need this. I look around. Am I in my room or his?

"Is this your room?"

He nods. "I needed to make sure you were okay. You were sick all night. That's why you're on the fucking floor." He paces and shakes his head. "What did you expect me to do?"

I walk over to the sink, run my hands under the cool water, and splash some on my face. That feels better. Then Coen hands me a toothbrush. I look at it, puzzled.

"It's yours..."

I nod and he leaves. I guess he wants me to brush my teeth. After doing my morning business, I walk out of the bathroom to find I'm in the penthouse. This room is definitely much larger than mine. Coen stands with his back to me, he appears to be looking out of the window. The sun is shining. It casts a light glow around him creating a stunning silhouette.

What.

A.

Guy.

"What are you doing here, Coen?"

"Taking care of you," he states, still facing the window.

"No, what are you doing here, in Orlando?"

He turns and walks towards me. His hand moves slowly around my waist and pulls me towards him. His mouth dips low and he whispers, "Taking care of you."

His hand inches up, skimming my outer breast. It keeps climbing and then grips my neck. His thumb brushes my upper lip. "The scarring is lightening up."

I nod and he continues whispering. "Been in any more fights?"

I nod, again. His brows crease and he scans my face, I guess looking for any more injuries or bruising.

I take his hand that is still around my waist and move it to cover my heart. "Here's where I took a beating."

He closes his eyes and swallows loudly. He pulls me closer and rests his forehead on the top of my head. We stand like that for several moments until we hear a strange trilling sound. Uh oh, the marching band has come back with wind instruments.

He gives me a quick squeeze and walks into the other room. I follow.

"Collins," he answers while pushing the phone to his ear. "Yes, Mrs. Paz, how are you this afternoon." Oh no. What time is it? "Of course, she didn't forget her hair appointment. I just couldn't seem to let her go." He chortles like they're sharing some inside joke. I am *not* liking this! "Can I have my girl for a smidge longer?" He grunts a few more times. "Yes, of course. Excellent. Looking forward to it! I'll send her down soon!" He makes a few more agreeable sounding noises and then ends the call. He turns to me smiling.

"Why does mother have your cell?"

"Because we're practically family, my heart," he states it as though this were obvious. "Now, we need to get you fed, showered, and changed in less than thirty minutes. You have a hair appointment at the spa and then makeup in the bridal suite." He marches over to where…wait, is that my bags?

"How…how…"

"Ssshhh love…" He puts his finger on my lips. "Go and get dressed, we don't have time." He pulls my luggage to the bathroom in one hand and my arm in the other. "Step to it!" he says as he taps my ass, and then he leaves the room after closing the door.

Apparently, the meds are taking their time to kick in, because this morning is all types of confusing.

After a fast shower and throwing on some jean shorts and a tight black Five Finger Death Punch tee, I make my way back to Coen. He's dressed and is sitting at a table reading the paper and drinking coffee.

He smiles when he sees me. "Feel better? Sit down…we have something to discuss and not much time to do it in."

"Thank you for collecting my things. This looks lovely, thank you." I smile while looking at the delicious set up of food. After sitting down, he pushes my seat forward and returns to the seat across from me. I grab a croissant and start digging in.

I see him glance at his watch. "Charlie, last night, while I was carrying you into the hotel, I came across both of your parents. As

I mentioned earlier, your mother wasn't pleased with the situation. I had to calm her down."

"Okay..." I'm edging him on. It sounds like there's much more to this story.

"I sat down with them, with you in my arms, and we spoke about a number of things." He looks at his watch again. It appears to be a Movado with a black face and silver links. It looks dark against his pale complexion, almost out of place. "Shit, we don't have much time. I wish I could explain things better." He stares at me and begins to chew on his thumbnail.

"Just spit it out."

I take a sip of the orange juice and watch him over my cup.

"We're engaged."

I spit. Yes, very unladylike, but I literally spit the juice out and start coughing. I may be convulsing, too. He runs around the table to pat me on the back.

"Just breathe, love. Take another sip." He puts the cup to my mouth and I try to swallow the liquid slowly. I mustn't have heard him right.

After catching my breath, I question. "Umm, would you mind repeating that? I don't think I heard you properly."

"By your response, I'm guessing that indeed, you did. I told your parents that we're engaged. I didn't like the way they spoke of you. I wanted to have a legitimate claim to make them stop."

Heat floods my cheeks. I can only imagine what atrocities they spoke of. As shocking as all of this is, I'm not mad. Again, it's more hurt. I slowly exhale through an open mouth.

"They believed you?"

"Of course. Despite what you think, I'm quite a catch, love." There's Cocky.

"Ha...yes, I know you are. But we've only known each other for roughly, what, seven weeks? And I've never mentioned you. I mean, this just...I mean..." I can't seem to track a thought. My parents, and by now with the gossip queens, my entire family, think that I'm engaged to Coen Collins. The same man who is on the Forbes top twenty bachelors of America list. None of this is computing.

"Charlie...relax, love." He smiles with softness in those arctic eyes while smoothing my wet hair. "I know I pushed...I shouldn't have said anything to them. But I could tell you were hurting. They made you hurt. I wanted to make things better. You were…" He takes a breath. I hate the way his voice is breaking. "Please… give me this. You can tell them…I don't know, that we ended or something later. You were hurting and it was fucking killing me, baby! Just give me a couple of days."

He closes his eyes and rests his head on my shoulder. "Won't they ask about a ring?" Meh, might as well enjoy some diamonds. What's done is done. Maybe having Coen here will take the heat off of me.

He lifts his head and smiles. "Just like that, huh?" I join him in smiling and nod. He kisses my forehead and stands. Reaching into his pocket, he pulls out a box and places it on the table in front of me. I look at him with a raised brow. This is handy.

He shakes his head and points at the box. "Don't look at me like that. I had Davis pick this one up this morning. If this was a real engagement, I would have had the piece created specifically for you. But, since we didn't have time…." He rolls his arm.

I open the velvet box and the light catches on the most dazzling looking stone I've ever seen.

Maybe this was last minute, but wow, he didn't skimp.

I slide the gorgeous addition onto my finger. "Well, it's not the most romantic proposal…" I smirk at him. "Is it from Cartier?"

He nods.

"You like that store, huh?"

"Whatever do you mean?"

"The bracelet you gave me, the one you won't let me return, was from Cartier, too."

"Yes, that's true. Why aren't you wearing it?"

"Are you kidding, it's huge and terribly gauche."

"Gauche? What about that snake you always wear…that thing is gauche!"

"Hey, don't hate on Sussurro."

"Who?"

"The snake thing…that's her name."

"Do you name everything? First your bike and now this Susisu?"

"Sussurro…it means whisper in Portuguese. I had her commissioned two years ago. She was made to my exact requirements. She's unlike any piece of jewelry you've seen."

"Well don't stop now, love. Tell me about your whispering snake charmer."

"Since you asked, she's precisely twelve inches long and is made of a specialized magnesium alloy that's as light as aluminum but as strong as titanium. Her tail is sharp and her head is shaped into a snake, the eyes ruby, and when you depress down on the two fangs, the individual vertebrae in her spine become lax. I can then lock her into another shape, as a necklace or even a straight line." She has many talents. Many useful skills. And like me, her looks are deceiving.

He looks pensive. "She's a weapon…." I don't say anything.

"Why do you need a weapon, love?"

Again, I remain silent.

"Is this why you fight?"

I can see the wheels spinning. Coen is processing. He swallows audibly.

"Does this have to do with the jagged scar?"

"Mother is waiting for me…" He nods in frustration but quickly hides it as he stands up and takes my hand. He kisses the new ring addition, his icy eyes locking in on my greys, searching again.

He keeps my hand in his on the ride down the elevator and across to the spa.

"I thought you'd never get here, really Charlie. I thought I raised you better!" Mother immediately greets us.

Coen stiffens and his voice becomes domineering. "It was my fault, Delilah. I'll hand her over for now, but please take good care of her." He quickly peeks to the side and I follow to see Davis walking towards us. I guess Davis is like an Amex card, Coen never leaves home without him.

"Delilah, this is Davis. I'm having him watch over Charlie. I'd greatly appreciate it if you'd accommodate my wishes and allow him access to her. I'm rather protective of my girl," he states and gives mother a grave look.

"Of course, Coen. I assure you, she's always safe with us."

"Really, because left in the care of her sister last night she was later abandoned while intoxicated. Forgive me if I take extra precautions." He looks upset. I'm glad I'm not on the receiving end of mad Coen…well, at least in this moment. I'll probably end up there at a later time.

"Right, of course. Come now, Charlie, we don't want to keep anyone waiting." She smiles briefly at Coen and then walks inside the spa center, assuming I'll follow.

I gaze up at Coen and smile so brightly that my cheeks hurt. "You're my hero!"

His smile doesn't exactly match mine, but it's there. "I'll be upstairs." He runs both hands through my hair and cups my cheek. He stares into my eyes, his beautiful blues grasping my gregarious greys. "Don't take any of their shit. You're smarter, kinder, and the sexiest little thing I've ever seen." He pushes his forehead to mine and then kisses me softly on the lips.

He pulls back and then comes in for one more kiss. "I'll see you at the wedding, love. I'll be the sexy fiancée watching your every move." He winks. "Be good." One more sweet kiss, he nods to Davis, and then walks away. I guess watching him walk away is a new hobby of mine.

Chapter 15

IF THIS WOMAN CONTINUES PINCHING my chin, I won't be held accountable for my actions. Damn that hurts. She keeps digging in as she applies god only knows what to my face. I've been sitting in this chair for a solid ten minutes getting shellacked and I swear my head feels five pounds heavier. Is that even possible?

"You have good skin. But your eyelids are a bit small." The makeup artist mother has hired to fix all the bridesmaids says in her thick Puerto Rican accent.

Mother jumps in, ready to dodge any type of compliment my way. "Yes, her skin is clear, she gets that from me, but those freckles are a disaster. Please make sure to cover them completely. I know there isn't much you can do with that obnoxious mole, but see if you can at least lighten it."

Twenty-three hours and fifty-six minutes. I can hold it together for the next twenty-three hours and, oh look, fifty-five minutes. Yes, one down and one thousand fifty-five to go. It's like I'm practically home, now. Not.

I hear my sister and her friends talking in the other room. I'm the last to finish makeup, naturally, so they're already getting dressed and passing out champagne. I guess my sister needs to be intoxicated to walk down the aisle. Not that I can really blame her, Gene isn't what I'd call drool worthy.

Allegedly, they didn't realize that I was no longer with the group when they left City Walk. At least that's what mother claims. Speaking of mother, she's back hovering over me. She and Joelle were first to dress, so I'm guessing she's bored.

"Charlie, why didn't you mention that you were engaged? You'd think I'd be the first to know though I suppose he seems like a charming enough man. What does Coen do, again?" She asks while analyzing the ring Coen placed on my finger only a few hours ago.

She's fishing but this is mother and if I don't give her something she will never leave me alone. "It was Jo's weekend and I didn't want to steal the limelight. Coen's the current CFO to Collins Corp."

"Collins Corp…" She's tasting it. Feeling it out. "He seems a bit old for you. I'm not sure if I approve. He didn't even ask your father for your hand." She huffs. This isn't going well, and I can see she's prepping for a verbal lashing. I sink in the chair to better ground myself.

"You just show up, drunk I might add, in the arms of a complete stranger. I was so embarrassed. And…and…you promised you'd keep your tattoo hidden. But no, it was on full display for everyone to see that god-awful monstrosity. Including the family! And don't even get me started on your clothing. I mean really, Charlie, those leather shorts were too short…and knee high boots? You looked like a street walker. Do you want to work on OBT or the Sunset Strip? Is that the look you're going for?" She fans herself with a hand trying to cool down before she melts away. *I'm melting, I'm melting.*

"You demanded that I change. I grabbed what I had and got downstairs before they took off without me. I swear to all things holy, I can never make you happy. Mother, go bother your *real* daughter and let me finish my painting in relative peace."

She gasps and walks away with an, "I never!"

Sadly, it's me that never's. I never talk back. I never stand up for myself. And I almost never get what I want.

So…never, never, never. So there. Yeah.

After the makeup torture concluded, I'm squeezed into my dress; amaranth pink in Mikado silk encrusted with contrasting black lace. It's surprisingly short for a bridesmaid dress, more like a cocktail dress, but with the bateau neckline I could easily wear this dress again, and hopefully, I will. But it's the hat that throws it. A hat? Yes, a hat. A big mad hatter hat, with a gigantic bow in the front dressed in the same shade of pink.

I would feel like the only one at a tea party, except all eight of the bridesmaids have to wear it. My sister is in a sleeveless traditional white gown that flows all the way to the floor with little embellishments. She has a matching neckline as ours, so maybe that's why she chose it. But no hat for her. Maybe she is secretly mad and looking for a tea party so she can be the white rabbit.

I know I certainly feel like Alice.

I think even Lewis Carroll would agree that everyone is indeed mad here.

The procession gets underway without a snag. I can see my parents under the chuppa next to my sister. They look so happy. Mother is crying while Abba stands stoic and proud. I shouldn't have snapped earlier. The last nine months of planning and stressing has culminated into this very moment. Maybe I should have been more understanding. Mother looks positively peaceful. I think she may even be glowing.

I'm always at a loss when it comes to interactions with my family. Like a little girl, I still strive to please them. A task I will never succeed in. Riddled with guilt and confusion, I fight the falling tears. But they're victorious.

Hoping to distract myself and gain the grounding that I again need, I scan the crowd hoping to find those gorgeous glacial eyes. I locate him instantly, and sure enough he's watching me. When he notices, his brows raise in flirtatious questioning. I can't help but send him an enthusiastic, though wet, smile. The man looks positively adorable in a kippah.

With the ceremony over, the reception begins. We are seated at one of the three tables reserved for the bridal party. My parents were kind enough to add Coen to the table, so he's seated next to me. Much to the joy of Joelle's head cheerleader and maid of honor, Kiki. She keeps leaning over and flaunting her tits hoping to catch Coen's attention.

"Coen, I just read an article about you last month in the Post. I heard you were approached to do some acting or was it modeling." She giggles while licking her lips and eyeing him up and down.

He clears his throat looking uncomfortable. I feel the need to intervene and squash poor cheer girl's libido thumping heart. "Well, my poor *fiancée* has so much on his plate right now, that he hasn't had time to fully weigh the options. But don't worry…" I lean over Coen and whisper conspiringly. "I've made sure to keep his endurance up." I wink.

He chuckles, then asks me to dance. Though this is the second time I've danced in this man's arms, I feel more relaxed this time. Maybe it's because I'm engaged. Ha. That's funny, being engaged to a guy that I've never even dated. We should probably fix that.

I lean my head back. "You know, my darling fiancée, you've yet to take me on a proper date. I'm thinking I should have given this engagement more thought." I'm laughing. I know this engagement isn't real and I'll return his ring once we get home, but, as long as I'm here…

His lips pucker in thought as his nose scrunches up. Adorable. His eyes spark as he responds.

"So true, the future Mrs. Collins. Please allow me to remedy the situation upon our Boston arrival." He leans down and kisses my nose.

I pretend to think it over. This game is fun. "Hhhmmm, I don't know. You're really not that enjoyable in Boston. I think I prefer Orlando Coen. Maybe we should stay here for a few more days?"

"Ahh, I wish. I have a meeting first thing tomorrow morning. Perhaps we can come back one day soon."

To that I chuckle loudly. There's no way I'll be stepping foot in this state for at least another three years.

"Are you flying commercial?"

He chortles. "Love, when you have as much money as I do, you don't fly commercial. If you'd like I can send the plane back for you."

"Actually Mr. Collins, I do…and I don't."

"What do you mean?"

"Didn't you do a background check on me?" I certainly did on him.

"The company did. It's standard practice when working with an outside partner on something of this magnitude, but I never reviewed it. I hoped I'd get to know you outside of what's on any paper." He winks. Yeah, I know exactly what he was hoping to get to know. "What are you implying?"

"Nothing, never mind." I'm embarrassed now.

"No, no, no love. You've piqued my curiosity. Something you're extremely good at." He pulls me tighter to him, my neck now craning north. He pops another kiss on my nose.

"I've made several good investments, that's all." I shrug, like that's all there is. On paper, he's worth more than me…

His returning shrug tells me that he's dropped the subject, and the way his eyes brighten, I wonder what he's picked up.

His fingers lightly caress the shell of my ear and continue a path across my cheeks. My eyes remain on his. The awkward hat is tilted on my head and is ensconced in thirty-seven thousand pins to hold in place; poor Coen has some obstacles in his path if he's trying to get close.

He closes his eyes and learns forward, breathing softly against my face. "I've missed you so much, love. What have you done to me?"

I lick my lips and sigh. He opens his eyes and they are blazing. Pure raw fire. It ignites me. I tilt up and taste his sweet lips. Barely opening my lips, I feel his tongue probe for more. I want to give him more. I want to be lost in this moment. I want to pretend I'm kissing my fiancée and he loves me with every breath. I want to be his world.

I don't want to think about the girls that hunt him down. The girls he plays with in his office on lunch breaks and coffee breaks, and who knows, maybe cigarette breaks. I don't want to think I'm just a little toy to occupy his time, while the merger settles. I don't want to think of how I may never see him again after the ink has dried in two weeks, and my part with CC is over. I don't want to think about how scared I am that every time I'm with him, he takes more of me.

I pull away from the kiss and press myself against him. I bite my lip hard trying to redirect all the pain in my mind and heart. I shake my head. Always such a silly girl. A weak silly girl.

"Charlie…" He's trying to get me to look at him. "Please love, let me see those gorgeous greys."

I squint my eyes a few times in the hopes of drying them out, and I pull back smiling.

"What's going on here?" he asks while his thumb rubs the crease in my brow. I can never get anything by this man.

"Just a busy weekend, that's all. Looking forward to getting home."

He nods but he doesn't buy my story.

The speeches begin and we take our seats. Next the cake, a boatload of pictures, and the night eventually comes to a close.

Despite a lack of an invitation, I'm glad Coen is here. I fed off of his strength. He made the mad hatter wedding more bearable. And by the end of the evening, both my parents were putty in his hands. He is a charmer.

Since he moved all of my belongings to his room or is it rooms, I end up staying the night with him. Getting out of the dress is a cinch since there's just a zipper, but I can't seem to take the damn hat off. I need extra hands. When Coen sees my mad hatter predicament, he volunteers. You would think he is scrubbing in for surgery, the way he sets me in a chair in front of the mirror and begins to meticulously remove each of the thirty-seven thousand pins. I should have recorded it. Half of the time his tongue was hanging out the side of his mouth. You could see the strenuous thought he put into this challenge as he mapped out each bobby pin as if it were a Jenga set ready to topple over.

I melt a little more.

Now we are both lying in bed, flat on our backs. I'm freshly showered and pounds lighter, in a "Keep Calm and Read On" tee and matching shorts with little books on it. He's shirtless, wearing only his briefs. What kind, no clue as I tried with every ounce of restraint to not stare in that general area.

"I don't like you being so far away." He reaches over and pulls me towards him. I swear, I'm like his personal ragdoll. He positions me with my head on his chest and my arm over his stomach. I immediately stiffen up.

"This is our first night together," I whisper.

"No, love, it's our third. Try to relax and go to sleep."

"Ummm, both times I blacked out. I'm not sure if that counts. I'm a terrible sleeper. Let me get my pills." I attempt to get up but he twists and is suddenly on top of me.

"Why do you need pills?" He's still hunting.

"I have sleep issues."

"Charlie…" He's giving me that look. The one parents give their children when they know they're lying.

"I...uh…I sort of suffer from PTSD."

I watch as his Adam's apple bobs, his eyes hard and etched into mine. He shuffles down so his eyes have a direct line. His body is completely cocooning me. This is both terrifying and exhilarating. He's still searching and I'm trying desperately to hold onto reality.

This is Coen. This is now. I am strong. I can get out of this if I want to. He won't hurt me. He can't hurt me.

He sees my distress and pulls back, leaning on his elbows beside my shoulders. "Are you a virgin?" he asks tilting his head.

I hesitantly shake my head back and forth. Is that why he wanted me?

His fingers create dizzying patterns on my cheeks and neck. He's trying to relax me while he continues his own search. He should know by now that I won't be found until I'm ready. And that day may never come. I was stolen and lost long ago.

"Coen, I need my pills, please," I whisper into his warm hand.

"Where are they? I'll get them for you?"

"Bathroom." I sigh in relief.

He climbs off of me, and despite missing his electric warmth, I can finally take a full breath. This man is intoxicating. His enchantment is insurmountable.

After taking the magical tablets, we assume the original position.

It takes some time before my muscles loosen, some time for me to make peace with the day and let go of images and thoughts. But slowly, I feel myself slipping into the darkness. Then I hear Coen whispering – or maybe I dreamt it?

"I won't ever let you go. Destiny has brought you to me. I'll patiently wait for all of you. Nothing less will ever do."

Chapter 16

I AWAKEN TO THE SWEETEST, SOFTEST kisses making trails on my cheeks and down to my neck. I can feel my hair being brushed aside as his lips dig deeper. He bites me lightly, chuckling. "Wake up, my sleepy love." He nuzzles his nose in my neck whispering in my ear, "I have to go."

"Okay." I laugh, rolling onto my back. I glance over at his glorious smile. He looks relaxed and energized. Ready to go. His hair is still damp from his shower and it's slicked back. The little curls are lost in gel. He looks crisp and clean in his suit.

He leans over and kisses my lips. Then rubs his nose against mine. Eyes open, watching even this close. He's like one giant snow storm heading my way. All icy yet somehow steaming hot.

"Somebody is a morning person." I point into his chest then stick my tongue out.

"If you keep showing me such tasty treats, I may have to take a bite." Hot dog! He wiggles his brows at me.

"Sorry, ice boy, you *may* have to invest in another store," I throw back.

"Oh, that's where you're wrong." His breath is hot as he licks my neck and continues down to my collarbone. He bites me there and moves to the hollow of my neck. I feel his tongue circle the tiny indention in the base. Then he softly kisses it. He twists back and sends me a chilling and rather commanding look with one brow raised. "All of my assets are already tied up into one venture. I'm afraid its sink or swim for me."

"Ummm, uhhhh, shopping…" What? Were? We? Talking? About?

There's a sharp knock on the door.

Coen rests his head on the pillow next to my ear. "That'd be Davis." He continues to tell the pillow. "I'm leaving him here with you."

"Co...that's crazy. I'm only here for..." Quickly do the math. "...less than ten hours. Besides, I'm on a commercial flight. There's probably no vacancies."

"Charlie, I won't compromise on this. It's either Davis stays or I drag you onto the jet with me now." He sits upright and crosses his arms. His eyes widen in waiting.

"Fine..." I sit up and push him backwards. "You win, Mr. Collins! But I can't promise that I'll send him back in one piece." I cross my arms, too.

He smiles and kisses my brow. "You're too cute when you're mad."

He gets up and walks into the main room. I follow.

"Hey, did you not see my fight? That shit wasn't cute!" I lift my arms and flex. Check out my baby guns. Pow, pow.

He continues chuckling and walking to the door. Opening it, he ushers Davis in.

"Don't let the little minx out of your sight. Apparently, your safety is in jeopardy. So watch her *not* be adorably cute!"

Davis walks in, grabs the handle to Coen's rolling suitcase, and places it in front of the door.

Coen saunters over to me squeezing my upper arms. "Feel like a late dinner, tonight?"

"We'll see what time I get in. You want me to call you?"

"Send me a text when you land." Kissing my nose, he adds, "I had an enjoyable weekend. Your family is strangely colorful."

"I'm glad you think so. Maybe now you know where I get some of my color from."

His opened lips press against my mostly closed ones. His warm fingers press into my neck. "I expect more of this in Boston," he says sternly. I think he knew I was going to back away. "I believe I owe you a proper date." He kisses me once more and then winks while backing towards the door.

He smiles giving me one last look over his shoulder, and then he's gone. I immediately feel his loss. The room feels colder, especially when Davis is left standing there.

It's only a quarter after six in the morning. I doubt anyone is up, yet. I leave Davis in the main room and decide to dress. With plenty of time to kill, I also pack.

I'm sitting in the living room sizing up a silent Davis when I decide to have a little fun with him.

"Davis, did you know that although I'm a corporate lawyer, I also practice trial law."

He shakes his head having no idea where I'm going with this line of questioning.

"On the rare occasion when I get to practice as a trial lawyer, I gain access to various judges, many of which know me by name." I chuckle and watch as he continues to stare blankly and nod.

"I've also become acquainted with several members of the police force." Again, a blank face.

"Are you familiar with Part IV, Title I, Chapter 226, Section 16A of the Massachusetts general constitution?" His face is still completely frozen, but I'm about to warm it up. Time to watch body language, I doubt he will break his state much.

"I think you'll find it applicable with your recent proclivities." I arch my brow so he sees that I'm about to get serious. "It states that, whoever in the nighttime or *daytime* breaks and enters a building, ship, vessel or vehicle with intent to commit a misdemeanor shall be punished by a fine of not more than two hundred dollars or by imprisonment for not more than six months, or both." I wait. He shifts minutely.

"Did you know that my building has seven cameras in the lobby, alone?" I watch him very carefully and see that although his face hasn't budged, his shoulders stiffen and he swallows.

"Five of them were dismantled on March 19th at approximately 4:58 p.m., but two remained online." I continue. "Do you know what I found when I checked the surveillance video?"

He shakes his head. "You." I smile and lean back into the couch cushion. Now it's my turn to be silent and watch. And I do. I wait. I want to see his reaction.

We fall into a silent game of truth or dare, neither of us budging or saying a word. The quiet room becomes alarmingly peaceful. I keep my guard up waiting on him to break and count down the remainder of my time in this serene prison.

It's just after eight when the phone rings, disturbing us from our wordless attacks, and I answer without looking thinking it may be

Coen or mother.

"Good morning." I try to sound chipper.

"Baby girl?" It's Gunner.

"Hey, what're you doing up so early. Is everybody okay?" I start to panic. Gun never calls this early, let alone is up this early.

"Yeah, everyone is fine. Nah, that's not true. We're a fucking mess. When are you coming back?"

"I should be in tonight," I say flatly.

We finish our conversation soon after, though I'm much more rigid than usual. No love you's, miss you's, just a straight goodbye.

Davis takes our bags and stashes them in the rental car while I venture out to say goodbye to my family for what I hope will be the last time for years. Jo and Gene are nowhere to be found, thank goodness. I find my parents downstairs at the hotel restaurant having brunch with my grandparents and a few of my uncles and aunts. I sit silently and listen to various conversations.

My dad and his siblings go back and forth talking in Hebrew, French, and Arabic. I think it might have been some game they played when they were kids. Every so often they laugh hysterically when one messes up. It's a funny little game, juvenile but funny. Once they notice I'm following them, they force me to join in. They think they can stump me. The pattern is easily decipherable; the first person speaks in Arabic, the second in French, and the third in Hebrew. This goes for questions or even a singular statement.

Mother tsks at the other end of the table while taking a breath in between chatting with my grandparents. I think almost everyone is heading out today.

"Charlie, what time does your flight leave today?" Abba asks in Arabic.

"Around three but I'll need to be at the airport by one thirty give or take." I answer in French while giving him my waggled eyebrows. Can't trick me old man.

"When will we see you next?" Aunt Perla questions in Hebrew.

"Anytime you wish." I respond in Arabic while winking at her. She knows I adore her, though I rarely have an opportunity to see her.

"When do you plan to marry the blondini?" Uncle Max chimes in, in French.

"Who knows?" Back in Hebrew.

This is fun. We continue this way, though for some reason it ends up being a game of twenty questions with Charlie. Mother must be jealous of her limelight being dimmed because she grabs Abba and demands that he spends time with her parents before they leave. Yes, apparently her parents trump her daughter. Foolish me for thinking that I could have bonded or connected with my family.

Feeling rejected, yet again, I quietly say my goodbyes to the rest of the family and sneak out without saying farewell to either of my parents. The sad thing is, I bet they never noticed.

Chapter 17

THE LONG WEEKEND TRAVELING HAS caught up with me and I'm exhausted. Davis collects my baggage and walks us to an awaiting car. From there we go directly to my place. Davis, of course, walks me to my condo.

I sent Coen a text that I arrived but I haven't heard anything back. I guess dinner is out. Out of sight, out of mind. A bit quicker than I had anticipated, but?

As we near my door, I hear male voices coming from inside. My boys. I smile to myself. I guess they couldn't wait to see me. There are two people that have keys to my place, Malice and Gunner. I'm guessing Gunner did the deed.

Davis immediately puts his arm out to halt my steps. I guess he thinks he's the only one who can do B&E.

"It's fine, they're my guys. Gunner has the key. I'm guessing they're waiting for me." The thought alone has me filling with warmth. How could I ever have been so foolish to think that they didn't love me? They're loyal to a fault. Their gigantic roughed up hearts nearly as big as my own.

Creeping closer, I hear their laughter. Davis does too, so I assume he no longer views them as a threat. Before entering my condo, I feel the need to thank Davis and have him relay additional thanks to Coen. He uplifted my mood this weekend.

"Davis, thank you for accompanying me, and please send my thanks to Coen, as well, for this weekend. I think I can take it from here." I nod towards my door.

"Of course, Ms. Paz. Have a lovely evening."

Oh, the ring, I almost forgot. I quickly go to take it off and Davis stops me. "Please keep it for now. That's a gift best returned to the giver. Also, Mr. Collins has asked me to apologize on his behalf. He was called out of town on business and isn't sure when he'll return."

Sounds about right. I should have known. "Thank you, Davis. Goodnight."

I turn my unlocked knob and enter my place. Ah, home. And filled with joy and warmth thanks to the trio of my heart. Walking in, with my bag trailing behind me, I smell pizza. Yes, my boys do it right!

As I turn the corner, I watch the guys laughing and gabbing. I feel my smile grow larger than the building. It's big. I love these three. They would never hurt me. They are loyal and fucking amazing.

There are three pizza boxes on the dining room table, two pepperoni and one pineapple. My favorite. There are a couple of slices removed. I guess the boys got adventurous, as usually they hate it. But they got it for me. They remembered, and they love me.

The talking stops and they all turn to look at me. I can't help but eye each one. Gunner is closest to me on the long side of the table, next to him is Trig, and at the head of the table, because he thinks he's the king, I find Bully. My smile grows. I can't help how much….

"Bully, there's no more beer, baby. She's got some tequila, though," comes a shrill sound walking out of *my kitchen*. My eyes widen as the same chick, Tricks, walks around the table and sits on Bullet's lap. Then she grabs a slice of *my pizza* and begins eating it.

I stand there white knuckling my suitcase handle. All of the warmth has left me and I'm chilled to the marrow of my bones. I think my heart has exploded and may no longer be in my chest. I put my hand over my heart for verification. But it must be wrong because nothing has changed. I'm still whole. How can that be?

They brought pussy…dirty random pussy into *my home*? *My sanctuary*? This was about us.

"Baby girl," I hear Bull mutter. I look up, but he isn't talking to me. Oh my fucking god, he's talking to *her*. Using *my nickname?*

I make some strangled animal sound. I feel like I've been standing here for hours watching this travesty unfold. Gunner notices and winces. Standing up, he calls out, "Charlie." He takes a step towards me, but the damage has been done. Doesn't he see me in pieces on the floor? I do.

Run. *Run!!!*

I put my hand up and another horrid sound escapes me. I can't seem to breathe. I refuse to let them see me like this. It's different, now. They feel like strangers and are hurtful. I run down the hall to my room, my bag banging against my legs as I go. Locking the door, I run to my bed and drop onto it. In my pillow I scream and fucking scream.

I hear banging on the door. It's Bullet, this time shouting my name over and over, pleading with me to let him in.

I shut down all emotion, locking it all away. Piece by piece…

It doesn't matter how many psychology and sociology books I've read. It doesn't matter how the chemical makeup of our bodies shift to produce epinephrine. In no way does it matter how my intellect works nor how logic should kick in.

Pain overrides thought. Emotion overrides pain.

I have to lock up all emotion and all thought if I'm to extricate the pain. Logic.

If I go out there, it's probable I'll hurt someone. Either with fists or words. Instead I text Malice to remove these strangers from my home. I don't elaborate. I just want them gone.

In less than five minutes, I hear the front door open and bang against the wall. Malice is here. When the condo next to mine went on the market, I quickly purchased it and moved him in. Knowing that Malice is nearby, is always a great reprieve. But none more so than tonight.

I hear muffled sounds and know he's yelling at them. Bullet is still near my door and Malice's footsteps can be felt through the vibrating floor as he makes his way towards him.

"You…get foock away from her," he screams with his French accent coming through harsher in his anger. "You have wirld! She give to you wirld! You spit on it. You not good man! OUT!" he roars. Then I hear something bang against my door. Are they fighting?

"Charlie….please baby…please come out…you don't understand…" I can hear his voice moving down the hall. Malice is getting rid of them.

More shouting ensues and then the door slams. A minute later I hear a soft knock on the door.

"Ils sont partis. Sortir. Je dois vous assurer que vous êtes d'accord."

They're gone. Come out. I need to make sure you're okay.

I climb off the bed and pad over to the door. With my eyes still on the floor, I open it.

"Ils sont stupides. Ils ne savent pas ce qu'ils font. Vous devez leur pardonner."

They are stupid. They know not what they do. You must forgive them.

I chuckle slightly before falling into his stiff arms while fighting back tears. They are stupid. They don't deserve my tears. One step forward and twenty-nine back. I'll never catch a break.

Poor Malice isn't used to my blubbering. I mean, who have I had to cry over? My family shit is the norm. The guys and I were always fine. We used to be, anyways. And, even though I've been on dates. I don't really date. I keep to myself for the most part. Even during my fights I never cry. Of course, I never lose. There was a fight almost a year ago, I hit the mat so hard that my shoulder popped out. My right arm was effectively useless and pain radiated everywhere. But I kept going and won. And I *never* cried.

Maybe it's my time of the month. Come to think of it, I have a desperate craving for some chocolate.

I didn't realize that we'd moved to my couch and I look over to the dining room. They left the boxes of pizza and the beer bottles are everywhere.

"Avoir le tableau donné à peu de charité demain. Je ne veux plus jamais le revoir."

Have the table donated to some charity tomorrow. I don't ever want to see it again.

He nods. I'm pressed against his side still sobbing.

"Avons-nous le chocolat?"

Do we have any chocolate? I sniffle.

"Oui."

Yes.

He gets up and walks away. Appearing a moment later, he hands me some chocolate chip cookies. Not what I had in mind, but this will work.

"Je ne l'ai pas acheter ces. D'où sont-ils originaires?"

I didn't buy these. Where did they come from?

"Ils sont à moi. Je leur ai caché dans votre maison en espérant de ne pas les manger."

They're mine. I hid them in your house hoping to not eat them.

What a freaky Frenchman. I snort, a wet goby snort. He's taking my mind off of things. Got to love the French for that.

"Pourquoi ne pouvez- vous pas les manger? Ils sont délicieux. Merci par la manière."

Why can't you eat them? They're delicious. Thank you by the way.

"Je mange tout le sac. De là, je ne mange un à chaque intervalle. Tout le sucre n'est pas bon pour moi. Je ne suis pas aussi jeune que je l'habitude d'être."

I eat the entire bag. From here, I only eat one at each interval. All the sugar isn't good for me. I'm not as young as I used to be.

"Je savais que je vous gardais autour pour une raison."

I knew that I kept you around for a reason.

I shake my head and shove the entire cookie in my mouth. I know, I'm gross. But I'm too upset to care. I grab another cookie and shove it into his mouth. He chuckles and grabs the remote to turn on the television.

We stay like that for the rest of the night. Shoving cookies in our mouths. Me fighting a round of tears every so often, ignoring my cell that's been blowing up.

Eventually, I fall asleep on him.

It's sad.

The one friend I have is the one I pay to be there.

Chapter 18

I AWAKE TO AN EXPLOSION. WELL, in my head anyway. My sinuses must have imploded overnight, as I feel like utter garbage. My head keeps throbbing, and every time I move, it feels like the world is tilting. I can hear the crackling of mucus shift back and forth. My eyes swollen, my nose drippy, I can already tell that today is going to be stellar.

I shower in searing hot water, in the hopes that the steam will alleviate some of the sinus pressure. After dressing and ingesting a million liters of Dayquil, I attempt a day at the office.

After my long weekend, work has piled up. I shift through my messages and find some serious issues on the CC merger that need my attention. I also notice that I'm scheduled in court next week. Trevell's case, the pro bono case I've been working on, begins at the same time as CC is scheduled to finalize the merger in Montpellier, France. I can't be in two places at once. I'll have to set things up for a replacement.

Coen might be my best in. Catch him while he's in a good mood. I hate bailing on him, but I think I can set things up where my absence won't make much of a difference. I try his number thinking I can leave a quick voicemail.

"Hey, love. Missing me already?"

"Ha, you're a funny man, Mr. Collins. Thanks for the flight upgrade, by the way. That was sweet of you," I speak through my goober filled nose.

"You shouldn't have had to ride commercial. Love, you don't sound well. Are you sick?"

"Ssshhh. Don't tell anyone. I'm trying to make it through my day." I chuckle a snotty snortle. "Coen, I hate to do this to you, but

I received a court date today on my pro bono case. It begins next Friday. It's a murder case and I'm hesitant to walk away."

"Of course, love. Can the CC team handle things solo?"

"I'll prep them. I can send my legal secretary. She's been working with me on the case."

"Anything for my fiancée," he says softly.

I'm about to correct him when I notice Gunner walk into my office, close the door, and sit in the chair facing my desk. He crosses his arms, eyebrows raised. He doesn't look like he plans on moving. I better hurry this along. And now I have an eavesdropper.

"Coen, à ce sujet. Je voudrais revenir sur le ring. Je suis sûr qu'il était coûteux et je ne me sens pas à l'aise avec elle dans mes soins."

Coen, about that. I'd like to return the ring. I'm sure it was costly and I don't feel comfortable with it in my care.

"Why are you speaking in French? Is somebody there? Do I need to send in Davis?"

"Je vais bien. Juste un ami déposer un déjeuner tôt. Je ne voulais pas que quelqu'un a mal interprété les choses."

I'm fine. Just a friend dropping off an early lunch. I didn't want anyone to misread things.

He sighs. "Charlie, there's nothing to misread. Hold the ring for now. I'll be back in a few days and we can have that date. Are you wearing it?"

"Non, Je l'ai laissé dans ma boîte à bijoux."

No, I left it in my jewelry box.

He hums his disapproval. "Ok, we'll talk about this soon. Text me later. I'll have Davis drop in to check in on you. Feel better, love."

"Bye." I sigh while looking over at Gunner and immediately go on the offense. "You should leave. I have a hectic day ahead of me and no time to waste."

"Look baby girl…what happened was..."

"Don't call me that! Obviously, it means nothing. An empty term of endearment," I interrupt.

"Charlie…"

"No, I'm done Gunner. Please leave."

"NO!" He jumps up, rounds the table, and grabs both arms of the chair pulling me towards him.

"Three years. We've been family for three years. What in the fuck is going on with you? You just shut down."

I push back at his chest interrupting him again. "Is that what this is? Me shutting down. Not you guys giving me shit then freezing my ass out? Then you have the fucking audacity to bring some nasty piece of ass into *my house*? Are you fucking kidding me?" I'm livid. Fuming and he's turning it around. Family, my ass. I try to stand, pushing him away, but he gets directly in my face and grabs my neck hard.

"Would you calm your shit and listen for two fucking minutes?" He squeezes and I go silent. It's time to medicate and my sinuses are pulsing tighter with the increased blood flow. I should have left work early and avoided all of this.

Despite his constricting hold, I lean further into him, daring him with my eyes. "Just relax, baby girl. I just wanted to talk. This got out of hand. I'm going to let go and you're going to join me by the chairs. Then we're going to talk and say what needs to be said. You got me?"

We're so close that I notice the tension lines in his forehead. I notice the coloring under his eyes and that his lips are more chapped than usual. Even his perfect rocker shoulder length hair is askew. Maybe he's taking this harder than I thought. No matter what, he was still a contributing party to last night's hurt fest.

"You hurt me," I whisper.

"Shit." He drops his hands and steps back.

"Last night," I correct him. "Last night you and Trig, and especially that bald asshole, *you hurt me*!"

He drops his head, the curly dark hair curtain blocking my view, and grabs the back of his neck.

"You're the last person in this fucking world I want to hurt. I swear to you! That's not why we came over. We needed to talk, as a band, as a family." He straightens up and props himself on the edge of my desk. "Look, in five weeks we start touring. The label wants to drop another single from *Fully Loaded*. We're supposed to be in New York next weekend to do a radio tour since we're finally starting to gain some momentum. We shouldn't be fighting. We've got to be a strong band to get through this."

"I don't know what to say to you, Gun." I sigh to the floor. He knows me better than anyone and he was the one with my key. He's the one I trusted, unequivocally.

"I didn't know he'd bring her."

"I don't care. You knew she was there."

"I fucked up. I'm sorry. Get over this shit and let's move on."

"No. What happened that night?"

"Last night?" he asks, confused.

I nearly growl in frustration, my patience is growing thin. "No. The last time we were at BedHead. When you all bailed on me and this shit storm started brewing."

"Oh, that night." He scratches his neck, again. "That was on us. Well, on Bullet really. He crossed a line."

"What line? What are you talking about?"

"The pact. The guys and I made a pact that we'd never cross that line. Never get physical...with you."

"You kiss me all the time. All three of you. We even sleep in the same bed, and I just...I just don't get it."

"Hhmmmm. We, ah, we can't fuck this up. You get me. Being with you, well, that would fuck this up."

"Jesus, thanks a lot! You've said what you needed. Please leave." I stand and walk to the window, effectively cutting him out and ending the conversation.

He follows, apparently not getting the hint, and wraps one arm around my top half, and the other bands me in across the stomach. His mouth is close to my ear and he's rubbing his scruffy face against my neck and cheek.

"Baby, you've got to understand, Bullet crossed that line. Trig and I beat his ass for it. He knows we can't lose you. We won't lose you. You're part of this, part of us. I don't know what you've got in this crazy brain of yours, but please get it through." He kisses my neck. "We love you, baby girl. I fucking love you."

He seals me to him. My back to his front. I willingly lean in. I miss him. He's supposed to know me. He knows how to hurt me and how to make things better. That makes him both dangerous and paramount.

"I have to think about things," I reply hoarsely.

"Okay, talk to me, though. Don't shut me out. You wanna kick Bullet's ass, I don't mind as long as you leave his hands in good shape. You could do one of your awesome little ninja moves." He chuckles and kisses me again. "I miss you. I hate missing you! Please stop making me miss you!"

I give him a half smile and turn to look him in the eye. His reflection in the window isn't doing him justice. "I got engaged," I say slyly and wait for the Gunner volcano to erupt. And he does. Even sexy rockers sometimes have a challenging time keeping their cool.

We spend the next twenty minutes talking about this past weekend and my fake engagement. He isn't Coen's biggest fan, to say the least. Other than saving me at City Walk, Gun saw no rationale as to why Coen was in Orlando. He made a point to repeatedly tell me how he doesn't trust Coen and that he will only hurt me in the end. It was disturbing to hear but wasn't entirely unexpected.

We mapped out a solid schedule for the next few weeks and then he left claiming that if I didn't start sending my daily texts and calls, that he would obsessively hunt me down and stalk me. It's not hard to do; I'm either at work or home, most days.

At least the throbbing in my head went away, if only it would stay away. But peace is a rare occurrence in my life and tends to have a fleeting shelf life.

Chapter 19

"GO AWAY!" I YELL THROUGH the door. Bullet is on the other side, but I want nothing to do with him.

I arrived home thirty minutes ago and I feel like absolute monkey poo. I'm in my comfy sweats and was finally sitting down to relax with a bowl of chicken soup that I picked up from the deli. It's still warm and has awesome fluffy matzo balls. The meds are finally working and I've found stuffy head zen. The last thing I want to do is get all worked up.

"Open up! I wanna talk."

"Go away! I'm sick and *don't wanna* deal with your shit!"

"Come on. I won't take long. I'll stay here all night if I have to. You know how stubborn I can be."

Damn. He's right. He is extremely tenacious. I open the door and walk away. Let him figure the rest out. I bury myself in the couch, padding the four blankets in all around me, and dig into my extremely satisfying soup.

He walks in front of the TV, blocking my view and straining to garner my attention.

I shake my head, seeing through his guise. "Clocks ticking, baldy."

"I don't like you hurting."

"Then you shouldn't have fucking hurt me!"

"What do you want me to say, baby girrr..."

"Don't say it. You don't get to say it anymore! Just like you won't be getting my lips. Just like you won't be getting my friendship. And just like you won't be getting my fucking heart!"

I stand up, soup now forgotten, and impede his personal space, my hands flailing everywhere to punctuate my points. "I didn't know about the pact. I just thought we were having a moment of, I don't know, something. I thought, maybe, we connected. But even if we didn't, even if what happened meant absolutely nothing to you, you still owed it to me to be a decent friend. To not shut me out. Shut me down. Then bring a, a, a female into *my home*!"

He looks over to where I was pointing. "Where's your dining room set?" He questions while quirking his head to the side.

"I lit it on fire during a sacrificial offering to bring a bout of herpes to your sensitive man parts."

"Right." He hisses and grabs my head pulling me towards his chest by my hair. "You don't really believe any of what you just said, do you?" I nod, because, well, I do, except for the offering. Although, I did think about it.

"What happened wasn't *nothing*. You hear me. It was beautiful. Watching you, in that way. So fucking beautiful. I've never seen anything more perfect than watching you cum. And knowing that I brought you there. That I was the first…" He stops and scratches his new beard. "I'm glad that Gun stopped me, Shooter. I shouldn't have touched you the way I did, and now, fuck… and now I can't get it out of my head."

He releases me and turns away, his hand rubbing his bald head. "You've got no idea how hard it's been to *not* touch you for the last three years. In the beginning, you were still just a kid. Remember? Now, you've gotten so fucking gorgeous. And that night you were wearing that sexy as sin shirt and were all wet. Your face was flushed, and fuck, I had to taste you. I know I screwed up. I know I took things too far, and that I hurt you. The really fucked part is, I wouldn't take it back."

He turns back around to face me. "I've never wanted anything more than you, baby girl," he whispers and I can see the moisture building in his eyes. "You think you're nothing, but what you don't get is, YOU'RE FUCKING EVERYTHING!" He puts his head to mine and breathes me in. "If I can only hold you in my arms as a friend, then that's what I'll take. That's all they'll let me take." He kisses my head. "I love you, Charlie! Maybe someday, you'll be mine to truly love."

He kisses me again on the head and walks away.

"Feel better, baby girl. Lock up after me."

I wonder if he meant the door or my heart. Because, I honestly no longer know...

Chapter 20

EDITH WHARTON CLAIMED THAT, "THERE are two ways of spreading light: to be the candle or the mirror that reflects it." I'm neither the candle nor the mirrored reflection.

Instead, I'm a crystal. I refract. I bend the light and create a masterpiece of color on the other side. Using wavelengths and depths, the color changes in my spectrum.

And although I'm the myriad of colors in its reverse, the light is still singular.

I am still whole.

Just colored in different shades and seen in different planes.

I am refraction.

This was how I used to feel. That I was broken light and in an element all my own. But I've decided that this is no longer the case. That I am, in fact, the mirror. A mirror that has broken into thousands of shards and pieces. I am reflected and refracted in those pieces. The colors are there but only when the candle, only when the light, is present.

I think I was the light once. I think I had a candle that had begun to glow, an ember. But it was snuffed out. And sadly enough, I think it was the mirror, the vicious shard that breaks the light, which eventually led to my death. The candle that lost all warmth in the vacuum where darkness exploded and entertained.

I was never a normal child. Despite how hard mother tried to make me so, my DNA claimed otherwise. I began walking too early. I spoke too early. I read too early.

At two, I began with tutors. Father insisted that I have the best education; a gift as great as mine deserved to be harnessed. Mother agreed, as Joelle was beginning Kindergarten and she was the 'normal' child, plus it kept me out of her hair.

With private education and access to the wonderful worldwide web, my knowledge grew. I was a sponge; language, mathematics, science, history and especially law. I loved law.

If there was a puzzle, an order, a complication to be solved it was met with enthusiasm and infatuation. I needed to solve that puzzle. Law provided that avenue. To hunt that loophole. To devour the status quo and evolve. I aspired to be the good guy.

As my education flourished in the realm of academia, both my parents realized that I lacked the social skills needed to advance properly in society. My sister wanted nothing of me and my closest confidents were my tutors. I couldn't relate to children my own age. They didn't make sense to me. They would say ridiculous things like, "If you don't play with me than I won't be your best friend." What nonsensical notions. I saw no value in their friendship and refused to pursue it.

My end goal was Harvard. Always Harvard. I would endure come what may, if I would be allowed to learn from some of the most sought after minds in the legal world.

Before allowing me to enter any type of higher learning, mother insisted I go to high school as it was some of the best years of her life. There are homecoming games and prom and a child shouldn't miss out on such crucial activities. They are a rite of passage.

It was horrid, I was a freak. I was never asked to any games. Why would I be? I graduated at twelve years old. Who wants a date that hasn't even hit puberty yet? Apparently, not the average pox-covered teenage boy. Friendships were nonexistent. Then in senior year, my sister joined the ranks as a freshman and led the 'Charlie is a geek' club. Needless to say, I never went to Prom or did any of those rites.

It was college that changed me forevermore. In the end, it was the University of Florida that won my acceptance. I would have preferred to move further away from home, but as it was less than a two-hour drive from Orlando, this was the only school acceptable. Beginning as a sophomore, I only had to endure two and a half years.

Mother insisted that I live in the dorm and the university paid extra for the RA to watch over me. I had a curfew and had to check in at the end of the night. I was warned repeatedly to stay away from any parties, mainly off campus. It was very strict. Not at all a typical college experience.

Puberty had finally found me and that alone felt like a huge accomplishment. By the end of my senior year, I had begun to smile and even have short conversations with others in my class.

I wore my hair in a shoulder length bob and would hide behind it whenever the need arose. My baggy clothes always covered me, despite the eternal Florida heat, and I never flirted...ever. I just wanted to learn. I wanted to be invisible. I thought I was.

The date was December 2nd, a Thursday night. I had just finished the last of my exams and was staying on campus until graduation. I was elated. I had survived relatively unscathed. There was a party that night at a fraternity house and one of the freshman girls on my floor, Krissy, had begged me to attend. We had been semi social and she was sweet, so why not? The last and only party. Although Harvard will have its own brand of party, UF is a notorious party school. Might as well try to act my age, well a few years older anyway.

With nothing to wear, Krissy and two of her girlfriends dressed me. I guess I was their Barbie doll guinea pig. A beer in my hand, a skirt too short and my goodies nearly hanging out, we were dancing away. I must have lost track of the girls because the next thing I knew, Tori, Krissy's friend attacked me on the makeshift dance floor begging for help. She claimed that Krissy was in the bathroom and crying for me.

Naturally, I went. I didn't know the protocol, but she was one of the few people I actually liked.

I followed Tori towards the bathroom, and when we entered the room I knew I had made a grave mistake. We weren't in the bathroom; we were in some type of study. In the back of the house. During a party. It didn't take long for me to realize what was happening and I immediately went to the door, but Tori stood in front of it and blocked my path.

I recognized no one in the room accept for a guy, James, who had been in my International Relations class. He had been sweet to me and we struck up conversations every so often. However, the four other huge men....yeah, I was done for.

I later learned that it was James' twenty-first birthday and I was his present. A pretty little virgin.

The biggest of the five men came to me, grabbing my arm; my instinct was to fight and so I did. Mistake number two. I screamed and punched him across the face, and in response, he shoved me into a large mirror. My head hit hard, splintering it and sending shards every which way. I grabbed a large piece from the floor and swung it at him. I managed to slice his forearms, but fared in slitting my palm and dropping my one and only weapon. My second wound of the night. In response, he picked it up, plunged the glass into me, and broke it off.

My vision splintered, my breathing ragged, there wasn't much left of me to fight. James easily had his way. Tearing my clothes and ripping into me.

I was fourteen…FOURTEEN.

Never had a date.

Never had a kiss.

Never had a boyfriend.

And never, ever had had sex.

They thought I was so much fun that they each took a turn. I begged for death. Wished for it. In total five men. To my fourteen-year-old self. Four would hold me down, while the other did his business. With each shift change, I would fight, between tears and screams. Until the end, when the last guy took his stance and wanted me from behind. A different way to torture me. By then my vision and consciousness was inconsistent. Time lapsed. I was no longer attached to my body. Eventually, I was out of the fight altogether. Slipping into blissful unconsciousness, pleading to never return.

I later learned that they had wrapped me up in a bed sheet and left me in front of my dorm. Naked, beaten and bloody. I was a dog to be forgotten. Used and disregarded. And ultimately, left for dead.

DOA…that's what they called it. I died upon arrival to the hospital. They attempted to resuscitate me several times, but were unsuccessful. My heart couldn't take it and I had lost too much blood. So on December 3rd, 2007 at approximately one fifty-eight a.m., I died at age fourteen. Even dogs have a higher life expectancy. I had flat lined. I was gone.

And then, I wasn't. Seven minutes and six seconds later, I was reborn. I wish I could say that I have some new profound view on life. Or that I can see the dead. Or something insightful. Maybe even a super power. But I'm just me.

I've heard that those individuals who have crossed over, even for a short period of time, can recant tales of lighted tunnels and loved ones lost. I had none of that.

I woke three and half weeks later in the hospital. I had suffered two concussions, so much so that they had to put in a stent for drainage. Due to traumatic brain injuries, my brain had swollen so severely that holes were drilled into my skull to relieve the pressure, and I was placed in a medical coma.

My left humerus had a displaced fracture, my right shoulder had been separated resulting in the tearing of the rotator cuff, a closed fracture in my right ulna, my pelvis had been fractured, and the ligaments in the anterior muscle torn. My face endured several lacerations and multiple bruising, as well as a broken nose.

Internally, I was nearly as severely damaged. Thankfully, my lungs remained intact, but my large intestines and pancreas were perpetually damaged. My spleen, however, could not be saved and a splenectomy was performed.

They questioned whether I'd ever be functional again. The brain is a fickle organ. But after three weeks and four days, I woke to a room full of people, every one waiting for answers.

When the police came in to question me, as the hunt for my attackers had been well underway, I lied and told them I had no memory.

That I didn't remember the brutality.

Didn't remember the betrayal.

Didn't remember the decimation of my sense of self.

Didn't remember the abject fear enrooted in my every cell.

The UF scandal made national news. Although nobody was arrested, all evidence was deemed circumstantial, and the university decided to close down the fraternity house. The victim, an unnamed minor, was brutally raped. This began a national ethical debate on whether the university system is flawed and caters to the fraternal presence on campus, allowing them to literally get away with murder. Regardless, it was a hot topic on the 24-hour news channels.

That is why when I find a distraught Coen Collins banging on my door at 7:28 a.m. on Saturday morning, I'm not surprised. I was the one who encouraged him to review my background check.

He managed to stay away all week. And the 'proper' date that was absolute, never came. I was too buried in my own work to notice, so I never followed up on his true whereabouts.

"Who's there?" I ask through the door. I know it's Coen, but I thought to delay the inevitable.

"It's me, love. Let me in." His coarse voice barely reaching me.

I crack open the door and usher him in. He's sporting loose fitting blue basketball shorts and a long sleeved white tee. But it's his eyes. They look bloodshot and tired. His hair is free of its usual gelled prison and in complete disarray. A curly blonde free-for-all.

Before I can fully turn around after closing the door, he has me secured in his arms.

"Tell me it isn't you. Tell me those animals never touched you." He's grinding this out, the words barely reaching me through his clenched teeth.

"Coen," I breathe out on a whisper. I mean realistically, what can I say? There's no way he's getting the complete story. Nobody has and nobody will. I won't recant any of it.

I decide to play dumb and make him out me. "What isn't me?"

He lets me go and walks over to the couch. Resting on his arms, he leans over it. I notice his back muscles tense. I don't like seeing him upset. I like Coen. Despite whatever whore-ish ways he carries, much like the rest of the XY chromosomal companions I have in my life, he has proven to have more discipline and may be even more dependable. Only time will really tell, though.

I walk over and rest my head between his shoulder blades. I'm barefoot and he's a giant. I bring my hands around him and squeeze. He smells good. I think I've missed his warmth. Coen is light.

"What would you like me to say, Coen? What do you want to hear?" I whisper into his back.

"Just tell me…you were at UF. Were you at that party? Was it you?" His voice gradually fades with each word. He doesn't really want to know. Nobody wants to hear. Not really.

"Coen…I, ah…I was at the party. The only frat party I've ever been to actually." I chuckle with that last part. It's sad and pathetic and kind of funny. Like screwed up funny, not ha, ha joke funny. "There's not much I can tell you. My memory is spotty." I leave it at that. I really don't want to have this conversation but he needed to know if he's expecting any type of intimacy between us. I never worried about any of this with Andrew. But Coen is another breed of man.

A strangled sound rips through his chest. I felt it and the chills awakened in its path alarm me.

And then, I'm in his arms. He's grabbed me tight and wound me into him, around him, and we are both rocking on the floor behind my couch.

I wish I could empathize. He's mourning over a naïve little girl that lost her life over seven years ago. I can't and won't mourn her loss. She thought she could hide, she thought she could find safety in words, in equations, in facts, in the greatest minds of history. She was pathetic. I refuse to equate myself with such gullibility and simplicity.

"Jesus, love. Holy fucking shit. I'll kill them. Give me their names and I'll fucking have them sliced at the knees." He sounds livid as his head rests on mine. I can't see his face, but I can feel the potency of heat he's radiating. He's undoubtedly pissed. I don't know why. You'd think this just happened yesterday. Or that it happened to him. It's over, though. Not that I've made peace with it, but I certainly don't dwell on it or use it to excuse myself. It is only a step in my evolution.

As for their names; yeah…they've become my mantra. All six of them. When I've hit a wall during my run, I run through them and break through to the other side. When I'm close to losing a fight, I cycle through their images and I massacre my opponent. When I'm at the board room table and someone sneers in my direction, I mentally chant those six names until it fuels me and pushes me to succeed.

I chant and chant and chant some more:

Tori McNeeley

James Evans

Shawn Patterson

Quinn Thompson

Chris Fletcher

Elias Munez

Always in that order. I'll never back down. I've seen the other side. I'm not afraid of it. I've seen evil. I've seen death. And I've survived both.

"You sweet man. I'd love nothing more, but as I told the police, I don't remember much." I sigh in an effort to end this line of questioning. I arch up and kiss him on the lips. Then remember that I haven't even brushed my teeth and need to pee.

Smiling sweetly, I whisper in his ear. "I have to pee, baby. Can you let me up before I burst on your lap?"

He pulls back showcasing a broad, full toothy, smile, though his eyes are a bit glassy and still rather red-rimmed. "You called me baby!" He leans forward and kisses me, another closed mouth sweet kiss. This one lasting longer than the last.

"Did you miss the pee part? I may look small, but I have a big bladder and you caught me still in bed."

"Oh, I thought you were trying out a new look." He smirks

while yanking on my tangled hair. I got him smiling…

A quick kiss on my nose and I'm released from his firm grasp. After a quick morning clean up, we spend most of the day hanging out. I made us loaded veggie omelets and we watched an on-demand movie. Our earlier conversation forgotten, we talked about his busy schedule. His father has been riding him hard, increasing his workload. I wonder what's going on with Greyson?

They leave for France on Tuesday and I know Coen is concerned. With this merger succeeding, CC will be revolutionized. I've decided that with the additional consumption of Renault Matra, this is the right time to watch their stock. After the merger is complete, I plan to buy out the market. I see a hefty profit in my future.

After a gourmet lunch of PB&J and in the middle of a riveting conversation over who's a better Presidential candidate, which his boneheaded ideologies need serious amending, his dad called killing our weekend fun. Apparently, Coen was needed again.

Chapter 21

THE PARTNERS AND LORI LEFT on Tuesday, as did the CC legal team and the Collins men. I never got an opportunity to see Coen again before he left. I'm not sure if he was just busy or if I'm simply not a priority. He called Monday night to check in and swore we'd talk while he was gone.

Realistically, I know better. The merger is nearly complete and so is my time with him. I don't have much to offer him now. It's for the best. I was repeatedly confounded by the man.

I've been busy with the murder case now that the CC merger is out of my hair. We have a solid case and I've been working heavily with the public defender's office. The band begins our summer tour the end of May and I needed to make sure that all of my bases were covered before we leave.

Trigger came over Thursday night for Chinese takeout. He wanted to check in on me. Those guys are such softies. I've made good on my promise to call or text Gun daily, but things are uncomfortable with Bullet. We haven't spoken since he came by my place last. I have no idea if he's still with that girl or any other for that matter. I don't fully understand what happened between us. And I most definitely don't understand the guys' reaction. But, in a world where I trust few and believe in little, they're who I have.

Friday afternoon, the trio, Malice, and I drive to New York for a radio interview with Octane, the hard rock channel on Sirius/XM radio. Our second single of our upcoming album is slowly gaining traction and we're in demand. It's an exciting time; to have our names out there like this.

We've had quite a Boston following, but I'd hardly say we're a household name on the national level. With our repeated airplay, things are definitely falling into rock and roll place.

We're grilled with the typical questions; what are your influences? What do you do for fun? How was the band formed? Yada, yada. Then the interviewer threw it out into left field and asked if we've ever fucked around with each other. He claimed that it must be difficult to have a chick in the band, as 'hot' as I am, surrounded by guys.

Gun got crazy pissed and went on the attack. *"Don't you ever fucking disrespect our girl like that? Do you fucking hear me?"*

Needless to say, the radio tour didn't go as swimmingly as the label execs would have wished. In a way, I'm glad the guys did that, as messed up as it is, they again proved how loyal they are to me. That I'm not just another prop but a true part of the band. I guess I need reminding.

Saturday night, we were invited to do an acoustic version of our music at a local coffee house that one of Trig's best friends owns. It was packed so tightly his patrons spilled out onto the streets.

There's something truly intimate about unplugging your instruments and then peeling down the layers to the root of the music. It felt more intimidating and soulful. For *Call to Arm*, Gunner retrieved his guitar and in a small circle, while squatting on benches, we sang and played so hard that I had to take a breather. It was beautiful. Raw and real and exquisitely beautiful. We were able to connect with the audience in a profound way. Vastly different from the rocking we do at BedHead or any of the coliseums or venues we rock on the roads.

But Bullet was standoffish. Despite the beauty, the intimacy we had all shared, he still walked away at the end of our set and hooked up with some chick. He never came back to the hotel that night.

Sunday was Mother's Day. Not just mine, but all mothers. You couldn't tell with the way she answered the phone. When I told her I was with the guys in NYC, she lost her mind telling me how I'd lose my fiancée by not acting like a proper woman. I finally lost it and told her he was in France and that our 'engagement' was over. She didn't take things well and told me how I've disappointed her yet again. Why do I bother calling?

Back in Boston and the week ahead looks to be fast paced. But it's the following weekend I'm looking forward to, we will be in

Vegas celebrating Tank's UFC fight. I'm ecstatic for him and to be a part of his special moment means the world to me. I've spoken to him several times and he's promised that he's sticking to his regimen and planning on winning this thing. I have no doubt. Nobody wants this more than Tank does and he has worked diligently to get here.

From Vegas, we head to LA to deal with last minute adjustments to our album before its release in June, and then go straight into touring. I've lightened my caseload in preparation for the tour. The partners have been amazingly flexible and forgiving with my schedule. Last year, I only took off six weeks, this year, our tour dates have increased to ten weeks, and there's even talk of extending it with touring in Europe. Although my caseload is light, I still have work that needs maintenance, which I'm able to tackle via skype, phone calls, and emails. Technology is a godsend.

I receive a huge flower display at the office on Monday afternoon. It appears that the merger went through successfully and CC sent the flowers as a thank you for all of the time I spent on the case. Although extremely thoughtful, it only seems to upset me more. A reminder that the merger is complete and I haven't heard a word from Coen.

By Wednesday morning, the partners and Lori have returned and regale the office with stories from France. Darrien had thrown a big party over the weekend to welcome everyone and celebrate. I guess things got out of hand because Lori seems to be going on and on about her random hookups. I can't say I'm sorry I missed any of it. It sounds wasteful. I'm all for a good party but even I know the right time and place to let go.

I'm out of the office as much as I'm in it. The jury selection is complete in Terrell's case and the offense has begun presenting its case. I've been spending an exceeding amount of time at the courthouse and the office. So much so that Malice has begun collecting me by eight every night, at times even kicking and screaming pleading for five more minutes.

May fifteenth, my twenty-second birthday. Although it isn't a *big* birthday it's still another year I've survived. The day started the same as the rest that week. Courtroom then office, and drowning in affidavits, amendments, and vague interpretations of the law.

It's late afternoon when I feel eyes on me. Looking up I spot a relaxed Bullet leaning against my door jam, arms crossed. He's wearing a black hoodie covering most of his face. It's a mystery how he even got in here or made it past Olivia. She's been obsessed since she learned I knew him. He's not smiling but looks fairly content. I wonder how long he's been standing there watching me.

"You planning on standing there all day?" I blurt. That must not be his plan because he walks in, closes the door, and then sits *on* my desk, practically on the papers I'm working on. Leave it to Bull to piss me off.

"Show some respect for the law, butthead," I whine, moving papers out of his way.

"I came by to set things straight."

"Maybe you should hold off on that. We're at my place of employment." Bullet is unpredictable and unabashed. Fantastic characteristics for a drummer, not so much in an office setting.

"First things first, I need you with me on Sunday." Just like that, he says he needs me. Maybe his brain has been absent for the last four weeks.

"I don't *need* to do anything. It's one of the awesome advantages of being me."

His lip twitches but then locks back into neutral. "Okay, Ms. No Need, I'd very much appreciate if you'd accompany me on Sunday." Better. He's piqued my curiosity.

"Okay, I *may* be available. What's Sunday?" I ask, standing up. My back has been hunched over for the last umpteen hours and I could use a little stretch. I take off my glasses and toss them onto my desk. I need full view of this animal.

He widens his legs and pulls me towards him then rubs his thumbs around the outside of my hips. My camisole is untucked and loosened with each thumb cycle. The soothing motion relaxes me and I lean into him. I missed this closeness.

"Rage has chosen to officially make Big D his old lady and the ceremony is Sunday. There's going to be a big family celebration and everyone's coming in. He wanted to make it official before we push out next weekend. I don't wanna go alone and refuse to bring one of the guys, so that leaves you." I quirk a brow.

"Ok, I want you with me. We can ride down on my bike. It's a nice drive, you know that." He pleads with me under his long lashes. He's the one who introduced me to the world of motorcycles. One ride and I was hooked.

Bullet's family life wasn't easy. His dad, Wrench, was the Sergeant in Arms for the Babylon Bastards Motorcycle Club or the BBMC. His mom, Gia, one of the sweet butts, died when Bully was born. He has a half-brother through his father, Rage, who's five years older. They both favor Wrench and share several similarities, though they have different moms. Rage's mom, Star, is a tough little firecracker. She's been Dallas' old lady for a couple dozen years now and is active in the BBMC since he's the current Treasurer.

When Bullet was seven, Wrench was arrested for manslaughter and put away for thirty years to life. With no other living relatives, Bully moved in with his brother and Star. He was already staying with them half the time anyway, so it made sense. Rage is currently the VP of the club, so I guess this Sunday will be a big deal. He and Big D have been on and off for years. They have a daughter together and live together.

"You want me as your bitch? I don't think so!" I'm throwing at him to see how he reacts. He knows I'm going. I love hanging out with his niece, Harley. She's crazy edible! I spoil her rotten and she loves her Auntie Shooter.

He chuckles and continues his slow circles, now his thumbs on the skin of my hip bone. "You want to ride next to me, birthday girl? I'm game either way as long as you get down there with me."

"Is my princess going to be there?" The most important question.

"It's her folks, so she'll be there for the barbeque. But the ceremony itself isn't exactly kid friendly." I've never seen an old lady ceremony. He's piqued my curiosity.

"Don't they just give her a property patch and call it a day?"

He chuckles darkly and licks his lips. I feel his breath sweep across my face.

"Nah, baby girrr…" I put my hand on his lips. We may be amicable but he did damage.

He sighs and I remove my hand. "You ever gonna let me call you that, again?" I shake my head. He's lost that right.

"Shit. I apologized. You're so fucking stubborn." He rests his forehead on mine. He may be frustrated with me, but he's got a smirk in his eyes. Circle, circle, circle. Each time he digs his thumb lower and lower and increases the pressure.

"You know me better than almost anyone, Bully. You knew it'd hurt me. But you chose to do it anyway. I'm not *your* baby girl anymore. I've got plenty of other names you can use, though."

He growls in frustration. "You and me, Sunday! And tonight the guys and I are swinging by for our girl's birthday dinner. We're bringing in Italian, your favorite, so you better make sure your sweet ass is back at your place by seven. Hear me?" I nod against him.

He kisses my forehead and stands up, pushing me back into my chair.

"Get back to work so you can get home on time. I got you a little something." He hands me a box. "It's not diamonds and money, but it's something for my baby gg…chick? Maybe just baby?" He winks.

He walks towards the door. "Happy birthday, Shooter girl!"

Looks like the day is picking up.

Chapter 22

"OPEN UP, SHOOTER GIRL. WE got food and we is huuuuungry!" I hear through the door along with several bangs.

I just got home and threw on black yoga pants and an off the shoulder Loaded Gun pink tee. My hair is a knotty mess and I'm smiling big. Opening the door, the guys stampede towards my kitchen.

I'm thrown over a shoulder, which I think might be Bullet's by the sway of the ass. I pat it…yep, a nice ass! My own is slapped in return. "Cut it out or I'm gonna have to take you to your room and show you what I'd really like to do to you on your birthday." He chuckles and rubs my bum a bit more.

Dropping me into a dining room chair, he smooches my head and joins the guys readying the food in the kitchen. I hear a pop and assume someone opened a bottle of wine, which is confirmed when Malice comes over and hands me a glass.

"Pour vous, la reine d'anniversaire."

For you, the birthday queen.

"Merci!"

Thank you!

Birthdays are fun with my gang around. I hardly even remember that my parents didn't call to wish me well. Or my sister. Or even Mr. Background check himself, Coen. I hardly remember that at all. Or so I keep telling myself.

We're laughing and eating. The guys surprised me with all of my favorites. I love anything with melted cheese on it and Italians know how to do it right! Manicotti, Ravioli, Stromboli, I'm in gooey cheese heaven.

Half way through dinner, they begin to throw out their renditions of comical Shooter stories. It's funny how I totally don't remember things their way. In fact, they're *always* the instigators, while I somehow get suckered into following them.

Like the time they thought we could climb through the air ducts at the Stafford Centre in Houston. They couldn't fit, so they shoved me in there. But I could only go in one direction, so I had to climb around the air duct system for nearly ten minutes trying to find a safe way down. Malice went ape shit, but once I was finally out, the stupid trio couldn't stop laughing. I think that's the *real* reason they keep me around. Comic relief.

We end the night on a high note with promises to hang out tomorrow night. Pretty soon, these guys will be all I see. I have to get my head back into that world. Our tour officially kicks off in two weeks.

They leave me a few birthday gifts on the table and lots of kisses and hugs on the way out. Bullet stands to the side as everyone makes their way out the door. Noticing it, Malice gives me a curious look, which I return with a shrug.

"I gotta speak with baby g…Shooter. You guys go ahead," Bully says still hanging back, arms crossed, daring anyone to say shit. Gunner gives Bullet a look I can't decipher and then walks stiffly away.

"Night guys! Thank you for an awesome birthday! Love you," I yell into the hallway and then close the door. He's behind me in an instant. I turn to look at him but I'm immediately caged against the door. His arms are on either side of my head and I feel his heat permeating. He isn't touching me, though. In fact, there's still about a foot between our bodies.

"Was there something you needed, Bullet?" I softly ask.

His hand comes down and his fingers caress the silver necklace he bought me. It has several charms on it, including a guitar, drumsticks, and a gun. The charms sit in the crevasse of my cleavage. His fingers lift the silver string and run them up and down sliding against my skin. His singular focus there, never meeting my eyes.

He breathes out against me. "You're wearing it." Of course, I wore it. He bought it for me, I thought that was why he bought it.

"Of course," I respond above a whisper. He's so close that anything louder feels like yelling.

His eyes realign to mine. I notice they're dilated and his breathing is gaining speed and strength. He moves his hands back to the door and presses himself against me, his nose barely rubbing my neck.

"Does that stupid preppy take care of you?" he whispers against my earlobe. The warmth causes shivers to spread throughout my body. I shake my head.

"I haven't seen him in almost two weeks."

He inhales deeply. "Jesus, I'm no good for you, baby. You deserve some rich dickless punk to take care of you not some loser that doesn't have a fucking clue about family or love or any of that shit." He takes another few breaths. "You deserve the world, Shooter girl! I fucking wish I could be the one to give it all to you." He rubs his nose deeper into my neck and grinds his lower body against me.

I rest my hands on his chest, needing grounding through him. "Why do you say that? Did you forget it was preppy frat boys that attacked me, that fucking killed me? Did you forget that it was tatted bad ass men that helped bring me back to life?" I voice louder than our little bubble allows. I push against him even more exasperated.

"Don't tell me what I need. Don't *ever* assume you know better. If that's who you think I am, then you don't know me at all?" I huff this all out and am shaking by the end. Why does he keep pushing me? He pulls then pushes. I'm in and then out. I can't take much more.

"No, you're wrong, baby. I do know you. I just wish I could have you." He pushes himself closer to me and I feel myself shaking against him, through him all while his hands grip the door so fiercely I wonder if he'll get splinters. The dumb macho man probably wouldn't even notice. He has a pain threshold on another level.

"Why can't you?" I whisper. It feels like I'm approaching a taboo topic. That I'm not allowed to enjoy him. I push him harder this time and squeeze around him. He's still leaning against the door, muscles taut and hands planted.

"Just leave." My voice elevates. "Why bother with me? Pull me in and then push me further out?" My stomach aches with these thoughts. I touch my scar, reminding me. Pushing me for more. I'm stronger. "We can't be alone if this is our every interaction."

I'm at a loss. There's no puzzle here to figure out. How can I when it's so obvious that he doesn't even know himself? I hang my head. I don't think I'll be able to survive the next few months if he keeps doing this.

I'm a few feet behind him deep in thought when he comes at me again. His hands rub across his bald head, and he looks upset and frustrated. His face is pinched and pained. "Stop thinking that shit!" he yells. "That's not what this is. This…this…" He sighs. Shaking his head, he reaches for me. "You…you…" He can't seem to finish his train of thought. I know the feeling all too well.

He drops to his knees and pulls me to him. He buries his head there. "I can't," he says over and over into my stomach, and with each word he moves his head from one side to the other. One hand clings and digs up my back and the other grabs lower.

I try to push away. "No, you don't get off that easily." He holds me tighter. "Go…just go. I don't want this anymore. If you don't want me then leave." I'm so frustrated that the threatening tears are burning my eyes. But my words don't stop him. He keeps holding me down. Holding me to him.

Eventually my top half falls backwards. Bull catches me before I fall and jumps on top of me. Not the position I was aiming for. "Get off," I screech, pushing him and trying to roll away.

He grabs my hands and holds them above my head. His body nearly crushes me, and his lips are only a breath away from mine. "Why are you doing this?" I cry out. Closing his eyes, he rests his forehead against my own, silently shaking, or maybe I still am.

"I can't let you go. I can't keep you. I don't know what to do," he whispers against my closed lips.

I turn my head to the right and close my eyes. This isn't how I wanted the day to end. I don't want to consume his delicious spicy pasta breath. I don't want to feel his body pulsing all around me. I don't want to notice the hurt in his stunning eyes or the way he keeps licking his full delicious lips. I don't want any of this. He pursued this. And he keeps hounding me.

"I need you, baby," he whispers into my ear and then trails his tongue along the outer shell. "I need you more than anything."

He sucks on my lobe, biting and nibbling at it while shifting over me. He starts to move, pressing his enlarging cock into me. Rock and nibble. Rock and lick. He digs his pelvis deeper into me and rocks from side to side. Then he continues with his slow torture. Rock and nip down my neck. My hands above my head, he leaves one hand locking me in place while the other trails down my body. He skims over my face, touching my parted lips, then follows by touching the necklace as it glides towards my breasts. He keeps his eyes on mine and continues the rocking torture.

I can feel the volcanic heat pooling all around me. My face is engulfed in flames, begging for eruption. "Bully," I whisper. Words are barely there. Thoughts are nowhere near.

"Fuck yeah," he grunts. "Give it to me. Give it all to me. Does it feel like I don't want you? Does it feel like I don't need you?" He pushes himself harder into me. The rocking tempo picks up and I can see the sweat building on his brows and upper lip. I whimper, aching to touch him, to lick him. I want to let go and give into the heat, absorb it through him, but I can't. He will just leave me later and hurt me, ruin me.

"Stopppp…please Bull." I whimper and try to pry my hands out of his clutch.

He freezes all movement and lifts himself off of me. "What's wrong…?"

"I…I can't do this." I look to the ground and wrap my arms around my knees pulling them to my chest. I slowly start rocking myself, trying to catch my breath and calm my heart.

"Are you scared? I won't hurt you. I'd never…" he whispers trying to touch my leg.

"But you will. You keep torturing me. Just go while you can. While we can still look each other in the eye." I plead. I can't lose him. He wants to be my friend, my lover, I don't know anymore, and neither does he. I'm too new at this game to play. I'll perpetually lose.

I keep my head on my knees, the rocking easing my fears and calming my now raging libido.

I feel him move away from me. Then after a few minutes of watching me, he comes to my side, squats, and whispers, "Our time will come. It *has* to." He kisses my head and seconds later, the

door slams shut.
Just like that.
Twenty-two sucks!

Chapter 23

ON FRIDAY, I GET ANOTHER visitor. It seems like my office is the hotspot this week. Coen enters and sits in the chair by my desk.

"Hey, love. You miss me?" he asks cocking his brow with a matching cocked smile.

"Sure. It sounds like the merger went well. How's the dust settling?" I give him a hesitant smile, unsure why he's here. He never bothered to wish me a happy birthday or check up on me. Why should I give him time now?

"Good, good," he states looking around. "You've got a new plant. Nice." He smiles hesitantly, slowly picking up on my mood.

"Thanks. My grandparents sent it, yesterday." I'm fiddling with my pen, trying not to make eye contact.

"I remember them. What's the occasion? Did you already win your murder one case?"

"No, it was my birthday." I utter vacantly, keeping my eyes on the twirling pen in my hand.

I hear his quick inhalation. "Shit, when was it?"

"Yesterday." I shrug. It's forgotten. Over. "Is there something you need, Mr. Collins?" I glance up to see he's carefully watching me.

"Fuck, we went backwards, huh? I'd hardly think that you should refer to your *fiancée* by his last name. We don't exactly have a formal relationship, do we?"

"I didn't realize we were in an actual relationship, Mr. Collins. You see, from what I've gathered, relationships aren't about convenience. And I'm pretty sure communication is essential. But what would I know?" I say all of this in one breath with a straight face. Nothing is flicking or ticking. After Bullet's bullshit and the jerking from both men I'm beginning to think that my no relationship status should remain steadfast.

He grips his hair, pulling at it. "Charlie, things got a little hectic in France."

"And before France and after France," I add.

"I missed you. That's why I came here. Not to argue with you. Look, all of the merger stuff is behind us now." He shakes his head, his voice softening. "Maybe we can have our date tonight, we can catch up and-"

"I have plans tonight," I say.

"Are you seeing someone?" He shifts in his seat, suddenly uncomfortable. His eyes are frosty and narrowed in on me, searching for the truth or some version of it.

"Just the usual suspects," I jest. I don't know if Bullet counts. I don't know anything on the relationship home front, any more.

"What does that mean? Are you with Andrew again?" He slams his hands on my desk and leans forward, getting himself worked up over nothing.

"I haven't heard from or seen Andrew in a long time now. My time is valuable, Mr. Collins. I have much to do, so if you don't need anything then please excuse yourself."

He clears his throat. "Well, Ms. Paz…" He articulates slowly while watching me. I don't think I've ever heard him call me by my last name and I don't think I like it. He stands and slicks his suit down. "We're inviting those of you that assisted with the merger to a party tomorrow evening. It'll be on the Collins' yacht."

"Sounds glorious. Thank you for the invitation. Please leave the prudent information with Olivia. Have a lovely day, Mr. Collins." I go back to my work effectively shutting him out.

He walks to my side of the desk. Turning my chair towards him, he leans down and cups my chin, his thumb rubbing my lower lip. His eyes are searing me.

"Charlie, we aren't done. I'm sorry I missed your birthday. If you'd let me, I'd make it up to you. I'd give you a lifetime of making things up to you. You just have to trust me." He leans forward and pecks my lips and then rubs my lip again. "Mine," he whispers and quickly kisses me again before he's out of the door.

It's my birthday weekend and I'm so tired of these alpha brainless assholes in my life thinking they can dictate my every thought and orgasm.

I decided to leave work early and do some serious damage to my credit cards by purchasing all new clothes and boots. I'm going to party in style. My hair is straight down, my makeup dark and smoky, lips blood red. I'm feeling the heat and dishing it out, wearing what might be considered a black leather corset, but it's strapped with buckles in the back. It's so tight, it makes my boobs pop up revealing lots of cleavage. My leather pants sit low and are cinched with more of the same belt buckle, but along the sides. It looks like I'm wearing only half the leather pants as the buckles are the other half. There's nothing underneath. Nothing.

I'm dirty, naughty, and I'm going to have a fucking good time, even if it kills me!

Malice drives us to BedHead and accompanies me into the main level. I set tonight up as my birthday bash, so the place is crawling with people. I grab a drink and head for the main bar. Show time! I signal to the DJ and put on my headset.

"Hello, Head-onites!" I scream into the mic as the lights embrace me. I laugh as I listen to the sounds of the club shift towards me, screaming in excitement. "How are we doing tonight, lovers?" More screams and I notice a bunch of good-looking men closing in on the bar.

"Allow me to introduce you to some of the sexiest women in Boston…my very own minxy mixologists," I scream and the girls climb onto the bar. Again, this part is all routine…well, when I'm in the mood to do it. My club, my playground, my rules.

"Starting with my right; we have the lucky Lola. Next is the bodacious Babs, killer Kelly, followed by delicious Debbie, smack that ass Sammy, and lastly sex kitten Savvy." The girls bow or wave as I go through each name and then they jump off the bar. Just like we do every time. But this time around, I'm going to change things up a bit.

"As for me, lovers, well some of you know me as…" I wait putting my hand to my ear. People all over shout "SHOOTER."

"That's right, they call me Shooter." I laugh. "And did ya'll know that I'm celebrating my birthday?" More shouts.

"Hhhhmmm, I guess that means I deserve some extra birthday love tonight. Who's willing to throw some extra love my way?" More screams and I look down and see a gorgeous guy eyeing me like I'm ice cream on a hot day, dying for a lick. Then the DJ kicks in playing Marilyn Monroe's Happy Birthday song to JFK, and everybody in the club sings happy birthday to ME!

I put my hand over my heart. Who needs family to remember you when you have an entire freaking club singing your praise? "Thank you lovers of BedHead! Now I have an important question: who has gotten HEAD TONIGHT?" Everyone screams and I see ice cream man licking his lips.

"What about you?" I ask pointing at him. He smiles and shakes his head 'no.' "No?" I ask, aghast. I reach down and try to pull him onto the bar. "Ladies, this gentleman.... what's your name, sexy?"

"Drake," he yells towards me still holding my hand. He wobbles onto the bar and stands possessively next to me. He has potential.

"Drake has been neglected in the Head department." I look at Drake, still holding on to me.

"Are you more of a giver or a taker, dearest Drake?"

He glowers straight into me and says, while licking his lips, "I'm a giver!" I sigh.

"Hhmmm. What should I do with you? Ladies, is there anyone interested in taking Drake up on his...um, giving needs?" Lots of high-pitched squeals and screams follow.

"Oh." I chuckle and shift my attention back to Drake. "I think you'll have your pick tonight!"

He leans over and whispers loudly. "But I want you!"

Game...Time to play. "Head-onites, Drake here thinks that I should take him for myself. What do you think? Maybe I should put him to the test? See if he's worthy?" More screams.

I look up into his eyes and say in the most commanding voice I can muster, "On your knees!" I think I may have just got a thousand times dirtier than when I walked through the club doors thirty minutes ago.

He looks confused for a second, and then his eyes widen in understanding. Welcome to my world, Drake. He looks down at the bar nervously, and then does another wobbly drop before landing on his knees in front of me. "Bring it, baby!"

I walk over to where he is kneeling and press his beautiful wavy chestnut hair to my crotch. That's right, the girl who has never really been touched there, just shoved a stranger's head...there.

I'm soaking up every move he makes as he sticks his tongue out and licks my leather-clad pussy without taking his eyes off of me. The entire club is shouting and screaming! I let him have a few more licks then laugh into the mic.

"Alright lovers, it looks like I'm gonna have to take Drake, here, back home with me to finish what he's started. You guys have a wonderful night and make sure you've got someone to tuck you tight into bed! Tip my girls well and tip them often. The BAR IS OPEN!" I scream and then the lights go down. I take off the headset and hand it to Savvy. Immediately, Malice and Zeke, my head of security, are there to usher me to the VIP. But this time, I take Drake with me.

When we get upstairs, I find that the whole place has been bday'ed up for me. There are black and pink streamers everywhere with matching balloons. Patron is waiting on the center of the coffee table with lined up shot glasses next to it. The couches are filled with the trio, friends and others of the female persuasion. I walk over to Gunner and kiss him on the cheek.

"Did you do this?"

"Nah, baby girl, this was all Bullet." I look over at the mastermind. After last night, I really don't want to see him. He has a couple of girls around him and I make it a point to eye each one.

Cade Stryker, from the band Stryker, comes over and kisses me hard on the lips. He smells like he's already started on the tequila. "Damn, you look like a fucking wet dream tonight! Shooter, happy birthday, baby." He goes in for another kiss but I pull away before he can reach me.

I hear someone in the background say, "Get him the fuck off of her." We went on tour with Stryker last year and are planning on doing it again this year. They're the headliners and we are one of the opening acts. I feel Stryker being pulled off me and then Bullet is in front of me glaring, almost maliciously. "What the fuck are you wearing?" he yells.

Set....

"Whatever the fuck I want!" I smile, my fuck you smile. He wants to pass me up, then he doesn't get a voice in what I wear, who I play with, or what I do. I grab Drake's hand and bring him to the couch.

"Hi Drake, I'm Shooter." I wink and hold my hand out. I guess it's a little late for introductions, but mother raised me with manners.

"Hi." He smiles brightly and I notice how perfectly aligned his teeth are. He has a little scarring in his neck region, but otherwise he's quite attractive. His eyes are expressive in a riveting shade of green mixed with specks of blue.

"What do you do, Drake?"

"I officially got out of the Corps a few months ago. Right now I'm working with my dad at his dealership and I'm sort of working as a model."

"Sort of a model?"

"I...um, I lost part of my leg in Afghanistan, and recently I've been working with a photographer friend of mine on various projects. It's still new," he adds shyly whilst looking down. This explains why he was nervous and a bit unstable on the bar. I just thought he was intoxicated. Now I feel like a big douche.

"So, you're a war hero?"

"I'm just a guy trying to survive. Adjust to my new life." He smiles and briefly looks at my cleavage. Poor guy.

I climb onto his lap straddling his legs. His hands immediately go around my backside. I can feel the heat off them through the open parts of my pants.

"I hope you don't mind," I whisper as I slide further towards him on his lap.

"No, I really like you and your music.Your club is awesome!" He clears his throat. He is so nervous.

"Yeah," I whisper and breathe into his ear. I dig my hands around his neck and pull him towards me. The brief revelation of intimacy I've had over the last couple of months has taught me well. I shamelessly grind myself onto him, over and over again, in a slow seductive rhythm. "Tell me more about yourself, Drake."

"Oh... I, uh, I." He's whispering in complete unintelligible gibberish. I continue my slow torture of this poor guy. I feel him getting hard underneath me. I lick and grind, then lick some more until I'm flying. No really, I'm in the air.

"Put me down!" I scream. Bullet has pulled me off of Drake and thrown me over his shoulder.

"You stay the fuck away from her!" he barks at Drake, pointing at him.

Gunner drops his chick and marches over. "Let her go, Bullet!

It's her birthday. She can do whatever the fuck she wants!"

I feel Bullet shake his head. "No way, man. Nobody is touching her! I don't give a shit what any of you say!" He's beyond pissed, I feel him vibrate underneath me. He slaps my ass hard. Then thinks better of it and does it again. He keeps muttering incoherently but I don't think he's drunk.

Trigger comes over and says something in his other ear. Bullet shakes his head and starts walking out of the club with me on his shoulder. I look up to see Malice not far behind.

As early as I'm being sent home, as mad as I should be right now I chuckle to myself and think…

Match!

Chapter 24

ON SATURDAY, I WAS UP and on the run early. First, hitting Tornadoes for a solid workout. The place seems empty without Tank. I can't wait to see him in a few more days.

Then I do some grocery shopping and other errands before getting ready for this afternoon's fun.

I decided to take Malice with me to the CC party. He fits in almost anywhere and I realized too late that I should have brought him with me to Florida, so I'm hesitant to leave him behind now.

He looks his typical tailored self in a tan suit and I'm dressed in a white pants set. The elephant pants end at my toes, mainly because I'm ridiculously short while the top is the same material and color. It's a half turtleneck and the shoulders are asymmetrical. One shoulder is completely bare while the other covers past my collarbone. Since we will be on the yacht, possibly over the open sea, I decided to French braid my hair to the side to keep it from flying away.

The party is called for four o'clock at the Boston Yacht Club out of Marblehead. We follow the crowd to the Collins' yacht and climb aboard. There are a lot more people here than the team that assisted in the merger. The yacht is so packed that Malice and I climb to the top deck for a breather. I don't recognize anyone and just want to get out of the way.

By the time we make it to the top, the yacht is already moving. Shit, we missed our out. Now we will be trapped on this thing for God knows how long.

"Combien de temps allons-nous coincés ici?"

How long are we trapped here? Malice asks while sipping his bottled beer. He must have read my mind.

"Je ne sais pas. Je ne pensais pas qu'il y aurait autant de gens ici."

I don't know. I didn't think there would be this many people here.

"Il est pas trop tard pour sauter le navire et nager."

It's not too late to jump ship and swim.

"Tu es drôle. Peut-être que nous pouvons trouver un peu de chocolat pour vous garder heureux. Je pensais que je l'ai vu un peu de nourriture sur l'un des ponts inférieurs nous sommes passés."

You're funny. Maybe we can find some chocolate to keep you happy. I thought I saw some food on one of the lower decks we passed.

We take a leisurely stroll around the floor, enjoying the chilled air. I rub my arms as we walk around trying to erase the goose bumps. Despite it being mid-May, the air feels cooler over the water.

As we make our way to the stairs I glance over and who do I see? Mr. Coen Collins surrounded by a bevy of blondes. Even from twenty feet away, I can hear their high-pitched squeals of delight as he regales them with…whatever it is he does.

Coen must have felt me because his eyes shift to mine. He sends me his dazzling I'm-Cocky-Coen smile and the air around me charges. Normally I would melt, but I'm tired of his disappearing acts.

He looks confused when I don't smile in response. Still surrounded, I glance at each of the women hoping to see…his perfect match? A more suitable playmate than myself?

I shake my head and look away. I shouldn't have come today. Malice places his hand on my back to usher me to the next level. His presence snaps me back to reality. I don't belong with the Coen's of the world. According to Bullet, I don't belong with him either. So, as usual, that puts me in the I-don't-fit-in zone. It's where I've lived for the past twenty-two years, it certainly isn't something new. I should be used to it by now. But I'm not.

I feel a hand on my arm half expecting it to be Coen, I'm surprised when I turn and find a smiling Andrew. The last communication we had wasn't exactly pleasant. I immediately grab onto Malice for support, which is foreign to me.

"Darling…" He leans forward and kisses my cheek, lingering longer than I'd like. He places his hand on my bare arm and rubs up and down. "You look beautiful. I didn't expect to see you." He seems to be in a pleasant mood, but still I lock my grip on Malice.

"Andrew, how are things? I believe I mentioned that I assisted with the legal aspects of the Collins Corp merger." I can't say that I'm surprised he doesn't remember. After all, it had nothing to do with politics or him.

Suddenly, I'm met with even more warmth as Coen comes around Andrew and pulls me to him by my waist. I glance at Malice, still in my firm lock, confused. Are they going to urinate on me and mark their territory? I should move. I just got these Gucci Espadrille sandals and don't want them ruined.

"Carpenter, wonderful to see you, again. How are things?" He smirks at Andrew and then kisses my shoulder. His hot breath lingers as his kiss turns into a small nibble. What is he doing?

"Hi, love," he whispers into my shoulder. Despite my obvious confusion, the chilled goose bumps are back, only this time for a different reason. Dang it. I don't want to react to this man.

Andrew watches Coen, and I notice the disdain grow on his face. "Collins, I thought you were interested in Morninglane?" He looks pointedly at me and raises his brow. Oh, right, Non-Boobs Betty, I wonder if she is here. "I didn't realize you were into my sloppy seconds."

OH NO HE DIDN'T!

I can feel my face blaze as I'm about to spring into action. He may have never attended one of my Cage fights, but he's about to get a front row seat now. I let go of Malice and am ready to pull back my arm, when Coen strikes into action.

He releases me and gets directly into Andrew's face. Andrew is shorter, so Coen has to tilt his head down. "What the fuck did you just say about my fiancée?" he grinds through clenched teeth. From my angle of his back, I can see the veins protruding in his neck and the tick of his jaw. His hands are tightly fisted at his sides. Through his rolled up sleeves, I can even see the veins in his forearms rising in anticipation.

I drop my arm and watch thoroughly dumbfounded. I'm pretty sure my eyes are wide and my mouth is hanging wide open.

"What? What did you just call her?" Andrew asks in shock.

"I said, you slimy piece of shit. If you ever denigrate the love of my life again, I'll cut you up into pieces and pass you out to your constituents."

That's the sexiest thing I have ever heard anyone say about me!

"And if you ever *touch* her again, I'll hold you down and let her moo goo gai pan your ass!"

No wait, *that* was the sexiest thing I've ever heard.

Coen releases Andrew from the stare down apocalypse, grabs my hand tightly interlocking our fingers, and leads me away. We get to the other end of the room and he pulls me to him. Hand around my neck, he leans down and breathes me in. "You ok?" he whispers to me. I nod in response. I look over his shoulder and see several pairs of eyes on me, including a pissed off looking Greyson. I hope he didn't see that little exchange, but I have a feeling he did with the way he glares at me.

I think about pulling away and notice Coen is still faintly shaking. I will wait this out while my head filters through everything. I can't believe he said that to Andrew. The gossip train will be steaming up any minute now and half way to Cali. I wasn't prepared for any of this. What was he thinking? I could have handled Andrew.

The rest of the afternoon is spent with me at Coen's side. Every time I attempt to move away, an arm snakes out around my waist, or around my shoulder. He won't let me take a breath without touching me or having me nearby. Even when Greyson comes over to pull him away, Coen refuses to let go of my hand.

I would say that I was a prop, but every so often he throws a question my way, or tries to bring me into the conversation.

"What do you think, love?"

"Charlie would love going there, wouldn't you, love?"

"We've got to see that one, love."

"I've never been. We should go, love."

"Charlie said the exact same thing…"

From my zoned out vantage point, I watch the women staring in disparage, glowering at me. I wonder what they think. Are they jealous like those two old bitties in the bathroom whining about Andrew or are they plotting my demise? Maybe they feel sorry for me. I look over at Coen. How could they not be jealous? He's stunning. If they knew he was just pretending, I bet they would feel sorry for me.

"Charlie, good to see you finally got out of the office," Brantley says coming over to join our little circle.

"It's true," I jest while shaking his hand with my left as the right has been Coen confiscated. "I do leave it on the rare occasion."

Coen shifts his attention to the new intrusion. "Brantley, how are you? Thank you for all of your hard work on the account." Apparently, holding my hand wasn't enough, because he releases it and puts it around my shoulder, drawing Brantley's attention.

"Of course, but as you know, it was really Charlie that took this merger to bat."

"Yes," Coen agrees and kisses my cheek, in front of my boss. "She's quite a woman!"

"She's quite a lawyer," Brantley corrects him. "I'm not sure how we're going to get on without you for the summer," he says to me, shaking his head.

I feel the pressure on my shoulder double and Coen stiffen. "Yes, it'll be quite challenging for all of us to manage without her." He nods while forcing a half smile.

After Brantley leaves, Coen whispers in my ear. "We'll talk about this later." Then he continues his conversations without me. Business as usual.

If we ever did get together, have an actual relationship, with dates, dinners, theatre, would this be my life? He's here and he's not. He wants to be with me and then I don't see or hear from him for weeks. I know he's upset now, but he doesn't have any right to be, does he? What is it with these men?

Chapter 25

TODAY IS A PERFECT EXAMPLE of the juxtaposition of my life. Yesterday, I was on a yacht with some of the most influential people in the north-east US, while today I'm on a bike heading for a barbeque with a bunch of tatted roughed up bikers.

Bully showed up at my place at around ten ready to go. And despite some intense arguing, I got my way and rode Abbey here, solo. Bully rides up first, nods to the Prospect who opens up the gates, then we are through and parking our bikes side by side.

As I'm making my way off the bike, Bullet comes over and unclips my helmet. He starts with the rules. I can't drink, I can't talk, I can't fight, I can't…I can't…I can't. Why the hell did I come, again?

I roll my eyes. I've been here enough times over the years that he'd know I got this by now.

He grabs my chin and sternly looks me over.

"I'm serious, Shooter. Can't have anything happen to ya!"

"Then why'd you bring me?"

He shakes his head and starts rummaging through my saddlebags. I bought some stuff for Harley and for Rage and Big D for their ceremony naming thing.

Instead of walking through the clubhouse, we walk around to the back. There are tons people here today. Lawn chairs are lined up in circles filled with all types of grizzlies, children chase each other screaming, and against the fence there are tables covered with food and the women standing guard over it.

"Auntie Shooter," is screamed from the sweetest little voice. I bend down and pick up the little thing running towards me and smack kisses all over her. At only four and a half, Harley has long dark blonde hair that's always a loose mess around her perpetually dirty face. But what I love the best about her is her eyes. She has her uncle's eyes. The world calls the color hazel so monotonous and uninspiring. But in my world it's interwoven strings of golds, bronzes, and yellows all ringed in glossy black. And at times, it's pure fire and rage.

I grab the gifts for Harley out of Bull's hands and run off to play. It's the safest route. I'm here loving my girl and staying out of trouble.

After we stuff our faces with burgers and chips for lunch, we end up on the ground with Harley doing all sorts of dreadful things to my hair. I have a backwards braid in the front, like a unicorn horn, and several barrettes, bows, and ponytails all around. Thank goodness she forgot to bring her makeup case today or I'd look like a Goth Barbie clown right now.

Zoning out, I watch Bull as he speaks animatedly with Rage. Bullet is wearing his cut today over a white tee. He looks to be in his element; he looks happy and he must feel my stare because he turns in my direction and smirks, then winks while he says something to his brother. Rage stretches his neck to check out his daughter's handiwork. They both start chuckling and resume their talk.

"Pssttt, Harley. Let's go tickle Uncle Bullet." It never hurts to have a coconspirator.

We stay low to the ground as we jump out and surprise Bullet and start tickling him relentlessly. We're screaming and laughing, and of course, over powered. Now on the ground he looms over us readying for another round.

"Run Harley, save yourself!" I scream and she runs towards her mom screaming about how 'Uncle Bull is gonna tickle kill Auntie.'

"Dirty girl, what have you started?" I stick my tongue out and he jumps on top of me straddling my legs and goes back to his torture. "Had enough?" He laughs out.

"Never!" I shake my head. "I've endured worse ticklers than you!"

He digs in for more when a booming voice above us shouts, "What are you doing to that poor girl, boy?" It's Dallas, Rage's stepdad.

"Well, sir, you see it's like this." I bat my eyes and play innocent.

"I was just minding my own business when this biker mauled me and began his vicious attack." I'm trying and failing to keep a straight face.

"Anyone ever tell you that you're full of shit, Shooter girl?" Ha, you'd think these hams were blood related the way they treat me. Bull laughs a real deep belly laugh and helps me off the ground.

"Oh, he's got you pegged, baby!" Bull slaps my ass. I glare at him and then turn my attention to the old man.

"You're real funny, Dallie." I lean over and give the bear a hug. He pats me on the back, laughing.

"You're just too easy little girl." He winks and then sits next to Rage, who has been laughing at us.

I straighten up and tuck a freaky ponytail behind my hair. "Ohhhh, you messed up my hair. I'm gonna tell Harley, you're in so much trouble." I give him the middle finger salute and saunter away.

As the sun sets and the air chills, the kids are forced to go home and go to bed. One of the old ladies is on babysitter duty, so Big D and some of the others can stay and party. I feel an immediate shift when the kids leave. The music is turned up, food is replaced with spirits, and the club whores plow in. There's a fresh round of men piling in, too.

Pretty soon, I notice everyone is forming a circle outside and Rage's hog has been moved to the center. I'm not sure where to stand since Bullet disappeared, so I join Star and Dallas. I skim over every face as we stand nearly facing each other and awaiting. I finally spy Bullet across the way, when Dallas stretches over Star to ask if I've ever been to an Old Lady patch ceremony. I shake my head, which results in his cackling into near convulsions.

"Oh, you're gonna love this girlie."

We wait a few more minutes when I notice Big D walk out in a robe. Wasn't she wearing jeans seconds ago, why's she dressed that way? She continues her journey until she's in front of Rage. Together, they listen intently as the Prez speaks quietly to them.

They both nod and Big D drops her robe in the middle of all these people staring at her. Holy fuck. I see all the men start smiling and grabbing at the girls around them.

Rage is wearing nothing but his cut and jeans. He grabs Big D's hand and leads her to his bike. He climbs on, unzips his pants, and pulls his cock out. I slap my hands over my eyes and I know Dallie saw because he's in near hysterics. He knew I'd react like this. Why the hell did Bull bring me to see this? I mean, I've seen sex tons but not Rage or D. Even with my hands over my face my eyes are squeezed tight with trying to block out those images.

I part my fingers to take a quick peek. Despite my disgust with this little ceremony, I'm still curious. Yup, they're going at it on top of his bike. I hear moaning but it isn't only coming from the center of the circle, it's coming from all around. I remove my hands and notice several sweet butts on their knees already sucking guys off. Is this a fucking orgy? Did Bullet really invite me to an orgy? No fucking way!

I look back to the spot where I last saw Bullet and notice he's watching me. There are people fucking and touching all around him, but he's watching the chicken shit with her hands over her eyes. He looks tense, too. His shoulders are pressed back and his hands fisted at his side. Raging Bull. He notices the shock still apparent on my face and walks over to me, cutting right through the circle to reach me. He passes right by his brother fucking his old lady but manages to keep his eyes on me. Grabbing me by one of the many braids that Harley gifted me and wrenching my head back, he smacks his lips hard onto my own. A hard possessive kiss.

Dallas starts laughing next to us. "When are you gonna lock yours down, Bullet head?"

Bullet glares at him. "Mind your own fucking business, old man." His gaze softens when he turns back to me. "You okay, baby?" I nod and swallow. This little event caught me off-guard. Why would anyone ever want to be an old lady? I mean look how you're treated. "You're wrong," he whispers closer to my ear. His soft words drown out the moaning and debauchery of everything surrounding us.

"This is the highest compliment a brother can give his lady. Their names will be tatted on each other forever. It isn't like divorce. You're a brother for life, an old lady for life. Some women wait forever to be given a property patch. It's an honor, baby. You should view it as you would a religious ceremony or something. With reverence."

"So, if you were in love with someone and wanted her to be yours you'd have to fuck her in front of all your brothers and whomever was there to watch and you'd be cool with that?"

He pulls back, his eyes brighter, the golds reflecting the moon's light. Fucking stunning. His thumb lazily traces my nose and down to my lips. "*If* I loved someone enough to promise them forever, I don't know, I think I wouldn't be able to share her. But then again, the thought of her wearing my patch, the thought of her branded with my name…" He closes his eyes and tilts his head back. After a moment of silence, he opens them and they laser in on me powerfully. "Anything would be worth that," he grinds out hoarsely. With that he kisses me firmly and walks into the house.

The ceremony finishes with a loud crescendo. There are screams of passion from all directions, including Dallas. Gross. Big D gets her property cut presented and after she puts it on, everyone cheers and officially welcomes her into their family. I run to the bathroom to take down my sexy hairdo and freshen up. I don't want to look like a total outsider, I already stick out enough.

Hair brushed, makeup on, clothes straightened and fixed, I'm feeling like myself again. That is until I walk out and notice the lights are dimmed low, and who do I see on Bullet's lap? Tricks. The whore who doesn't quit, like herpes or some other STD, which she probably has.

He's so engrossed in his conversations that he's not paying attention to her. Yet, there she sits, her stench lingering. I walk to the bar, hoping for a little something to ease the nasty that has crawled up my spine. Next to the bar, a rugged looking guy, who I've never seen asks, "Pussy or property?"

I know what he's asking. He wants to know if I'm a sweet butt or an old lady. "Neither."

"Can't be neither. Either you're property or you *are* pussy."

He eyes me up and down, stopping at my tits. I don't know what he sees. Compared to the other ladies here, I may as well be wearing a bourka. I'm in skinny soft denim jeans and a loose fitting V-neck black thermal t-shirt, partially tucked in the front. Nothing about me says sex kitten here. Normally people know to not fuck with me, but this guy appears to be new...not a Prospect, though. He's wearing the same cut as Bull and the rest, but he seems rougher.

May as well have some fun, it looks like everyone else is. "Well there..." I raise my brows expectedly waiting for him to provide his name.

His gruff voice spits out. "Gage." He quirks a shapely brow with a deep scar running through it. I notice his murky brown eyes and his tan weathered skin. I can't make out his age since it's clear the road hasn't been kind to him; maybe late twenties to mid-thirties. He's nicely built, though, and stands close to six feet tall.

"Gage. I assure you, I'm *not* pussy!" He doesn't look like the type of guy who's used to hearing the word 'no '.

"Well, sugar, I think it's time to change things." He grabs my arm and pulls me to him, handling me much rougher than I'm used to. I land harshly against his chest and I feel his big meaty hands on my ass. I can't see anything around the bear, so I don't know if Bullet or his family notice.

I give him one warning. "I really don't like to be touched. You should back the fuck off before you force my hand." I'm not in the mood to cause a scene, nor do I want to piss Bully off and break one of his rules.

But Gage laughs. "Oh, you sure are cute, sugar. I think we're gonna have us some fun together." He leans in trying to shove his tongue in my mouth.

Jerking out of his reach, I jab my palm into his chin, thrusting him marginally backwards. Before he registers my next attack, I land an uppercut and cross, throwing him off balance. Next comes a knife-hand strike landing half an inch below his Adam's apple, which instantly closes his throat. Unable to breathe, he lands on his knees while gripping his neck and hyperventilating. I hastily spin around as a Tornado Axe kick strikes across his chin. Hands loose, eyes roll back, and he lands flat on his back, motionless. Only seconds have elapsed since the onset and poor Gage is out, at least for the next few minutes.

I stand, straightening myself, and timidly look behind me. I'm hopeful this little interlude went unnoticed until I detect the unwanted attention. Eyeing the crowd, I'm yearning to avoid an irate Bully. No such luck. The snarl on his face substantiates that he bore witness to the entire debacle. Even the prominent vein in his forehead looks like it's reaching out to lash at me.

Where's a cute four-year-old to save me when I need one?

I should stick to tickle fights and unicorn braids.

I might not be equipped to navigate the adult world.

Chapter 26

THE WEEK FLEW BY. I was pulling ten-hour days on top of my time in court and had barely heard a word from Coen. He was mad that I was leaving for the summer, so instead of spending what little time we had together, we were apart. Man logic?

By Friday, I had endured enough and was determined to see him. We were leaving for the airport and on my way out I decided to stop in at CC and hand deliver the 'engagement ring.' Just knowing that I still had it, made me nervous. He needed it back and I needed to give it to him.

When I reached the receptionist's desk, I gave them my name and waited to get thrown out. I was struggling to come up with a legal reason of why I should see Coen, when the receptionist politely said to go right on up.

On the thirty-fourth floor, I walk down the hall with that creepy déjà vu feeling lingering. Bypassing his vacant secretary's desk, I knock on Coen's closed door and after almost a minute, heard his call for me to enter.

He was on the phone barking orders at the caller. Unsure what to do, I stood in the door frame fiddling nervously with my fingernails. Is this what people feel like when they visit my office? Waiting for permission to move about the space freely? Finally glancing my way, he breaks out into a brilliant smile. His eyes light up and then...they turn cold. His face hardens and he abruptly ends his phone call.

"You're leaving," he says flatly, while studying whatever work lay in front of him.

I clear my clogged throat. "Yes. I wanted to stop in and say goodbye."

He doesn't respond, but continues working. Frustrated with being ignored, I walk around the desk and place the ring on the paperwork he's so focused on. As I turn to leave, he grabs my hand and pulls me onto his lap. His hand rubs across my cheek, his thumb padding the bridge of my nose. He looks lost and sad as he sighs, leans his head onto my shoulder, and whispers, "Don't go."

I want to ask him, why? Why does he need me to stay when we never see each other? When I don't feel like I matter in his world. But instead, I rest my head next to his. I play with his hair at the base of his neck and enjoy this moment. It would be peaceful if I didn't feel his sadness slinking into me. He inches his head to the side and begins peppering my neck with sweet little kisses. His hand that has been playing with my cheek glides to the base of my neck, holding me closer.

His lips part and charge into mine. I taste him and can't help but emit a soft moan. I feel him smile against my lips and then he dives in for more. The pressure on my neck, the pressure on my lips, everything feels like its swelling and pulsing. He's so slow with his movements, so careful, I can't help but fall into it. His tongue sweetly tangles with mine and his left arm lowers to slide up my bare back. His skin on mine is sinful. Everything is buzzing and electrified. I pull him closer to me and shift on his lap so I can feel more of him against me.

I don't want this to end. I don't want to pull away. I want to dive. I want to drown. I want....

"Coen, this shit-storm you've got brewing with that..."

Oh shit...oh, shit, shit, shit! Greyson just barged into Coen's office and is staring at us.

"What the hell is going on here?" he demands.

"You should really learn to knock, father," Coen says flatly still clinging to me. I try to get out of his lap. The bucket of ice chilling my veins has ensured that happy times are indeed over, but I can't budge.

He squints his eyes and points. "Is that the little lawyer? The one you were trumpeting around with all weekend?"

Okay, so he's not a fan.

"You damn well know her name, father." Coen sighs. "What is it that was so important?"

Greyson glares at me and puckers. "Why's she here?" She? I

thought I had a name? One Greyson couldn't wait to get his hands on.

"Can this wait? I'm in the middle of something."

"With her?"

"Get out, father!" Coen shouts, his voice rising with each word.

Greyson throws one last disdained look my way then exits the room with a slammed door.

Still on his lap, I clear my throat. "I should go. Malice is waiting downstairs and the guys are at the airport."

He takes a moment to respond, contemplatively. "When will I see you?" His voice is more somber than usual.

"I don't know." I run my fingers over his brows, trying to relax the tension there. "We have a packed schedule but there are some shows in the area during late July..."

He gazes into my eyes as his fingers continue to draw abstract paths on my face. He leans forward and kisses my now swollen lips, all tingly and heated.

Standing up, he gently places me back on my feet. He picks up the ring on his desk and without uttering a word, he places it back on my finger while keeping my eyes frozen in the icy waters. He leans down and kisses the ringed finger, then holds that hand and walks me to the elevators. All the while, we are trapped and secluded in our silent bubble.

This man is utterly mystifying. I have no idea what is going on. The elevator dings and he guides me in. Pressing the first floor, he digs himself against my front without saying a word. He breathes me in, but doesn't kiss me. He continues staring now that he's anchored me into place. I don't know if I'm seeing anger there, or hurt, or some other unnamed emotion. I wish he would talk. Just say it! Say anything...

On the ground level, he knits our hands together and leads me out. Again, there are no words. People greet him and he nods, but continues walking in silence. At the front of the building past the glass doors, we find Malice waiting next to a town car. Coen pushes me against the car and then motions to Malice.

"Puis-je avoir un mot en privé?"

May I have a word in private?

Malice looks to me and I shrug in response, unsure of what Coen has in mind. He nods in response to Coen and the pair walk a few feet away and stop. I'm too far away to hear the conversation, but I notice the tension in Coen. Malice nods a few times and then both men walk back towards me. Malice climbs into the car while Coen wraps his hands around my shoulders.

He kisses me so passionately, so intensely, that I swear this must be our end. This *is* a goodbye kiss. I've never been kissed this way. It feels like the end. My heart suddenly hurts and I'm scared to let him go. What's happening?

He pulls back, his lips still resting on mine but with his eyes open. "It's too late for us," he says *into* me. I shake my head. I don't know what to do. He got in. Somehow, in some way, he got into my heart and I don't want this to end. I feel the panic growing. My eyes start to burn and my lips start to tremble.

"Ssshh, love," he whispers, trying to sooth me with his touch and his delicious tantalizing breath. I need to memorize such details if I'm to survive his departure. He smiles this horribly tragic smile and I snap my eyes closed in response. I changed my mind...I don't want to remember any of this. Block it out. Don't feel. Don't feel his sweet lips. Don't feel his warm arms. Don't feel his heart beating in sync with mine. Don't feel!! Please, don't feel.

"Charlie," he utters softly. "Give me my greys, love." I shake my head. I don't want him to see how he's destroying me. He kisses me on each eyelid and chuckles softly, sadly. Then he pulls back and tucks me into the car. With my eyes open, I focus on the ground keeping them a safe distance. He reaches over and buckles me in. Then he grabs my left hand and kisses the boomerang returning ring there.

"Soyez bon, mon cœur."

Be good, my heart.

With my head still hanging low, he kisses my temple, then backs away and closes the door. Closes the chapter of us.

Bringing an ending to the never would be fairytale that I was momentarily swept up in.

Chapter 27

THE FLIGHT TO VEGAS, THOUGH eight plus hours, goes by quickly. I barely talk to anyone and barely notice anything. My thoughts are still lost in that icy storm that has caught me up in hurricane force winds.

We shuffle into our rooms at the MGM Grand, where the fight will take place; Malice and I in one, and the trio in the other. As soon as we settle in, I text Tank to let him know we're here.

He's staying at the same hotel a few floors up in the penthouse suite. There wasn't any room for us there. He has a full staff with him plus his family. I love how supportive they are over everything he does.

Sadly, with all of the preparations for tomorrow night's fight, we don't get a chance to see our guy. He has weigh-ins and a press conference that he gained us access to but it's not as good as a Tank tickle or a hug sandwich. Those are irreplaceable. By the time Saturday night comes, I'm dying for some Tank time. Hopefully we will get to spend some time together after the fight.

There are so many people in the arena tonight that we are crammed in like books lining a bookshelf. Some straight, some diagonally, while others smoosh on top of each other and seem to be crammed into every nook and cranny. The volume is nearly painful but the energy level intensifies everything, like every breath is magnified. Every step feels colossal as we find our seats down the narrow walkway. There are people of all walks of life vying for a view of the great Tank. Tonight is his introduction to the world of UFC. Tonight, the world will find out what I have known for almost six years – that Tank Remmington is one of the greatest fighters that have ever lived. Truly, he's a beast in the cage, a master of the metal. He is speed unrecognizable to the naked eye.

The guys and I grab our seats and begin the arduous process of waiting. I hate waiting. I find myself yanking on my Tank t-shirt twenty thousand times. My nails are being chewed to shit and that's only to free up my lips for when my nails have all been desecrated. I even go so far as to start cracking my knuckles, which finally snaps Bullet, who is on my right side, out of his Zen mode.

"Jesus, did someone slip you crack or something? Calm the fuck down."

"Shut it, I'm just nervous for him." Guys are incredibly self-centered.

"Baby girl, you've seen him fight how many times? He's unstoppable. He'll be fine." He shakes his head and chuckles. "You're not even this nervous when you walk in there."

He's right, of course. I know Tank will be fine, win or lose… though I'm pushing for the win. I guess it's just that this place seems so immense compared to our little fights. It feels so legit. So real. It makes my fights look like playground scuffles.

But it's really about Tank. He wants this so badly. This is his dream. He has been working for this moment for nearly a decade. And it's here. And I get to share it with him.

More people shuffle into the grand space and I find myself drawn to watching the men in suits. There's a whole slew of them in the front rows accompanied by beautiful women. Blonde, long thin tanned legs, full plush lips, gigantic boobs, and matching butts. They all look related, like they sell the platinum blonde hair and silicone with a group discount rate. My self-confidence running fairly low these days, I start to compare myself. In a room compacting all of this testosterone, it's sort of unavoidable.

My legs are nowhere near that length and are thicker with muscle. My dark hair is normally so straight that curling irons run screaming, with no gorgeous waves or curls to create any lasting volume. I'm a freckled, moley mess. No flawless porcelain skin. No creamy milky luminous skin. Nope, I am ethnically ambiguous, which is a much better way than saying, "What are you?" I've been told I look Greek, various types of Hispanic, and even Italian. I rarely get the mix that I actually am or even close for that matter.

One of these women would be a better match for Coen. I can almost picture the platinum duo on a red carpet, walking arm in arm, doing the queen wave. They would be stunning and though possibly fake under the picture perfect guise, it would still be beauty to behold. I guess things are better this way. He would be better without me and my short legs, and my freckled, moley ambiguousness.

As I'm busy convincing myself of the inevitability of Coen's absence, Malice, sitting on my left, elbows me. Looking up, I see he is alerting me to the arrival of Tank's family who sit to the left of him. I guess this means the festivities are about to begin. We are all seated in the reserved section, in the first two rows, which means we have tremendous views of Tank and his takedown.

Again, my bouncing resumes. This time it seems to generate from my back and I'm vibrating in my seat. If Tank doesn't hurry this thing along, he might find me in the octagon with him. I have too much energy surfacing with no output.

After another eternity, Tank's fight song booms through the loud speakers, which seem to be everywhere. I almost start tearing up when I hear my voice. Tank chose a Loaded Gun's song as his entrance piece. *Fully Loaded* pounds through as my softhearted guy marches down the aisle sporting the most callous face he can muster. From my view, I spy his sharpened brown eyes under the silk hoodie. He's laser focusing right now with pristine precision. His face is a mask of concentration and I dare not shout his name or try to touch the sacred zone. His management crew, along with Tony, follow behind him into the octagon and the announcer greets him and begins his stats. As a newbie in the UFC ring, he gets a few boos. Immediately, I feel myself readying to throw down. Who said that? I want names, faces, and social security numbers. How dare they mess with the great Tank?

I can tell he isn't affected. He remains perfectly calm while disrobing and begins bouncing on his toes and loosening his fists at his side. He is sporting new digs, and it looks as though he has several sponsors plastered on his blue shorts. I guess I've been out of the loop a bit. I haven't seen Tank in nearly two months, and even in that short period of time, I can see a huge difference. He looks leaner and has more muscles; a perfect specimen to enter this arena. Like a Spartan readying for war. All he needs is a sword and shield, though that's against the rules here.

The next guy is called in with his blaring country music and enters the octagon followed by a round of his stats. He's been here before, so the crowd goes ape shit at his arrival. He's definitely the fan favorite and even the suits rise to cheer on their great warrior.

After everyone leaves the octagon, minus the fighters and referee, I feel the tension in the air rise. It might be the pounding of my heart but it's as if everyone gathers in silence to await the first blow. To await the announcer's go ahead to begin the fight. I'm so busy concentrating on not jumping out of my chair that I miss the taps and rules and the fight begins.

The audience chants and boos collectively and we all wince every time a blow lands. We are one unit divided into halves. You can even feel who belongs where. I tune it all out and try to find the mechanics in it. Tank has been studying his opponent's moves for months now. He should have these patterns down but as hard blows land against Tank's chest over and over, I wonder why he isn't striking and taking advantage of the obvious weakness. Maybe he doesn't see it. Maybe it's new or an over compensation for an injury. He's doing a great job at keeping his arms raised and avoiding facial contact but I'm not sure if these injuries are sustainable.

Tank's training is in boxing, wrestling, and Muay Thai, hence these are his strengths, and by extension mine, although my wrestling technique is nowhere near as keen as his. He is missing opportunities to strike and it is killing me as I watch helplessly from the sidelines. Is this what everyone feels like when watching me fight?

The bell finally rings and Tank has one minute to get it together. His manager and the cutman run in to check him over and give him outside pointers. This is a non-championship contest, so there are only three rounds to impress the judges, and at this rate, Tank is going to lose. His only hope is for submission or knockout. The first round was lost. I can tell that his manager is wrapping up and my nerves force me up and over to the octagon.

"He's dropping his arm," I scream several times in the hopes that Tank will turn my way and see what I'm talking about. After the fifth time, he turns and spies me. I show him my left hand and how it's dropping. He nods and goes back to paying attention to the professionals. His face is swollen with cuts, and the Vaseline they've used to stop the bleeding makes the area look shiny and distorted under the heavy lights. Bullet pulls me back to my seat chastising me the entire way. *This isn't a participatory sport*; he keeps trying to convince me.

The bell dings all too soon and they are back at each other's throats. With nothing to chew or bite, I literally start pulling my hair. This is excruciating. My fights are always over in the first round.

They are locked in a front clinch and with inches separating them, there's no room for any true momentum to build.

"Use the elbow, use the fucking elbow," I shout repeatedly while bouncing on the balls of my feet. There's no way I can sit for this. I may be escorted out if he doesn't finish this soon. Thank goodness this entire thing will be over in less than twenty minutes. Something must have clicked in Tank's brain because he finally reacts with a diagonal elbow straight to the chin. Bam! His opponent releases him and takes a few steps back.

"Strike!" I scream along with the vivacious crowd. He throws a quick jab and then the haymaker follows to the cheek. Tank's opponent stammers and then drops to his knees his eyes rolling back and he face plants to the mat. He's down. TKO!

Unilaterally the crowd jumps to its feet, though I've been there for the duration of the round, and the uproar begins. It's glorious. It takes Tank a few seconds to register what has happened. He barely moves until he sees the referee check on his fallen opponent. His team runs into the octagon and immediately start congratulating him. They throw his shirt on him, registering more corporate sponsors, and they check over his injuries to make sure he is presentable for the final judgment.

In the background, I can hear Joe Rogen commenting on Tank's technique and how this newcomer is officially on the must-watch list. I beam. Bullet grabs me and spins me around kissing my head over and over. Everyone congratulates each other.

Both men are present and when the final judgment is officiated, Tank is declared the winner. I can't help but join in when he smiles this magnificently. The announcer throws questions at him left and right while Tank attempts to answer and appear coherent. Though his face is swollen and cracked, he flourishes in the moment. He spies me several yards away facing him and blows me a kiss. I blow him twenty kisses in return and scream how much I love him. I think about a thousand other women do the exact same thing, but he will always be my Tank just like I will always be the skinny little teenager that walked into his gym looking for salvation.

It isn't every day that you get to watch your hero achieve greatness.

Chapter 28

THE TOUR IS EXHAUSTING. THE physical aspects are draining. Every night we go out there and play like there's no tomorrow. We meet people after people. Faces after faces. And we watch the world behind a window; a window of our tour bus, a window of a speeding taxi, or even the window of our hotel rooms. In the end, it starts to feel like framed pieces of moving art.

As a corporate lawyer, I spend most of my time pouring over legal contracts and briefs. Not surprisingly, this is a rather solitary and hushed endeavor, quite the opposite of my time in the thralls of screaming hard rock. However, my usual adjustment period has lapsed and I should be settled in by now. But during this tour, I feel restless.

After Vegas, we flew to Los Angeles to meet the label executives and talk about our upcoming album release. With our latest single climbing the charts, they want to really push our record. They shelled out a boatload for us to film the video for our single *Fully Loaded*. I can't wait to see the finished edit. The director's vision was dead on and filming it was a blast.

There's also talk of a European tour at the end of the year. The guys are game but I'm still dragging my feet on a final decision. I don't know if this is the right move for me.

The trio need this. They need the fame, the attention, and most definitely the fortune. While I do this because I need them. Despite how uncomfortable things have been with Bullet, I still need him...I need my trio. I know it's a selfish pipedream; the guys will eventually fall in love and get married and then I'll be in the background, in the past. I mean, that's how it's supposed to be, right?

It's the weekend after Independence Day and we're at a two-day festival in Wisconsin. The weather is absolute shit and fits my mood perfectly. It's hot with the crazy July heat, but it's rainy and drippy, so there's mud everywhere.

Since we aren't one of the main headliners, we don't hit the stage until tomorrow afternoon. That means that while we aren't performing, which is most of the time, we have the opportunity to walk around and munch on the different vendor's food goodies and watch the various bands. It's also a cool time to connect with our fans.

Our bus finally parks by the other tour buses and we get out to roam, eager to shake the day off. We've been trapped in that over-sized tin for almost a dozen hours, even I was antsy for an escape.

Rule number one on the road and at any festival is to never go anywhere alone. This is drilled into me over and over by all the guys on the bus. As the only girl, they tend to worry about me the most. But in reality, any one of us could have a miserable outcome if we don't take heed.

The trio go in one direction looking for easy hookups while Malice and I meander about. All in all, it was a fairly decent mud drenched day. Malice and I caught all sorts of vendors and I purchased several skirts and lots of snacks. We ate hamburgers in lawn chairs and then crawled into bed after watching two of my favorite bands play. We kept to ourselves and nobody noticed us thanks to my incognito appearance of sporting a trucker hat, a flouncy colorful shirt and some denim Daisy Dukes.

The guys never returned and I can't say I'm not heartbroken. For all of their talk, they tend to leave me solo an awful lot lately. I think I even heard Malice head back out for a late night beer.

While lying in bed, I hunt the internet for Coen news. It has become my nightly ritual, especially since I haven't heard a word from him. I glance down and look at the ring. I shouldn't wear it. I should have returned it as I had intended to. I switched the ring to the middle finger, as it doesn't attract as much attention that way. I wish I could just stick it in a drawer and be done with it. Be done with him. But I can't. And the more difficult life feels here, the more tension that builds on this bus like a shaken soda can ready to burst, the more I feel that I no longer belong here.

My Coen stalking is interrupted when I hear giggling coming

through my door. The bus is set up so that when you walk in, you hit the living area, dining area, and kitchen area. Then there's a small door dividing the sleeping area that houses six sets of bunk beds, three on each side. In the back of the bus there's a small bedroom with a tiny bathroom, which is mine since it has a lock on it. That's a necessary feature when dealing with rowdy, usually intoxicated men.

Rule number two on the road is that no chicks or partners are allowed on the bus *ever*! I hear the high pitched laughter again, this time followed by a deep rumble. I climb off my bed and inch towards the door, my cell still in my hand. I listen to the intruder to see if I can pick up on who it is. All I can hear are moans.

I'm so creeped out. What if someone stumbled on our bus accidentally? What if it's fans being sinister? I decide to muster my courage and get closer to the door. I need to know if I should alert anyone to this.

As quietly as possible, I slowly pull the door open. Only a tiny crack of light can be seen at first. Then as the door reveals more of the images in front of me I gasp and slam it shut.

I should've known better. I knew he'd take things too far. He's upset and trying to hurt me. But after roughly six weeks of dealing with this shit, I don't see why I'm here anymore.

Bullet knows the rules.

I'm a rule person…I live by the rules.

I need the rules.

The rules exist for a reason.

You break the rules, there are consequences.

The next morning, I wake up before everyone. Grabbing Malice and my Black Penguin, we journey to the stage where we'll be performing later today. I hang out backstage and talk with the performers as they exit. They're all in the same boat as Loaded. We're starting to get some notoriety but still have dues to pay. There aren't many females on our stage, except for the waiting girlfriends or wives or the fuck-of-the-moment groupie. But I hang out and chat with them and their partners when they get off stage.

Stryker comes over while I'm waiting for the group to arrive.

"Where's the rest of the gun patrol?" He smiles coyly at me. His band is performing on the main stage tonight. They get prime time air and love to throw it in everyone else's faces.

"Stryker, don't you have women to roofie? That's how you get laid, is it not?" I'm in no mood to play nice. After Bullet and his twat finally settled, I couldn't seem to sleep.

The jerk eyes me up and down while licking his lips. "I'd love to show you how I get my women, delicious Shooter." Gross, I think I just threw up in my mouth. I roll my eyes and attempt to walk away when he chases after me.

"Seriously, sexy, why haven't we been fornicating all over this tour?" he asks sounding surprised.

"Because I have standards."

"You know they're just using you." He throws and I willingly turn to catch.

"What do you mean?" I feel myself heating up.

"I know about your double life. They use you for your talent, your money, and your connections."

What? How does he know any of this?

He must be able to read the confused look on my face. He walks over and cups my chin then softly whispers, "Come on, baby. I know you aren't this dumb. I wouldn't know any of this if they didn't tell me, right? They don't deserve you…" He knows exactly where to stick the knife.

Stryker is a manipulator, but how does he know about me?

He continues his torturous ripping of my soul. "I'd take care of you. I wouldn't leave you alone all night and fuck away with tramps. Not if I had you waiting for me."

This is just another way of him trying to get in my pants. He's been dying for a taste of me for over a year.

But, as I always say, the best lies have some truth.

I look over and see Malice watching with wide eyes. He heard everything.

"Savez-vous ce dont il parle?"

Do you know what he's speaking about?

He shakes his head, but I can see the sadness growing in his eyes. I bet they mirror my own. Either he knows and is afraid to hurt me by revealing this truth or he's only just learning of this, as I am.

"Je ne le crois pas. Ils t'aiment. Tu le sais."

I don't believe him. They love you. You know that.

"Je ne sais pas quoi que ce soit, pas plus."

I don't know anything, anymore. The words catch in my throat.

Our manager, Rick, comes around the back and heads towards us looking confused.

"Where are the guys?" he yells.

"I haven't seen them." I shrug.

"If you were in my world I'd never leave your side, sexy Shooter," Stryker coos.

I turn to Mal. "S'il vous plaît le faire partir."

Please make him leave.

I know I'm a baby but Stryker throwing lemon juice on my paper cut is turning the slit into a burning infested mess.

As I'm making my way to the stage, I see all three of my band-mates running in the same direction. They all look like absolute shite and like they just woke up.

"Baby girl," Gunner calls out as he runs over. I continue walking and ignore him. I need to get through this set and then I will be able to fester on the thoughts Stryker has implanted in my manic mind.

I run up the steps to the stage and wait for the guys. There's no curtain; it's basically just an open platform and a massive field. In my opinion, this is how music should be. No hype. Just the performers and the audience connecting in the key of sanctified rock.

It does help, though, when the band is better prepared, and when they aren't stabbing each other in the fucking back.

"Hey, we looked for you this morning. Where the fuck did you go?" Gunner asks, always playing the concerned best friend. I wonder how much of it was actually real…

"I was here, Gunner. Waiting for you guys." I say this too softly. Too revealing.

His brows crease as he walks over to get a better look at me. "What's wrong?"

Both Trig and Bullet slink closer to hear.

"Nothing," I say clearing my throat. I turn to Bullet and stare. "Just couldn't sleep well, I guess."

I watch as he swallows and looks away. Coward!

They call us on set and we find our rhythm. We give the fans a show that they'll never forget. Despite the trio's obvious disarray. Despite the mud and rain. Despite my heart and soul crashing into nothingness they get a good show.

Tori McNeeley

James Evans
Shawn Patterson
Quinn Thompson
Chris Fletcher
Elias Munez
I can do anything.

When we close and run off the stage to make room for the next group, I feel the guys surrounding me. I keep walking. I hand my guitar to Malice, and keep walking. I don't sign autographs, I keep walking. When they yell my name and question what my problem is, I keep walking.

I keep walking.

And walking, and walking.

I feel like Forrest Gump. Just keep going and never stop. I know I won't like where I'll end up so what's the point?

But I know I have to stop. So, I eventually do. I turn to find Malice and I drop. My legs incapable of supporting the emotions swirling and churning inside me.

I try to think of those six horrible names to pull myself together. If I can live through that, I can live through anything.

I lived through death, but I can't seem to live through life.

"Nous allons trouver la solution."

We'll find the solution.

I shake my head. There is no solution.

"Que fais-je?"

What do I do? I ask Malice.

I continue clinging to him until the sun begins to set and the air around us chills. We melt into the muddy ground as people pass us. He holds me. I'm so lost in my head that I'm paralyzed, and afraid of saying goodbye to my three lifelines. How could I stay with them if any of this is true? I have to get back to the bus, though. I'm getting cold and hungry, plus both Malice and I are covered in dried mud and probably smell. We're a sad duo.

"Es-tu mon ami?"

Are you my friend? I finally gain the courage to ask. I mean, I know he's my employee, but is he my friend?

"Non, vous êtes ma famille."

No, you're my family. I lean over and squeeze the crap out of the poor filthy French guy. Maybe, if I *know* I have someone in my corner, I can get through to the other side. Because right now, I'm not sure if I can.

Mal stands up and holds his hand out to me. I reach up taking it and we walk back to the bus together. I'm terrified what I'll find when I get there.

I climb the steps with lead feet. As I walk in, I hear the guys yelling at each other. I notice that Gunner's collar is ripped, Bullet's nose is bleeding, and Trigger has a growing bruise on his cheek.

They all freeze as I enter. I keep my eyes to the floor. I can't do this to them. They were a unit before me. Once I joined, they had to make pacts, and now they're beating each other and narrowly missing performances. This isn't what I want for them. I doubt it's what they want for themselves either.

"Shooter, baby?" Bullet croaks.

"Rules are in place for a reason," I whisper to the ground. My throat is still closed and scratchy, so even my whispers sound broken.

"I'm sorry…please?"

Gunner comes over and reaches for me but I duck. "He's a fucktard. You know this, baby. But we're fine, right?"

I shake my head, never reaching his eyes.

Trig tries. "It was just a bad day, baby girl."

I don't respond but stay firmly rooted in this moment, waiting to see what they will ultimately force me to do. At least a minute or two goes by.

Gunner comes at me again. This time he cups my face and tilts my head his way. "Don't do this. We love you! We need you."

I'm not sure what to say anymore and the day has drained my fight. "Maybe we should figure some things out," I whisper while biting my lip.

Gunner must take this as a good sign, as he smiles softly still tilting my chin. "Yeah, baby. Anything you want." He looks into my eyes for a quick moment then pecks my lips softly. His hand falls to my lower back and he ushers me to the little benched table.

I'm on one side with Gunner, and across from me is Trig and Bullet. We're drowned in silence while counting the stupid specks on the table…well at least that's what I'm doing. They might just be staring at it for all I know. Malice comes over with a big bowl of ice and some dishrags. He throws it in the middle of the table and walks away. Silence is certainly not golden tonight. That would be the case had my stomach not chosen that moment to growl. Loudly. Bullet jumps up and comes back a moment later with a yogurt and bottle of water. He places it on the table in front of me never meeting my eyes.

"You should eat, baby." His voice is hoarse and soft.

It's a distraction, so I do, but not because he told me to.

"Shooter, we were really worried about you this morning. And then you ran off and we've been losing our minds all day with trying to find you. You know you can't do that shit, especially here at a festival," Trig says firmly.

"I was with Malice. And you three slept in thanks to your late night proclivities," I deadpan.

Bullet clears his throat and looks to Gunner. I watch their silent exchange but I get nothing. I really want a shower. This is going nowhere fast. Time to lay my cards on the table.

"Look, um, things haven't been right with us for a while now, and I'm not sure if this is working," I finally break through. We spent the next two hours hashing out our issues. Well, they did majority of the talking. I stayed mostly silent. In the end, I agreed to stay. Bullet promised to behave, though I don't entirely believe him. They claim that everything Stryker said was fabricated, and they have no idea how he knows about me. Only time will tell.

After a searing hot shower, I crawled into bed exhausted. Again to my nightly ritual of Coen stalking commence. He's in the news, as always. There was a charity fundraiser last night and he was seen with several beautiful women, though he arrived alone. I wonder if he's ok. It's too late to text, so I decide to send an email.

I address him as Mr. Collins. I know he hates that, and I'm checking to make sure everything with the merger has come to its full conclusion and to his satisfaction. I scroll through my social media and learn that my sister just found out she is pregnant. I love how nobody had time to call or tell me but managed to post it on Facebook.

As I'm about to shut my cell down, I find an email from Coen.

Ms. Paz,
Thank you for your concern over my satisfaction. I assure you that I am far from satisfied. We need to remedy this quandary immediately. When will your services be next available?
In need of immediate assistance,
Coen Collins

Since this is my work email and it appears he's awake, I decide to text him.

11:49 CHARLIE: MY APOLOGIES ON YOUR DISSATISFACTION, MR. COLLINS.

11:50 COEN: YES, IT IS MOST DISTURBING. A PLAN IS NEEDED TO CORRECT THIS MALFEASANCE.

11:52 CHARLIE: PLEASE ADVISE.

11:53 COEN: WHERE ARE YOU?

11:54 CHARLIE: BED.

11:54 COEN: GGGGRRR

11:55 CHARLIE: NOT SURE WHAT VERNACULAR THAT IS.

Instead of responding he calls.

"Hi..."

"Hi, love. Ah, I've missed hearing your voice."

"You should've called."

"I wasn't sure if I'd chase after you and drag you back once I heard your voice. Are they taking care of you, at least?"

"I don't know. We got into a big fight today. Well, it's been building and it just sort of finally erupted."

"What's going on? Is there anything you need me to do?"

"No, it's just that…I guess our relationships are changing."

"And that bothers you?"

"Yeah, I thought we were...I don't know. More than family. The guys are my best friends. I don't really know where that leaves me if they're gone. People are saying things to me about them. And Bullet is purposely pushing my buttons."

"I know you love them but maybe it's time to open yourself to other relationships. I'll be here no matter what you need."

"What about the last thing you said to me. How it was too late for us?"

He chuckles. "It *is* too late, love."

I fail to see why that's funny. "Coen?" I nearly growl feeling frustrated with yet another male in my world.

"I meant that destiny has already joined us on this path. We've found each other. It is too late for either of us to find another way. This is it. I won't let you go."

With that, he melts my heart. We talk a little more and then hang up with promises of tomorrow.

I fall asleep with a smile on my face, my first real smile in weeks.

I awaken in the early morning hours to something warm on my back. Immediately, I slide my hand under my pillow to clutch the knife I store there. My instincts aren't screaming at me but I'm covering my bases.

"Put it down, baby. You know I won't hurt you," Bullet murmurs as his hand shifts over my stomach. Why can't he just let me be? Despite my better judgment, I release the knife. I can always grab it later.

"Go away. In case you didn't notice, I was sleeping."

"Naw, I can't sleep and it looks like you're awake."

"Go find another bed to occupy yourself with. You've closed this one down *forever*!"

He digs his nose in my neck and with his two arms banded around my front, I'm sealed to him with no hopes of escaping.

"Well, then, consider this a grand reopening," he moans while grinding his front to my ass and licking up my neck.

"I watched you fuck some chick last night and now you're here like I mean something to you? Go fuck yourself!" I try to move, but he pulls me tighter to him. "Dammit Bull, let me go." I mean this in so many ways, it's not even funny.

"Settle down and go back to sleep. It's not like we've never slept together. I just want to hold you for a while."

I fuss a little more, still tense. Then he starts humming. As he hums, he loosens his hold on me, but leaves his arms circling me and his body close to mine. Between his warmth and his devious humming vibrating through my back, I reluctantly fall asleep. Easily falling back into Bullet.

Sadly, I'm never too far out of his reach.

Chapter 29

THE TRIO KEPT THEIR PROMISE and were well behaved for the rest of the tour. Things were still a bit tense but we managed. On the bright side, Gunner and I got closer on this trip. He didn't seem as into the 'easy life' as the other two. As for Stryker, I guess I let it drop. He hit on me at almost every venue and I incessantly wondered what he really knew about me. I'll get Malice to do some follow up research in the coming months.

Coen and I texted, emailed, or spoke nearly every day. So when I show up at his office, unannounced, I'm not sure what I'll find. I walk to his new PA, Turner's, desk.

"Hi there. I was wondering if Mr. Collins had a moment to speak with me?" I question.

He looks bored as he eyes me. I'm wearing a black and white long flowy skirt with a white camisole, my hair messy and down. Not really Coen Collins' usual visitor. "Mr. Collins is an extraordinarily busy man and is currently in a meeting. And you are…?" He squints his eyes at me like I look familiar to him, but he can't place me.

"I'm Charlie Paz. We worked together on the Renault Matre merger." I smile so he knows I'm friendly and not here to do any harm.

"Oh." He stands up. "Oh my gawsh, I'm so sorry. Of course, you are! And I'm Turner, Mr. C's new PA." He grabs my arm and drags me into Coen's office. "You sit here and I'll grab Mr. C for you. Do you need anything to drink?"

"Thank you, I'm fine. I thought you said he was in a meeting."

"That was before I knew who you were, little filly. I'll be back in a Jiffylube jiffy." With that the adorable Turner saunters out, leaving me bathed in the serene silence of Coen's ginormous office.

Seated in the chair facing his desk, I notice the back of a picture frame. I glance at the door then jump around so that I can get a better view. Rounding his desk, I find that the picture is of the pair of us. I've never seen it, but it looks as though it was taken at the yacht party. Coen's hand is on my bare shoulder and we're gazing at each other, almost longingly. We both wear gorgeous smiles across our face, and even from the distance and angle of the shot, his beautiful eyes are sparkling in my direction.

I completely fall head over heels with this picture and pick it up to further examine it. It has managed to pull me into that moment and I find myself beaming with the charming happy couple. God, Coen is gorgeous. I'm in awe of his magnificence. By standing next to him, at least in this photo, even I look lovely.

"Love?" I hear from the door. I look up and see the splendor that is Coen. His perfect voice edged with excitement.

I grin with my teeth tucked around my bottom lip. I feel like I'm smiling too big and I have to catch my lip before it runs away. He dashes over and pulls me into his arms showering me with kisses. I breathe him in, reacquainting myself with its calming way.

With his hands woven in my hair he pulls back to look me over. "Jesus, I missed you!" He rubs his nose along mine, kissing every other freckle. I chuckle and pull him closer.

"I missed you, Coen." I gaze into his dazzling eyes and try to relay how much with them. His smile broadens and his hand circles to my jawline. He watches his thumbs glide across and land over my lips.

He leans into me and whispers. "You can't leave me again, love."

Falling into his glare, I nod. This trip was hard. I'm ready to be back on solid ground.

He licks his lips then softly rubs them against mine. His lips parted, I feel the air escaping. He pulls my lower lip into his mouth and his tongue darts out to taste me. He moans, the vibrations traveling through his mouth and into mine. He lightly bites my lip then licks it to ease the lasting sting. A few more soft, slow, powerful kisses and I'm back on Earth. He pulls back smiling. Resting his forehead on mine, he closes his eyes and moans.

"I'm in a meeting but I can't leave you."

I run my fingers up his strong neck and through the soft curls around the no-gel zone. "Maybe we can see each other later?"

He shakes his head, eyes closed as he moans. "No, later isn't good. I need now." I half chuckle half groan as he moves to my neck. Soft large hands pull down the strap of my tank top, lightly scratching along the way as his kisses follow down to my collarbone. Woah! What is he doing?

With one hand in my strap, the other pulling me into him at my waist, I'm lost. I feel every hair on my body stand and bow in greeting to their new master. The goosebumps rise in respect. And my nipples tighten painfully, expectedly awarded in his revelry.

"Charlie, is it too late for us?" He licks across my neck to slide down the other strap, baring more of me to him.

"Yesss," I answer. It's too late for us to choose another path because ours has already been destined.

Pulling back, he smiles and tucks some relentless strands behind my ear, his fingers grazing the outer shell. He glances down at his wrist watch, sucking in his cheeks, deep in thought. Brows furrowed, face pinched. "I probably have another hour or so here. Why don't you go home, pack a bag, and then head to my place? We can have dinner together." Dinner doesn't require a packed bag.

"I, um, I start work tomorrow."

"Okay. I'll get you there." He smiles while righting my straps then he leans down and kisses each shoulder. "Okay?"

I nod reluctantly. I've missed him terribly but I'm not sure if I'm ready for the next step. Those imposing pearly whites return in a massive smile. He sends a heavy wet smooch my way, then grabs my hand and walks me towards the door. I still have the frame in my hand and want to know more.

"Coen?" I lift the frame while raising my brows.

"That's my favorite one of us."

I nod. "I like it, too." I give him a sweet smile and he returns it with one of his own. Then he kisses me again on the lips, takes the frame out of my hand, and puts it back on his desk. "Where it belongs," he murmurs.

We walk out to the elevators and as we pass Tucker, I give him a little wave.

"He seems like a good guy," I whisper to Coen.

"Yeah."

"Why did you get a new PA, again?" He never actually told me, but I phrase it this way so he'd think he did and answer. Instead, he simply shrugs.

Climbing into the elevator car, Coen pulls me against him. "Should I have Davis pick you up?"

"I think I can manage fine." I roll my eyes and tuck some hair behind my ear. He notices my hand and frowns.

"Where's the ring?" Oops, I forgot about that. I stuck it back in my jewelry box a few weeks ago.

"I didn't want to lose it on the road so I haven't been wearing it." He sighs and looks frustrated.

Clearing his throat, he pushes on. "You're not on the road anymore."

"We aren't engaged, Coen." I state this slowly, not leaving room for any misinterpretations. I think we have missed some steps along the way.

He looks wounded as he nods and looks away. He ushers me to my car, kisses me goodbye, and warns me that I should be at his place by six…no exceptions. Looks like Cocky Coen has turned into Bossy Coen during my absence. I'm not sure which Coen is more enjoyable. Maybe I should ditch them both and hunt down Fun Coen. I've met him a few times. He has definite potential.

Chapter 30

I RUN A FEW ERRANDS ON my way home and arrive with plenty of time to pack. I'm not sure what's on the agenda for the evening but I'm a little nervous. Okay, maybe a lot nervous. Coen is ridiculously friendly with the ladies; he has experience and demands and I doubt I can supply those needs. My physical self is slowly awakening into normalcy, but I think my mind is far from ready.

What if I have a flashback and lose control? What if I shut down and go into a Charlie coma? If he sees me like that, I doubt he'd be interested in me. I never really cared about any of it with Andrew or any of the other guys I briefly and superficially dated but Coen has molded himself into an entirely new category.

I knock on his door at exactly five fifty-five, with five minutes to spare. He answers the door in a white t-shirt and low navy basketball shorts, barefoot. His appearance has altered? I frown bringing up pictures in my head, trying to make a quick comparison to spy the culprit.

"What are you doing?" he asks, sounding concerned.

"Oh, um, nothing. Why, what's wrong? You going to let me in?"

"Your eyes were flicking back and forth. It was like you didn't see me." He pushes the door further open and grabs the bags out of my hand.

Could I be any more of a freak?

Closing the door behind me, I finally admit how much of a nutso I am to the poor guy.

"You look different. I was just trying to puzzle it out. I was in my head." I shake my head like a dork and make some weird phony laugh sounds. Run, Coen. Save yourself from the freakhood of

Charlie.

He walks over to me and gently tucks some hair away, and then glides his hand down my neck. "You have a photographic memory, love?" I nod and shrug with some quirking of my lips.

"You were looking at pictures of me in your head?" I nod again. My voice has run and hid from the sheer humiliation, can't really blame her.

I watch his mouth as it tilts on one side. I scan his face looking for fear or disgust. I have freckles, freaky eyes, and disappear for months at a time. Instead I hear him sigh. "So perfect…" He leans down and kisses my forehead. "Come on, love. Dinnertime."

We make our way to the kitchen and Coen has me sit on those enchanting stools again. I breathe in the scrumptious smells of lasagna and garlic bread. Yum!

"Did you cook for me?" I jest.

"I had Marie prepare it. I'm just heating it up for us, love."

"And Marie is…." Your lover? Your slave? Your live-in-do-what-you-will person?

He laughs. "Look at you getting territorial. I think you've made my night, love. And we've only just begun." Oh, that cocky man. Stop reading my thoughts. "She's my housekeeper. Quit looking at me like that." He bops my nose triggering my blush.

Dinner is wonderful. I guess Marie has her uses, though I will need to investigate further to make a proper judgment call. We spend most of the evening chatting about CC and the changes that have occurred. He tries several times to convince me that I'm limiting myself by staying at Morgan and Freeman. He wants me to head his legal team at Collins Corp. After turning him down for the fourteenth time, I finally told him I'd think about it. But a move to CC is highly improbable.

I'm not a happily-ever-after type of girl and this won't be your typical happily-ever-after story. I know that. I always have to be prepared for that. I always need an out.

He catches me mid-yawn and demands we head to bed. The last few months are catching up with me. He leaves me upstairs in his room to do my business, while he tackles some emails in his home office.

I must be more tired than I thought because after changing, I crawl right into his bed. I don't even wait for him to join me; I just close my eyes and feel myself drifting into sleep. Sometime later, I'm woken by movement. Then my entire body shifts as Coen angles me over him. My head resting on his chest. It's firmer… yes, there it is…that's what's different! He's bigger. Has he been working out?

"There that's better," I hear him mumble softly. I nestle myself deeper into him and despite the firmness of my new pillow, I drift again. As I begin my descent, I think I hear him whisper, "Welcome home, love."

I scream. He's holding my arms down. There's so much pain. I feel the chill the dripping liquids leave behind, but I'm no longer fully connected to my body to interpret where it's coming from. Everything is heavy and there's so much pressure. I can feel my bones twisting and snapping as I'm being held from every angle. I can't catch my breath and I feel my stomach revolting from the painful intrusions. I'm drowning. Let me drown. I want to drown. I keep screaming, though. Maybe someone will hear and save me. I can't save myself, no matter how hard I try. I can't fight. My bones and muscles have been shredded. My vision is blurred with the swelling blocking my view and distorting the images. Then I see their ugly faces above me…

I jerk up screaming. I'm shaking. Where am I? On the floor. Where? I'm rocking now with my knees tucked in. I'm scared to look around. I repeat that I'm okay over and over again. This isn't the first time I've awoken this way. It used to be nightly but it has gotten better over the years.

"Love?" I hear in a broken voice a few feet away from me. I look up realizing that I'm next to a wall in Coen's bedroom. By the wetness on my face, I'm guessing I've been crying.

"Coen?" My voice is hoarse. I must have been screaming in my sleep. It looks as though he turned on the lamp on his nightstand. When I finally focus, I see his lip is bleeding. "Oh my god." I cover my mouth with my hand. I know I did that. I ram my head back up against my knees and sob. I'm such a fucking mess. This is why I can't date. This is why I have to keep people at a distance. I was so tired that I forgot to take my pills and look what happened.

I feel his warmth encircle me completely as he picks me up and carries me to the bed. He's rocking me in his arms whispering that he's okay. But I know he's lying.

After what feels like ages, I finally settle down with the weird jerking hiccups of exhausted cries. I look up to examine Coen's perfectly sculpted face. His lower lip is covered in dried blood and the area is bruised and swollen.

"We should ice that." I brokenly whisper.

"First, tell me that you're okay." He's concerned for me?

"I'm okay." His hands trace the dried tear paths running down my left eye and he whispers softer.

"No, love, tell me that you're okay…"

"I need to take care of you first, please." I plead with my watery eyes.

We walk to the bathroom where I have him sit on the countertop. He directs me to the first aid kit and I get to work on cleaning him up. Thankfully, the slit is small and doesn't need stitches.

But the guilt eating me is insurmountable.

I get his lip settled and then grab some ice out of the freezer by his closet. Only a man would have a full size fridge in his bedroom. It's paneled in the matching wood that circles the back wall.

He crawls back into bed and waits for me. I shake my head emphatically. "I can't. It's too late for me to take my pills. I just don't…I can't..." I bite my lip hard. I need to focus.

He gets up and walks over to me. Arms on my shoulder, he squeezes.

"Charlie, I need you in bed with me." His jaw is clenched and I can see his pecs twitching. I shake my head trying to snap it out of Coen's magnetism. I glance at the time. It's only ten till four. Dammit!

I push at his chest to get some space and start pacing in front of him. I stop and take a moment. "First, tell me what happened."

"I don't remember. I'm tired, love. Let's get some sleep. Having you in my arms is the best medicine." He holds them out for me to climb into. Not that easily swayed, Coenlicious.

"Please tell me, Coen. I need to know if you want me to move past this."

He sighs, rubs his hands on his face, and then sits on the edge of the bed. "Okay, but I need you in my arms. Those are my terms, councilor." I quirk a small smile. He's adorable.

"Your terms are agreeable, Mr. Collins." I sit next to him and lean on his shoulder. I yelp when he picks me up bridal style and carries me to his side of the bed. Placing me down, he follows then lifts me and places me in the 'sleeping with Coen' position that I've become familiar with. His arms circle me tightly and he kisses the top of my head. I scoot so that I can rest my chin on his impressive pectoral muscle. I want to look at him while he speaks.

His soft voice echoes harshly into the darkened room as he explains how I woke him. I was screaming in my sleep and thrashing wildly. He wasn't sure what to do, so he attempted to wake me out of my nightmare. Instead, according to Coen, he only made things worse. I tried pushing him away, and when he kept trying to touch me, I punched him. Then I started rocking in the corner. He kept trying to call to me but at a distance as he didn't want to further agitate me.

By the time he's done recanting his story, my eyes have fallen heavy. My head rests peacefully in its spot and Coen's fingers hypnotically comb through my hair. Gosh, I love that. His soothing voice has lulled my troubled thoughts and eased me back into the realm of sleep. He knew what he was doing when he laid us down like this. I have a feeling that I'm more than outmatched by this worthy opponent.

Chapter 31

WE DEVELOPED A ROUTINE. I don't remember mapping it out or analyzing its topography. It just happened. One minute it was August and the next October.

Work was hectic and nonstop. On my off hours, I was usually with Coen. I rarely saw the trio and neglected my music.

It wasn't until I was getting ready for a charity event in mid-October that I had my little freak out. I had managed to find a stunning Herve Leger sleeveless bandage gown in rose gold and was hunting for the perfect matching shoes in the closet when I noticed a gorgeous pair of Rene Caovilla pearly T-strap leather sandals on one of the shelves on my side of the closet. And that's when it hit me…my side of the closet.

I freeze and find myself sliding onto the bench in the middle of the dressing room. I regard Coen's side of the closet. Everything is color coordinated and organized: filled with an array of suits, tuxes, and his favorite tees. Then I glance to the other side and notice a full assortment of female clothing. There are work suits, designer ball gowns, sheath dresses, casual clothing, and then the shoes. I gape at the lighted shelves holding a plethora of heels that I don't recall ever purchasing.

I pull open one of the jewelry shelves and note that sitting before me is all the jewelry that I thought Malice had returned, plus several newer pieces that I've never seen. In fact, I've never seen most of the items in the closet. Coen would tell me to pack a bag or have Malice grab some clothing for me but I didn't bring this much over. And come to think of it, I haven't done any laundry or brought anything to the cleaners in quite some time.

I look at the riveting heels in my hand. They're my size. I stand and check the sizes of the gowns, even the one I'm wearing I didn't purchase. But it fits. I grab the drawer pull on the side panel spying my undergarments. But these aren't mine. There are name brands like La Perla and Agent Provocateur, I have never ordered anything from there. I'm a straight laced Victoria Secret kind of girl. Hey, if it's good for an angel, then why not me?

But these are my clothes, aren't they? Is more of me here? I check the bathroom and sure enough my toiletries litter the shower and bathing areas. My toothbrush stands proudly next to Coen's. My makeup lines the vanity area. When did all of this happen?

I remember that Coen set up his garage codes in my car. He wanted me safe, and I understood that. I remember the house key on my key chain. He said he wanted me to have it, and the entrance codes for when he was running late. Oh my goodness....

There is only one correct conclusion; I'm living with Coen Collins.

Staring at the mirror in front of me, I watch the heat pool into my cheeks. I feel the panic beginning to boil. I am living with him. I am living with a man I've known for all of seven and half months. A man that was once my employer. A man that could potentially leave me at any moment. My hands rise instinctively to my throat, trying to coax the air into moving easier from my lungs. I can't be living with Coen. I mean he's wonderful but I am me.

I am not a roommate!

I'm panicking and can't seem to force my breathing into submission. Coen is downstairs doing some last minute work in his home office, so when I see his reflection in the mirror, I'm further startled. Eyes wide, eyebrows raised, entire face and neck flushed, hands shakily white knuckling my throat, and I can see why he would be concerned.

"What's wrong, love. Talk to me!" he shrieks grabbing onto me and twisting me towards him. He pries my hands from around my neck. "Can you breathe? Do I need to call an ambulance? Charlie, talk to me!"

"We…we…we live…to…gether?" It's a whispered question as the air is still stalled along its pathway.

His brows furrow and his icy eyes absorb me. I see him scan me over and over, searching for the right answer.

"Charlie," he begins softly, as if he were talking to an injured child. His hands cup my jaw and begin that soothing rubbing motion. "Yes, love, we're living together. Is that what you needed to hear?"

I look up to him. He's so much taller in his dress shoes while I'm standing barefoot. Larger than life. "Coen, I still have my condo, my stuff?" I question it because at this point I'm not even sure.

"Yes, I was deliberately moving you in at a gradual pace. I know you get overwhelmed easily, love. I was just trying to lessen any uneasiness." At this point, everything sounds practiced, confident. He's been waiting for me to notice. How long has this been going on?

"But...but..." I begin to question still trying to calculate.

"Ssshhh, love." He kisses my forehead. "We'll be late. You need to finish dressing." His hands roam down my neck to the open back. "You look breathtaking, by the way. Can't wait to see the finished product." He winks, pecks my lips, and is out the door.

I lean against the countertop for support as my mind recalls the conversation. Coen only confirmed what I had just figured out, but he never explained why. Why is a really big deal!

The charity event was effective, though I don't remember much of that evening. Well, other than I saw Andrew with Mandy Morninglane. Talk about sloppy seconds. Even Coen noticed and we had a good chuckle at Andrew's expense. Just like at the yacht party, Coen always keeps me at his side. Charlie this, Charlie that. I did get a little frustrated when he told one gentleman that I was thinking of fronting the legal team at CC. I can't wait for that one to hit the office tomorrow.

I was so exhausted by the end of the night that when we got 'home' all of the pestering thoughts of cohabitating were lost. Pajamas, check. Nightly bathroom ritual, check. Climb into bed with new favorite pillow, check. Sometimes Coen will bring his tablet or his phone to bed, not quite finished with his work, but *every night*, he insists we fall asleep together. I have no doubt that I'm being conditioned. If I ever have to sleep without my pillow, I doubt I'll get any actual slumber.

I think at this point we act more like an old married couple than two live-in lovers, well, minus the lovers part. We touch all of the time. We kiss all of the time. But we have a PG rated sex life. If things start to get intense, Coen pulls away.

This relationship is exactly the opposite of what I assumed men wanted. The commitment, married, live together, all in your business stuff; that was to be feared in Manland. The sex was what you hope to regularly achieve in Manland. And since the majority of my friends are indeed residents of Manland, I assumed this to be accurate. If this were the case, then where does Coen reside? Chickland? Either way, I have a feeling I'm screwed.

Just like I had anticipated, the day started in the rumor gutter. I was in a conference with Brantley and Tom for nearly an hour trying to reassure them that I was happy. Happy, happy, happy. Gag!

I receive a text from Tank asking if I had time to meet for lunch. We ended up around the corner at an outdoor eatery catching up. According to Tank, I've been Missing in Action. He's right, too. I've been so MIA that I don't even know what my address is anymore.

During lunch, I realized that I haven't properly trained since my last fight in March. I've never gone this long between fights. Tank was worried that he was the cause. I tried to explain that between going on tour and then trying to fully catch up, I've been neglectful. Coen has a well-equipped gym in part of his basement. I use the treadmill daily and lift weights when I have time. But now that seems like excuses. If I want to train, Tank will work with me. He says he learned some new techniques in Vegas that he is dying to show me. The prospect of having an advantage in the cage is too good to pass up. I promise to recommit and ask him to schedule a fight for me after Thanksgiving. That should give me plenty of time to get reacquainted with that punching bag...or person.

Going through our nightly rituals; eating, discussing our day, getting ready for bed, I neglect to inform Coen of my newest fight prospect. It's not that I was avoiding it, I just forgot. So when I wake that morning early, despite it being the weekend, Coen goes on alert.

"What are you doing out of bed so early? We always sleep in on the weekend." He's still in bed, and without me in his arms he throws them over his eyes.

"I promised Tank I'd meet him at Tornadoes at eight," I respond while putting on my shoes.

He sits up and glares at me. "What do you mean? Why do you need to go to Tornadoes? We have a perfectly equipped gym, here."

Agitated, I reply sharper than necessary. "Because I need to spar."

He throws the covers off and stands before me in just his boxer briefs. Hands balled on his hips, his lips thin, he growls, "Why do you need to spar?"

"Because, Coen, I'M A CAGE FIGHTER!" I enunciate every single word to enforce perforation.

"NO!" He shouts…at ME! "NO, you're NOT a cage fighter. You're a lawyer!"

I finish tying my shoelaces and stand before him, my hands shaking in a painfully tight fist at my sides. But when I finally speak, I'm deceptively calm. "You're obviously mistaken, Mr. Collins." With that, I grab my cell and keys and head towards my car.

I hear him following me and yelling at me. "No, you don't. Don't you dare Mr. Collins me! We're beyond that! Charlie, you don't get to walk away!"

He reaches out to grab my arm and swings me toward him. I stop myself from falling into him with the momentum and jerk to a stop. I can feel the anger bubbling at the surface, dying to be unleashed. I need to keep it together.

"Charlie," he says softer this time. His eyes are begging for me to bow to his every will. Apparently, he thinks I'm his personal ragdoll.

I purposely soften my face and crack a small smile. He thinks he has won me over and loosens his grip. "That's my girl," he whispers with a growing smile.

I step back and respond with, "No, I really never was!" My right eyebrow quirks up and I feel my smile darken.

I quickly make my way to my car and out to Tornadoes. By the time I get there, the shaking in my hands is mostly gone.

Tornadoes isn't what one might call a pretty gym. For one, when you walk in, you're hit with a malodorous smell formed from layers and layers of man. Sweat, body odors of every spice, feet, a faint tint of male cologne and soap, and the under layer of cleaning products. It's not for the faint of heart.

There are varying types of punching bags hanging from exposed beams in the ceiling. The favorites have frayed edges and discolorations. There are a few cardio machines on the side wall too, but even those have seen better days. Nothing here is shiny. The free weights and kettle bells line the opposite wall and there are benches and bars nearly everywhere in between. There are mats on the floor marking the sparring areas but everyone wants to be in the cage.

No yoga or pilates classes are held here. There is no glorified pool or tanning beds. There is a hot tub but I don't go anywhere near it! There's no ladies locker room, so I change in Tank's private bathroom in his upstairs office. I usually don't shower until I get home. The trade-off, Tank.

Since I'm already in my workout gear, I head straight to the treadmill to run. I told Malice that I'd be here this morning and I spy him hitting the bags in the far corner. I can't hear him but I can imagine all of the grunting with each punch.

After twenty minutes on full speed, I see Tank hopping down the steps from his office. He notices me and nods his head encouraging me to move his way. Calmer and sweaty from my draining run, I grab my stuff and get ready for today's lesson.

He looks at my hand and frowns. "No way, Charlie. I aint gonna wrap your hands with that rock on there. Get rid of it or ya don't get to play."

I look down and notice the Coen ring (I refuse to call it an engagement ring) on my left ring finger. I remember Coen insisting that I wear it. At the time, I didn't think much of it but it certainly looks imposing sitting there.

"Right…hold up a sec!" It's never a good idea to leave jewelry of any type in a gym. But in this gym, with these guys, with this crazy expensive rock…I need backup.

I walk over to Mal intruding on his pounding time.

"Je ne peux pas porter ce. Pouvez-vous regarder pour moi?"

I can't wear this. Can you watch it for me?

He takes the mini golf ball ring and stashes it in his pocket then angles his head for me to run along.

Back on the mat, hands wrapped, Tank has me run through our start up routines and then goes to town. I learn his new techniques and fail repeatedly. I'm slower. I'm weaker. And by the end of nearly two hours, I'm completely drained.

"What the hell is wrong with ya, babe? Where's ya head at?" Tank grabs my puny weak arm and pinches the skin. "Ya got no muscle. Ya goin' soft?"

"Ouch!" I pull back. "No, I aint going soft. I just have some work to do. Which is why I'm here, nut job!"

He continues pounding me for another hour. I've fallen or been flipped so many times that I know I'll be covered in bruises. I can't believe I've been so lax on my health regimen. I look down and pat my stomach, and notice that even that is softer. I used to have pure muscle, now I'm afraid to look. I could easily be taken out by a grandmother at this point. I'm an embarrassment to the sport.

With my head low, I unwrap my hands. Tank stops me and throws his arms around me. "Sweetheart, we all go through periods like this. It's no biggie. Ya gotta get up on that wicked horse and ride. Ya feel me?"

He's right. I have to get back in the swing of things. I play music for the guys. I lawyer for my mind. But this is for so many reasons. I never want to feel weak again. I never want to feel fear and not have my body respond because it's too broken. It's about staying strong in the mind as well as the body to allow them to fully connect. At least on my level.

"I feel you, big guy. Consider me on my come-back tour." I wink at him.

He cracks a smile and starts belly laughing, his head raised to the ceiling. "Hell, yeah it is! That chick will never even know what hit her come November. You're lightning babe! Swift and sharp, so let's get ready to slice, milady."

He slaps my ass and sends me on my way. I'm so out of shape that we never even made it to the cage. Malice and I head to the door together. He showered and is back in his normal dark suit, navy this time.

"Vous rentrer à Collins?"

You heading back to Collins'?

"Non, nous sommes dans un combat ce matin. Je besoin d'espace."

No, we got in a fight this morning. I need space.

"Faim?"

Hungry?

Heck yeah! But I better limit my carbs if I'm going to tighten up. I'm craving meat and lots of it!

I nod and he climbs into the driver's side of my car. I see several missed calls and texts when I check my phone, which has been hiding in my bag all day.

7:28 COEN: CHARLIE, ANSWER YOUR DAMN PHONE!

7:42 COEN: PICK UP THE FUCKING PHONE, WE NEED TO TALK.

7:58 COEN: OK, GET YOUR WORKOUT IN AND WE WILL TALK WHEN YOU GET HOME.

10:37 COEN: WHEN ARE YOU COMING BACK?

10:54 COEN: PLEASE, LOVE.

11:07 COEN: YOU ARE COMING HOME, AREN'T YOU?

Wow, I was thinking of returning later in the evening after my shower but now I think some time apart might do us some good. I dial his cell.

"Love, where are you? What's taking so long?" He sounds exasperated.

"Coen, calm down. My workouts always last this long. I'm all sweaty so Mal and I are heading home to shower and then off to grab lunch."

"You're on your way here." His voice sounds chipper, suddenly.

"No Coen, my condo."

I think I faintly hear a growl. I eye Malice to see if he heard it but he's pretending not to listen.

"Coen, how about I come by tomorrow evening and we can have dinner together? I will even cook."

"No, Charlie. That's unacceptable! I can't sleep without you. I need you here!" Talk about negotiations, Coen isn't even trying to meet me halfway.

"Just one night, Coen. Things are just…they're moving too fast. I'm not saying throw the brakes on, I just need a pause. Can you try to understand?" My voice is soft and steady. I'm not angry, just confused.

"Go have lunch. I'm at the office now. Father dragged me in and now I'm knee deep. When I'm done I'll call you. Have your phone

ON YOU!" He still sounds upset, though.

"Ok, babe," I answer even softer.

"Charlie..." He groans and drags my name out. "You don't know what you do to me, love."

With that, he hangs up. I relax my head back in the leather seat and wait our return. I'm going through the last months in my mind. August....September....October? What is in October? Did I do...? I sent that in? Bills? Florida family? No way! Trio family? Trio...Gunner? Trig? Bulllllll?? Bullet...oh shit!

I jerk up and immediately dial Bullet's number. No answer. I don't bother leaving a voice mail, as he never checks so why bother.

"Après le déjeuner, je me dirige pour voir Bullet."

After lunch I'm heading to see Bullet.

It's Saturday, so he'll probably be working at his tattoo shop. He and a high school buddy of his, Lyle, opened it nearly a decade ago. *Loaded Ink*. I didn't know Bully when I got my ink done on my eighteenth birthday, so he has never worked on me. But he's extremely talented. If I ever decide to add more ink, I will definitely go to him.

After a shower and change we are out the door. We tackle one of those cafeteria-style places for lunch and grab every meat product on display.

With full bellies, clean bodies, and a renewed sense of purpose, we trek to the shop. Although, I've been here a boat-load of times, the last was before our tour, so it's been a while. When the tatted chick at the door greets us, I'm not surprised she hasn't recognized me.

She eyes me, probably sizing me up. "Welcome to Loaded Ink, what can I help you with?" She's cordial, but there's an undertone. I eye her back. She's seated behind the desk but from what I can see she looks like one of those retro forty chicks but covered in tatts and multiple piercings with large gages in her ear. Her cherry red lipstick and heavy eye makeup match my own and we are both sporting black clothing, but hers is more revealing.

"Is Bullet available?" I know it came off as demanding but I don't appreciate being sized up that way. Not in my Shooter garb.

"He's with a client, right now." She smiles callously.

"Do you know how long he'll be?"

She sighs and looks frustrated. "Why? He's booked for the rest of the day. If you wanna make an appointment, I can check the books. But since his bay-and hit the top 100 his schedule is booked solid."

We made the top 100? How am I so oblivious?

"Shooter?" I look over at the waiting area and spy a few guys hanging out. One guy stands up and walks over to me. "Holy shit, you're her!"

Malice immediately goes on guard and blocks the new guy's path. He crosses his arms and stares down the newbie.

"Mal, c'est d'accord."

Mal, it's okay.

"Hey." I smile at the new guy around Malice. "You all waiting to get tatted?"

The newbie beams. He has shoulder length red hair and a matching full beard. "Yeah, I'm actually up next with your boy." I nod doing that weird head bob thing people do when they don't know how to continue the conversation. Back to chick.

I glare her down. I think she knows who I am now. "I'll just let myself back there, good?"

"Yeah…um, sure. He should be finishing up." Oh, now she's helpful.

I walk down the hall checking the separated cubicles as I go. I know which one Bull hangs out in but I'm being nosy. Walking a few steps into his area, I quietly watch while he finishes up. It's never a good idea to alarm someone holding a gun, even a tattoo gun. His machine goes silent and he wipes the excess ink away and then looks up at me. He's working on a stunning replica of Ganesha, the Hindi deity of elephants, on a guy's back. I can tell he's been at it for a while.

"Hi, Bully," I say softly. The machine may not be on but it's still in his hand. And we haven't really spent any time together since our tour ended.

"Hey, baby girl, whatcha doing?" He's still seated and looks a little confused. I try to read him, I don't sense any anger, so I continue.

"I tried to call earlier, I just need a minute."

"Yeah, okay." He looks back at the big guy he's working on. "Bro, do ya mind if I talk to my girl for a sec?"

The guy lifts his head and glances at me. "Sure man, take care of yours." Hmm, cool guy.

Bullet puts his gun down, stands stretching his back for a second, then grabs my hand and ushers me to the back office outside of his working station. Still holding my hand, he closes the door and glides his hand to my upper arm. His other hand moves to my hair brushing it from my shoulder. He's watching me. I feel like I haven't seen him in forever.

He clears his throat. "So, baby girl. You got something you wanna tell me?" The way he presents it, though, is as if he knows something. I have a feeling we will be talking about two different things. Might as well get mine taken care of first.

"It's Harley's fifth birthday on Monday. Are they throwing her a party?" I have gone to every party for the last three years. I would hate to miss it.

He removes his hand from my arm and rubs his nose with the back of his hand. "Naw, they aint doing anything this year." He's lying. He doesn't want me to go to her party. He's that upset with me? We've grown apart that much?

I take a step back and turn away from him. Oh wow, I didn't expect this.

"Now your turn. Tell me what you came here to say." His voice is hollow and deep.

I don't know what he's talking about. "What do you mean? I wanted to know about Harley," I answer while turning to face him.

"Charlie, quit bullshitting me." He puts his hands on his hips and glares. He about never calls me by my name, so this must be something big.

"Bullet, would I lie to you? I honestly don't know what you're talking about."

His brows furrow and he reaches into his back pocket. "Shit," he murmurs. "Give me your phone." I pass it to him and he taps it a few times. "What's the pass code?"

"1 2 0 3," I answer, still wondering why he's being a dick.

His eyes look up from my phone. "Really?" I nod. Then he types in and mutters. "That's fucked up." I scrunch my face. How does he know what that code means? Does he?

He messes with it for a bit and then passes it to me. I look at the screen to see a story printed in today's *Boston Globe*. The headlines read: **COLLINS: BACHELOR DAYS ARE BEHIND HIM**.

The article goes on to explain that Coen and I are pleased to share the news of our engagement. It gives specific information of my employment, and that Coen and I live together, as well as a vague account of our relationship timeline and how we met. Underneath the article there are several pictures, mainly from around town over the last month, and even one from the yacht party. In most of them, I'm wearing the Coen ring.

I feel the blood drain from my face. Reaching for the chair behind me, I sit down. Why did Coen leak this information out? He's never even asked. I don't understand.

"You really didn't know?" Bullet squats down next to the chair to get a better look at me. I shake my head and he grabs my left hand searching for the ring. "You're not wearing it?"

"Bully, I had that ring all summer. I wore it on my middle finger, remember?"

He looks confused. "You're living with him, though. Malice told me that you're there every night."

I shrug. "Yeah," I whisper.

He reaches over and grips my neck and looks deep into me. His eyes are flaming, a brilliant bonfire sparking to life. "What are you doing, baby girl?" His thumb rubs my jaw softly.

"I don't even know." I sigh. "I really like him, though."

"Yeah?" he croaks out.

"I think so. I mean, I've never really cared about someone other than you guys, Tank, and Mal. I don't know how this is supposed to go."

"Hhmm, does he make you smile?" I nod. "Does he take care of you?" I nod. "Does he let you be you?" I don't nod. Instead, I bite my lip and continue getting lost in the fiery depth of Bullet's eyes.

He nods and continues his soft movements.

"Is Harley having a birthday party tomorrow?" Wondering if I will get a different answer.

"Yeah, baby girl. I don't think you should be there, though." He looks down and drops his hand. Standing up he whispers. "It's just too hard." He leans over, kisses my forehead, and walks out the door.

As I walk dejectedly to the front of the shop, I hear a familiar growl echoing in my ear.

"Where you been, Wifey?" Lyle comes behind and squeezes me.

I laugh and fall into him. He has been calling me that since we met over three years ago. He claimed that we were married in his dreams before we actually met. I think he is adorable, incredibly strange, but harmlessly adorable.

He's a few inches shorter than Bullet and at least twenty pounds lighter, but with the same bald head and coloring, they could pass as brothers. With one true distinction, Lyle doesn't have Bully's dazzling eyes.

"Is that my favorite husband?" I arch my neck trying to catch a look at him. The man has tatts everywhere including his head and face, but despite his looks he's a big softy.

He crushes me further into him. "You breaking my heart, Shooter girl? I hear you're off to marry another guy. Say it aint so!"

"Never!" I exclaim. "I'm yours till my end of days."

"Then let's proclaim our love to the world!" he sings in the grandest British accent and carries me in his arms. I can't contain my laughter as he swings me ceremoniously towards the waiting area.

"Alas dear people of Loaded Ink…I shout my love of Shooter to the valleys!" he purses his lips in a regal snarl.

"Put her down, dumb ass." Bullet walks over smacking Lyle on the back of the head. "She belongs to some rich shit now."

"Ow, fucker." Lyle sets me on my feet and rubs the back of his bald head. "Quit crushing dreams. She knows who she belongs to!" He pulls me to him and waggles his brows. "You know some pompous ass can't do to you what I can." He smirks deviously then bends down and licks my cheek.

Bullet grunts. "Lyle man, don't ya got tatts to do? Malice, get your girl. I gotta shop here to run."

I turn my attention to Mal, who is watching me in return. I feel my face heating. I'm upset and hurt. Malice won't listen to Bull but he knows his shit is upsetting me. Mal quirks a brow wondering what I will do next.

With the miserable disconnect from my brain, I pull my arm back and throw a swift uppercut to Bullet's jaw. He never saw that coming, and sadly, neither did I.

His head jerks to the side and his hand comes up to touch the bruising skin, his eyes wide as he gapes at me.

With a chilling dark voice, I respond. "We both know that's been a long time coming."

I can't stop the disgust now evident on my face. We have moved from best friends, to something more, to this. I'm slowly hating him and it's shredding my soul. He's cutting Harley from my world and it appears he's doing the same with Lyle. Well, fuck him!

The shop has fallen silent, except for the gasps that came with my hit. Oh well, let them think I'm a cold hearted bitch. I flick my hair over my shoulder, straighten myself to my tallest height, and saunter out with an extra sway to my hips. Might as well own the bitch act.

I keep walking out of the door and into the car. I'm pretty sure I heard the pinup chick call me a 'bitch' but then again, she's right. I've never hit anyone outside of the cage or mat or in self-defense. This feels like absolute shit.

Malice climbs behind the wheel and begins the journey home in silence.

"Je pense que je l'ai finalement perdu mon esprit."

I think I've finally lost my mind, I whisper to Mal.

In response, he reaches across the consul and clasps my knee. Giving it a quick squeeze, he then goes back to normal Mal demeanor.

My cell phone ringing disrupts the thought provoking silence. Pulling it out, I half expect to see any one of the trio calling to bitch at me for my outburst. Instead, I find the devil herself.

"Mother," I sigh. This can't be good.

"Charlie, how are you? Oh, of course, I know how you are. I just heard all about your little announcement from the girls this morning. It's about time you got him back and made it official." Her voice is extraordinarily chipper and the 'girls' she is referring to, is the standing appointment she has at the salon. Oh no, it isn't just the salon employees but her friends all meet there every Saturday morning to get their hair styled, cut, dyed, what-have-you, and then they do brunch.

I'm in such a horrible sulky, snarky mood, that I decide to have a little fun with her.

"Oh mother, you know how terribly delayed the Globe is with its information. You'd think with someone as prominent as my husband, they'd be better equipped. What can you do?" They never called on my birthday and never notified me of Joelle's pregnancy.

My father included. I owe them nada!

"Husband? You're already married?" She gasps, fully on alert now.

"Mother, you know we've been engaged on and off since last spring. Coen couldn't wait. We had a lovely ceremony on his yacht. The same one that was in one of the pictures the Globe printed."

"Charlie, you'd think as your *mother* I'd be invited to my own daughter's wedding. I can't believe this."

"No, you're absolutely right. We were sailing your way when we heard of Joelle's pregnancy. I certainly didn't want to take you away from her. It's such a sensitive time. Anyway, we had a blast. Greyson, Coen's dad is good friends with Mick Jagger, so he joined us once we docked in the Bahamas. Oh my, that man is carayyyzy!" She loves the Rolling Stones, so I thought to add salt to the wound. "Anyway, we had a grand party on the yacht. Then Mick called up Johnny and we all went to his place. You should have seen Johnny Depp's place. Gorgeous!" I picked up that tidbit from a magazine I read once. I guess a bunch of celebs have homes down there now.

"Then Johnny and Mick started playing for us. It was chilling…I mean total impromptu but freaking beautiful." I sigh dreamily, remembering my fake wedding.

"Charlie, I can't believe this." That's because I just made it up. "You should have at least called. You're right, Joelle's pregnancy has been rather trying, the poor dear. The girls were just so excited for you. After everything, we didn't think you'd ever get to this point. I mean, Joelle's married and pregnant already." I wonder if she knows that I'm only twenty-two. Most people my age are still in college. Perhaps the Botox is killing off brain cells.

"You're so right, mother! What a relief to find a man willing to love me."

"Yes, of course I am dear. Well, you make sure you and your husband come down soon. Abba will be heartbroken. Don't worry, I'll smooth things over for you. I better run, we have an anniversary party tonight at the Rosen Plaza, and I need to get ready. Send my best to that handsome husband of yours! Bye."

"Bye, mother." I hang up with a small smile on my face.

My boyfriend / fiancée / husband is trying to manipulate me in our relationship as well as change everything about me. My best friend is pretty much cutting me out of his life, piece by piece, and

I just punched him. My mother is a cruel clueless bitch. My body is revolting against me, and Tank won't let me get away with it. Loaded Gun's single made the top 100 on the Billboard charts and I never even noticed. There's only one solution...

"Crème glacée, chocolat, et beaucoup d'alcool est nécessaire."

Ice cream, chocolate, and lots of alcohol is needed.

Grabbing Chinese on our way in after our essential stockpiling, we headed back to my place to indulge. Mal stayed for a while but then bowed out making up some excuse about needing to go to bed. It was only nine o'clock at the time and I could have sworn I saw a faint blush. If my female instincts are correct, I think he has a date.

Not long after Malice left, there was a knock on the door. Having no clue who it could be, I screamed at the door in a sing songy slightly slurred way. "Whoooo iss it?"

I hear a deep chuckle followed by, "Open up, baby girl. I think I need to join you." It's Gunner. I wonder if he still likes me.

I swing open the door harder than I meant to and it bangs against the wall.

"You waaant sommma this, too?" I put my fists up and start circling them.

He laughs and walks in, closing the door, then grabs my hand and guides me to the couch. "Sit, baby girl. I think I'll help myself." He pats me on my head then disappears.

I grab a chocolate bar that's on my coffee table with the rest of my chocolate haul and start munching. Chocolate is the answer to every dilemma. Since I have several, I should really indulge. It seems only right.

He plops down next to me cracking a beer. Taking a big swig, he puts it on the table, then grabs my hand. "Look at me, baby."

I glance up to his eyes. He must find something he doesn't like in there because he picks me up and pulls me on his lap, wrapping me in his warm thick arms. Ah. Gunner is so good for my shredded soul. Like chocolate.

"You're hurting, I can see it. What needs to happen?" he asks.

"More chocolate?"

He chuckles and rubs his right hand up my arm while the other tightens on my thigh. I nuzzle into him. "Gun, I don't know what to do anymore. I can't handle things," I whisper, suddenly sobering in his embrace.

"Well…" His voice rumbles through me. It's soothing. "Maybe start with *not* punching people." I purposely angle away and furrow my brow.

"You mean there are *other* ways to communicate?" Again he chuckles and sloppily smooches my brow.

"We need to get things straight or none of us will walk away in one piece. And I don't mean just you. We're all losing our shit."

I don't know what he means but I know that we are breaking as a band, as friends. "Gun, I didn't mean to hit him. The things he says to me now, he doesn't even want me at Harley's birthday party tomorrow. He's cutting me out. I just reacted and it was wrong of me."

"Yeah, baby. You may be tiny but you pack a mean punch. As for Bullet, I can't really say what's going down there. He's hurting, too." He kisses my brow and then pushes my head on his chest. "You gonna tell me about this preppy asshole?"

We spend the next hour or so eating chocolate and discussing the Coen situation. Gunner isn't a fan. I'm still unsure who contacted the Boston Globe. In reality it could have been anyone. I'm not as quick to blame Coen as Gun is.

I'm nearly asleep when Gunner kisses me on the head, tucks me into the blankets on the couch, and leaves me for the night. Lost in confusion and a chocolate hangover.

Chapter 32

I'M SOUND ASLEEP WHEN I hear someone key the lock on my door and enter my home. I'm not too concerned since it could only be Gun or Mal. After a few squeaky steps I hear clothing being removed. I think a shirt, maybe pants, but I definitely catch shoes peeled off. Then someone slides onto the couch behind me and pulls the covers over us. By scent alone, I can tell it is Coen.

I start to mumble incoherent sounds and he reacts by spooning me to him. "Sshh, it's only me. I can't sleep without you, love." He moves one hand over my stomach while the other glides under my head. He kisses the back of my head and then urges me back to sleep. Reluctantly, I listen with ease.

I awake with soft rubbing movements on my bare lower back. It's relaxing. I bury my head into my warm pillow and try to get comfortable. I feel Coen's light chuckle underneath me. With my arm around his middle and my leg wrapped around his, the couch still feels too small.

He groans. "We might fall off if you keep wiggling on me like that."

Opening my eyes, I look up at him. Even with the awful couch-head he's sporting, he's still stunning. The way the sun slips through the window gives Coen a radiant glow. Coen is light.

"Morning, love." He brushes his lips softly against mine.

"Morning," I respond in my scratchy morning voice then snap back into sanity. "Coen, do I want to know how you got into my condo?"

He chuckles and shakes his head. Davis. No doubt.

"Can I ask you something?" I bite my lip and look down. I hate all of this fighting.

"Of course, love. Anything, always." I can see the determination lying there.

"Did you, by any chance, um, speak with the Globe? About us, I mean?" He looks confused.

"I thought you did? I saw the article myself, yesterday." He shakes his head. "I haven't said anything, I swear. Charlie…" He sighs. "I'm so afraid of losing you that I wouldn't do anything to jeopardize this. As it is, I've been losing my fucking mind since you left yesterday." He leans forward and pecks my nose.

His hand glides up my spine. "Charlie, I never want to hurt you. Please, believe me." He moans and flips us over so he's hovering above me. He grinds his morning happiness into me and then drops his head. I feel his breath fan across my lower face and his soft messy hair tickle my lips. He's trying to control his breathing. I run my fingers over his back, relishing his warm solid skin beneath my fingertips.

"Coen, I don't know what's going on between us. You mean a lot to me and…Um, I know I'm not perfect, but…you can't…I just have to be me. I have to do me." He catches my eyes. "This feels…Coen, I'm….I'm kind of scared." I whisper the last word, as if it's malignant to speak it aloud.

"Ah, love, you don't get how perfect I think you are." He shakes his head and brushes the hair from my face. His lips reach out and suck in my bottom lip and he pulls back licking his lips. "Charlie, I love you." He reaches into my eyes conveying his feelings.

I gasp and he takes advantage of my parted lips to sear me with another passionate kiss. His tongue caresses mine as he moans into my mouth. The vibrations and his taste meld into a Coen sensory overload and I love every minute, his revelation melting me further into him. He continues his rhythmic grinding and I feel the heat spreading through my body centering on my pulsing clit. His grinding motion increases the electric current humming through my body, charging my every cell. I'm on fire, lost in his icy storm.

"Charlie, I fucking love you!" he exclaims fervently, while his hand slides up my ribs and his thumb glides over the bottom of my breast, I can't stop the moan from echoing in his mouth. He pulls back to meet me, his eyes heavy and dilated.

"I won't let you go. I don't give a shit if we're engaged as long as we're together. I don't even care where we live. I'm not gonna lie." He circles his pelvis against my core and I moan at the new movement. "I want you to have my name. I want my mark on you, love. We can go straight to the marriage, fuck the engagement and wedding shit. I just want you…I want this, love."

He leans down and continues tormenting me. His kisses have turned forceful and he nibbles across my lips and down my jaw. His tongue darts out creating wet lines and curls against the long column of my neck. I can feel the yummy scruffy grating against the moist trail he leaves behind. He nibbles gently then whines, "More." Grabbing my shirt at the base he slowly pulls it up my body, his hands scoring a dangerous path along the way. He locks his eyes with mine as he pushes it over my head and off me.

He moans. "Oh, Jesus love." He looks down at my pierced nipples then plucks at the hardened nubs. "Please tell me a female did this." He leans forward and sucks the golden ring into his mouth. The pulling sensation merging with his hot mouth is insane. I arch into him begging for more as the writhing meows keep generating from somewhere in my being. "So fucking good," he whispers into me.

"I..I, it…was a gggirl." I lick my lips. I've never felt this…this skin on skin. I've never been this bared to anyone. He takes full advantage and continues his tongue thrashing on one breast while his hand pulls and twists the other. The sensations are bathing me in heat and ice and wet and dry. I can't tell where or what. I just know it's all so fucking good.

"Coen." I can feel the coiling building, my lower areas completely engulfed in flames. I rock up against him to increase the pressure and friction, my thin yoga pants receiving quite the work-out.

He continues biting, sucking, and that incessant rocking. "Oh, god. Please don't ssstop." The building pressure is volatile and demanding. He rises further above me, jerking his hips into me forcibly, and plows my mouth with everything he has. He needs me as much as I do him, in this moment.

"I'll never stop, love. You're mine to please, mine to love, mine to fucking worship. Only mine. Nobody will ever touch you again. I love you, Charlie, more than anything." His voice breaks with his movements.

He reaches down and pulls his cock out of his boxers, sliding the material down. Holy shit! I start to freeze up.

"Just need to mark you, love. I need to own you." The heat coming from his rather impressive cock is insanely pleasing. Now each time he rubs my clit through my pants, everything intensifies. I glance down my body to see his beautiful shaft. The veins look so thick under the thin angry skin. It looks so hard, so strong, and strangely authoritative. He grabs my ass and traces over to my upper thigh pulling my leg up. I scream. This position is much more potent, I can't last much longer.

"Hang on, love. I won't let you fall alone, together, baby. For fucking ever, love, together."

Having faith in his every word, I grab harder onto his lower back pushing him into me. Cutting into him with my chewed up nails, I feel his muscles flexing and clenching, and the building only escalates.

"Jesus, now Charlie." He bites my neck and I lose all sense of time, space, and reality. Nothing. Else. Exists. The coiling pressure releases me and I spiral out of control into drunken oblivion. The electric currents combust and I explode all around Coen. Everything tingles and ignites and I'm aflame. I can't find my fingers as they cleave to Coen praying that he won't let me float away. He screams my name over and over again, grunting how much he loves me. Then we both slide down from our heavenly grace and cling to each other. I shake with the spent energy.

Coen's arms gave out at some point and he rests his full weight on me now. His moist hair brushes my cheek as he places tender kisses on my now scoured sensitive neck. I feel the warmth left behind from his cum and I like it. It does feel like he marked me, like I am his. His strong chest smothers my soft. His hard pelvis is firmly rooted to my own and my legs limp with exhaustion.

I lightly scratch my nails up and down Coen's back as we regain our footing. I feel as if I've just given a huge piece of myself to him and I'm incredibly vulnerable and bare. I don't know how people do this with randoms.

We connected. We merged on a different plane, a different realm, maybe. I've never felt this.

"Am I hurting you, love?" he whispers while licking the shell of my ear. His hot breath potentially in route to reignite the dying flame.

"No," I say with a huge smile on my face. He feels heavenly

exactly where he is.

He pulls himself onto his elbows, resting next to my head, and smiles back at me. "You're so fucking gorgeous." His eyes are glowing orbs. "I want to put this smile on your face every day," he whispers while his fingers softly circle my swollen lips. "I want you dripping with passion for me, aching for only me, every fucking day and every night you belong to me. I'll give you this." His voice drops an octave. "I'll give you anything to be mine."

He kisses me with his finger still on my bottom lip, pulling it down. Then he grinds into me again and moans. "Shit." He scoots back and sets his forehead on my chin. "You're too potent, love. I have to pull back." He chuckles as he rises to his knees and delights in what he sees while looking down at me.

His fingers slip into my mouth. "Suck," he whispers. I open my mouth and wrap my tongue around his fingers as they enter. I suck them in deeper until they're fully saturated. I've never sucked anything, other than a lollipop or Popsicle, so I close my eyes and imagine that. Only I taste his salty Coen flavor.

He moans and pulls his fingers out, then trails them down my chin, down my neck, through the valley of my breasts, and into the remaining cum on my stomach. He draws two C's there and then picks up his fingers and brings them back to my lips. My brows furrow and my eyes narrow. I don't know about this part. He sees my indecision and murmurs a soft encouragement. "Taste me, love. Everything I am is yours."

Fortified with his words, I open and allow him to slide his fingers across my tongue and into my mouth. Sealing my lips, I suck in his juices, cataloging the new flavor and texture. This is Coen. This is mine. He closes his eyes and tilts his head back with a groan.

"It's too late for us, love. We're forever. Destiny has marked you as mine, and now you see that she has made me yours." Astonishingly enough, I am beginning to understand what he means.

Though I've never been one to have faith in destiny, through Coen's eyes, I suddenly believe almost anything.

Chapter 33

AFTER SHOWERING SEPARATELY, WE ENJOYED a relaxed breakfast and spent the rest of the morning and afternoon cuddling. My thoughts drifted to Bullet and Harley several times. I wanted to text him. Tell him to give her a big kiss from her auntie. But I doubt he'll ever speak to me again. I can imagine Harley's face when Bull pulls up and she sees I'm not there. I wonder what lie he'll tell her. Maybe he'll be cruel and tell her I don't care for her anymore. That would break her little heart. The thought alone breaks mine.

I wonder if he took Trig or Gun with him. I bet Gunner wouldn't tell me. He'd try to spare me.

How fucked up that I'm thinking about Bullet when I'm with Coen. That has to be cheating on some level.

Later that night, we order in. With dinner set out on the table and our forks fully in motion, Coen plans our week and soon we are readying for the day to end.

He had Davis bring over a few complete suits and his toiletries. I know this is simply a logical move on Coen's part. He's made it clear that he'll be staying the night. But the thought of his clothes next to mine in *my* closet, in *my* world, well that's sexy. Though I think it's mainly to give me the illusion of more control. Who knows if I have any at this point, but I'm down with the delusions for now. He was rather cross when I told him about my upcoming fight, perhaps it's time for a little Charlie History 101 lesson.

"Hey babe," I call out from the bed. It's after ten and I'm ready for our little talk and then sleep. He went into the living room twenty minutes ago for a work call. Even from here, I hear him yelling every few minutes, which sounds like an aggressive discussion. With no response, I get up to check on him.

Padding across the condo, I watch as his hand tugs at his hair. He's sitting on the edge of the couch, elbows on knees. He looks miserable.

"I told you, I don't fucking care!" he replies to the caller, appalled. "You ever do this shit again and I'll leave you." His head still bowed, I can see the straining of his muscles on his forearms and neck. He wants to attack. "You think I give a shit about money." He laughs darkly then growls. "You can't touch my trust or my fucking shares. No…No. You hurt my girl again and I'll cut you off." He nods in response to whatever is being said. "Hand it over to that arrogant old prick, then." More hair pulling. "Fine, but she's part of the package. Better get fucking used to it." He nods some more and then sighs. "Okay. Tomorrow." Then he clicks off the phone, drops it on the table, and rips deeper into his hair. He's going to be bald in no time at this pace.

I clear my throat prompting him to look up in surprise. "I didn't mean to interrupt. You've been gone a while and I was getting concerned."

"Sorry, love. Got caught on a call." Standing up, he rubs his face a few times, then grabs his phone and wraps me in his arms. "You sleepy?" I smile for him and nod while he ushers me to the bed.

Instead of assuming the nightly positions, we lie side by side facing each other. "You want to talk about it?"

"No, it was my father. I questioned him about the Boston Globe leak and I found the culprit." He sighs and closes his eyes. I want to cheer him up.

"Mother and I had a bit of a brawl yesterday. I wanted to shut her up, so I told her we were married." I say this casually but I know he'll eat it up. He snaps his eyes open, the excitement bubbling behind them.

"Married?" he asks with a smirk. "Should I ask where and when we had our faux nuptials?" At least he's smiling again.

"I told her that we took the yacht and sailed to the Bahamas."

"Hmm, I love the Bahamas. This could work." He waggles his brow. "What else?"

"I sort of mentioned that Mick Jagger was a friend of your dad's and that he called in Johnny Depp to party." I bite the side of my lip. Saying it all out loud it sounds completely farfetched. The fact that mother believed it, says so much about her parenting skills.

He bursts out laughing. "And she believed you?" I nod, picking up on his good mood. His laughter is contagious. "Oh, that woman!"

I let him enjoy that ride before I hit him with another.

"You ready for a little Charlie history bedtime story?" I ask shyly. I don't like to discuss my past.

Nobody knows everything, only bits and pieces, and even those parts are vague.

He looks concerned and starts to tense. I lean onto my back and wave him over. The only way I can do this is to not see his reactions. He scoots closer to me and I pull his head down onto my chest. I comb my fingers through his now curly and gel-free hair.

"If you wanted another round with the big man…" He grinds his front into my upper thighs. "All you had to do was ask. I'd love to oblige." He grabs the top of my tank top and pulls down to expose my right breast. Then he sucks most of my breast into his mouth.

"Quit it!" I can't help but laugh. "I'm trying to have a heart to heart." Pulling up my top, I grab onto his lower jaw in one hand squishing his lips together in a guppy-like pout. "No play. Coen listen." He grunts in response and I shake his head up and down. "Good boy." I wink at him.

"Okay." I put his head back and begin petting it, both to relax him and myself. "So, remember how you came to me before the tour?" He nods against me. "You know, about the UF thing." I wait as he slowly nods again. "Well, um, what I want to tell you is what happened after the…the, uh, after. What happened after." I exhale after spitting that last part out. Shit, this is harder than I thought.

He looks over at me. "You don't have to tell me any of this, love." He arches up, gently kissing my lips slowly.

I shake my head and rub my fingers through his scruffy yummy along his jaw line. "I do! I need you to understand."

He thins his lips and quietly takes his original position.

"Ok, so bear with me here. I've never spoken about this." He squeezes me, reassuring me to go on.

"Anyway, when I was finally released from the hospital, I was still very broken. I mean physically and with my internal injuries. I was scheduled to be in physical therapy for the next few months and was basically cemented to a wheelchair." I clear my voice and try to shake off the images cycling through.

"But those injuries paled in comparison to what really weighed me down. I lost my faith in humanity, and worse, I lost faith in myself. I thought I could be invisible. That if I stayed the course and didn't rock the boat, I could skate by untarnished. Well, that wasn't the case. I was naïve and weak, and so fucking pathetic. I look back and I hate that girl."

And I really truly do. I don't even think of us as the same person sometimes. She was Charlie prototype, and I am Charlie 2.0. I continue strumming my fingers through Coen's beautiful golden locks. It's connecting me here and not there.

"Quite the wakeup call, right? Anyway, mother, being the dear that she is, didn't know what to do with me. I was afraid to leave the house, afraid to let anyone near me, and she would glare at me with this strange mix of despise and pity." I chuckle sadly remembering her face when she would look at me. She pitied me, rather than aching for her daughter's innocence being ripped away. Rather than angered at my assailants, she pitied *me*. I mean who would love me now, right?

"After about three months of my parents throwing me onto therapist after therapist, they sort of gave up. I wasn't eating and lost all of my baby fat. My hair had been shaved short, thanks to the stitches, and there was nothing in my eyes. I would look in the mirror and didn't recognize the stranger looking back. They sent me to Israel to stay with family. My cousin was heavily involved with…well, let's just say that he had connections and I was deemed useful. As a minor, I couldn't legally get paid without my parent's involvement, so I traded for two things. The first, was some type of under the counter financial compensation, and the second, was training." He tenses and I try to reassure him with more stroking.

"I was scheduled to start Harvard the fall after graduation, but after the incident, they allowed me to postpone to the following year. That gave me roughly a year in Israel. I mastered several fighting styles, including Krav Maga, and I trained in other fields. When I finally arrived in Boston, I was now sixteen and stronger than ever. But I had to keep it up. I researched underground MMA fighting and learned about Tank. Once I stepped foot in his gym I knew that I was where I needed to be." I take a deep breath.

"Tank furthered my MMA education. I learned about boxing

and wrestling and various MMA styled grapples and holds. He mentored me and helped make me stronger. I can't be weak again. I can't get back to that place. I need this, Coen. I need it!" I state that last part firmly. I want him to understand, to relate, and then to encourage and support me.

I can't believe all that came out. I've never shared, and even when I was forced to see a therapist when I was younger, I would vaguely skim the details or makeup rainbow stories.

Coen takes several minutes to absorb what I said in silence. I continue stroking his hair and the feeling of his weight and heat bring me solace. He grounds me.

He finally lifts his head and looks at me and thankfully, there isn't pity nor anger there. He shifts his body over mine and drags himself higher so our eyes connect intimately. Hands softly stroke my hair and he kisses my lips gently. I almost don't feel the pressure there.

"I love you." His voice is hoarse, like he's been fighting tears. He nods as if agreeing to something and then kisses me harder. "Thank you, Charlie."

More kissing follows and it quickly turns passionate. Tongue and teeth. It's rough and needy and I'm not sure if this is about him trying to please me or Coen trying to comfort himself. With my clothes still on he kisses, licks, nibbles, and bites down my body. He pulls up my shirt and I feel his nose rubbing up and down my scar. His staggered breath against my stomach and yummy scruffy trailing behind.

"I'll never let anyone hurt you again, love. You have to believe that. If you want to spar, then I won't stop you. But I don't think I can handle another fight." He takes a deep breath, and on the exhale I feel the moisture welding to my skin.

"It killed me the first time, and now, well, you're my whole life." He leans his forehead on my ribs and his hands grip my hips on each side. I know he is trying to convey the strength I feel in them to me, but he still doesn't get it. My intentions are forsaken.

He continues his ministrations as his hands smooth up my sides lifting my shirt above my breasts. He slowly slides down my body spreading my legs as he goes. Since sleeping with Coen I've switched my nightly outfit to a tank top and old boxers. Coen is a mini-furnace.

I feel my boxers and undies being pulled down as his soft hands scrupulously navigate. When I feel the cool air caress my skin, I lock up. My every muscle tenses.

"Coen?" This is…more.

"Please Charlie, I need this. Just a taste, love." His growl sounds more like a whine.

He opens his mouth and sucks in the area below my navel, scraping his teeth as he goes. Slowly his tongue darts out and he circles it several times and then dives in. His tongue loops into my navel ring and he pulls it vigorously into his mouth, sucking aggressively. I moan, this sensation new and exciting, and push his head further against me. Scoring his scalp as I wedge my fingers in his hair.

He releases my ring after a few more tongue spelunking exercises, then heads south. He nips at the skin just above my pubic bone with his perfect Coen teeth and then eases the sting with his perfect Coen tongue.

Strong hands dig under my thighs and grab hold of my giant globes, filling each hand near perfectly. They knead and mold and manipulate my body to their every whim. His nose digs into my pubic hair as he breathes me in. I'm not bald, just trimmed, and I've tried to keep up with the bikini lines, but shit, I'm a woman. I hope he likes that.

He must like it because I hear him moan and look down to see him grinding the bed. Oh goodness, that's hot. With my legs spread, he has no barriers to his prime objective. He looks up and meets my eyes while hovering just above my vagina. I feel the heat emanating from him. His eyes are so heavy that icy blue is consumed in the black of night. He smirks and I watch as his tongue slowly darts out and barely licks from my perineum all the way to my clit. The touch is barely there and yet I'm quivering.

"Oh god," escapes me. All logic is traveling at the speed of light to my center in the hopes of achieving another life altering orgasm. He chuckles and the rumbling brings me closer to the finish line. More please.

His hands on my ass push me further into his mouth as he takes hold of my clit and viciously sucks, his teeth grazing the sensitive pink flesh and creating a seismic wave. His firm tongue trails pointed lines back and forth from my opening to my clit and then his tongue slides slowly in. Flattening his tongue, he licks leisurely in and out pressuring the skin there. My fingers fall from his hair as I grab the pillow behind me and arch my back in a twisted bow, only held by the pillow and Coen.

I can't stop the wild screams that keep traveling up my throat. My mind on hiatus all I feel is sinful guilty pleasure and I don't want to stop. Soon the coiling returns and the build is reaching higher and higher. My muscles tighten in anticipation, my mouth open to the sky desperate for more air. Oh god, this man is killing me with pleasure.

I'm so close and the tremors are slowly gaining in intensity and length when everything freezes.

His finger is in me. Someone is in me. They are hurting me.

"Stop!" I scream with everything I have. I jerk and wrap my arms around my naked legs and rock.

They are going to hurt me. It hurts. Stop. Stop. They have come back. Please, stop. Stop. I keep rocking. Leave me alone. Stop. I can see their faces hovering above me. Laughing. They hit me. They hold me down. Pain everywhere. Make it stop. Please, stop. I keep rocking. Stop.

Chapter 34

I COME TO IN COEN'S ROCKING arms, wrapped in a bed sheet like a burrito across his lap. His head is down and he keeps muttering how sorry he is and to please come back to him. His voice is raspy and it all sounds broken and muted.

"Coen?" His head pops and I notice his eyes are red rimmed and his face flushed.

"Oh god, Charlie, I'm so sorry, love. Please baby." He grabs my head and throws himself into the curve of my neck. I feel him shaking and then hear a whimper. "I'm so sorry." The trails of moisture beading down my back are breaking my heart. He pulls back and looks deep into my eyes. He kisses me so hard, it's bruising and filled with so much relief.

I pull back and gently cup his cheeks, dragging my thumb over the wet trails.

"I'm the one who's sorry, Co. I, uh…I'm broken. They broke me." I can barely get the words out when I feel my lower lip tremble and my eyes water. No matter how hard I try, I'll always be that broken girl.

"Noooo," he wails. "No, this. This is a process. Just don't leave me, love. Don't ever leave me like that again. You were in my arms, but you were gone." He leans into my hand and kisses the other. "I won't let you go. Quit those thoughts now. You can't fucking give up on me. It's too late!"

He repeats that last part over and over while sealing his head to mine. He continues his pacifying rocking motion until we both feel settled.

He picks me up and carries us to 'his' side of the bed. He sits down with me still in his arms and then lies down while positioning me atop of him. I don't know if he fears I will run away or if he just needs to maintain physical contact. Either way, I'm glad I'm trapped here in his safe embrace.

Maybe he can save me? Maybe he can protect me from the bad guys out there? The realist in me doesn't believe any of it, but there's a small part of me, a growing part, that has jackhammered the stonewall around my heart and let Coen slide through the cracks, who thinks he might be the right guy for the job.

We lie in uncomfortable silence in the dark with only the sound of his too-fast beating heart to keep my thoughts from drifting bleaker. He's still here. I cling tighter to him while wondering how much more he can take. I've punched him, I've wigged out, and I've shut him down more times than I should admit.

"I know I'm going to have to say it a thousand times, and I don't fucking care. I'll tell you every time you need to hear it. Every time you doubt, every time you question, every time you hesitate, I'll tell you how much I love you!" His voice booms in the quiet darkness.

I squeeze him tighter to me. I wish I could say those words back. I know that's what's supposed to happen, I've seen enough Rom-Com to recognize. I know he needs to hear it. If not now, then soon. But the love part, that's scary. I love Tank. I love the trio, though lately I've even questioned that. I love Malice. And maybe, in some fucked up way, I love my family. But this emotion I feel towards Coen, is different. He isn't my best friend. He isn't blood. I don't know what he is so how can I know where he fits? Which category to assign? Which box to throw him into?

With my head swirling in images of love, I stop on one of Harley, her beautiful smile and stunning eyes. That's pure love. I never felt that innocent complete love that you do with a parent. Or that of a child. But when I think of her and the way she looks at the world, how she loves with her whole self, never knowing anything but happiness and warmth, that is pure love. I can't help but have a small case of envy. I wish I knew that feeling. To love completely with my whole self, not the filtered watered-down version that living has created.

I allow these thoughts to weigh me down and lull me into a restless sleep.

It's still dark when I lean over and kiss Coen's forehead while brushing the hair off his eyes. Without me in his arms, he has turned onto his stomach.

"Mmmmm," he moans, and then reaches out for me. Realizing I'm not next to him, his eyes pop open and squint at me trying to see in the dark. "What's going on? Come back to bed," he whines.

"Sorry, babe, I'm in training. I have to get into work early to knock out my caseloads, then off to the gym. I didn't want you to worry when you woke up and didn't find me." I lightly stroke his cheek and his eyes close on a moan. "Maybe we can have an early lunch later? If not, swing by after work, ok?"

He looks so sweet all curled up on my pillow, well the one I used to use before he became my pillow. He nods and pulls me down on him. I squeal in delight as he flips us over and is now hovering above me, his eyes suddenly bright and alert. He strokes my lips and then leans down for a swift taste. Minty, I'm sure.

"Thank you for sharing part of your story last night, love. It meant the world to me." He kisses me a few more times. "I have a late meeting tonight but will join you in this very spot…" He rocks us side to side. "…later on. I need you in my arms." He latches on to my lower lip sucking it harshly into his mouth and groaning. "Mmmm, before I forget, where's the ring?"

Oh, I forgot it with Malice. I'm sure it's fine and well, but let's test Coen. "I'm really sorry, babe. I was so upset and wasn't paying attention. It must have slipped off. I don't know where it is. I'm sure it's insured, though."

He tenses and swallows audibly. "Um, I did have it insured." He sits back on his haunches and bites his lip. Uh oh, maybe I pushed too far. He looks upset.

"I'm sure we can pick up another at Cartier. You said it wasn't a commissioned piece." I watch him closely as I sit up.

"Actually…" He scratches the back of his head, yanking on a few strands. "I had it cleaned and appraised there. The piece, the ring, it was um…it belonged to my mother. I brought it down to Florida, because, I've kept it close since I met you, Charlie. I knew I wanted us to be together."

I throw myself in his arms and squash him with all my might. I kiss his cheeks and lips repeatedly. This guy is fucking crazy yet ridiculously sweet. "I'm sorry, Coen. I can't wear it when I spar. Malice has it. I never lost it. I'm sorry, baby." I keep peppering his face with kisses feeling like a total douche now.

He chuckles and exhales an 'oh, thank god.' He pushes me back weighing me down again. "Now, where were we?" He waggles his eyebrows as his eyes grow bigger. "Breakfast?" He licks up my neck and grinds himself against me. "Yummy, Charlie for breakfast is the best way to start my day. I am a growing boy." He grinds harder to get his point across.

"Coen," I giggle like a teenager. "I've got to go. I have a fully encumbered day ahead of me." I push his head away from me and catch his eyes. "Be a good boy and maybe we can play later?"

He nods still smiling.

"Text me when you get to work, so I know you're okay. Maybe you should have Malice drive you." Back to bossy Coen mode already.

"I'm good, silly. Or I will be once you get off of me." I push at his chest a few times to reiterate the point.

He reluctantly lets me up. Standing, I grab the oversized glasses on the nightstand and put them on. "Are those prescription?" he asks with furrowed brows.

"Nope," I announce while popping my 'p.'

"Why do you wear them?" He stands and pulls the frames from my face to scrutinize the offending piece of plastic.

"That's a complicated answer." I grab them back and with a sharp finger sliding up my nose, return them to their spot. "Bye, babe. Have a good day at work." I smooch him a sloppy full impact kiss and walk out.

Our new routine begins. Me up early, changing the world one company at a time during the day, then hitting the gym for three hours and back to my place for a steaming hot shower and healthy dinner. Coen usually walks in the door around seven thirty, sometimes already haven eaten, and we chat, lounge around, or make out incisively.

I'm not sure how I feel about the new routine. It's a definite upgrade from the last, but I'm still missing something. Tank has been a living savior. I worship that man's skills. I feel myself strengthening, and the loose bits firming up. I sleep better now, too. I haven't been using my pills as regularly as when I was at Coen's.

Two weeks before Halloween, I get a *Loaded Guns Alert (LGA)* group text from Gunner. This is Gunner's or any band member's way of saying we need to get shit done, NOW! We never take an LGA lightly. And I'm not about to start just because Bullet and I are shitheads.

We're scheduled to headline at BedHead on Halloween, so I'm guessing we're due for some serious practice time. I think that's what the LGA was sent out for. I show up at Gunner's house straight from today's workout. I'm a sweaty mess but stopped at a gas station for toiletries and a t-shirt. I'll grab one of Gun's boxers or something.

When I knock on his door, Trig is the one to greet me. "Hey, baby girl. Where ya been?" He pretends to send a few swift punches in the air. I notice he's letting his beard grow in. Already, he looks so different.

"You gonna let me in or am I gonna freeze my ass out here?" I put my hands on my hips and give him my best stare down.

"Uh, oh, guys," he screams into the room. "We've got a wild one here. Maybe she needs some reminding that real men don't take that lip." He arches his brow and then throws me over his shoulder. Fuck, what is it with these guys and letting me walk?

"I'm all sweaty, Trig. Put me down."

He spanks my ass. "Nope, you're due."

Next thing I know, smack. Then another smack, followed by another fucking smack. Then someone eases up and plays bongos with my burning bum. I scream. "Put me down. I'll take all three of you on at once. Try me motherfuckers."

I hear Bullet laughing at my expense. "You kiss your pompous boyfriend Richie Rich with that mouth?"

Knowing that I'm stuck in this position while they freely mock me, I arch my body while rocking and then throw myself as hard as I can backwards. Trig lets me loose and I go flying, bouncing off the hardwood with my arms extended and then land surreptitiously. I stand to my full height and look around the room. All three men are standing nearby staring, my throbbing butt reminding me that they are indeed twats. Still holding the plastic bag in hand, I motion to the hall, "Shower," then walk away to take one, ignoring their laughing at *my* expense.

Eased muscles, tender ass, clean Charlie, I hurry and dress. My hair is wrapped in a towel and my shirt covers to my upper thighs, but I forgot to grab Gun's pants. Deciding it's safer to dart across, I ditch the towel, crack open the door, and make a run for it. Right. Into. Bullet.

"What's the rush, little lady?" He holds me at arm's length and slowly looks down my body, licking his lips and arching one brow. "We need to have some words."

He walks forward and I walk back. "Bull, I'm sorry for what happened at the shop," I whisper still on high alert.

He takes another step towards me. "You're gonna make it up to me." Was that a question, a command, or maybe an assumption?

I shake my head. I'm with Coen and I don't want to hurt him. Not that the idea of hurting Bull is at all pleasant. I step back and hit a hard wall. Damn, I'm trapped, again with this man.

We're both barefoot and he purposely steps on my feet. But not in a painful way. His toes wiggle gently on mine. It feels like a light massage but kind of dirty.

He clears his throat and I look up into his amazing solar eclipsed eyes. The black orbs are surrounded by endless fiery light in fiercely epic shades. I wonder if constellations linger in their depth.

His hand goes low and cups my bare upper thigh, and then he glides up. He moans when he realizes there's nothing underneath. He continues climbing until his hand is full of my burning bum. They hit me hard, plus all of Tank's beatings. He groans and leans against me.

"Are you fucking him?" he asks in a low voice.

I shake my head and he nods with his lips pursed.

"He love you?" I nod, slowly once.

"You love him?" I shrug. I don't feel like I love him but maybe I'm on that path.

He picks up my left hand, looking for the ring. He arches his twitchy brow when he sees it isn't there. I'm not comfortable wearing it, although it has only been a week since the Coen/ Charlie baby blowout, I refuse to wear it. Besides, he hasn't asked. And I don't think I'm ready to even entertain the thought of marriage yet.

"He's forever?" Now both brows are down awaiting my answer.

"I don't know," I whisper, biting my lip. I think I just pulled the skin off there. Shit, I can taste the metallic flavoring coating my tongue.

He pulls my lip from under my teeth with his thumb, looks

down at the small red dot, and then glides his thumb across it. I can see the red streak as he puts his thumb in his mouth. Pulling his thumb out, he sucks his bottom lip followed by his top into his mouth, then quirks a smile.

"Mmmm, I love the way my baby girl tastes."

I narrow my eyes, confounded in thought. What is he doing?

"How was Harley's party?" I ask while widening my eyes. I want to throw him off.

He links his fingers at the top of his head and I can't stop my eyes from centering in on the beautiful ink covering that generous sliver of skin exposed with his rising shirt. He clears his throat and I know I'm caught. I scan up and see how pleased he is with himself. But come on, he knows he's beautiful. In a Stephan James beautiful type of way. Muscles, tatts, dazzling perfect smile. I mean, what was I thinking about again? Harley…right, back to Harley.

"It was good," he replies cautiously.

"Bull, are you trying to cut me out?" I ask with a bit less gusto.

"I can't." His hands cup both sides of my face. "My baby Shooter girl."

"Hey, did you climb in the shower with her? Leave her the fuck alone man," Gun shouts from somewhere in the apartment.

"I wish." He pecks my forehead and then another swiftly to my lips. Giving me a hard once over, he then strides away.

After pulling some of Gun's sweat pants on, I meet the guys in the living room and we get down to music business. We discuss the lineup and rehearsal schedule until the show and things start to feel like old times.

Gun let us know that he has been speaking daily with our label. They love how our record sales are increasing. Not only that but we're getting a real 'we don't give a shit' image. With what happened in New York City with that radio DJ and then the circulation of me punching Bull in the face, word of LG is going strong. One of the clients at Bull and Lyle's shop videoed the entire debacle, including what I said to Bullet afterwards. Apparently, the clip has a couple of million views and people want to know more about the band. It appears I'm getting a nasty reputation, too. I guess I'd rather be known as the ball-busting bitch than something else.

Rolling Stones wants us back in New York City in early November for a photo shoot and a complete write up on the band. That's insane! Outside of our video shoot and album covers, we've never had a full on photo shoot. Wow. Talk about intimidating.

Gunner also comes down on Bull and me, hard. *Do we not give a shit? Don't we know better? Quit acting like fucking pussies?* Hey! In the end, I know he's right. I've been childish. Bullet keeps digging under my skin, like a mosquito bite or something. I'm from Florida, and it's our state bird. I *know* mosquitoes. You want to ignore it, but no, you scratch and pick at it and then it scabs up and looks gross. Bull is equal to that yuck right now.

I cook for the trio and we spend the rest of the evening talking; catching up on the daily grind and indulging in the unusually low ball brand of humor that my trio is epically known for that I lose all sense of time. That is until Coen calls.

"Hello?"

"Where the fuck are you?" He sounds furious, no 'hi' or 'how are you?'

"I'm with the guys, calm your tits."

"Wait, what did you just say to me?" He practically screams in my ear. Trio talk must be rubbing off on me.

"I just meant that everything's copasetic."

"You need to come home, Charlie. It's getting late. Say goodnight to your little friends." With that he hangs up on me. I'm in such awe that I simply stare at the unsightly devise wondering, '*What the hell*?'

"Uh oh, lover boy sounded pissed," Trig says and I can't stop the shade of embarrassment that creeps across my skin. They heard him yelling at me. I look over at Bullet and he appears to be as livid as Coen sounded seconds ago. His nose is flaring like his namesake, Bull.

Without wanting to cause any trouble, I stand and try to compose myself. "Well, I should get going. It's getting late." I glance at the clock to see its nine thirty-two. Hardly late, but apparently so.

I grab my things and lean over kissing Gunner and Trigger on the heads with a couple of 'love you's.' When I get to Bull, he stands up. "I'll walk you out." With his hand on my back, he walks me to my car.

"Baby girl, you don't deserve to be treated like that. I mean, shit, does he yell at you like that all the time? Does he fucking hit you? I'll kill him, if he does." He growls and I can see his teeth grinding in anger.

"Bull, I'm fine. He must have had a hard day or something." I try to sooth him by placing my head on his chest, just above my tattoo, the one hidden in his shirt, the one I desperately miss but will never voice aloud. In response, he wraps me in his arms and breathes me in.

"I'll kill him, just say the word," he murmurs into my hair.

"I know, Bully." I rub my hands up and down his back, feeling the tension there. The chilly late October air is whipping my hair around freezing me in place. "I hate fighting with you. Promise me, no more." I search his face, noting the growing indifference.

"I can't promise that, baby girl. I try and all, but things are changing. My head ain't right. Sorry."

I nod and disentangle myself. That one hurt like always, he's good at it.

On my drive home, I think about how I should react to Coen; go on the offense or play the good little girlfriend. Should I pick a fight or acquiesce?

I ponder my new dilemma for the duration of the entire forty-minute ride back. I know I lost track of time, but I was with the trio not scoping out the corner for my next trick. He's overreacting, and this isn't the first time. If I keep being a doormat, then he'll keep treating me like one. I make up my mind and with each floor passed in the elevator, I feel my determination strengthening. That is until it opens and reveals a rather flushed looking Coen in sweats and a tight tee. His arms are crossed and I see the tension pulsing through them. Uh, oh.

He stares at me as I walk out of the car and stop a few feet away from him. Is he expecting me to apologize? Excuse my contemptuous behavior? Doormat Charlie no longer, I copy his pose and put on the meanest face I can muster. I think it's mean until I notice his lip twitch a bit, like he wants to smile.

"You should have texted me," he states calmly, his face a neutral mask.

"Yes..." That's all I'll give him until I know where this is going, and hopefully it's not in the hallway. In my periphery vision I notice Mal's door is still closed but I wonder if he can hear our argument and feel the insane antagonism.

"I don't like coming home and finding you not here," he begins.

"I don't like getting yelled at. And while we're discussing our dislikes, I really do *not* like being manipulated, and conned into living together, I never said I was ready for that. We've barely dated and yet everyone keeps congratulating me on my upcoming nuptials. Even Brantley said something the other day about maternity leave, how he'd gladly wait for me and they'd be exceedingly accommodating. I'm twenty-two, Coen!" I rub my fingers against my eyes and try to stop the building pressure. If he gets to be mad then I do, too.

"Tout va bien ici?"

Everything okay out here?

Malice finally emerges shirtless, and crosses his arms. As he stands just outside of his doorframe, I hear a voice behind him asking if something's wrong.

I quirk a brow. He does have a date. Or maybe a boyfriend at this point. I wouldn't know, though, as he doesn't share anything.

"Retour à votre date."

Go back to your date. I answer gruffly. Either people keep me in the dark, manipulate me, or ignore me. I'm so tired of all the nonsensical men in my life!

I charge past Coen, through *my* door, in *my* condo. I rush to the bathroom, pull off my clothes, and grab my pills to pop. I'm putting today to bed. Why should I stay up and alert when Coen is only going to argue and try to sway things?

He follows me into the bedroom and watches me from the bed. He's already undressed and in position. I climb in to join him but curl onto my side facing the wall. I want nothing to do with routine tonight.

I can feel the bed shift as he moves towards me. Pulling me back into him, spooning me. I arch my back in response and try to wiggle away but he pulls me closer.

"You might as well quit, I won't let us go to bed apart." I feel his words as he spouts them against my hair.

"I'm tired, Coen. I don't want to fight. I'm done for the day."

"So, about this baby we're having. When can we get started on that?" He chuckles.

"Coen, I swear to…" I'm trying desperately to pull him off of me so I can do some bodily harm.

"I'm just kidding, love. Relax, Charlie. I'm sorry how things elevated tonight. You're right, I overreacted." He lightly brushes his nose against the shell of my outer ear and breathes out, "I'm sorry, love."

I sigh. I have too much on my plate to whine about some overbearing boyfriend moments.

"Goodnight, Coen."

"Goodnight, Charlie." He kisses me a few more times and then everything is silent. I wait to hear the evening of his breaths. My mind in motion, I'm lost in a sea of images. Even the pull of the pill doesn't lull me to drift away, though I'm eventually lost to it. Surreptitiously surrendered.

Tomorrow came too soon and I awoke on Coen's chest. I honestly don't know how or when he does it, but somehow I always end up there. I escape the condo without any interference and drown myself in the minutia of work. It may not be stimulating but it's occupational.

During my lunch protein shake break, I text Tank to let him know to delay the fight until after the photo shoot. It would make me look pretty badass to have a few bruises and cuts, and it would most definitely go with my 'new' image, but I doubt the label would be thrilled with me. As it is, I'm walking on thin ice.

Malice stops by to check on me but I'm fairly unresponsive. He has an entire hidden life that I'm not privy to, and I find it rather offensive. After we stare at each other for fifteen minutes, both of us grunting and barely speaking words, he leaves warning that he'll be at the gym when I get there.

After an abusing afternoon at the gym, I limp to my condo door when I hear arguing. Quickly unlocking it and barging in, I find Bullet and Coen in a face-to-face battle of wits. No fists appear to have been unleashed at this point, but both are at the ready by their sides.

They each stop yelling and back away from each other when they see me enter.

"What's going on?" I ask numbly, taking a moment to scan each of them, quickly looking for any injuries or tells.

Coen crosses his arms and glares at me. "Your little friend was just leaving!"

"Little friend," Bullet chimes in. "I'm bigger than you, Richie, you pompous fuck!"

"I told you she doesn't want you. She upgraded, now get the fuck out!"

"Whoa, whoa, whoa! You…" I point to Coen. "Bullet's my best friend. Why are you talking to him like that?"

"Why the fuck are you defending him? He came to our home, picking a fight with me," Coen retorts growing angrier by the second.

There are so many things wrong with that last sentiment. "I'm not." I really am, though. "I'm just trying to figure out how two of the most important people in my life are practically attacking each other? Anyone want to share?"

I look at Coen. He looks to Bullet and then to the ground. Next, I drag my attention to Bullet. I openly stare with raised brows and wide eyes giving him the go ahead and tell me look.

He walks over, kisses my cheek, and whispers, "You look so fucking sexy all flushed and sweaty like that. Love you, baby girl." Then he glares back at Coen and points at him. "I'll be watching, mother fucker."

After the door closes behind him, I scowl at Coen. "What the hell just happened?"

"You tell me. He certainly isn't my friend."

No. I guess he isn't. Abandoning any hope of a prolific conversation, I run and shower. Dinner is painfully reserved and full of dead and debilitating air. I'm drowning in it so severely that I can barely taste my chicken and broccoli.

"Were you ever going to tell me that you're leaving in two weeks?" Coen asks killing the silence with a death blow.

"Last night we fought, tonight we fought. When would have been a suitable time to bring it up?"

"Anytime!" he shouts and throws his bundled napkin on his plate. "I don't want you to go! These guys are a bad influence on you. That guy," He points to the closed door, like Bullet is going to walk through it any moment. "He's in love with you. I can see it in his eyes. I don't want you near him."

"Wait, are you *forbidding* me A) to go to New York City and do the Rolling Stone piece and B) to spend time with Bullet?"

He smiles in satisfaction. "Yes, I'm so glad we're in agreement." He stands, grabs our plates, and takes them to the sink. I'm left flabbergasted.

I storm up behind him while he's washing the dishes. "You need to leave," I say in an empty voice. I thought he loved me. How could he possibly take such a big chunk of my heart away and not think it would kill me?

He turns off the water as his hands firmly grip the edge of the sink, still facing away from me. "I don't believe that's going to happen, Charlie. You see, I won't let you go."

"Coen, if you can't accept me, then you need to leave. Bullet is part of me. If you don't like it leave!" I breathe in my calm trying desperately to preserve it.

"Charlie, I know how you feel about them, but put yourself in my shoes. I won't stand for my future bride to be in constant company of partying Neanderthals."

"Maybe we aren't on the same page. I care for you greatly, Coen, but I won't give them up. Perhaps we both need time to cool down."

I see his head nod a few times, the resignation evidently clear. "As you wish, love." He grabs his keys and cell and storms out the door. I even hear him lock it from the outside.

I don't trust him not to crawl in bed with me in the middle of the night, so I call Malice to see if I can stay there. He doesn't answer and with thoughts of that possible date the other night, I don't want to disturb him. He deserves happiness despite all the secrecy. I call Gunner, next. Another no answer.

I have a key to Trig and Gun's place, so I quickly pack an overnight bag and a work outfit and head that way. I'll analyze what just happened with Coen later. My thoughts are too muddled to strategize a proper Coen response. This will take time to finesse and finagle. I need a safe haven to shelter me until I've been fortified.

Chapter 35

FOR THE ENTIRE WEEK I barely hear from Coen. The guy who 'couldn't sleep without me' was doing just fine. Of course, I didn't give him an option. After that first night at Gun's, I started to stay at Malice's place. Coen is too clever and I'm not sure if I trust him to have my best interests at heart.

The trio and I practiced every day. We even got into the Halloween spirit by picking out matching costumes for Saturday's concert. I heard the local hard rock station mention us repeatedly and our single was thrown into Musicland rotation. It was mindboggling.

Coen stopped by the office as Halloween neared and forbade me to go to New York City. I tried to explain that this was an amazing opportunity for the band but he refused to budge on his viewpoints, as did I. Despite our arguing, I miss him greatly and feel his absence increasingly weigh me down.

With Andrew, I could easily cut him out and not think twice about it. With Coen, I gave too much of myself. When we spoke, we connected. When we ate, we bonded. When we touched, we unified. I miss his gentle touches and kisses. I miss his smile and laughter when he thinks I did something adorable. I miss him. I hate missing him. I'm amazed how one part of my life could be thriving while the other dwindles into oblivion.

The Friday before Halloween, I receive a text from Bullet asking if I want to go to Harley's Halloween party at her church. Apparently, my girl asked specifically for me. The weather is creeping to freezing and poor Abbey will have to hibernate until the spring. But on the back of Bullet's bike, he catches all of the wind and cold. That man is so big he could be a wall in front of me. He gets the wildly chilled air while I enjoy the view and the freedom, once more this year.

I decided to go as a ninja. I'm dressed in black from head to toe with only a slit where my eyes are visible. Besides, it's her church's party, so I can't exactly dress like a naughty police woman, naughty schoolgirl, or naughty anything. Covering up, especially in this weather, is the way to go.

Bullet didn't bother dressing up. Instead, he has his white thermal under his cut and ripped jeans. I rarely see him wear his cut outside of these family events and I wonder why. He's a club member, though he doesn't do much, claiming he lives outside the main area. I suspect more to that story but it isn't like Bull is a heart to heart type of guy. If he wants you to know something, he'll tell you, whether you want to hear it or not.

Harley was dressed as one of the *Frozen* characters, Elsa. I should know as she's made me watch that movie a trillion one times. Most of the BBMC family was there, too. Not that Gage character, though. I guess he didn't think he could get through the church door without engulfing in flames.

We stayed for a couple of hours talking, dancing, and eating some fantastic pot luck. I swear pot luck is the best thing ever invented. Well, besides chocolate.

It was so much fun that I even convinced Dallie and Wrench to dance with me, though Bull refused. I did watch Harley get a dance in with him, though. She has her uncle wrapped around her finger. It's seriously adorable, and I must find a way to harness this newfound knowledge. The possibilities are endless.

On our way back, Bull dropped me at Gun's place. He doesn't trust himself enough to have me sleep at his place, and since we arrived back so late, I didn't want to disturb Malice. Neither guy is home, so Bull insists on staying with me.

I clean up, change into sweats, and make my way to the couch. Bull has already grabbed all of the extra pillows and blankets and has made the couch into a bed for me. I climb in and use his thigh as a pillow. He scrolls through his phone while combing through my hair. After such a long day, I fall asleep in minutes, excited to see what the rest of Halloween will bring my way.

After waking up solo on the couch, I ended up staying the entire day with Gun and Trig. We practiced for a while and then our manager, Rick, showed up with lunch to give us the rundown for the next week. We're expected at nine in the morning on Tuesday to go over the shoot. There will be two days of shooting followed by the interview. We'll be staying in New York City to do any additional shooting, if the magazine sees fit, and spending the rest of the week promoting the new single we're about to release.

Bullet joins us and we all get dressed in our costumes for the night. I thought we should go as the Scooby Doo gang. Trig said he'd even dress as one of the chicks and I could drag Malice on as Scooby. But I was overruled. That's what happens when you're with a bunch of dumb boys. So when we walk on stage in our full blown Kiss costumes and started rocking *'God gave rock and roll to you'* there was a curious reaction from the crowd. Some people screamed for Kiss while others cheered for LG. Despite my tits and obvious height deficiency, I made an excellent Gene Simmons.

When Gunner finally piped up and the crowd recognized his voice, the entire club came alive. It was Halloween after all, and time to play.

On Sunday, I stop at Coen's. I still have the key so I let myself in after realizing that he wasn't home. I feel like we've drifted apart and need to decide where we want this relationship to go. Together. I don't want to be told.

Malice had been safeguarding Coen's ring for me, not knowing what to do with it, I leave it on the kitchen counter with a note. I want Coen to know that I stopped by and that I haven't given up on us. I explain that it doesn't feel right to wear the ring with the way our relationship has deteriorated. Maybe when I return we can find a way to mend things. I don't know what to think anymore. Is saving this relationship the right thing do? Or is it time to resign from relationship bankruptcy before it bleeds me dry?

Chapter 36

WHEN WE ARRIVE AT ROLLING Stones, they throw their fashion editorial ideas our way. Like Janet Jackson, they want us to do a nude shoot. Since we seem to have been caught several times as aggressors this has manifested into our calling sign. Our new vibe. They want something avant-garde, for LG to be noticed. In order to encapsulate that, their plan is for me to be bound with a mouth gag and a blindfold while the boys carry me horizontally. This is how they want to present and introduce LG into the world of rock.

I shift my eyes to Bullet. They want me tied up, but I can't do that as I'm scared it will trigger another attack. I can't freak out on set.

Bullet picks up on my unease. "That won't work for us," he barks in his scariest 'don't fuck with me' voice.

We spend the next thirty minutes dissecting this shoot to find some agreeable solution. Back and forth pecking at imaginary images they're trying to sell us on. We finally reach an agreement and we are sent to hair and makeup. I like this part. They are doing my eyes crazy dark and have added intensely long eyelashes.

It isn't until I'm sitting in the hair stylist's chair that I realize that my tattoo will be fully exposed and visible. Normally, this isn't a big deal, but this will be a link to Lady. I'm usually partially covered as Shooter and fully covered as Charlie. I know, thinking about myself in the third person is slightly demented, but hey, we all have issues. Having a still on the cover of Rolling Stones will draw attention. Loads of attention. Linking me will be easy once someone recognizes my one of a kind phoenix, crafted specifically with my needs.

I excuse myself from the chair and try to hunt down Bullet. I don't know what to do. Is there a way to airbrush it out? Should I even try that?

Trotting down the hall in thongs and a robe, I find the guys a few doors down and make my way over to Bully.

"Do you mind if I have a word?" I ask his makeup stylist. I guess they're putting powder and stuff on his bald head. His eyes are lined in chalk and give him that haunted zombie look.

The guy looks at Bull who nods in answer. "What's wrong, baby? You look crazy sexy by the way." I smile, even though I'm having an internal freak-out, I love how he always finds some way to compliment me...well, when it suits him.

I lean forward and whisper in his ear, "My tatt is gonna be stilled on the cover."

He digests what I said and thinks on it. I can see his eyes working. The colors change into lighter swirls and they narrow. "Whatcha wanna do?" I shrug. I want to be authentic. I'm just worried about the repercussions.

He studies me further. "Do you want more protection at the fights? This will come out, eventually."

"What do you think I should do?" He smiles his dazzling smile, the one he saves for me. When it suits him.

"You know I'd support you no matter what you do, baby girl. But, as sexy as you are in the ring, I hate watching you get hurt. I can't tell you how many times the guys have had to hold me back because all I wanna do is run into that fucking Cage and carry your ass out."

He strokes my cheek with one finger then he looks lower and notices that I'm leaning forward with an open robe. I look down to follow his eyes and see that he has a clear view of my left breast. I quickly stand, readjust the flaps, and tighten the belt. I look around and find that nobody is watching me, well, except Bullet.

I feel myself flush under the caked on makeup. I look down avoiding his eyes. He stands and pulls me to him with an arm around my waist. He quickly looks behind him to see the guys immersed in LG chatter with the cute girls on set and grinds himself against me. "How am I supposed to do a damn photo shoot with a fucking hard on, Shooter girl?" he growls softly in my ear while pulling my lobe in-between his teeth.

"I'm with Coen, Bull. You know you can't say stuff like that to me," I whisper back, denying any eye contact.

He growls again and bites my lobe hard. "Richie's a fucking pussy!" He slaps my ass and walks away. "Gotta take a shit," he calls over his shoulder to the boys. I'm pretty sure that isn't what he's about to do, and as wrong as it is, I feel myself delight in the thought. Bullet is about to spank it thanks in part to my boob slip. My girls are ruthless.

Gunner questions what's wrong and I explain to him about my tattoo. I guess it's time to merge. I liked compartmentalizing everything but I knew it wouldn't last. Gun and Trig have my back, at least for now.

The shoot goes painfully slow. First off, we're all naked. Well the trio is anyways. The photographer said they could wear that nude hammock thingy, but nooooooooo, the boys thought it was lame. That leaves me standing there staring at them completely in the buff while they wait for me to disrobe. Being the wuss that I am, I insisted on the hammock covering my girly bits down under however, there was nothing but pasties to cover the girls. They are too merciless to be subdued in pasties. So, they are free to roam the set as they see fit.

"Come on, Shooter, we wanna see!" Trig yells to me.

I ever so carefully remove the robe, one side at a time while trying to cup my boobs simultaneously. The robe falls and I'm left in a very stringy nude thong thingy with one hand on each breast. Not at all uncomfortable. Suddenly, the room is bathed in silence and all I can hear is my heart beating out of my chest screaming for me to run back to the dressing room.

Bullet clears his throat. "Shit, let's get this done so we can go home and spank it."

"Okay, asshat trio, how's this supposed to work, again?"

"I got her tits!" Trig comes over to me and starts to pick me up when Bull pushes him away.

"Fuck no, brother. Tits are mine."

"Dibs on her pussy!" Gunner jumps in. My eyes widen, possibly beyond the realm of my face. What is happening here?

Bullet growls. "Fine, I get tits, Gun pussy, Trig, you're on legs." With that Bullet walks over to me and smiles devilishly while leaning in. "Fuck you look sexy as hell, baby girl. Gonna make me chafe my dick today or you gonna help out?"

I look down at his hardening cock. Wait, that's right they're all nude and going to be holding me? I glance at all the guys and their hardware. Oh dear, lord. Coen is going to kill me when he sees this.

I finally get placed the way the photographer wants. He has moved arms to make sure there's no nipple exposure and that thong straps aren't visible. As he starts to take shot after shot, I realize that hard things are being pressed in certain places.

"Trig?" He's on my legs, not exactly a turn on for most people. But I'm pretty sure that I can feel him growing down there. He has a Prince Albert piercing, so the metal is strangely cool against that heat of my flesh.

"You better keep your shit loose man. Don't you fucking get hard on her," Bully growls and inches forward to eye Trig.

"Sorry man, I can't help it. The four of us naked together is fucking hot. I've fantasized about this a dozen times. My wood aint going nowhere."

"Gun?" I notice something poking my ass cheeks. Could this shoot get any worse?

"I'll fucking kill you, Gun. Get your cock away from her." Bull is slowly turning red and looks meaner than mad. All the while, I hear click, click. Oh gosh, this is going to be our cover?

"Chill bro. She aint fucking yours. Besides, her ass is fucking insane, you tell me all the damn time."

"Bull?" I can't look back to see him.

"Shut it, I got your pierced nips scratching against my arm. You're lucky I haven't spurt on you." He chuckles. "Yet!"

Then the photographer wants to twirl me so that I'm facing the boys. In an exceptionally careful move, all three arms twirl me. Now I have my tits against Bull's cock, my pussy, though covered, against Gun's cock, and my, well Trig still has my legs.

"Oh Jesus, get me though this." Gunn starts shaking while he and the guys are directed with hand placement.

I look up to Bullet staring down at me. He's so incredibly hard it hurts my boobs when his pierced man muscle is pressed against it. His eyes are unusually dark with red and brown swirls that can barely be seen beyond today's black orb.

He whispers, "Richie Rich or not, I'm gonna fucking taste ya!"

My eyes widen and I shake my head. That isn't going to happen.

This day keeps getting worse. I barely hear the photographer as he directs the trio to look a certain way or hold me in such and such position. I'm too focused on what's being held against me.

One more pose for the day. They want one of the guys cupping my tits behind me and the two guys kneeling at my feet biting my thighs, hands hugging my hips to cover my goodies there. Naturally, there's a three-minute discussion on who will get my tits again. They walk away from the area to discuss this life altering tit holding dilemma.

The photographer looks at me questioningly and I shrug, maybe it's deemed an honor? I hear some raised voices and then a head sticks out every twenty seconds and glances at me, then back to the conversation. Eventually, they come to a conclusion and head my way.

"Decision made?" All three nod, and all three look pissed. We get into the new positions with Bullet cupping my tits, yet again. His hands are simply supposed to be there for coverage and support, like a sexy tatted human bra. Harmless, right? Not in Bullet world. Nope. He slowly and casually kneads them. Then his thumb joins in on the circus act and starts a slow gentle rub of the area over my breasts. Instantly, I'm chilled with goosebumps. The boys by my legs take notice and apparently decide to join in on the Charlie tilt a whirl torture.

Gun's and Trig's arms drape over the other side of my hip, criss-crossing me to hide the bikini me. Their faces are so close to my hips and my nether region that I can feel their exhalations...there. It intensifies when they start to lick and nibble on my hips. One on each side. I grunt in response, still trying to keep my posed face, in an effort to stop these shenanigans before I implode. Instead, I'm met with smothered chuckles. All three are eating this up.

"You dirty, dirty girl, Shooter. I bet you love this. Your nips could cut glass right now." Bullet breathes behind me, sending a warm wet trail across my neck. The goosebumps continue and dominate. My every thought is fixed on the three warm bodies attached to me. Oh gosh, please speed this up. The heat from my makeup-covered face is creeping down my neck and I don't doubt it will consume me soon.

Gunner leans over to the space between my legs and inhales loudly. "Fuck, if you taste half as good as you smell, I'll gladly run away with you and make you mine." I can feel the moisture building down there. My little nude thong thingy is going to be drenched and everyone will see. Trig decides he wants a whiff too, and leans in.

"Hells yeah! I got you covered, baby girl." He glances up at me winking, and then slowly sticks his pierced tongue out and licks a trail from my hip to my navel. I'm shaking with exhaustion in trying to control my libido.

"Fuck that, I got her covered." Bull squeezes my tits and thrusts his cock against my lower back. "Don't I, baby girl?" Without a usable brain to respond with, I whimper. Throughout this entire time, I'm vaguely aware that people keep redirecting us and that pictures are being captured. My sole focus is on not combusting, and getting dressed.

Click, click, click. The shoot comes to a close. I bet today's pictures are going to look like shit, though. I can't imagine what my face looked like. Gunner climbs my leg like I'm a pole and stands across from me.

"You wanna finish this up later, baby girl?" He winks and waits for a response.

Bull, who is still cupping me, drops his hands and pushes Gunner's chest. "Fuck off, bro. We spoke about this shit." Resigned to their fighting, I quickly cover up and extricate myself from this precarious encounter. As I'm running down the hall clutching the robe to my chest, I hear them laughing behind me.

I hate boys.

We have to return for one more shoot tomorrow. The photographer promised that this one will have more clothing. That doesn't tell me much when I wore near nothing today.

After finishing the day, we head back to the hotel. I shower for about an hour trying to get all of the crap off of my face and body and unstick the pound of product from my hair. Bullet might be onto something with the shaved head.

Before bed, I text Coen. A brief 'hi, everything is good, hope you had an okay day', type of text. We are still on shaky ground and my thoughts are everywhere when it comes to him. The distance is doing me some good, though. Like I can breathe better out of Coen world, which might be all of Boston. Maybe we were never meant to be? Maybe we are? I can't wrap my head around that man.

As I lie in the dark hotel room, I try to process the day. Coen never called or texted back. I guess he didn't like that I left him the ring. I also left Malice in Boston. I have the guys here and with all of the people around us, I thought it would be too much. Plus, I think he is getting serious in his budding relationship. He keeps me in the dark but I catch him humming or smiling at random times. An obvious shift in his perpetually sour mood.

At around midnight I hear a knock. "Who's there?" I ask thinking it's probably one of the guys.

"Baby girl?" Oh yes, the guy that's hell bent on torturing me. I crack open the door and stand blocking any paths.

"Yes?" I scan him noticing that he's freshly showered and barefoot. He's wearing a tight black Deftones tee and grey sweats.

"Can't sleep." He pushes past me, pulls back the covers on my bed, and climbs in.

"Well, by all means, join me in my slumber fair gentleman of phallusville." I roll my eyes and climb in next to him. Why the men in my world have insomnia issues, I have no idea. Maybe I should look into that.

"Do you miss Richie?" Ha, they've changed Coen's name permanently.

"I guess. We slept together every night. I never thought I could do that. I never knew what it was like to have someone to come home to. Someone to hold you through the rough moments. To share your idiotic thoughts and your shit day with. Now, it seems like it's gone. It barely started." I sigh. I guess I really do miss him. "You know I punched him when I was trapped in a nightmare, and then another time I wigged out on him while we were a... playing. He deserves someone who isn't as broken as me. There are plenty of perfect little debutants out there, maybe I'm not the right woman for him. He deserves more." Thinking about this is making me want to cry. I feel the burning drippiness in my throat and nose.

"That's bullshit and you know it. He aint all that. And you, fuck, baby girl, you're you!" I snort in response.

"Thanks, Bully. I guess that means, yeah, I have no clue where you went with that!"

"You're perfect, baby girl, and if he can't fucking see that, then you let him go." He sighs loudly. "When you really love someone, you'd give anything for that person to have that happiness. You'd even set them free if you thought they needed to find a better man." He swallows audibly, and I watch his large Adam's apple bob.

"What if you lose them?" I whisper back. "What if it's the biggest mistake you'd ever make?" I sink closer to him and drop my head on his chest. I listen to his heartbeat increase as he rubs his hand over my bare arm. His hands are so calloused, scratchy, and rough. It should bother me but it never does.

"Naw, if you'd really do anything, let her find some Richie shit to buy her everything she deserves, or give her freedom to climb in a cage and come back all bloody, or even beat the shit out of some shifty eyed, bow legged, asshole rapist for laying his fucking dirty paws where they don't belong or how...."

I stiffen. What did he say? He freezes too and his heart rate triples. I've never said anything to anyone. How would he even know who, let alone where to find him? But he said that 'R' word and he was correct with the funky eye and bow leggedness. Oh my goodness, Bullet is the one that attacked him last year, isn't he?

He clears his throat and continues stroking me. "You sometimes talk in your sleep, baby," he whispers so softly I almost don't hear it.

I think back to the surveillance video I watched. It was just over a year ago when Elias Munez was attacked. Someone must have been watching him and scoping the cameras because nothing was ever recognizable. They knew exactly where he would be and when, near his place of employment. The two assailants had dark hoodies covering their faces and dark jeans. They also had gloves on.

This was a premeditated attack. I couldn't find a motive but instinctively knew it was personal. The assailants were violent and with combat boots repeatedly kicked and beat Elias. There was never a weapon drawn, and no evidence found on scene. Elias claimed to have never seen either assailant's face.

He was paralyzed that night and is confined to a wheelchair. He's alive, though. Now I'm left wondering who was with Bullet? Gunner? Trig isn't that violent? Maybe one of the BBMC members? This was several states away around Lexington, Kentucky. Not exactly right next door. This had to have been meticulously planned.

I should be disgusted. I should chastise Bullet for taking actions into his own hands. I should be appalled by such violence and lack of regard for human life. Why aren't I? Instead, I kiss his rough cheek, snuggle up, and drift peacefully into sleep. My nightmares too afraid to touch me with a big bad Bullet at my side.

Chapter 31

TODAY'S SESSION IS SCHEDULED TO be much tamer than yesterday's as in I get to actually wear clothes. My hair has been teased out and my makeup is even darker than yesterday's. But the real kicker is my outfit, a skin-tight red leather dress that hangs just below my ass. It comes with matching skin-tight tall leather red boots that pass my knees. My lips are an intense blood red, and I'm rocking spike bracelets and a choker.

I walk onto set and find the trio shirtless wearing leather pants and barefoot. Trigger's hair is spiked into a Mohawk, Gunner's is jelled to look curlier, and Bullet's, well the boy has none. The photographer sets us up; the trio is on their knees in front of me, where they totally belong, and I stand behind them. Each guy has a thick black leather dog collar connected to a leash that I have in my one hand and a long bull whip in my other. Every once in a while, the photographer or his assistants tell me to whip it or rake it over the guy's backs. I'm not hurting them but the possibility, in the name of publicity, is there.

I have to say, this is the best day ever!

After the grueling shoot, we're done for the day. Tomorrow we get to sit down with the Rolling Stone's journalist to speak about our recent fame and activities. The life of a rock star, if they only knew.

We are back at the Sirius/XM studio on Friday introducing our newest single, *'We Make No Excuse.'* This time, Octane has invited a female DJ to interview us. I guess they thought the trio would be on better behavior and I doubted she'd ask such numb-nut questions.

I tune out as always, one of the many reasons why I'm not the leader of the group. I have no patience for it. Luckily Gunner is in his element. He's chatting with the DJ and has her eating out of his hands in no time. Bullet plays video games on his cell, and Trigger chats up with the random walkabouts. On air though, we are polished. We do a live acoustic performance, which I completely loved, and then introduce the single with a short story of what it's about and how we wrote it.

But I can't seem to focus. Today, I feel off, almost itchy. Like something is going to happen and I need to be ready for it. I don't know why, though. I spoke with Malice this morning and he's doing well. Coen and I have started talking during the evening hours, but it isn't all warm and melted chocolate. Last night, he sounded distant and told me that when I get home, we have decisions to make. He thinks it's time we stop playing games and take our engagement seriously. He still hasn't asked me to marry him but he's insisting that I wear his ring. This prompted yet another argument resulting in him yelling and telling me we will deal with this upon my return.

I grab my cell to shoot Tank a quick text to see how he's doing since he's the only one I haven't touched base with, when I find that Coen has called me half a dozen times. He didn't text and never left a voice message. This has me on high alert as the chills multiply and crawl up my spine.

I quickly excuse myself and call Coen. No answer. I call the next best thing, Davis. Again no answer. Now I'm starting to worry. I access the Boston news to see if there's anything listed when I see a recent headline that catches my eye. **GREYSON COLLINS, COLLINS CORP CEO RUSHED TO HOSPITAL AFTER COLLAPSING IN BOARD ROOM.**

Oh no, Coen. I run back inside the room and explain as quickly as possible that I have to go and tell the trio to grab my stuff from the hotel. I run down the three flights of stairs and into a taxi screaming to get me to JFK airport. I call Malice and tell him to book me the next flight and to pick me up at the airport.

The rest of the ride to the airport is in silence as I mentally beat my ass for not being with Coen. He didn't want me to go to New York and I went. Now he needs me and that thought is eating me alive. I'm so jittery that I can't stop my legs from bouncing, which gets worse the second I step out of the taxi. In my haste,

I overlooked my dress. I'm in full Shooter garb at JFK on a Friday afternoon. This isn't good. I have people following me, taking pictures, when all I'm doing is trying to not scream and throw punches to get them out of my face.

After I finally make it on the plane, I check for any updates on my cell every two seconds until I have to shut my phone down. This is killing me. Poor Coen. He must be devastated and I'm not there to comfort him. And all I want to do is throw my arms around him.

I feel sweaty, fidgety, and nauseous so when the stewardess offers drinks during midflight, I gladly accept a rum and coke. I need to stop shaking and get to him. I want Coen. I need to touch him and to know he's okay.

We sluggishly disembark and I practically run once I'm off the plane. Malice is waiting for me and drives us to Beth Israel. I question him for the entire duration of the ride wondering if he has heard anything about Greyson or Coen. Apparently, the news is reporting that Greyson has had a heart attack and is currently in critical condition.

Malice pulls up to the hospital and I run straight to the information desk. "Excuse me, which room is Greyson Collins in?" I ask, gasping for air and flushing from the adrenaline build up.

"Ma'am, I'm not permitted to say. You reporters have a lot of nerve. Let the man heal in peace."

I interrupt her rant; I don't have time for this. "I'm his son's fiancée. Give me his goddamn room number before I make a mockery of this entire establishment by exposing your shitty customer service and blatant disregard for patient families to the dozen plus reporters outside," I scream and slam my hand against the ridiculous podium she looks down from.

"Well, excuse me if I...."

"There's no excusing you if you don't give me that fucking number!" I scream.

"Ms. Paz?" I turn to see Davis stalking towards me from the elevator banks.

"Oh thank god, Davis. This vile woman refused to be cooperative and give me your location. Where's Coen?" My frustrations and worry are taking over any form of human kindness today.

His face turns angry as he snarls at the annoying woman and

motions for me to follow him. "Mr. Collins has been most eager to see you. I was just on my way to make contact with your label since we've been unsuccessful in reaching you."

"I was in the air. How's Greyson? How's Coen?"

"I'm afraid neither one is doing well. I think you'll bring much relief to Mr. Collins, though. He has been quite upset these last weeks."

We ride the elevator silent, lost in our own thoughts. I have stopped the jerky fidgety mess of movements but I still can't remain subdued. I need Coen. The doors finally open and I follow Davis. I've been told that Greyson is currently in surgery.

I find Coen with his head low in his hands, resting on his knees. His tie has been loosened and I can feel the despair radiating from him.

I cautiously walk over but he doesn't seem to notice me. I softly stroke his hair while I whisper his name. "Coen? Baby?" His eyes dart up and I see the grief in them. His brilliant icy blues have dulled as if the ocean has begun its mourning. It breaks my heart. He looks relieved to see me but he isn't moving. I continue stroking his hair and lean forward to kiss his forehead. He closes his eyes and hums. I don't know what to do or how to ease his pain. Without much thought, I follow my instinct and crawl into his lap, holding him close to me. His head against my chest, my fingers in his hair, I finally begin to settle.

Slowly, I feel his hands creep around me and pull me to him. "Charlie?" he questions softly, as if he doesn't know I'm there.

"I'm so sorry, baby. I'm here and I won't let you go." I ache so much for this man. Truth be told, I'm not a Greyson Collins fan, but I'm a huge fan of Coen Collins' heart.

I continue holding him while he seems lost and empty in my arms. I keep trying to rub the warmth back into him, letting him know I'm here and that he can break while I help him rebuild. Although I do backup singing with the band, I'm not much of a singer. But now, as I surround myself with this faded version of my sweet broken man, I can't stop the tunes from coming. It starts off as *Frere Jaque*, and then moves into *Hush, Little Baby*. It makes me feel better and I hope Coen, too. Malice has since arrived, and along with Davis watches our exchange.

Coen looks up at me, his eyes still blank and lost. "Charlie, my dad died."

I brush his smooth cheek. "I'm so sorry, baby."

He arches up, indicating he wants me to kiss him and I softly and eagerly reply by pressing my lips against his. His hand slides into my hair pulling me closer to him and kissing me fervently.

When he releases me, his eyes have regained a bit of spark but they still remain lost. "Don't leave me again, love." I nod, feeling horribly guilty. All I want in this moment is in my arms.

I lean my head against his shoulder and breathe him in. My Coen. I love that smell. "I'll never leave you, my Coen." He makes a grunting noise and then picks me up bridal style.

"Babe, what are you doing?" I whisper, trying not to bother any of the other hospital visitors or staff.

"Give me this, love. I need to hold you. I won't ever let you go again." He carries me past Malice who looks at me questioningly. I give him a brief nod, indicating that I'm fine and to go ahead and leave.

Coen carries me straight through the hospital lobby and outdoors to the waiting car, but first he has to bypass the reporters. He stops and scans each face when they start shouting questions.

"Greyson Collins…" he shouts loudly and waits for everyone to quiet. "…Passed away this afternoon. I'll alert the media to any further developments in regards to the burial services. Thank you for your interest and concern for my father but I'd appreciate if my fiancée and I could have time to grieve properly. Thank you."

He carries me towards the car and sits with me still in his arms, now resting on his lap. He leans his head against my chest and I again stroke his hair, his cheek, anything I can reach from this angle which will bring him comfort. He closes his eyes and asks me to hum again. And so I do.

That night, trapped on the couch, he barely said a word as I lay in his arms. My stomach alerted me that it was past time for dinner, so he finally relented and released me with promises to return.

I heated up a large piece of Marie's lasagna, grabbed a bottle of wine and two glasses to join Coen on the couch. Placing everything on the coffee table in front of him, I try to make him comfortable. I undid his tie, unbuttoned his shirt and removed it, so he was in his white undershirt and trousers. Squatting, I untied one shoe and removed it followed by his dress sock, and then I did the same to the other side. Coen watched me, his eyes not fully connecting with mine but signs of life still evident. He was not lost to me.

"Are you hungry, baby?" I ask while climbing back onto his lap. He shakes his head and pulls me back to him. I lean over, grabbing my plate and fork a small piece, blowing on it softly before holding it to his mouth. His eyes never leaving mine, he eventually opens his mouth. I give a small thankful smile in return.

I make a silent promise to myself that I'll take care of this man. I don't know if I love him in the true sense of the word, but I love him enough to hate his pain.

We sit like that for a while. I fork a piece for myself and then a piece for him. I crack open the wine and pour it into one glass; one sip for him another for me. He never says a word but his eyes are alert and continue to examine me.

I crawl off his lap and return our used goods to the kitchen. When I come out, he's still sitting on the couch, in a blank stare. His eyes aren't as alert as when I left. I walk over. "Come baby, let's get you a bath and then bed." He doesn't nod but when I reach my hand out to his, he takes it. All good signs I think.

Although I never lost a parent, I've felt loss and I know to not give up on him. We walk up the stairs. His hold in my hand isn't resistant so I know he is present with me.

I walk him over to the deep set garden tub and turn on the water. Then I pour in some of the bath salts he had purchased for me. I don't use them usually but hope the lavender smell will have a calming effect on his thoughts. Though they aren't visible, I can feel them churning.

I squat on the ledge of the tub and take my boots off. Again, he watches in silence. Nothing but the bath filling breaks the complete stillness. My lively Coen is lost. I grab the edge of my shirt and pull it over my head. Next, I unbutton my pants and shimmy them down and off. I stand before him in just my undergarments. No reaction. I place my hands on his warm chest and glide them down to the ledge of his shirt. He is nearly a foot taller than me, so when I attempt to get it over his head, I fail and practically fall on top of him.

Normal Coen would have found that comical, but lost Coen simply takes the shirt from my hands and pulls it over himself.

Then he falls back into his lost Coen disposition, hands limp at his sides and face a blank mask. I unhook his belt and undo his slacks letting them pool to the ground. We stand in our underwear staring at each other. Although we have been naked in bed, we have never bathed or even showered together. This feels more intimate and by definition more intimidating.

I reach behind me and unhook my bra, and slowly pull the straps down, letting it fall off my breasts and to the floor. I continue to hold his eyes and track any emotion. Still none. I pull one side of my undies followed by the other, until it too pools on the ground.

I reach forward and trace the edge of his boxers with my short nails lightly scraping his warm unblemished skin. Then trail them to his hips and push the garment down and off. Though his eyes are still somewhat dismissive, he is hardening, which means he isn't completely unaffected.

I lace my fingers with his and pull him over to the tub, and we both climb in. I seat him and then scoot in behind him. He is stiff and needs coaxing to fall back into me. The emotion building in me is positively painful. I'm breaking for this man. As selfish as this feels, I need him to come alive and love me again.

Lightly washing him with a loofah, I continue my humming. His shoulders relax and tension slowly ebbs away. I can't stop myself from peppering light kisses across his neck and shoulder before me. He smells of Coen and despite this horrible mourning, the truth is, I have missed him.

"I've missed you," I whisper pressing my lips to his ear. I squeeze my legs around his waist and my arms around his chest. His hands move to mine bringing them to his heart.

"Tell me you love me…" These are his first words in several hours and they emerge broken and hoarse. He has been holding back tears. I can hear it in his voice.

I take a minute to think on this. I do love him, but I don't know if it's the same love he feels for me. Would it be lying? As I take too long to decipher my thoughts he turns to look at me over his shoulder, and the second our eyes make contact, I whisper the words, "I love you, Coen." It doesn't feel like a lie, I've fallen for him.

As soon as the words leave my lips, he closes his eyes and I watch as the first tear falls. He pulls me to him and I'm thrown onto his lap as the water spills over the tub. His head buries in my neck and I can feel his violent trembling.

"You're my only family now. I can never lose you." He tightens his hold on me as his shaking fades. With Greyson's passing, Coen is indeed the last Collins. His mother was orphaned as a young child and raised by her grandparents, which have long since passed, while Greyson, an only child as well, lost his parents several years ago. This realization further saddens me.

His wet hands tangle into my hair and pulls back hard to capture my eyes. "We'll be wed soon. I won't wait. I need you to bear my name and my future." His eyes are the darkest I've ever seen, the icy blue merely a light rim around the intensity of the blackened void. He pulls me forward so quickly that I slam into him, and my lips swell immediately with his roughness. His tongue takes, prods, and plucks against my own. "Tell me," he growls. "Tell me we will marry."

"Coen," I whisper while my hands softly stroke his chest. "You've never even asked." I lean forward and kiss his neck. I have to avoid the zeal in his eyes. He looks nearly manic. The highs and lows of the last few minutes are unsettling.

His hands still in my hair yank roughly, forcing my neck back. "This is me, telling you, that we will be married. No asking, Charlie." His jaw ticks as he grinds his molars. It takes a moment for me to understand that he wants a reaction. I slowly nod my head, which must have been what he desired since his lip quirks into a side smile. His eyes soften and he releases the tension in my hair while his hand slides down my neck and smooths the wet hair over my shoulder. Leaning forward he gently kisses my lower neck and glides his tongue up my ear.

"Mmmm, I've missed you too, love. So fucking much!" While his tongue glides up to suck under my earlobe, his hand slides down and cups my breast. "All mine, Charlie. It's time for me to take what's mine."

His teeth scrape across my neck and then latch on, sucking and biting me. His hand, which has been resting on my hip, glides across and lightly skims my navel travelling lower until he finds my clit. His thumb begins a slow circular motion while his fingers rub back and forth. I'm straddling his legs and didn't realize how close his cock is to me until I feel the head thump against me. What's happening here? Is he going to…? I start to feel the panic build. Yes, the coiling has begun to intensify but my head is reeling. The heat broadens across my cheeks and down my neck, straining for the oxygen stalled in my lungs, I see spots in my vision. How can I be orgasming and panicking at the same time?

"Coen, I can't. I can't." The shaking begins and now things are blurry with the moisture building in my eyes.

He clamps my head. "Look at me, Charlie. I love you. We're one. I need to be inside of you, to become a part of you. Focus on me. Who am I, Charlie?"

I try to focus as he said. To lock in on his eyes, to recognize the color, the shape, the way they make me feel. "My, my fiancée?"

"Good," he leers while continuing the circles on my clit and dancing with his fingers. "Keep your eyes on me. Grab my cock, love." Slowly, I slide my fingers down from where they settled on his chest and graze across his mass of curly hair. In the water everything feels lighter, different, and I force myself to stay grounded, connected in this moment. I won't let my past dictate how I navigate my future. Coen is my future and he needs me here.

My fingers gently graze his cock and skate up and down the length, testing it, familiarizing. My thumb goes around the base and I try to close my fingers but Coen is too thick to latch onto. I realize my gaze has fallen to my actions and in trying to see through the water, I look up to catch Coen watching me with a small smile.

"That's it, love. Remember, he's yours, bring him home." I swallow, my throat dry. I don't know if I can do this.

He leans forward with parted lips and sucks my top lip into his. This time the pace is slower and the heat builds hotter. The tightening is intensifying and I can feel my muscles twitch in upcoming release. "Now Charlie!" he growls into me while biting my lip.

With shaking fingers, I bring him to my opening. My thigh muscles are burning and everything feels quaky. I feel the pressure as I try to slowly bring him inside of me. My eyes have again dropped to watch his entrance, but in a moment of fear I jerk up to lock in on his eyes. I need them. I need them to bring me into the shallow waters and safeguard me.

His smile has fallen and his face looks tense. The muscles nearly as locked as my own. "You're doing great love, don't stop," he grinds out through clenched teeth. His breathing is labored and matches my uneven breaths. We might lose consciousness in this bathtub if things don't ease up soon.

His eyes in sight, the coiling still churning, with a full breath I whisper loudly, "Don't lose me."

I slam him into me and then scream. My body arches violently and my muscles lock horribly. The coiling is gone, the stormy waters evaporate. I am pain. That burning. It haunts me, rips me, tortures me. It was far worse than the ripped limbs and smashed bones. It was invasive and immoral.

"Charlie! Look at me, love. Look at me!" His hands come around me and pull me back to him. Coen? "Stay with me, Charlie. This is me, this is yours, this is us! Stay!"

I have to blink a few times to find now. I'm with Coen. I can feel him throbbing inside of me while my body burns with the stretching it's doing to accommodate him. I'm shaking and can feel the ripple travel through me. This isn't an orgasm, this is me making Coen mine, and he making me his. Mind over matter. I am stronger than this.

I lean my sweat-covered forehead against his chest. I don't want to move. I just need to find my breath. Closing my eyes, I breathe him in, and then wrap my arms around his neck.

"That's it, love." He kisses my brow. "You're doing great, Charlie. I love you so much." He grunts a few times in between, reminding me that this isn't easy for him, either.

"What do I do now?" I ask softly into his ear.

"I have to move. You feel too good, my love. Ready?" I nod and shift so that we are face to face. His hand sweeps up and glides some hair which has plastered itself to my wet cheek and neck, behind my ear. His smile is dazzling and shines brightly for me.

"You're my world. Right here, this is our future. It's the path that destiny has designed for us. You can't ever stray, love."

A soft kiss and then his hands grab my thighs and move me up. The pressure there eases but then increases when he slides back down. Up and down. Up and down. His hands move me and I don't resist. He is with me and with each cycle, the pain absconds. The water around us gets caught up in the stormy hurricane of Coen and escapes over the ledge. The sounds of grunts and gasps reverberating through the tiled marble has become the symphony.

His face is a concentrated mask while his eyes rage icy blasts. My hands lock on his shoulders as I try to find the patterns to match his drive. The heat that remained in my face and neck has slithered down and engulfed me entirely. My skin is ablaze with sensitivity and erupting from the inside out. The tension that was lost earlier has reignited and is building deep inside. Even my toes can feel the pulling begin.

Up. Down. Up. Down. The heat is immense and I find myself shaking in an entirely new way.

"Coen?" I nearly scream. This is too big; I can feel my vaginal wall soak him in. Squeeze and pulse, everything feels like it is throbbing.

"It's good, love. I've got you. I'm almost there." His hands firmly locked in place on my thighs, he leans forward. "Your tongue, love. Bring it to me."

I lean across pressing my open lips to his and entangling our tongues. His taste, his hands, his cock throbbing and slamming into me. I let go and let myself free fall into the abyss. My body again arches back while I dig my nails into his shoulders trying to hold onto him. Even with my eyes closed I can see the spots dancing behind my lids. My mind goes numb and every thought centers on the pulsing movement between my thighs. I'm hypersensitive to every hair softly scratching there. I can feel the ridge of his head as it bumps across the plains of my inner walls. Everything is tense and alive and explosive. I don't even realize that I've been screaming his name until I hear him grunting and screaming my own.

I finally understand what he meant when he said that we needed to connect on this plane. In this world, it's different. He is part of me. I am now part of him. I want this. I want this future. I want this life.

Chapter 38

I AWAKEN IN COEN'S ARMS. MY warm stiff pillow is the best the world will ever offer me. I can already feel the rigidness in my muscles. My lower body throbs reminding me what we did in the tub.

I must have woken him because I feel his soft hand rub up and down my back. "You awake, princess?" I shake my head no, which earns me a little chuckle.

He rolls us, so that I'm on my back, his hands smoothing my hair away so he has a clear view of my eyes. "Hi." He smiles brilliantly my way.

"Hi."

"We're skillful orators in the morning." Chuckling again, he grinds his heavy cock against my upper thigh and plants a sweet kiss on my lips. I can feel they are still sore from last night. I think even my scalp is tingly. Coen sexed every part of me. "You sore, love?"

I nod and whisper, "Yeah."

He climbs high up my body. His right arm shifts above my head and curls back down to caress my cheek while his left raises my chin. "What we did, Charlie." He looks down and swallows. After a moment he regains whatever thought he lost and finds my eyes. "It might not have been the way I'd planned or what I envisioned for our first time, but that doesn't change its significance. You and I, Charlie, we're imminent. Infinite. You feel this." He pulls my hand to his heart. "You're the only reason it beats. Your soul is my religion, your body my sanctuary. I can't survive without you. I won't!" He growls that last part.

My own heart stutters with his electrifying revelations. I don't even realize I've been crying until I feel him wipe away the tears.

"Sshh, love. Don't cry, my heart." He smiles and quirks his head to the side. He looks like a little puppy getting ready to cause trouble. I can't help the giggle that escapes me.

"You're a nut. You know that, right?" Scrunching up my nose to drive home my point, it only excites him further. He licks my nose while laughing. Jumping out of the bed and marching to the closet, I watch his beautiful smooth watertight butt wander away. I do enjoy watching him.

Intrigued and incredibly nosy, I follow him to see what the crazy man is up to, when I notice he is digging into one of my jewelry drawers. Spying me hovering by the doorway, he walks over and grabs my left hand.

"This is never to come off, again. You belong to me, Charlie Rose Paz." I look down as he slips the ring on. Was that the equivalent of a marriage proposal? This man does nothing normal.

I salute the boss man and begin to saunter away towards a much needed bathroom moment when he grabs me, pulling me back.

"I don't think we properly sealed the deal, love. I think you need a more thorough sample of my commitment level." He pulls me to him. My back to his front, I can clearly feel his intent.

He pushes me against the wall and my arms shoot up to stop myself from face planting.

"Coen, baby, slow down. If I wanted to be bruised up, I'd be in the Cage." I chuckle, finding my joke amusing. Apparently, he didn't because he bites my shoulder and pushes himself harder onto me.

"Not funny, Charlie. The only marks you'll ever bear are the ones I give you every day when I make you mine. This is my art, love. No one else will ever color it, again."

My heart skips and I'm suddenly bathed in serene warmth. Logically, I know that what he's saying should upset me but I want him this way. I want him to own me in these moments. I don't want to think or worry or hurt. My brain deserves a vacation and with Coen at the helm, I gladly hand it over.

He continues to devour me, to assault me in the most deliciously wicked ways. Tongue, teeth, hands, I can no longer tell what touches me, only where. When he enters me from behind, I scream, but not in fear or pain. In relief as I relish the feel of this closeness. I've never felt such connectivity. We climax together and return to this world, together.

We shower and dress and then it's time to tackle the hefty day. I call on Turner, Coen's PA to organize all of Greyson's funeral arrangements. We are going to need the funeral service and burial followed by a reception in Greyson's honor. Coen wants to wait until late next week so everyone can visit and pay their respects.

I phone my group of merry men to let them know what's going on with Coen and that I'll be out of reach until things settle. The trio isn't thrilled with me bailing in the middle of an interview but they know I don't mess around when my loved ones need me. Tank understands and says he will cancel my fight until I'm ready to move. The partners were apathetic and encouraged me to take all the time I need and to let them know if I require any assistance with my case files.

Coen refused to go into work or to leave my side. We did everything together for the remainder of the week. When I ate, he did. When I worked out in the basement, he did. When I showered, he did. I guess he was serious about the entire commitment thing.

He was in a somber mood for the most part and wanted nothing to do with any of the arrangements. When I had Turner meet us at the house to discuss the ceremony, Coen barely spoke. He remained next to me but would defer to me on everything. "Whatever you think, love?" Or, "I trust your judgment."

In the end, Turner and I coordinated everything while Coen gave the final okay. It was rather challenging to plan a funeral for someone I didn't even like. Greyson wasn't the most pleasant man, and for some reason he wasn't particularly fond of me. But I didn't do any of this for him, I did it all for Coen.

By the time Friday morning rolled around, Coen had fallen deeper into his stoic stance. His beautiful smile was lost and desolation rolled off of him in gigantic tidal waves. Dressed in complete black and with his facial hair unruly, he looked like a different person. I stood next to him, apparently my new place, in a long sleeve black sheath dress with black stockings.

Turner and I had sent out over three-hundred and fifty invitations and by the time we reached the church, every seat was filled, and many people were standing along the back. Who knew so many people were waiting to pay their respects? Coen didn't want to sit by with idle chatter, so he insisted that we be one of the last ones to arrive. As we passed each pew, I felt eyes all over me. It made my skin crawl. I didn't dare look, though. I was here for Coen.

Taking our seats alone in the front row, Coen wrapped one arm around me and held my hand with the other. The priest gave a lovely eulogy on the many accomplishments of Greyson and how he impacted our world. Afterwards, Coen had asked that a few of Greyson's friends speak. Then came Coen's turn. I was almost afraid that he would drag me up there with the way he continued to hold my hand, but finally he climbed the steps and onto the podium solo.

His calm remained as he spoke briefly of his childhood and summer vacations. How his father attempted to make up for the absence of his mother, and finally how he introduced him to the world of Collins Corp. He ended by saying that his father's legacy will live on through the next generation and how he hopes that when he and I have children, that we do Greyson proud.

The gravesite burial was somberly beautiful. A few words were exchanged and then we each took turns walking to the casket and throwing a rose onto it. Coen pulled me along commencing the rose dropping portion of the service, and then we stood to the side while everyone took part and shared their condolences with us. Many individuals I didn't recognize, while several I knew from the office or through other charitable exchanges.

Not wanting to have the reception at Coen's house, Turner and I chose to do it at The State Room. It made catering and clean up much easier and we were able to accommodate not only those attending the service but any additions, as well.

I find several Collins Corp employees and even a few from my firm, mulling around. But it is Darrien Renault who catches my eye. He's off to the left speaking with a gentleman who I'm not familiar with. Something about this deliberation has my hairs raised. I need to be a fly on that wall. I manage to slip out of Coen's grasp, with promise of a swift return, when I casually make my way over. I stop at a group nearby and vacantly join their conversation, while keeping my ear to Darrien.

He and his conversationalist are speaking in German. I suppose they thought they'd be less conspicuous this way.

Darrien*: "It's important to strike while the iron is hot, my old friend.*

His son isn't as knowledgeable nor as ruthless. It'll be an easier take over from the inside."

Strange guy who I now hate says, "What do you suggest we do, as all our funds are tied up? Are you implying a buyout? We can start with stocks and see where we go from there."

Darrien: "*Yes, I think that may be the best route. What we need is patience to see where the boy takes the company. Then we tackle the board. Careful, that's his fiancée, there."*

Strange guy, now looking around, eyes me casually. "There's a pretty thing there. Do you know this brunette? I'd like her for the night. Possibly two if she's good on her knees." He chuckles and pats his belly.

Darrien: "*That's Collins' bride, fool. You don't touch her."*

That's when I take my cue and jump in. I need to get this guy's name. Even though I've never met Darrien face to face, we have had some intense phone and skype conversations. He is, to use the term loosely, an asshole!

"Darrien, et toi?"

Darrien, is that you?

"Oui, vous devez être la belle Charlie qui a capturé le cœur de la jeune Collins. Félicitations à vous."

Yes, you must be the beautiful Charlie that has captured the heart of the younger Collins. Congratulations, he says while kissing both my cheeks.

"Merci, je l'ai eu de la chance. Et merci pour assister les services de ce matin. Vous étiez un visage accueilli dans la foule."

Thank you, I have been fortunate. And thank you for attending the services this morning. You were a welcomed face in the crowd.

"Vous parlez trop gentiment de moi. S'il vous plaît permettez-moi de vous présenter un de mes amis, Gunther Droblowski, il est mon partenaire dans plusieurs de mes activités financières et voulait être présent pour partager ses condoléances."

You speak too kindly of me. Please allow me to introduce a friend of mine, Gunther Droblowski, my partner in many of my financial endeavors and he wanted to be present to share his condolences.

I stretch my hand out to shake. After Darrien told Gunther not to touch me, I'm curious to see how well his pet follows commands. He latches onto my hand and brings it to his swarthy lips. Apparently, not well at all. He speaks to me in English with his thick German accent.

"You're quite a beautiful lady. Perhaps there's still hope to steal you from Collins, yes?" Not likely buddy. I dislodge his lips from my hand and smile sweetly.

"Oh, you're a handful, Gunther. I better get back to Coen. I just thought to thank you for your support today."

I continue smiling as I walk through the crowd and pull out the cell that has been resting in my pocket. I send Malice a quick text to find out everything he can on Gunther. He and Darrien are definitely up to something and I'm going to find out what it is.

For the remainder of the evening I'm a statue at Coen's side. He clings even tighter now that I left him. He seems to be uncomfortable with all of these people wanting to talk about the good old days with dad or when a few of Coen's college friends want to rehash their glory year stories. I fabricate some excuse about a headache and we make our exit fairly unnoticed.

That night, while we are lying in bed. I ask Coen about Darrien and if he has any concerns with him. Instead of responding with a concrete answer, he is dismissive and somewhat patronizing. Coen is an incredibly intelligent man. He ranked in the top one percent in his graduating class at Stanford for the MBA program. He can't be this naïve. Surely, he knows something is amiss, otherwise why did his father literally work himself to death?

Chapter 39

COEN REFUSES TO LEAVE THE house. He doesn't answer his calls and he even gets upset with me when I mention anything about my work. Apparently, the thought of letting me out of his sight, even now, throws him into a tailspin. I thought after we laid Greyson to rest, that Coen would ease up, but it feels as though things are worse.

When I brought up Thanksgiving being only a week away and that I usually cook and have a big feast with the guys, he shot it down flat. Instead, he said he feels like he needs to get out of Boston. I can't blame him. Losing a parent, even one you don't like, must be hard. I reluctantly agree. This, at least momentarily, makes him happy. He gets right to work making all the arrangements and tells me that he will take care of everything, that all I need to do is pack a bag. I think it's the first time he's touched a computer in two weeks; a step towards normalcy.

He's so engrossed in planning our vacation from well, our vacation, that he lets me slip away. I get to the office and attack the mounds of messages on my desk. Phone call after phone call, updating clients. I even get one from the Boys and Girls Club that I have to turn away. I can't take on any more work when I'm not in the office to do the actual work. It's so horrible. I hate neglecting my responsibilities. I'm not this person.

While I'm busy typing as fast as my little fingers can muster, I see a shadow in my periphery walk through the door. I don't have time for chit-chat. I'm trying to dig through the millions of emails patiently waiting my response. I keep going ignoring the intruder, when they clear their throat. Frustrated, I look up to find Coen.

"Hi baby, I have some work to finish. Everything okay?" I continue clicking.

"You were taking too long," he says monotonously.

"Sorry, I'm about a month behind and many of my cases are time sensitive. I'm going to be here a while longer, or maybe I can bring some of this home with me?" I don't want to push too far but he has to understand that I have responsibilities. He may shirk his own but that won't fly in my world.

"Charlie, we're leaving tomorrow for a week. What's the point of catching up? Can't you pass your files to someone else? We'll be married soon and I need you with me as my wife." Though I'm trying to ignore him, I can hear the pout in his voice. If this is what parenting is like, then I'm waiting another ten years to have kids.

That's when Tom walks by and spies Coen. I stiffen when he ambles his way into my office. "Mr. Collins, good to see you. Again, I'm so sorry for your loss." Coen stands up and the two shake hands.

"Good to see you, Tom. I'd like to return the thanks in letting me keep Charlie at home. You have no idea how vital she is to me." Coen looks back to me then winks, as if I'm supposed to be 'in' on something. Uh, oh.

"Of course." Tom looks at me nervously but I shrug in response. I have no idea where Coen is going.

"I'll need more time with her. I hope that doesn't present a problem." Coen dominates Tom. Tom's short bulky frame is nearly stifled with Coen's immense presence.

Tom flushes nervously and wipes his hands on his trousers. "Well, um, the truth is, we really do need Charlie in the office. We have many clients that specifically ask for her."

Still only a foot away from each other, Coen tsks loudly while crossing his arms over his long sleeved charcoal grey sweater. He's an intimidating man and I can't help but feel bad for poor Tom.

Sadly, I move away from the substantial amount of work still calling me, and go stand next to Coen. I rub my hand up and down his back in an attempt to comfort him and calm him down. In response to my touch, he immediately relaxes and his arms go limp by his side.

"I'll need her longer. We plan on honeymooning soon and I'm afraid that I refuse to share her. It isn't like she needs money; I assure you Tom. I plan on taking excellent care of my wife. Personally, I think the extra stress isn't necessary and that her talents would be put to better use elsewhere." He looks over at me and then kisses my brow. I'm getting upset. What is Coen getting at?

"I must say, Coen, although I'm thrilled to hear of your union I do need to know if she can't keep up with her caseloads. We'd need to find someone to replace her. Surely, a businessman such as yourself understands."

"Absolutely, thank you for understanding, Tom. We really appreciate it!" I stand there, dumbfounded.

"Charlie, we're really going to miss you but I can see you're on to bigger and brighter things." He pats my shoulder then walks out.

My eyes widen fanatically. Coen reaches over shutting the door then plants himself in front of my desk. With arms crossed above his head and his legs crossed lazily, he looks relaxed. "Hurry up, love. We still have to pack before our plane takes off tomorrow morning."

"Did you…What did you do? What the fuck did you do? Holy shit, Coen! What the fuck?" I'm getting more frantic with each word that slips through my clenched teeth. How dare he interfere in my life?

He casually stands up and walks towards me but I dodge when he tries to touch me. "Charlie, calm down. It was bound to happen sooner or later. Think about it. How could I have you representing my competitors in mergers? There would have been too much conflict of interest. You're going to be my wife, love. My wife. A Collins can't represent another company. You had to have known that."

I can't even focus right now. My entire life I've worked towards one goal…to be a lawyer! I was a freak, a weirdo, the kid who never fit in. But it was all tolerable because I knew my end goal was within reach. I knew I could make a difference. And once things happened at UF, I learned there was a different way to do things. That it is who you know and how much you have in your bank account that really makes a difference. Innocence, guilt, they are sold to the highest bidder. I was just taking a detour, and now I've been completely derailed.

The air has thinned and isn't reaching my lungs. I can't breathe. I grab my neck, trying to open the constricted airways. I reach over and nearly fall on my desk. With my hands outstretched clawing the edge, I tip my head down. Coen comes in behind me and makes wide circles on my back.

"Love, everything is fine. If it's about money, I'll cover whatever you need." My head jerks up so fast, I nearly head butt him.

"Money…you think this is about fucking money? I don't care about money!" I scream.

"Shhhh." He covers my mouth like a fucking child. I shove him away. "Love, you've got to calm down. Someone will hear you."

"I don't fucking care!"

Cupping my chin, he gazes longingly into my eyes. "Calm down, love." His thumb moves back and forth while he leans down to rest his head against mine and continues in a soothing honey dripped voice. "I've got you, calm down. If you want to work with business, you can have any division of the company you want. I don't fucking care as long as I get you to myself at the end of the day. You want to work on your pro bono cases, again, I don't fucking care, as long as I have my wife when I need her." His lips press gently to my forehead, then work their way down my nose, and finally to my lips. "I love you, Charlie. I'll give you anything you want as long as I get you in return."

His soft kisses turn more eager and I'm suddenly hoisted onto my desk with his pelvis digging into me. Since I hadn't prepared on today's work visit, I'm still in my casual clothes of leggings and a big sweater. I'm reminded of this when I can feel him easily through my thin leggings as his thick fingers glide under my sweater to cup my breast roughly. "Tell me you love me and you're not mad," he growls as he bites my neck and his coarse beard scratches against me. What was he asking me, again?

I push against him. "Coen, you can't just jump in like that and switch my life around. We spoke about this. You swore you were done with the whole manipulate Charlie thing, remember?"

He grabs his large, stiff cock and straightens his shoulders while rolling his neck. "Love, the opportunity presented itself. Obviously, it wasn't premeditated. I was just getting anxious with you not at home and I had to stop by. Speaking of, let's get going. We need to make up immediately and I know all the ways I can properly apologize."

Then, the stupid sexy beast licks his succulent lips. First the bottom, then the top, and so slowly, too. If the necking and kissing thing didn't have me soaking my panties, then that look alone would have done it. Oh, goodness me. He must notice my change of mood because he grabs my hair and pulls my neck back while getting right into my face. "Or I could fuck you on your desk. Give the office gossips something really juicy to talk about?"

His lips part and he keeps them just a millimeter away from mine. Eyes wide, moisture pooling in all the wrong and right places, I allow this man to take me to the dark side.

Right there.

On.

My.

Desk.

He apologized three times. Job be damned.

Coen flies us into Nassau, Bahamas, and then we take a short boat ride to a neighboring island. Although he doesn't own it, it's incredibly secluded. I know this because he repeatedly tells me so and suggests that I forsake all clothing for the majority of our visit.

It ended up being the oddest Thanksgiving. We took the boat into Nassau to find a grocery store with hopes of purchasing a turkey. Being an island, they eat mostly fresh seafood, so we become brave and forego tradition in order to create a new one. We end up at a little café and I try the fried grouper and grits while Coen gets more daring and tries iguana with a creole sauce and a johnnycake on the side. Coen laughs the entire time he eats it, and at one point tries to shove it down my throat. He even makes weird slithered tongue motions pretending to be the iguana. For dessert, we share a lovely fruit plate of papaya, melons, passion fruit, and mangoes and then top it off with the world's tastiest rum cake. The cake is so intensely saturated with rum that Coen and I can barely walk out of the little outdoor café straight. We nearly fall countless times due to giggle pains alone.

We end the night in each other's arms on a blanket under the vast stars by the beach…until a horrid sound hits my ears and a putrid smell hits my nose. Then Coen moans miserably and runs faster than Flash Gordon. Apparently, Coen and iguana don't see eye to eye. I roll over laughing, still high from my dessert. The thought of the iguana coming back to beat up my big guy has me laughing so relentlessly that I can't stand up, and since Coen is, indisposed of, I keep rolling until the giggles melt away and drift into the night sky.

A few days later, we board a yacht home. It wasn't a Collins' yacht, but it was astonishing. We spent most of our time wrapped in each other's arms in our room. Coen decided that my freckles served as a hidden message meant for only him to decipher. Needless to say, he spent the first day trying to decode the meaning of the freckles and moles that destiny had left for him. He quickly gave up after I dismissed the bear he claimed was hidden on my back that he swore meant I was to bear him twenty kids.

The following morning, I awoke to an empty bed. Panic immediately engulfed me and I started screaming for Coen. It wasn't until a few minutes later, after I had thrown his large ugly Hawaiian shirt on, that I noticed a white envelope attached to a white rose on the side table.

Charlie,

Even with those bugeyed glasses, you caught my attention. The first time I saw you, I knew it was too late for me. That destiny had brought me my future, and it was up to me to grab onto it with both hands and never, NEVER, let go!

A question implies that there's more than one answer and more than one solution. There isn't in our case. I cannot ask. I need you too much. This last month has proven over and over again. Destiny never offered us a choice, but I assure you if she did, it would be you a trillion times over, my heart.

Join me as we take the next step. We don't need family or friends. Just the two of us. The world is waiting for you, love, and it begins with my heart.

I have left something for you in the closet. I'm on the deck waiting my sweet love.

Destiny's gifted.

Yours,

Coen

I clamber to the closet to see what was left for me. It's a white dress. Holy shit, it's a....wedding dress. Coen wants to get married.

Like, right fucking now.

My legs give out and I'm on the floor pulling my knees up. This isn't a surprise as he has repeatedly mentioned that he wants to wed soon. I thought I had time, though. My mind is trying desperately to rationalize this, to bring sense into this chaotic storm that Coen continually produces. I spy my purse under the bed and crawl over to it. I try several times to get some cell phone reception, but in the middle of who knows where, there is none to be found and I can't call anyone.

Without a voice to connect to, I scroll through pictures of the guy's Thanksgiving dinner that Gunner sent. To say it broke my heart would be an understatement. I don't think I ever fully understood the word 'family.' Lines have been blurred so much this year that I question what the word even means anymore. But the trio is my connection and I'm not with them.

I stare at a photo of Trigger shoving mashed potatoes up Bullet's mouth and into his nose. He looks pissed, too. I can't help the smile that crosses my lips when I look at how silly my gang is.

After today, it will be different.

Feeling slightly lost, I decide to write a pretend text to Bullet, since there's no reception to fully send it. Maybe if I pretend a bit, I won't feel this overwhelming sense of doom. I probably shouldn't feel this way on my wedding day, even a surprise one.

8:17 CHARLIE: HI BULLY, I HOPE YOU AND THE BOYS HAD A FANTASTIC HOLIDAY. IT SURE LOOKED LIKE YOU DID AND THAT YOU HAD SOME PRETTY GIRLS TO FEED YOU TOO. WELL DONE! I'M SORRY I NEVER CALLED. COEN TOOK ME TO THE BAHAMAS AND WE STAYED ON ONE OF THE LITTLE WHALE CAY ISLANDS. THE PHONE RECEPTION WAS CRAP. AND NOW I'M ON A BOAT TRAVELING BACK TO BOSTON.

I ACTUALLY JUST WOKE UP AND... WELL, I GUESS I'M GETTING MARRIED. IT'S A LONG STORY, BUT HE'S WAITING FOR ME ON THE DECK AND THERE'S A PRETTY WHITE DRESS IN THE CLOSET AND YOU KNOW I NEVER WAS

THE BARBIE-TYPE OF GIRL, AND HAD NEVER PLANNED A FANCY WHITE WEDDING WITH MY DAD GIVING ME AWAY. THEY ALREADY THINK WE'RE MARRIED SO WHAT'S THE DIFFERENCE, RIGHT?

I JUST WANTED TO HEAR YOUR VOICE, BUT I CAN'T. I KNOW YOU'RE GONNA BE MAD AT ME AND I'M SORRY. I HATE THAT THOUGHT. I HATE FIGHTING WITH YOU AND THAT'S ALL WE REALLY DO ANYMORE. I KNOW THINGS WILL BE DIFFERENT. THAT THEY HAVE BEEN DIFFERENT EVER SINCE COEN'S DAD PASSED, BUT I WANT YOU TO KNOW… THAT I LOVE YOU… BECAUSE I REALLY TRULY DO.

GIVE EXTRA HUGS TO HARLEY FOR ME. XOXO

It's not until a few teardrops land on my cell while I'm busy typing that I realize that I have been crying. Coen's dad died less than four weeks ago. It will kill him if I don't go up there.

December 1st, 2015 is the new date that will change this Charlie forever. The day that I become Charlie Collins, assuming we fill out the proper documentation upon our return to Boston, otherwise, this is just ceremonial, I think.

I quickly change, twist up my hair, and add a light coat of makeup. I'm not sure how one looks for their groom on a boat with nobody around but the whales and sharks. I opt out of shoes, as there's no way I'm wearing heels on the deck while we are moving.

Hesitantly, I climb the steps one at a time until I'm greeted with the salty air. The light is so shockingly bright that I shield my eyes. Then I see him. My beloved. He stands in the middle of the deck dressed in a linen button up with matching linen pants. His hair is a mess and his beard appears to be gone.

Frozen to the spot, I stand there. As stunning as this man is, I'm terrified of what this will do to me, to us, to the trio. He must see something cross my face because his smile drops and he trots over quickly and cups my face.

"Breathtaking, love. So fucking breathtaking." His smile returns, prompting mine. "You got my note, what do you think?" I tilt my head back to look up at him.

"Coen, I, ah…"

"Look, I know this isn't a big lavish affair. We can do that later if you want. We can do anything you want. Anything. I just thought, you told your mother we got married on a yacht in route to, or in our case from, the Bahamas." He sighs and kisses me a few times on my forehead before running his nose against my cheek. "Please Charlie, I know it feels fast, but I need you. I need this." A few more kisses and he straightens up and links our fingers together.

Then we walk hand in hand to where the captain is waiting. We stand on a rug with flower petals strewn everywhere. A woman I've never seen, hands me a small bouquet of white roses. I hesitantly take them, thank her, and face Coen.

The Captain begins his speech but I get lost in Coen's icy eyes. They look clear and alive today. I can tell he's truly happy and I want that for him. I want Coen to only feel this happiness and if I'm the one to give it to him, then all the better.

His fingers reach out to skim my bare shoulder then slips down to cradle my hand. He repeats everything the Captain says while gazing into my eyes. I'm mesmerized by all I see there. As the words cross over his sumptuous lips, his eyes moisten. Then he dives into his pocket and pulls out a diamond encrusted rose gold ring to slip next to the monster diamond that he tricked me into wearing months ago. I guess this does feel like a long time coming for him.

The Captain turns to me and asks me to repeat the words. Without much thought, I do. I don't focus on the words though, just on this magnificent creature that stands before me. Committing to me. Me. He has thrown me so far out of my comfort zone that I no longer know where I left it last. He has that effect on me. He wipes at his eyes a few times but never lets me go. I think I need him to hold on, too. Then we finish and the Captain tells me to get the ring. I look wide-eyed at Coen, brows raised in question. He dives into his other pocket and hands me his ring. I study it for a moment. Twisting it, I see the inscription; 'It's too late for us…C&C.'

"It's inscribed on yours, too, my love." I nod and when the Captain tells me, I slide the ring onto my almost-husband's finger. Shortly thereafter, he pronounces us husband and wife.

I climb up on my tiptoes and angle my head as far back as I can. I feel the tears falling, but I don't bother to wipe them.

"Hi," I whisper.

"Hi," he whispers back, smiling.

"I love you."

His eyes well up. "I love you too, Charlie. So much. Thank you for becoming my wife."

"Thank you for loving me."

I crush my lips to his and he wraps his arms around my waist and picks me off of the ground. The next thing I realize, we are spinning and both of us are laughing. I kiss his sweet lips repeatedly, relishing in every crease. My husband. My fucking husband. Holy shit, I'm married!

When he finally puts me down, I notice that all of our wedding 'guests' are gone leaving only the two of us on deck.

"Where are we going? We're at sea, so it can't be far."

"Ah, Mrs. Collins, you underestimate your husband? So early in the marriage?"

He smiles while peppering me with an obscene amount of kisses as he walks us back to our room. We stop in the living room area that has been set up with champagne and food for our mini reception. We eat, we drink, and then my husband spends the next two days of our journey consummating our marriage where he whisks me away to other worlds again and again.

Chapter 40

WE ARE HOME FOR ONLY a few days when I get my first visitor. It's Monday and Coen finally decided to go into work today, though he swore it would only be a half day. As I'm currently unemployed, Coen even had Davis empty my office while we were away, I am left at home. I thought about going to my condo and bringing over some of my favorite pieces, but I'm not sure if I want us to live here or buy a new house. Maybe one closer to downtown.

I open the door to find an enraged Bullet.

"You're fucking married?" he screams before even entering the house. I'm so shocked that I find myself stepping backwards leaving the door wide open. He barges through and slams the door shut. I'm guessing he read the announcement that Coen's PR team put together publicizing our marriage.

"Is everything okay, Mrs. Collins?" Marie asks from the kitchen area. She looks concerned and has a phone in her hand.

"I'm fine, Marie, thank you. This is a friend of mine, and he's just excited." I attempt a smile.

She takes a moment to study Bullet, then her sight bounces between us until she comes to her decision and ducks back into her cooking world. I instantly turn and glare at Bullet.

"What the fuck is wrong with you? Coming into my home yelling at me? Fuck you, Bullet," I whisper yell at the psycho asshole.

"You're home? This aint your fucking home, baby girl, and you know it. What game are you playing? Richie is going to slice you open."

"Don't talk about my husband like that!" I forget to whisper and so instead I yell.

"Your husband?" Bullet looks like he got punched, and takes a step back. "So, you did do it, then? You really married him?" His voice is broken and he looks pained.

"No, no, no." I vehemently shake my head. "You don't get to do that. You wanted me to find someone. You said so yourself. Don't fucking look at me like that." I point an accusatory finger his way. How dare he! With as many times as he pushed and pulled, you'd think he'd be thrilled at the prospect.

"Oh god!" he moans while digging his back into a wall. He throws his hands on his knees and leans forward. Is he going to be sick?

"Are you okay? Bullet?" I'm afraid to get closer to him. "Bullet?" He stands rubbing his eye then chuckles darkly at nothing funny.

"Jesus, Shooter. Or is it Charlie, now? Maybe it's just Mrs. Richie, how about that? Whoever the fuck you are, whatever brainwashing shit he threw at you, maybe you remember that we were hanging out just over a month ago. Just the two of us in bed all night long together. Do you remember, baby girl? Or did that pompous preppy asshole take your memories as well as your fucking thoughts?"

"Nobody brainwashed me. Maybe people ripped my fucking soul to shreds and tossed me around like a god damn yoyo, but all Coen has ever done is love me."

He grunts. "He don't fucking love you. He's gonna change you!" He's back to screaming at me.

"You change for the people you love. It's what you fucking do!" I scream back with my fists balled up by my sides. Why is he doing this?

"Why aren't you at work, Char-leee? Did Richie make you quit your job? Oh, I know, he wants you barefoot, pregnant, and in the fucking kitchen like a good little housewife? Oh wait, he already has someone in the kitchen, so I guess that leaves you with the barefoot and pregnant part."

"Get out!" I scream. He hit a nerve and he knows it. "Get the fuck out of my house!" I'm so angry that the tears are nearly falling. My voice is cracking.

"My wife said to get the fuck out of our home!" comes booming from the entryway. I guess he just got home, and I wonder how much he heard.

"Your wife," Bullet mutters looking down and closing his eyes.

I feel a strong arm come around my waist and pull me in. Coen's scent envelopes me and begins its usual calming effect. I close my eyes and try to push out the heartbreaking look that Bullet gave me moments ago.

"Charlie..." It's broken and hoarse. "You don't have to do this, baby girl. You can…" He swallows audibly. "We can figure things out, you know."

"I'd appreciate it if you would refrain from calling *my wife* little pet names. I suggest you leave. It's obvious you've upset her, and unlike some, I don't like to see her unsettled." Coen grinds out the last part.

"Shut up, fucking Richie. I ain't talking to you. Shooter, do you hear me, baby?" I shake my head as the tears finally break free. He didn't want me, he told me time and time again.

"You're wrong. I can see your thoughts all fucked up in there. He's got you so fucking backwards. Just think for a second. Think of the band. Fuck, think of me, baby girl." His voice keeps cracking but everything is blurred behind my tears.

"I'm not going to ask you again. Leave." Just then Davis makes himself known.

"Charlie? It's not too late." With that Bullet walks to the door, opens it, and goes right through, slamming it shut behind him.

Coen pulls me into his arms and tries to console me while I try to stifle the stupid tears.

"You did great, love! I'm extremely proud of you." He kisses me and carries me upstairs. "Do you want a bath?" He's trying to comfort me, but I'm not in the mood. I shake my head while keeping my eyes closed. He lays me on the bed and crawls in with me. It's just after two o'clock, give or take, hardly bedtime, but a brief reprieve in Coen's arms feels promising right about now.

I mull over thoughts of Bullet. Our relationship has been horribly strained for so long, I'm not sure if it's anywhere close to saving. I try to focus on Coen's even breathing, hoping it will lull me to sleep and ease my troubled thoughts. But nothing is working. Thanks to Bull's impromptu visit, not only am I thinking of him but also that I need to tell Coen about the Rolling Stone's shoot. The January issue should be out now and I've been so caught up in everything Coen that I neglected to tell him what happened.

He's going to be livid depending on what photos they chose. Bullet cupped my tits for the world to see. Oh yeah, Coen is going to love that. Feeling anxious and knowing that a nap is nowhere in sight, I try to gently extricate myself from my painfully warm and clingy husband.

"What's wrong' Where are you going?" He wakes pulling me tighter to his chest.

"Can't sleep, I'm too upset."

"Do you want to talk about it?"

Hhhmm, talking about my feelings for Bullet with my husband is a bad idea! Instead, I jump up and straddle him. Rubbing my hands up and down his broad naked chest, I try to strategize.

"So baby, remember when I went to New York to pose and be interviewed for *Rolling Stones* magazine?" He nods while watching me. He's relaxed but alert. "Well, the photographer had this lavishly brazen vision as to how he wanted to showcase the band. It was quite clever, if you think about it." I continue my movements and then bend over to kiss his heart and sit back up.

"As your wife, I would have approached things differently, but as your whatever-the-hell we were, it was sort of laissez faire. We were barely speaking, and although I've been a good girl, I assure you, the images are a bit.... revealing?" I question that last part. Truth is, I haven't seen anything. I left before we got to review the final shots. I don't even know if they came out okay let alone what was used.

Coen chuckles and grabs my hands, halting them from their now frenzied movements. "Are you talking about January's edition of the *Rolling Stones* magazine where my wife is featured on the cover whipping a bunch of assholes into submission?" I nod slowly while mentally sighing in relief.

Flipping us over so I'm on my back and he's hovering above me, I yelp. "Co?" My hands are pushed above my head and he grabs them in one hand locking them there. With the other he slowly brings it down my body, stopping to knead my breast then carrying on down to my thigh, which is suddenly jerked up.

"Yes, my naughty wife," he moans while circling his hardening cock into my pelvis. "I do believe that I bought a copy today. But don't worry, I only read the article." He waggles his brow as I laugh at his goofiness. "I certainly didn't jerk off to the sexy images of any rock goddess in my office." Leaning forward he licks the side of my neck and then nibbles on my earlobe. His hand smooths across my stomach, pulling up my tank as it climbs higher back to his favored breast.

"Se-eh-xxee? You think I'm sexy?" I can barely breathe let alone speak as he assaults my body.

"So fucking sexy, love. My wife is the hottest female on this planet." He continues biting me as he grinds repeatedly into me. His boxers do nothing to hide his arousal.

"But Charlie…" He glares at me, his darkened fire storm marginally receding. "That's it, no more. The thought of any man beating off to you, to your body…" He shakes his head. "That fucking kills me. This, is mine!" He leans forward and bites my nipple through my bra. I whimper in both pain and pleasure. "And this, this is mine."

His hand dives down and glides straight into my panties cupping me and then shoving a finger inside of me. Instinctively, I arch against him and groan. Oh goodness. I can't tell if he's pleased or pissed with the magazine images. He releases my locked hands and roughly grabs my chin. "All of you is mine, Charlie Collins. Forever, you are mine, and those little friends of yours will never take you away from me."

He slams his mouth against my own. It's teeth and tongue and he's rough and relentless. It almost feels as if he's trying to prove a point. When he finally releases me, I try a thought.

"What?" I struggle to snap out of my daze but his physical onslaught carries me away. Coen wins in the end. He always seems to win.

I text Bullet several times over the next few days with no response. I hate how we left things. I hate all of this fighting and this constant up and down he's constructed. However, I do get in touch with Gunner. We meet for lunch early the following week and catch up. I know I have been MIA, but I can't figure out how to balance things. He tells me that Bullet went to spend the Christmas holiday with his family and is staying at the BBMC compound for a while. Trig's birthday is the day after Christmas, so he went back to Colorado, where he's from, to celebrate with his family.

Gunner is left here alone and when I asked if he wanted to join Coen and me, he said he already has plans. He didn't expand, leaving me curious. We left on good terms and he swore that next year will be better for the group, as after all, we have now been together for four years. Another anniversary I missed.

Later that week, I start back up at Tornadoes. Coen isn't thrilled, and though I have Malice with me, he now insists I bring Davis, as well. There's nothing like having two grown men, which stick out in their polished suits, follow me day in and day out. I feel like a toddler being watched by her parents, well, maybe gay parents.

We end up in Coen's log cabin in Aspen celebrating our first winter holiday season together and even stay to usher in the New Year. We received countless invitations to various parties, balls, and gatherings, but Coen insisted we'd be alone for our first holiday as a married couple.

It was weird being so far away from my friends. I sent gifts to Gunner to pass out to the guys, and even one or twenty for Harley. I miss that little girl. I wish I could see her, but with the way things are going with Bullet, that isn't likely to happen anytime soon.

Later that month, Coen and I get into a heated argument over Tank's next UFC fight. It's in Dublin in early February and Coen refuses to let me go. He doesn't even give a valid reason or attempt to compromise. I've never missed one of Tank's fights. It feels traitorous to do so. He's one of my best friends and it's my job to support him. I refuse to bend on this one.

The trio is going and insist that I join them. They are even talking about staying a week later to see the sites. Mainly they want to see the Guinness Storehouse, and they've never been to Ireland. I travelled to Dublin a few years ago with a company I was overseeing, but hardly left the hotel or the company's building. Plus, anytime I get to hang out with the trio these days is an added bonus.

With Joelle's baby due mid-February, Coen claims we need to be available to fly down. Why does he care? My family couldn't give a rat's ass if I'm with them during any special 'family' event. He was there, and had a first-hand account of how they view my presence. The heir and the spare. They have their child, and then they have me. Why would I want to expose myself to that malignity? Hell, they barely cared that I got married. They never bothered to send condolences when they learned of Greyson's death, they never called for any birthday, any holiday. Even my father, he's so busy placating mother that he forgets me all together. If they wanted me with them during this baby's birth, then it's only to show off. To show me that they have this perfect family and how I'm not really a part of it. Or, they want money or elaborate gifts.

For Jo's wedding, she asked me to buy her a car as her wedding gift. At first, she wanted a Mercedes Maybach, an almost two hundred-thousand-dollar car. I laughed at her. She has ridiculously extravagant taste for someone on a teacher's salary. Then she asked for something that she claimed was more reasonable, a different Mercedes sedan, the E class, which was less than half the price of her original demand. I eventually succumbed to her pestering. She is notorious at getting her way. She whined and called me daily until I gave in. Once the car was delivered, I no longer received any more calls. Nothing. Truthfully, I prefer it that way. Totally worth the sixty G's I spent.

I don't know how to get around Coen. He still insists that we sleep together every night and as we lie side by side staring at each other, he tries to talk me out of my angry funk. I tried to convince him to accompany me but he's having issues at work and is afraid to leave things, or so he says. If he can't leave town, then I can't leave town.

On fight night, I purchase the pay per view ticket and watch my guy with a bowl of popped corn, a bag of chocolate kisses, and a huge bottle of wine. Coen was out late, due to a meeting and I was left alone. I gave up being with thousands of people, including some of those most important to me, to end up sitting home, alone.

Naturally, Tank won. The man is a machine in the Octogan. Utterly phenomenal. I could get hypnotized watching his movements as he dodges and jabs. His floor work is intense; I am so jealous. At least on TV, I get to pause and watch things in slow motion over and over again. It's simply amazing. In my humble opinion, he's an artist. I can't wait to give him a huge hug and tell him how proud I am.

A week later, Jo has her baby. Mother doesn't call me, she calls Coen. He has become her favorite son-in-law and he is enjoying being gushed over. I get it, as he never really had a mother. But hello, Delilah isn't exactly mother of the year let alone mother of the minute.

It turns out that my nephew's Bris (Jewish circumcision) will be in a few days and mother insists that we will be there. Without even consulting me, Coen agrees. It's funny, he couldn't leave work for Dublin but has no problem leaving it for Orlando.

We end up in Florida and I pretend to enjoy a Valentine's themed Bris. While the mohel is snipping away, they pass out jam-filled chocolate penises. The room is decorated in pinks and reds and the entire morning is gauche and haughty.

The only saving grace is that the luncheon is catered and utterly delicious. Lox and bagels on an empty tummy is sublime. I sit with my grandparents while Coen sits with mother and Joelle. All the seats were filled when I got there and my loving husband simply gave me a dismissive hug. He later said it was improper to grab me and throw me over his lap, so what could he do? He could have sat with his wife. He knew that I never wanted to go in the first place. On top of everything, later that night in the hotel, he tells me I'm too hard on mother. That I need to open myself up to her and see that she is really trying. Trying for what?

On the flight home, I do my best to ignore him. I'm exhausted with fighting and trying to appease him. If I care about someone, he tries to push them out of my life, and if I don't care about someone, he tries to pull them in. I can't seem to get a firm grasp on his thinking.

That night, when we're finally ready for bed, I lie there facing the wall away from him.

"Not happening, love. You know exactly where you belong and where you'll stay." He picks me up and twirls me around. I land on top of him and his arms brand me to him. "You can be mad at me but you'll never deny me."

I'm pressed so tightly to him that I can't even slide my hands between us. He sighs and loosens his grip. I slip off him and land on my side. "Charlie, I know we've hit a few bumps lately, but remember, they're just bumps. We still have a long road ahead of us. Things aren't always going to be smooth but do we give up? No! Besides, I'd never let you. I'd never let that happen to us."

"You don't seem to understand me the way I thought. You pushed my friends away only to try to replace them with people who hate and hurt me. I won't be going to Orlando any time in the future. Next time you accept an invitation without my consent, you can go without me."

"Charlie..." He snaps and climbs on top of me. "I was just trying to give you what you need. I thought…"

"No, you didn't think, you assumed. Incorrectly, I might add. What I need is to be surrounded with the people who actually love me. Who actually care about my feelings and my wellbeing. I thought you were one of them. Obviously..."

"Don't you fucking go there!" he yells a millimeter away from my mouth. The spittle flies all over my face and I shut my eyes tightly. "I worship the ground you fucking walk on. I'd do anything to…" My eyes slam open.

"No, you wouldn't. You refused to let me go to Dublin and you threw this entire family shit show down my fucking throat when I was dead set against it. How the fuck is that giving *me* what I want? How?" I scream the last words and try to buck him off of me. He's so much heavier that all I do is hurt my back and tire myself out. He stays silent until I cease all movements and lie there like a weak wet noodle.

"Are you finished?" I close my eyes and turn my head away from him. I'm shutting this man out, even if he's squishing me with his gigantic man weight. "Shit. Charlie…look at me, love." I pinch my face even tighter. If I could cover my ears and hum 'Mary had a Little Lamb' right now, I totally would.

He leans forward and whispers that he's sorry. Blazing kisses burn a trail up my neck. "I love you. I didn't mean to upset you. No more Florida, I promise. I won't talk with your mother anymore if it upsets you. You're my priority, love. Always."

My eyes slowly open. With them closed, his touches are severely amplified and I can feel the slow simmering in my veins. "And the trio?"

He shakes his head. "There's no way in hell I would have felt comfortable with you going halfway across the world without me. Do I regret my decision? No fucking way!" He bites my top lip and molests my mouth. "I won't let them take you. You belong to me, Charlie! Me! I take precedence. Do I need to remind you how I love you? How you belong to me?"

I want to shout out 'No' but with Coen the answers seem to always be 'Yes.'

Chapter 41

FUCK! I FEEL LIKE SHIT. I squeeze my eyes tight trying to ward off the next wave of nausea. I've been standing either across the toilet or over it for the last forty minutes. Coen and I are scheduled to be at the Cardiac Health Research event for the hospital in less than an hour. I had spent the entire afternoon getting my hair and makeup professionally done. Then…bam, my guts feel like they're literally spilling all over. I sniffle and wipe my eyes with a clean piece of toilet paper.

I must have eaten something bad at lunch. Coen is slated to be one of the speakers tonight, and he can't miss this. We donated one and a half million dollars to further cardiac research in honor of Greyson. Coen thought it would be a great way to raise awareness for the hospital and get other donors to contribute handsomely. I thought it was a great idea and even volunteered with organizing tonight's event. But at this rate, I'll never see it.

"Love, you feeling any better?" He brings me a cold bottle of water and some pain medication. I gently shake my head. "Maybe try some medicine?" he replies. He runs a washcloth under water and places it behind my neck. It feels heavenly and I sigh with relief then down the meds.

"Better?" He smiles, his perfect white teeth on full display. He looks stunning in his tux, minus the jacket. I touch his chest and savor the warmth there. Closing my eyes, I take a deep breath. I don't want to miss this. Get it together, Charlie!

I feel his lips press against my forehead. "You're a little warm, love. Please don't push yourself." I nod and concede. He's right. I'm an absolute mess. I look up at him. He's polished tonight. Perfect shave, hair locked into gel hell. Sigh.

"I wanted to be there with you," I pout. There's nothing worse than feeling like shit, as it brings out my inner whininess. He bites his lip while he ponders things.

"Maybe I can call Jameson to take my spot. They don't need me, just my name." He watches as I shake my head. Lips pursed, eyes narrow, I'm determined to make this man do good in this world. "Don't look at me like that. I can't leave you like this."

I push at his chest and walk to the bedroom while clutching my unsettled stomach. Sitting on the edge, I remove my delectable Prada heels and carefully climb into bed. "See, baby. I'll be fine. I'll probably fall asleep the second you walk out of the door and stay that way all night." I feign a smile while closing my eyes. See, all better. When really I feel like I might puke at any second.

He sits next to me and I feel the heat of his hand caressing my moistened, overheated skin. "I don't like this, love. Maybe I should call Malice or have Davis watch you."

"No, go! If you wait too long, you'll be late. Go! Wow those billionaires and make me proud."

He chuckles and leans over pressing his head against my temple. "You're such a handful, you know that, love?" He kisses me a few times, procrastinating his departure.

"Baby, if you delay any longer you'll be late."

"Fuck..." He's still resting against me. "Can't we just make out and be sick together. Then I won't have to go either." He smiles brightly when he catches me opening my eyes.

"Babe, I swear, I'll be fine. I promise to text you if I feel even the slightest bit worse. Promise."

"You're a terrible liar, love." He chuckles some more and then groans. "Okay, okay, okay. I'm going." He presses one last kiss against my forehead, and then stands. "I shall do your evil bidding, Mrs. Collins." He grabs the jacket that's been by the foot of the bed and throws it over his arm. "I'll come home as soon as my speech is given. I love you, Charlie Collins." He stares, waiting for me to return the sentiment.

"And I you, my darling husband."

"Sleep, my love. I'll be home and have you in my arms in no time." He snaps the lamp light off and cracks the bathroom door closed, so I'm still bathed in that sliver of light. He blows me one more kiss before walking through the open door.

My stomach still feels restless, but I'm starting to feel better. I scroll through images of Coen. He has been a part of my life for nearly a year now. I could barely stand him when we met and now I adore him. I probably wouldn't know how to breathe without him.

After another twenty minutes, I start to feel myself again. I sit up and drink more of the water that Coen left by the bed. I feel the chill it leaves in my empty stomach. I test things out by sitting up. No dizziness, which is a good sign. I walk to the bathroom and brace myself for what my reflection will reveal. Yep, raccoon eyes. Ughh. How that man did not run away screaming, I'll never know? He must truly like me. I sit at my vanity and start to clean myself up. There isn't a whole lot. My hair is still nicely in place, although I have to smooth some strands back.

Hmm. I think I can do this. I check the time and see that the party has only just begun. Cocktails will be served for at least the first hour. If I hurry, I can still make it in time for Coen's speech.

Excited by this new prospect, I quickly redress and I'm out of the door in no time. Davis drove Coen tonight and since I don't have time to wait for a taxi or Malice, I climb into my Audi. It takes me roughly thirty minutes to reach the hotel, but I make it with plenty of time to spare.

I quickly make my way through the entry way and into the ballroom and then freeze. Shit, I'm too short. There are men in tuxes everywhere, and at least two hundred guests in attendance. There's no way I'll find him like this. I walk to the edge of the room and snatch my cell from my clutch. He said to text if I needed him, so I'm hoping he has his phone close. As I'm about to dial, I spot him…being pulled by a woman.

Who's that? I watch as they make their way out of the door and into the hotel hallway, and I quickly follow. She's quite tall and thin from behind, and it looks as though he is trailing her as she pulls him along. What's he doing? He has a speech in fifteen minutes. With their long legs, I quickly lose them in the darkened hallway. Across the way are the bathrooms, so I begin to head in when I hear a bump behind me. I notice a sliver of light appear under the closed door and hear more bumping.

"What are you doing, Mandy?" More thumping and a loud bang. "You're so tense, Co-Co. I'm just trying to relax you, baby."

"Cut it out, I'm married now." Then another loud thump.

Oh my god, what's happening? I feel like I'm about to pass out when I notice the cell in my hand. Without much thought, I hit video and record. This can't be real. It must be my imagination. He would never do this. We've only been married for a few months. He loves me. He will stop her, I know it. I clutch my stomach and try to stop the new rolls of nausea creeping through me.

"Oh, I bet your cold bitch of a wife couldn't suck you off for shit. I know exactly how you like it, remember baby?"

I hear some noise and a zipper. Oh fuck. I whimper, then remembering where I am, slap my hand over my mouth. The other hand shakes while recording the door.

"Fuck you, Mandy. Get off, oh fuck...that feels good. Shit. You need to…oh god, don't stop." I hear slurping noises. I keep the hand pressed against my mouth and bite down on it to stop any additional whimpers from escaping.

"I know how to treat you, baby. Just sit back and enjoy. I'll make you cum so good, baby." Then more sucking and I swear I hear that son of a bitch moan. He likes this? He wants this?

"Fuck, this is, this is…oh, fuck, so good. Shit!" I stand there, like the fucking fool that I am and listen until he finishes. I hear every groan and moan while my heart stops beating all together and I die what must be the slowest death in history. My entire body has broken out in sweat and I stand there shaking and nearly convulsing. How could he?

"Oh god, Charlie. Oh god." I look around to see if he sees me. No, I'm the only fool in this hallway. The rest of the world moves on. The rest of the world is living as my life comes to an abrupt ending. I never stood a chance.

"You taste fantastic, Co-Co. Want to fuck me, now?"

"No, you fucking whore. Get away from me. My wife…she's going to. Oh, Jesus. What have you done to me?"

With that, I walk away and quickly shut off my phone, shoving it back into my clutch. They will be emerging from that closet any moment now. I try to gather myself as I go and not wilt into the ground. This is the second time in my life that I've really felt the sting of betrayal. The last time, I died. This time, it's a thousand times worse.

As I walk towards the hotel lobby, I see Davis standing with his hands interlaced in front of him. He clearly sees me and looks concerned. As he's about to step in my direction, I shake my head and put my finger to my lips. I know he owes me nothing, but I hope he knows better than to be a gossip. His eyebrows furrow and he steps back into place, neither affirming nor denying my request for his silence. Oh well. What the fuck do I care at this point? Nothing.

I drive home in a daze. I undress and climb into the hot shower. Maybe, I can wash it all away. My hair wet, makeup off, I throw on a huge sweatshirt and sweatpants and climb into bed. Despite the warmth of the clothing and hot shower, I'm freezing and I can't stop shaking. Even my teeth are chattering. But I know that no amount of covering will warm me. I'm cold because Coen Collins has killed my soul. I'm dead inside, so how will I ever find warmth again? I won't.

I grab my cell, which is next to the bed and press play on the video. I'm questioning reality and need to know if this is really happening. But, it is him. My husband. My love. The man I gave everything to and gave up everything for. I'm such a fool. I thought I had left the stupid girl behind me at UF, but I didn't. I guess I just covered her up with muscles and music. Stupid, stupid, fool.

I put down the phone and try to think of what to do next. I have no real job. I barely have my friends. I still have my condo but I'm married. It's different. What can I do?

I hear the door to the garage close. Coen is here, and my heart beat triples. In a split second decision, I decide to wait and see what he does. Will he tell me? Would that make it forgivable? I resolve to feign sleep for the interim.

He walks into the room and stops by my side of the bed, but keeps his distance. I can tell by his body heat and scent that he isn't terribly close. He watches me another few seconds, then goes straight to the shower. He's in there at least twenty minutes and I swear I hear him crying at one point. But it's hard to tell, even with my ear to the door.

He eventually comes out and climbs into bed behind me, spooning me. I feel his warm bare arm wrap around my waist and pull me tightly to him. He's shaking. He kisses the back of my head and whispers. "I can't lose you. It'll fucking kill me." He buries his face in my hair and continues his quiet whimpers and cries. He apologizes repeatedly, all in hushed tones, still thinking I'm asleep.

"I love you, Charlie. More than my own life. Please know that, love." He kisses my ear and then settles himself.

I feel a few more hiccups of after-tears behind me and then his breathing evens out. Soon after, I gather he isn't going to tell me. I'll never be able to trust Coen again. That the love I felt for him has been cheapened, dirtied. I realize I have to find a way out and that the countdown has begun. Let's see how good my acting skills are.

I awake alone to a sunny Saturday morning. Why the sun is up and how the Earth continues to rotate, I have no clue. Don't they know what happened last night? I need out. I dress and head downstairs. My stomach is still feeling off, but nothing feels as off as my heart right now. My heart wins.

I find Coen in the kitchen, wearing low slung sweats and no top. My mouth immediately waters for a taste and then my brain kicks in and chastises me.

"Morning, love. How are you feeling today? Any better?"

I try to fake a smile. "Yeah, it must have been a twelve-hour thing."

"I made some breakfast. I was going to bring it up to you in bed, but you're up. Why are you dressed?"

"I'm gonna hit Tornadoes." This is the part where he would usually put up a fight.

"Oh, okay. I guess you really are feeling better. Do you want something to eat before you go? I made a veggie omelet, just the way you like, and an English muffin." He's sweetly smiling, but it looks like he isn't readily meeting my eyes.

"No." I croak. "Maybe some water, then I'm off."

"Sure, anything you want, love." He reaches into the fridge to grab a bottle then holds it out to me. I reach forward and he pulls it back. "Do I get my morning kiss?"

I lean forward and wrap my arms around his middle and place my nose over his heart. His stupid cruel heart. I hate this fucking heart. I hate that I can breathe him in and it brings me peace and warmth and I want to drown in it. I hate myself so much right now. Just two more minutes. Keep it together, two more minutes.

"I love you so much, Charlie Collins. So fucking much. You know that right?" His voice cracks slightly but he tries to cover it with a laugh. Yes, laugh at the stupid girl. It's all so fucking funny. I nod my little lying head and kiss his deceitful heart.

"Give me my lips." He pulls my ponytail back and it snaps my head. Then he lays his soft beautifully perfect lips against my own. I hate his lips. He kisses me painfully soft and lets it go on past its expiration. Closing his eyes, he whispers. "Hurry home to me, my heart." I nod and then grab my stuff and walk away.

I run to the car and hightail it out of there. Walking into Tornadoes, I hope the smell will wash away Coen's. I want to get in the cage, I want to run, but instead, I climb up to Tank's office and plop myself on the beat-up plaid couch, resting my head on the arm rest. I let the sounds carry me away and hope that today will be over soon. I ache everywhere. I couldn't possibly exercise. I don't even know why I'm here.

"Baby?" I look up to see Tank crouched down in front of me. When did he get here? "Charlie, ya ok?"

"No..."

"Ya feeling sick or something? Ya look wicked pale, babe. I called your name like three times, where were ya?"

I shrug. "Coen cheated on me last night." Boom. It's alive now. I can't believe I said that.

Tank nods slowly. "What do ya wanna do?"

"Dunno?" His thumb strokes my cheekbone.

"Oh baby, I'm so sorry." He puts his head to mine. "Ya want me to take ya somewhere or call someone to getcha? Gunner, Bull?"

I shake my head. Why? So they can tell me 'I told you so?' No, thank you. This is so embarrassing. I feel like the biggest fool, why the fuck would I want to share that?

"Malice?"

"No, I can..." I swallow, my throat is so dry today. "I can call him, later."

He climbs onto the couch and holds me next to him. I try to find his warmth and allow it to penetrate this icy chill, but it doesn't. He gets a knock on his door sometime later and needs to go downstairs. He asks once more if there's anything he can do. After convincing him that I'm fine, he kisses my head then excuses himself.

I take a moment to gather my thoughts and call Malice. I tell him what happened and mail him a digital copy of my recording. At first, he thought I misheard, but after he listened to everything himself, he swears death. I don't want that; I just want to survive the Coen Collins aftermath. If it's possible. I tell him what has to be done and he swears that everything will be in order.

After our conversation, I sit and stare at the paint chipping near the ceiling for almost an hour. Then decide that I need to return. See what I can get out of the man who swore to love me forever. The greatest liar the world has ever known.

When I walk in, he's waiting for me. "How was your workout?" I nod. I'm so tired. This stress is eating me alive. "I made some lunch if you're hungry."

"Sure."

"Perfect. I was hoping you'd feel better, so I ran out to that deli you like and got your favorite."

We eat in silence, clean up, and then make our way to the couch. "How about a RomCom?" Hell to the no!

"No, not in the mood. Maybe just some Food Network action?"

He scoots towards me and pulls me to him. We sit for a couple of hours staring blankly at the screen, each clearly lost in our own thoughts. I decide I want answers, so I straddle him and make close eye contact. I rub my hands over his gorgeous bronzed shoulders. I hate these things.

"I forgot to ask how last night went. How was your speech?" I smile, letting him think I'm clueless.

"Good, the people were extremely receptive and we made quite a dent."

"Wonderful. Did anything exciting happen?"

He shakes his head and diverts his eyes. "Nope, same old, same old." He pinches the bridge of his nose a couple of times. He's lying and he missed a perfectly good opening to tell me.

Suddenly, my head feels incredibly heavy, like gravity has taken a hold, and I rest it on his shoulder. Please don't lose it. Hold it together. He rubs my back as I try to stop myself from physically harming him. "I missed you so much. I should have stayed home with you." Liar! Liar! Liar! The dizziness begins and I moan. "You okay, love? Maybe you need a doctor?"

"No, I'm fine. Probably just pushed myself too much. Maybe a bath will do me some good."

"Okay, love. You want me to draw it for you?"

"I'm fine." I try to scoot off of him but he grabs me and leans in for a kiss. I pull back and he freezes up as his eyes widen.

"Charlie?"

"I'm sorry, baby. What if I'm sick? I don't want you to catch it."

"Fuck that! You're my wife." His voice cracks at that last word. He's having trouble with it too. "I'd rather kiss you and be horribly ill than never kiss you again and live to be one thousand. Give me my lips, love." This time when he leans in, I take it. I close my eyes and relish this moment. It's killing me, but who knows how many more kisses will be left for me? I shouldn't have any as it is.

I run upstairs and marinate in the bath for far too long letting the tears drip down. They are silent. My life is already gone; this is just saying goodbye. I slip my head underwater to see if things will improve from this vantage point. Maybe a solution will appear. Instead, a hand dives in and pulls me out.

"What the fuck were you doing, Charlie? Oh god, you scared the shit out of me." He grabs his chest and sits in the water puddled on the floor. He puts his head on his knee and I watch him breathing deeply.

"Coen, I was wetting my hair to wash. What the hell is wrong with you today?"

He gives his head a good shake. "Jesus, you're right. I'm so sorry, love. I just walked in and you were under, and I freaked. I'm sorry. Do you want some company?"

"No, I'm fine. I'll be out shortly. Guess I lost track of time."

I finish up and Coen goes into his office. For the rest of the day, we both walk on eggshells. This is torture. By the time we're in bed, I'm thoroughly wiped. This acting stuff is exhausting! And I'm pretty sure I suck at it.

"I was thinking that maybe we could buy a new house. What do you think?"

"Yeah, that'd be great." NO! No it would be terrible!

"Yeah? How about I schedule some time with a realtor this week. We can search for something or we can build if you'd like. We could get a huge kitchen and a professional gym set up in the basement. I'll make sure we get a huge one. Oh, and if we buy a place with a large amount of property, we could even build a small home for Malice. I know how you hate him being so far from you. Would you like that?" Yes, please stab me then twist the fucking knife some more.

"That would be wonderful, Coen. Thank you!" I've been asking about a new home for the last month, but now…yeah!

"I'd do anything to make you happy, Charlie. You know that. Anything, just say the word."

"Thank you, Coen. You're too good to me." You lying, cheating man.

I fall asleep in his arms. And then I wake in his arms; the arms that once symbolized love and happiness. He touched her with those arms. He broke my heart with those arms. I hate those arms.

Sunday is as uncomfortable as Saturday was. And it ends nearly the same way, only this time Coen wants to take me on vacation… again. In another week plus, we would have been in each other's lives for a full year. He wants to celebrate. I want to die.

It's Monday morning and we're dressing for work. I am going into CC this morning to address the legal department and check on things. He loves it when we go in together.

"You have a busy day today?" he asks while shaving, and gliding the razor in slow fluid strokes. I get lost in the movement. He's so glorious. These will undoubtedly be the moments I miss. The details. "Charlie?"

"Oh, yeah. Sorry. I have to check in with legal then I'm off to see Juanita." He smirks and steps towards me, his face still a quarter covered with shaving cream. He's only in his trousers and I love his smooth flawless skin. I used to think he was too perfect for me, but now I know better.

"You see something you like, Mrs. Collins? It's yours. You can have this whenever you want." I hold in a whimper. He's so cruel. If it was mine, then how dare he give it away?

I swallow and bite back the tears. Stupid foolish girl to believe any of his lies. I smile politely. "I have to finish getting ready, baby. You know once we start…"

"I don't care if we're late. I know the boss." He smirks and bends down to kiss me. He grabs hold of my bottom lip with his teeth and tugs me into him. Then opens wider and weaves his tongue next to my own. He moans and I freeze. The last time I heard that moan…

"Coen, I'm still not feeling so great." I clutch my stomach, this morning's breakfast threatening a return appearance.

"If you're not better by tomorrow, we're calling the doctor. I'm not joking, Charlie. I'm getting worried."

I nod. He doesn't need to worry about me. I won't be his problem for much longer. We drive to the office separately and I busy myself with my tasks. I have a full plate this morning and a timeline to hold. After the legal team debriefing, I gather my things and head to Coen's office to have him sign off on all the needed paperwork.

His door is cracked open and when I push it, I find Coen hunched over his desk, his head in his hands. He looks miserable. My nonexistent heart aches for him. We could have ended differently. But he chose this. He chose to cheat on me. He chose to hurt me. He chose to hurt us both.

"Hey baby, can I get your John Hancock on these?" He jerks up when he hears my voice and wipes at his eyes. "Everything okay, babe?" I wander closer clutching the papers firmly to my chest.

"Yeah, yeah. Come here. You're exactly what I need."

He reaches his arms out to me and when I get closer he pulls me onto his lap. I put the papers on his desk and rest my arms around his neck. He smells so good that I take a moment to inhale his rich scent. It was my favorite smell once. I brush some hair behind his ear. It's getting long and he'll need a cut soon. My fingers continue tracing his ear, down his neck to the collar, then back up over his lips and nose and across his icy storming eyes. I love those eyes.

"I love you." I confess, while desperately trying to keep the tears at bay. This might be the last time I tell him. I did my part. I loved him. I tried my hardest. I changed. It just wasn't enough.

I wasn't enough.

He fists my hair and clenches his jaw. "I love you, Charlie. More than words will ever spell, more than any language can ever define." Again, he slams his mouth to mine, his fevered kisses frenzied and manic. He's losing his grip. He skims his lips down my neck and then bites my ear. Sucking and nibbling he molests my innocent ear with his lascivious tongue.

With my neck still hyper-extended, he has his way without much resistance. "Mine," he chants softly over and over again. It's building into a mantra of sorts and I can feel him beneath me hardening. "I can't ever lose you," he murmurs into my neck as his hand roughly grabs my breast. "Forever." He keeps voicing his random thoughts.

"Coen…baby, I have to be at the courthouse soon." I rake my fingers across his hair and down his neck. I kiss him softly a few more times. "I still need your signature, my love. Then I have to return everything to legal." I kiss him again, a distraction.

"Of course, whew. I got carried away there for a minute. We'll finish this at home." I watch his flushed cheeks return to their normal shade and his eyes gain focus. I smile and grab a pen.

"Here, boss man. Now go ahead and sign your life away, but hurry up before you make me late." I giggle. I'm so funny. Not!

He reaches across me and signs at all of the lines I point to as we go from page to page to page. Once we hit the last page, he throws the pen on the table and twirls my hair around with his fingers.

"When will you be home?"

"Oh gosh, that's hard to say. I guess it depends on how the day goes."

I stand and collect the papers, shoving them back into their file. I lean my knee on the chair between Coen's legs and stare down at the man who wrecked my heart. The man who I promised my every future step to. My fingers crawl all over his face, smoothing out the creases in his forehead and the little crinkles around his eyes. I memorize his eyebrows and the little bump on the bridge of his nose. I carefully study his ear and how the skin connects to his neck. I soak all of this in and let it infuse me and pray that it will be enough to get me through. Because, right now, I don't know if I can do this.

I allow myself to share those forbidden words one last time. "Coen Collins, I love you. I always will." I say them with more determination. I want him to know that at one point, he had me. All of me.

"And I love you Charlie Collins. More than life itself. Hurry home to me, love." I nod and smile back. I kiss him one last long hard kiss. A goodbye kiss. A real one this time. I avoid eye contact when we pull away and wave at him over my shoulder when I walk through his door.

Walking across the hall to my office and quietly closing the door I lean against it. Oh god. I did it. I close my eyes and try to center myself. What's next?

"Vous n'êtes pas obligé de le faire, vous savez."

You don't have to do this, you know.

I open my eyes to see Malice sitting in my desk chair.

"Que proposez-vous -je faire? Pardonne et oublie?"

What do you suggest I do? Forgive and forget?

"Il va le tuer."

It'll kill him.

"Et moi dans tout ça? Comment suis-je de survivre après cela? Je ne fais rien ... il l'a fait!"

And what about me? How am I supposed to survive after this? I didn't do anything…he did!

"Je pense juste que vous avez besoin de plus de temps pour réfléchir. Vous êtes trop impulsif."

I think you need more time to think things through. You're being too impulsive.

"Bonne chose que je ne donne pas une merde en ce moment. Tout est-il pris en charge?"

Good thing I don't give a shit right now. Is everything taken care of?

"Oui."

Yes.

"Tout comme je demandé?"

Just like I asked?

He nods numbly in response.

I walk to my desk, go through the paperwork Coen just signed, and take out the one I need. I pull apart the duplicate and fold it into thirds, handing it to Malice. Then I hold out my hand and Malice places a black velvet box in it. I open it and then stare at my left hand, which holds the two rings that I swore to Coen I would never take off. I continue to stare at it then bring my right hand up to try to remove it, but I can't as it hurts so much. I try to focus on the way he sounded when he let that traitorous woman touch him. I try to hold onto that anger and let it fuel me, but I'm sinking.

"Enlever."

Take it off. I hold my hand out to Malice.

"Non, si vous ne pouvez même pas prendre les anneaux hors tension, puis comment pouvez-vous le laisser?"

No, if you can't even take the rings off, then how can you possibly leave him?

I shake my hands out to the side and bounce on my toes to loosen myself up. I've been in the cage against scarier opponents, so this ring is nothing. I pull on my ring finger and I can't. Shit. Look at me, now. I'm a fucking weakling. Malice is staring at me, pursed lips, nostrils flaring. I have to do this.

Finally, with shaky hands, I try again. This time I get a firm grip on the rings and yank as hard as I can. They slide off and I throw them at Malice as if they were poisonous. He shakes his head in disappointment and places them in the ring box that I left waiting on my desk.

Frustrated, I grab my belongings and take one last final look at the space. I haven't been here long, so there aren't many memories. But it represented my future with Coen. Something else I have to say goodbye to.

I leave the office and head to Malice's condo. I let myself in and see he has the computer monitor all set up, waiting for me. The truth is, I'm a cold hearted bitch. Coen had me all muddled with thoughts of love and happily ever afters.

I text Malice to let him know I'm at his place then I turn the monitor on and click a few buttons. I get to see everything. Like I said, I'm heartless.

The display is a little grainy and the movement jerky, but today, I'm a fly on the wall or more precisely on Malice's lapel.

He knocks.

"Come in," is heard after some shuffling.

"Malice, comment allez-vous? Tout va bien? Charlie, est-elle d'accord?"

Malice, how are you? Is everything okay? Charlie, is she okay?

"Oui, elle m'a demandé d'apporter quelques cadeaux pour vous."

Yes, she has asked me to deliver some gifts for you.

"Cadeaux?"

Gifts?

"Oui, elle a dit que vous agissiez étrange et qu'elle voulait faire quelque chose pour vous. Voici la première"

Yes, she said that you were acting strange and she wanted to do something for you. Here is the first.

Malice reaches into his pocket and pulls out the first wrapped box. It's small and has a sweet red bow on the top. He places it on the desk.

Coen reaches over and pulls off the lid. He looks inside with questioning eyes and then grabs the USB flash drive.

"Il est une vidéo pour vous de regarder. Branchez-le sur votre ordinateur."

It's a video for you to watch. Plug into your computer.

"Que faire si il est racé? Elle pourrait ne pas vouloir que vous le voyiez."

What if it's racy? She might not want you to see it. He smiles devilishly. You wish.

"Elle approuve."

She approves.

Coen hesitantly plugs it into his computer. He has to click on a few boxes and then the image appears. A door. He looks confused.

"Augmente le volume."

Turn up the volume. Malice demands.

"Oh, I bet your cold bitch of a wife couldn't suck you off for shit. I know exactly how you like it, remember baby?"

Coen's eyes go wide when he recognizes that voice. He shakes his head. "No!" He yells at no one. The video continues and he clutches his hair.

"What is this? Where did you get this?" He screams at Malice and walks over to him. Malice is quiet. I can make out Coen's face more clearly from this distance. His eyes are red rimmed and he is shaking. "She was there?"

You can hear the groaning and moaning.

"Fuck, this is, this is…oh, fuck, so good. Shit!"

"Oh god. She was there. She heard this." He leans over and clutches his stomach. "Oh god."

Then you hear those horrid slurping noises followed by my own whimpering. Coen looks over to the video and sees it shaking, and hears my labored breathing and sniffles. He puts his hand on the screen and starts crying. "Charlie. Oh god, baby, I'm so sorry."

He wipes his eyes and turns the computer off. Before he has had a chance to turn around, he sees the new gift that Malice just dropped on the desk.

"Not another one. I can't take it."

"Elle veut que vous l'avez."

She wants you to have it.

He timidly reaches forward and pulls the lid off, revealing the black velvet box underneath. He looks up at Malice. And essentially at me. Then he places the ring box on the desk and carefully opens the lid.

He starts screaming, I hear the pain ripping from each syllable. "NOOOO. NOOO," he wails over and over as tears stream down his face. "NOOO, she's my wife. I won't let her go. Noooo! Charlie!" He's screaming and sobbing. He lays his head on the desk and continues bawling. It comes from deep within.

But I'm a horrible cruel person and I'm not done.

I hear Malice pull out the folded piece of paper and walk over to Coen who looks up with tears streaming down his face. He tries to wipe it away with the back of his hand.

"I won't let her go. I know I fucked up. But I'll never let her go. She's my wife. My everything."

"Non, elle est pas."

No, she isn't.

He puts the paper down and Coen quickly snatches it up. His moist eyes scan the document and then he starts shaking. His hands cover his face and the horrible sobs continue. This time with no hope in them.

I gave him back the last piece that he gifted me. His name. This morning I had him sign the annulment papers I drew up. I don't want his money or his company, only freedom from him.

I'm just Charlie now…good old Charlie Paz.

Coen will go home to find that all of my belongings have been removed. And when he tries to enter my condo, he will find a new family living there. I have effectively eradicated myself entirely from his life. Or vice versa. The old saying rings true, hell hath no fury like a woman scorned.

Chapter 42

"HHELLO?"

"Shooter girl, you wanna tell me why Richie came to my shop starting shit?"

"Bully?"

"Baby girl, what the fuck is goin' on?" He's growling.

"I, I, uh, I don't know."

"What's wrong? You seem off."

"I'm sort of having a bad week."

"Where are you?"

"At home."

"With Richie?"

"No."

"At your condo?"

"No."

"Charlie... Where. The. Fuck. Are. You?"

I give him the address to my new place then hear some muffling over the phone. "Lyle, Lyle, get the fuck over here."

"Charlie, listen to me baby girl. Don't move, okay? I'm on my way. When I get there, I need you to answer the door, okay?"

I nod.

"Charlie, I need to hear you say it."

"Okay. I'll answer the door."

"Good girl. I'm on my way."

He hangs up and I continue staring at the devastation in my hand. I'm stuck on the ledge of my tub with this atrocious stick in between my fingers. This can't be happening. This nightmare of my life keeps throwing me under.

Two lines have become my undoing. Parallel pink lines. Faint pink lines. Eternally parallel lines that will never meet. Endless lines. Something so benign that will change everything.

What am I going to do?

I hear a knock on the front door. Bullet must have invested in a teleporter. "Who is it?"

"It's me. Baby girl, open the door."

I attempt to open the door when I realize I have the stick in one hand and my cell in the other. I can't seem to let go of either. I somehow maneuver around both and open the door.

"Shooter, what the hell is going on?" Bullet barges in and scans me over. I have no answer. I don't even know what's going on anymore. I shrug, and I guess that's when he notices the stick in my hand.

"What's that?" he croaks out and points to the atrocity still resting firmly in my grasp.

"It's a stick. I peed on it."

He nods. "Are you…um….are you?"

I nod. "There's two lines."

"Okay, baby girl. You wanna put the stick down?"

"I can't. I think it's stuck."

"Okay."

He gently wraps his hand around my back and ushers me into the kitchen. He somehow pries the stick from my hand and my cell, then washes both of our hands in the sink. His arm returns around my shoulder and he brings me over to the couch, sitting me down. He squats in front of me.

"I…need a minute, okay? Do you have a porch here?" I nod and point at the glass door off to the side. "Okay. I'll be right back. Just sit here." He grabs the remote, switches the TV on, and then pulls open the groaning glass doors. Zoning out, I watch him. He's lighting up a cigarette and leaning over the railing with his bald head hanging low. After about five minutes, he comes back in, takes off his black leather jacket, and sits next to me.

"You started smoking again?"

"Yeah, it has been a rough few months." Slipping his arms under me, he pulls me over his lap.

"So, we gonna talk about you getting knocked up?" I shake my head. "You wanna talk about why your douche bag husband came to see me?" I shake my head.

"I haven't seen him since Monday." He glances down to see that my rings are gone.

"You wanna tell me why you haven't seen your husband in four days?" I hold up my finger, indicating that I need a minute, and climb off his lap, get my phone, and then return. I scroll through it, get to the video, and hand it to him.

"You want me to watch a door?"

I nod and rest my head against his shoulder. Closing my eyes, I try to block out the horrible noises and focus on Bullet. This is the first time I've felt any warmth in nearly a week. It relaxes me and I feel my muscles softening in response. Let the tension melt away, at least physically.

"Fuck…he's dead. So fucking dead. Why didn't you call me? Call someone?"

"Why? You were right, he did slice me open. Did you really think I could handle you rubbing it in my face?" My voice is monotone, there are no emotions left in me.

"Jesus, baby." He rests his head against mine while closing his eyes. "I would never have said that. Shit, you've been sitting here alone all this time?"

"Yeah. I guess."

"Why aren't you at your condo?"

"I gave it to a family. They needed a place to live. Their daughter is standing trial for murder two."

"Oooo-kay? And what are ya gonna do about your husband?"

"I don't have one."

I explain everything that happened Monday. I feel so detached like I'm retelling the storyline of some character on a movie or in my favorite book.

"What about the baby?"

"What about it?"

"Are you going to tell Richie?"

"I'm not sure what to do anymore."

"You should see a doctor. You need to get everything checked out."

I nod. Yeah, I should probably do that. That's what a responsible adult would do. A mom should know something like that, right? Already I'm fucking this up.

I call my obstetrician and schedule an appointment for Monday. One week after my failed marriage concluded in a fiery inferno,

I'll hear my baby's heartbeat for the first time.

We order dinner and Bullet stays the night. Unlike the evil man that impregnated me, Bull sleeps in boxers, not boxer-briefs. He sort of has a thing about it. For every birthday, holiday, what-have-you, he requests boxers. It's almost a game we play, to see who can get Bullet the craziest pair. So when I check him out in his boxers, it is purely for competitive purposes. Not in any other way and certainly not because he is a perfect physical specimen rendered with a virtuosity of tatted art. Tonight, he is wearing Fun Boxers, one hand points up and says 'the Man,' and the other points at his Mr. Happy and says, 'the Legend.' Why this cracks me up, who knows?

"Don't laugh at my cock, baby girl. Missile is very sensitive." I start laughing even harder. My sour mood be damned.

"Missile? What?" My face is all twisted with trying to keep my giggles in. Poor Mr. Happy.

"Yeah, baby girl. I'm Bullet..." He points to his chest. "This anaconda is Missile..." He cups his man meat. "And these guys are the rounds." He smiles as he cups both balls. That's it...tears fall I'm laughing so hard. I know the strangest people! Unable to stand, I fall onto the bed clutching my stomach and continue laughing.

"Oh, it's funny, huh?" He jumps on top of me and starts tickling under my arms and my stomach. I can't breathe I'm laughing so hard.

"Stop, stop. It's not funny. Your Mr. Missile is wonderful!" I clutch my stomach, protectively.

"Fuck yeah, he is! All the ladies think so!" I give him a dirty look while rolling my eyes and throw him off me, his back hitting the bed hard.

I lie there panting, trying to catch my breath. I wish I could take my sleeping pill tonight, with all the thoughts in my head, I'm not sure I'll get any rest and I'm so tired. But...the baby. I don't know if I can take it. Something to ask the doctor on Monday.

Rolling over onto his stomach, he hovers to my side. "You're gonna be okay. I'm gonna take care of ya." He sweeps some of my hair to the side and leaves his thumb tracing back and forth over my lips. "I missed you," he whispers while watching his movement. "I won't let you go again." Softly pecking my lips, he leans across me to turn the lamp off and then twirls me so that he can have my back. Spooning me the way he likes, he kisses my head a few times. "Sleep, baby girl. I gotcha."

"You sure you want to be back there? I think I heard that pregnant women are rather flatulent."

Snickering he asks, "Ya saying you're gonna fart on me?"

"Well, I'm not currently in the mood but if I fancy a fart, you better watch out and hide your missile."

"Shut it, Shooter girl or I'm gonna have to spank your sweet ass."

Every morning, Coen calls and leaves a voice message. Sometimes, when I want to twist the knife inside my heart deeper, I listen. He tells me he can't sleep without me. That he can't live without me. How sorry he is. Yeah, it sure sounded like he was sorry when he was grunting and saying how good that bitch's mouth felt around his, or rather *my* cock. Today, though, I listen.

I'm going to have to tell him. I'm going to have to do something.

Bullet left earlier this morning. He has a full lineup at the shop and then he's heading to the BBMC compound. He wanted to take me, but I can't stand the thought of everyone knowing that my marriage was an absolute fuck up. I mean, what does that say about me? I wasn't even married for three months. THREE MONTHS! That's all the happiness that God allotted to me. All the shit and struggle and I only get three months to be happy.

And now....now I have to bring him back into my life. Eventually, watch him fall in love and marry another woman. A man like Coen isn't going to stay single for long. As for me, I've given up on the notion of love. Well, in the romantic sense anyway. I will love my child. That will be my new passion. My son or daughter. The thought makes me smile.

Monday morning comes along. It's a leap year and today is February 29, which I'm taking as a positive sign. Something rare, special, to be recognized and appreciated. I need to be more appreciative of all the blessings in my life. Despite my current situation.

For some insane reason, the trio pack decided they needed to be at my appointment. Malice swung by and picked me up, while the gang met us there. This is going to be terrible. I'm nervous as it is but add the trio and it's bound to be a circus. To be honest, I could use all of their support, so I gladly take it.

Everyone stares at them as they walk into the waiting room. Bullet spots me first and picks me up and throws me across his lap kissing my brow. It's comical as they gather themselves into the cramped undersized chairs and wait for my name to be called. When it finally is, all three stand up. "You can't come back with me."

"We sure as shit can. Or should we get LOUD?" Gunner elevates his voice with each word causing every head to turn. Blushing, I grab him and follow the nurse.

They have me urinate in a little cup, then weigh me, then ask me a billion questions, and finally they drain me of roughly half my blood.

"She's a tiny thing, you're gonna empty her. Shit, save some for the baby at least." Bullet crosses his arms and glares at the nurse.

I apologize profusely and then we are ushered into a smaller waiting room for the doctor. I have to undress my lower half, so I make the guys wait outside and count to hundred, then come back in. I wore a long black skirt today with knee high boots, so changing comes easy and I'm on the table in no time. The guys come back in and start goofing off before the doctor enters.

"Congratulations, you are indeed pregnant, Mrs. Collins." God, I hate that name. "Is Mr. Collins here to congratulate?" She looks at each of the trio.

"I'm the father," Bullet pipes up. My head snaps in his direction. What?

"I'm the father," Gunner adds, crossing his arms and puffing his chest out.

"Hell, I guess that makes me a daddy, too." Trig puts his hands on his hips while straightening himself.

The doctor looks at me questioningly and I shrug. Yup, she probably thinks I'm a whore. Don't know who the baby's daddy is. Call Jerry Springer.

She internally checks me and does a pap smear, then tells me that I might be further along and need a sonogram to confirm my due date.

"Baby girl, tell her how you're missing parts." Bully's brows raise and he looks at me expectantly. How does he know?

"Um, yeah. He's right. I had a splenectomy and had some damage to my pancreas. Will this pose a threat to the baby or the pregnancy?"

"Yes, that puts you in the high risk category. Many women have complications during delivery and need a caesarian section. We will need to keep a close eye on your health. I'll go ahead and prescribe you an iron supplement, if you aren't already taking one, since you'll most likely become anemic. Have you felt fatigued?"

"Yes, but I've been having trouble sleeping as it has been a difficult week for me." I try to smile but I hear Bullet grunt and watch him turn away while scratching the back of his neck. He's upset, again.

She exits the room and tells us that the sonographer will collect us soon. I'm so excited. I was thrilled at the thought of hearing my little peanut, but to see him/her...heck yeah! I maneuver my skirt under the weird hospital cover thing and stay barefoot until we are called to the next room.

When we finally are, Bullet carries me to the room, while Gunner grabs my stuff. "Didn't want your pretty little feet to get dirty," Bully whispers while smiling.

He plops me onto the examining table in the dark room and stands to the side. The other two come in and wait by my head while Bull holds my hand. He seems so nervous. The kid isn't coming out anytime soon. The clinician whips out a long rod and rolls a condom onto it, and I look over at the guys to see all three sets of eyes grow huge. "What are you doing with that pole?" Bullet growls. I try to calm him down. This isn't going to hurt, I hope. He still has a seriously tight grip on my hand and when the timid lady, who looks to be around her late twenties, shoves it inside of me, all three guys grunt.

I give them a singular eyebrow raise, babies. Immediately, the room is bathed in a strange thumping sound. It sounds like a washing machine on a high spin cycle and the screen before us comes to life. Life inside of me. I squeal in delight and Bullet rubs my arm.

The clinician, Emily, clicks on images and measures parts. Then she stops on the little heartbeat. My mini-me has this speedy little ticker beating to the beat of his or her own drum. The guys chuckle and comment on how he's a boy and they can already tell he'll have some serious rhythm. They are fighting over what instrument he will play. I remain mesmerized by that little ticking thing. I feel a warm breath by my ear. "Can you feel it?" Bully asks, kissing my cheek. I shake my head and continue staring down. I don't want to miss any of this. I know they will take the picture away soon.

Emily explains that it is still too early to know the sex of the baby, but that my due date is August 30, which makes me roughly 15 weeks pregnant. I'm already in my second trimester.

She assured me that everything looked good and not to worry. She printed pictures and then Gunner asked if he could get a set, so the poor thing printed over a dozen copies. The guys started cooing that a baby Shooter would be here soon.

I freeze when I notice Emily's eyes widen. "You're Loaded Gun? Oh my gosh, I'm such a huge fan." She looks down at me. "You're Shooter? Can I get an autograph?" The guys look at me apologetically, but it's too late. What if she spills to the press or something?

"Yeah," Bully replies and walks over to her. "Just promise you'll keep this to yourself, yeah?"

She nods as her mouth hangs open. Leaning forward she asks for a hug and he obliges. He gives me a small smile that I can't seem to return.

We wrap up, dress, and I make my next appointment for two weeks. The doctor wants to keep an eye on me and is emphatically encouraging me to take things easy. Sure, failed marriage, lost job, lost home, finding out that I'm pregnant…not stressful at all, doc!

We grab a late lunch together and they drill me about my future plans. How can I make plans when the future keeps changing on me? Bull stays by my side for the duration of their pestering but remains mostly silent. He's been acting weird.

The next month passes fairly smoothly. I had my second appointment two weeks ago and it wasn't nearly eventful as the last. This time, I get another sonogram but most importantly, I will find out the sex of my baby. Since the guys scared poor Emily, I decided not to bring them.

Sometimes, they are too much for sane people to handle. Bullet moaned the most, but eventually gave up. He's been really sweet to me lately. I missed having the trio around. They are my best friends and my odd little family.

Coen has been persistently calling, at least three to four times a day. As far as I can tell, he still doesn't know where I'm staying. I've kept myself busy with running on the complex's treadmill and doing light weights. I have also heavily connected with the DA's office on Juanita's case. They have already begun the preliminary work, but it looks like it's a case of being at the wrong place at the wrong time. The Offense DA is seeking a full sentence and granted her a plea bargain with a guilty admission in exchange for fifteen years in a federal prison. Poor thing would never survive and I won't let that happen. This one is going to court.

As I'm waiting in the smaller room for the doctor, a nurse opens the door and ushers Coen inside. "Here's your wife's room, Mr. Collins." He thanks her and then stands next to me. He's subdued and doesn't utter a word while I'm freaking out with a million questions rolling in my head. How does he know? How did he find me?

The room is suffocating in complete silence, our personal thoughts doing the only speaking. I don't look at him but I feel his presence and smell his familiar Coen scent. I can only close my eyes and pray this will be over soon. It was wrong of me to keep this from him but I was going to tell him. Eventually.

The doctor walks in and Coen immediately introduces himself as my husband and even shakes her hand. I don't bother correcting him. She reviews my urine sample, chastising me on my low iron levels. She also found protein in my urine and wants me to come back next week to watch it. I agree to take better care of myself and she leaves to get Emily. From my periphery, Coen looks concerned, yet he remains silent.

We walk across the hallway to the sonogram room and Emily introduces herself to Coen, who makes her aware that he is my husband. Emily looks at me in confusion, remembering the trio. I shrug helplessly.

She lifts my shirt and plops some cold jelly on my stomach. Placing the little wand there, we get bathed in that glorious sound again as the picture comes to life. This time, I can see more detail. Fingers and even a full head of hair. We stay silent listening to the whooshing sound. Again, Emily takes measurements and reveals that I'm having a little...girl. Pink, pink, pink! My heart returns and explodes with joy.

I glance at Coen and he's smiling vibrantly and wiping his eyes. I bet he didn't expect this. She prints today's pictures and hands them to Coen. We leave her room and walk to the counter to make my next appointment. He remains silent by my side.

We stride out of the office and into the main waiting area where Malice looks concerned when he spies Coen behind me. I widen my eyes at him, giving him the I-don't-know-what-to-do look. Malice marches over, takes my elbow, and ushers me to the parking lot. Coen follows and when we arrive at the car, he pushes past Malice and buckles me in, his hand lingering over my growing stomach. It's not really noticeable, yet, but I have to wear stretchy clothes now. My little baby bump seems to get bigger every day.

He makes eye contact and holds it. I don't know what he is expecting, so I do nothing but stare back trying to get a read on things. He is stone-faced giving me nothing. I notice the darkness under his eyes. He also looks as though he's lost some weight and his hair is longer than usual.

He's wearing a sweater with a polo underneath and jeans. Not exactly office attire, even for late March.

He leans forward and kisses my brow, lingering there for slightly too long, and then shuts the door. I watch him quietly walk away, his hands in his pocket, head down. That's when the pregnancy hormones check in and I can't stop myself from tearing up. I shouldn't miss him. I sure as hell don't want to miss him.

Later that night, as I'm mulling over my next course of action, I hear a soft knock on the door. I peep through the little peek hole and see a distorted Coen. I carefully open the door a tiny bit and peer at him.

"Open the door, love. We have some things to discuss." I know he's right. I know all of this is unavoidable and that I'm the one in the wrong so I take a few steps back and watch as my ex-husband walks through my door. His hands are full of bags, so he pushes the door open with his shoulder and then closes it with his elbow. I'm still rooted on the spot. What do I do?

"Nice place, love, although I prefer our home." He takes a second to look around then leans forward and smooches my forehead. He proceeds to the dining room table and drops all of his bags unloading some food and smiles back at me when he sees that I'm watching.

"Come on. We have a lot of ground to cover tonight. I brought some food. I have to keep my girls happy." Still staring blankly at him, he comes over and interlocks our fingers with one hand while the other cradles my face. "Hi."

I know this is my cue for a reply, but I can't speak. I feel my face tightening and my muscles locking down, perhaps readying for a fight. Has he forgotten the last month and how he hurt me? Am I supposed to play the part of the jilted lover reunited now? That can't happen. I don't trust him anymore.

His thumb strokes my cheek while I zone in on his eyes. I hate missing this man. He has proven how little he thinks of me time and time again and I fall for it. I try not to notice the sparkling happiness coming from him. The way he's smiling at me, like I am still his world. He lied. I was never anything to him.

I bite my lip and look away. This is all too much. Too intense. "My greys, love. Give them to me."

"No." That didn't come out as forceful as I'd meant it to.

"Jesus, if I thought you were breathtaking before, that's nothing compared to how spectacular you look now. Carrying my daughter, Charlie. There has never been a more perfect sight." He tries to catch my eyes but I continue looking away. He leans down pressing his lips to my ear. "I told you it was too late for us. Destiny demands her way. Our lives are interwoven, we'll always be together. Always, love."

"No," I cry out and try to shove him away from me. He's too close. He doesn't budge an inch. "No! You're wrong. You have to be wrong. You would have never hurt me otherwise. I don't believe you or anything you say." I try to hold the tears at bay but my chin trembles and he, of course, notices.

"Let it out, Charlie. It's okay, I deserve this. I know I hurt you, love. And you have to know how fucking sorry I am. I am exceedingly and irrevocably sorry. Please, I'll spend the rest of my life and beyond making it up to you. Anything. I'll do anything. We can take things as slow as you want. We can seek counseling...anything. Please!"

"No. Go away and leave me alone. I hate you. I hate you!" I punch him repeatedly in the chest. I hate him for making me love him. Making me marry him. Making me give up all the things I loved to be with him, and then losing it all. I nearly lost everything. Nothing will ever be the same. He changed me.

I can't stop screaming and punching and crying, and I can't see or think. I'm a big tornado plowing through this man trying to get him to move away from me. But his arms band me to him and we fall to the ground in a tangled mess. My face feels red hot and I can't stop the tears, which brings on the snot. He still won't let go and keeps cooing in my ear to let it out. Let what out…I'm trapped. I'm here and he's right, I will be tied to him forever, now.

I cry and cry. Fucking pregnancy hormones on top of my miserable heart breaking. I barely realize that I'm on his lap straddling him when his warm hands glide up and down my back. He's pressed so tightly to me that I can feel his heart beating as frantic as my own. My head is on his shoulder, and I have no remorse in rubbing my snot-filled nose against his cashmere Henley. Take that, shirt! I can't beat up Coen, but I can take down the shirt. Score one, Charlie. The tears finally dry up but the snot and hiccups continue. I don't move. I'm not sure where to go from here. I suddenly feel so tired and my heavy eyes close. All that fighting and emotion knocked me on my ass.

Coen's hand glides up my back and cups my neck through my hair. "I love you, Charlie, and I already love our daughter. She's perfect isn't she?" I nod into his neck, murmuring my agreement. "Have you eaten dinner?"

"I was just about to start." I hiccup some more. With each movement my nipples scratch up against his chest. I forgot, I'm not wearing a bra. My boobs have swollen and feel rather tender, so the quicker these puppies are free the better. I chose a thin black tank and a pair of Bullet's stolen boxers with little yellow ducks on it for bed. But now, next to Coen, in his arms, I feel too exposed. He brushes his rough scruffy chin against my bare shoulder.

"I brought dinner for my girls."

"I'm not hungry," I lie. Maybe he'll leave. The truth is, I'm always hungry now. My stomach rumbles to embarrass me further.

"Maybe you're not, but our little girl needs to eat."

"Can't move." I sigh. Even my head feels too heavy, weighed down with all the shit thoughts that Coen shoved in there.

He chuckles and lifts me up, cradling me to him. "I'll take care of both of you."

He kisses my brow and walks us to the table. Sitting down with me still in his lap he grabs a few bagfuls of food. The smell that permeates the air is heavenly and I think my little mini takes notice because the growling gets louder.

He chuckles. "That's it my little Charlie Jr., tell mommy that she needs to feed you." I tilt my head and pinch my face at him. Charlie Jr.? No way!

"You've got to be more creative than that. Charlie Jr. is soo not going to happen." He laughs as he grabs a container filled with salad and pours the dressing over it. He gets a forkful and places it to my lips. I quirk a brow and tighten my lips. What is this man doing?

"Please, love. The doctor said you needed more iron. It's a spinach salad." His face is pleading, although he's still smiling sweetly. I hate him.

"I can feed myself." I reach for the fork but he pulls it out of my reach.

"I know. Please, let me take care of you. Besides its good practice for when…cupcake gets here?"

"Cupcake?" I shake my head closing my eyes in shame.

"How about I leave you to the nicknames and I'll focus on keeping you both healthy and loved, okay?"

"You've got the nickname part right."

"Charlie," he says warmly. He places the fork on the container and slides his hand under my shirt rubbing back and forth across my baby bump. "This is mine, love. No matter what irrational thoughts mull around that gorgeous head of yours, even you can't deny me this. I need this. I need her. I need to know that although I failed my wife, I won't fail my daughter. If this is the only connection I get, to touch her this way, to feed you both, you need to give that to me. And with that, I'll work on fixing what I fucked up. I'll bring our family together, love. This baby….our daughter…was made with love."

I start to fidget, as I want to get off his lap. "No, I know you know it's true. We love each other! She's a perfect example of how true love manifests even in the darkest of times." He shakes his head. "I won't let either of you go. Never, love. Maybe you don't wear my rings but I've already branded the ring around your heart." He takes a deep breath and closes his eyes. I want tonight to be over. "You're both mine. It's my job to take care of you and I'll do exactly that. If I have to fight you every step of the way, that's what will happen. But I won't lose either of you."

He kisses my head and picks up the fork to feed me. I'm now physically and emotionally drained. I don't know if I can beat him. A strong fighter knows when she can't win and she taps out. I wish I could do the same.

He feeds me the entire salad and a baked chicken breast. He brought some fruit for dessert but I'm too full and sleepy to eat. He puts me down on the couch and cleans up after dinner, then he brings me the rest of the bags. Inside, I find several baby books. He pulls one out of my hands.

"That one's for me. It's for expecting fathers. I want to learn everything so I can take better care of you both."

I'm studying a stuffed pink giraffe when he adds, "Charlie, I was wondering if you've thought about where we're going to live once she's born."

"What do you mean?" I throw the books and stuffed giraffe on the coffee table and dig deeper into the couch, resting my head on the back and closing my eyes to focus on Coen's voice.

"A baby needs lots of things; strollers, swings, highchairs. This place isn't very big. Is it yours?" I shake my head. I didn't buy it, and I moved all of my belongings into storage.

"What about coming home, to our place? There's plenty of room."

My head snaps and my brow quirks up. I glare at him. Is this man for real? "NO!"

"Okay, love. How about we table this discussion for a bit? But you're what, eighteen weeks along? We'll need to make a decision soon."

"I'm nineteen weeks." My eyes squint at him.

"Right, right. I should probably know that. See what I mean, I need to do a better job at taking care of you?" He exhales loudly. "You ready for bed, love?" I am. I'm excruciatingly tired.

"Yeah. this visit has taken its toll. Thank you for dinner, it was wonderful. Let me walk you out." I stand up and walk towards the front door, when I realize that he isn't joining me. "Coen?"

"About that. I don't think we should sleep apart anymore." He stands and cups my shoulders. I want to scream.

"Let me make this perfectly clear, I don't want you to stay." I annunciate each word while thinking calm and soothing thoughts of the nice warm bed waiting for me.

"I get that, Charlie, but I'm not about to put you or my daughter at risk. That isn't going to happen. So, I'm staying." He purposely enunciates every word, just as I had.

"Fine. Then goodnight! The spare room is down the hall, second door on the left. If you so much as touch my door, I'll change my mind and have all my band mates and Malice stand watch from now on. From inside *my* room. You get me?"

He nods, though his lip tweaked up for a second in a half smile. He thinks he's won. He should have figured out by now that I don't play fair.

Chapter 43

WHEN I WAKE UP, I'M alone. Thank goodness. It's Tuesday morning and I have no office to go to.

Now that Coen has found me, I feel comfortable in going to Tornadoes. I'm not allowed in the cage but I can still get a solid work out in. Dressed and ready, I head to my kitchen for some juice when I notice Coen sitting at the table waiting for me.

"Morning, love. You hitting Tornadoes today?" His feet are up on the opposite chair as he reads the morning paper and drinking coffee. He's dressed in a tight white t-shirt with sweat pants that hang too low. Even from my view I can see that.

"Yeah, I need a workout." I reply over my shoulder as I walk into the kitchen to grab a cup of juice. I need to take my prenatal vitamins and my extra dose of iron. He comes up behind me and wraps his arms around my stomach. "So how's my little…." He waits for me to provide a name.

"I guess I'm still thinking on that. I think she's okay. She certainly hasn't told me otherwise." I notice a brown bag on the counter and walk over peeking inside. "Yum, bagels. When did you get these?"

He smiles proudly. "I had Davis bring some things by this morning. I thought since I'm staying here, until we make other living arrangements, the least I should do is feed you."

"Coen…" I hop up on the kitchen counter facing him. "I'm not sure about any of this. It makes me uncomfortable." I grab a raisin bagel and start digging in. I don't even cut it or toast it, I just rip it apart piece by piece and pop it into my mouth.

"I know this isn't the most conventional relationship, love, but I have faith that we'll make it work. If anything, we'll do it for our daughter." Coen leans against the counter spreading my legs. He watches me as he deliberately leans forward and bites my bagel.

"Mmmm. So good."

His hands are flat on the counter next to my thighs and I feel the heat blazing through him. He's purposely teasing me, trying to ignite a response. Sadly, my body is already hardwired to his. The connection is out of control. My hormones are erratic and I shiver wildly at this man's closeness. This is terrible. I can feel he's hard when he presses and rubs himself against me. I whimper, unconscientiously, unable to stop the elicited sounds.

Just then there's a knock on the door and I throw Coen aside to get to it. Oh, thank goodness. I swing the door open without even asking who it is. I find a handsome Bullet waiting on the other side. He's wearing a black hat low on his brow and a loose tee and jeans under a black leather jacket. He smiles when I open the door.

"Good morning, baby girl. You up for some breakfast?" He steps into the room and kicks the door shut behind him. Then he wraps me up and smooches my nose. A big old sloppy kiss. I giggle like a silly teenager.

Someone clears their throat behind us and Bullet stiffens. He looks down at me. "You've gotta be fucking shitting me. What the absolute fuck, babe?"

"I'd appreciate it if you didn't molest my wife and daughter." I look back to see Coen cross his arms, his face tense with anger.

Bullet's chin goes down and his eyebrows rise.

"Can I talk with you in private?" I squeak out and grab Bullet's hand leading him to my room.

"Where you going, love? I thought we were going to work out?"

Ignoring Coen, I walk into my room and lock my door.

"Shooter, what the fuck?" I hush him with my hand over his mouth and motion with my head to follow me to my bathroom. We walk in and I close the door, only to turn around to see Bully leaning against the bathroom countertop. Arms crossed, he has that I'll-kick-someone's-ass attitude radiating everywhere.

"He showed up at my appointment yesterday out of the blue."

"You didn't tell him to meet you there?"

"Bull, I haven't seen or spoken to him in over a month. I was sitting in the appointment room and he just walked in. Then, he showed up here last night. I didn't even tell him where I lived." I walk over and rest my head against his chest.

He rubs my back and I can almost hear him thinking. "He stayed the night?" I nod against his chest taking a moment to breathe him in. He smells like laundry, fresh air, a hint of cigarettes, and Bullet. "Did you two…um, did you fuck him?"

I freeze and take a step back. How dare he ask me that? I glare at him, my eyes narrowed to slits.

"I had to ask." He grabs me and pulls me back into him. I listen to his breathing and relish in his warmth. "Why is he still here?"

"I think he's trying to win me back."

"Ya think, Charlie Brown?" Before I switched my name, Bullet decided I wasn't just a Charlie. So, I got a plethora of Charlie's; Charlie Brown, Charlie Chapman, I even got Charles Darwin. Bullet has a history of name changing.

"He refuses to leave. He says that my baby is his daughter too, and he needs to protect her or some bullshit reason."

"You're having a girl?" He smiles and runs his hand around my neck, cupping me gently and messaging the knots. I close my eyes and purr.

"Yeah, a girl." I can't help the smile that plasters itself to my face.

"She's gonna look like you. Dear lordie, two of ya running 'round causing trouble." He embraces me tightly. "You happy, baby girl?"

"I think so." I murmur, the sound barely audible with my face pressed against his solid chest.

"You know you don't need him. The guys and I will take of you."

I nod. "He's her dad, Bull. What can I do? I tried to leave, you know that."

"Best fucking month, too."

Laughing, I slap his chest. "Seriously, what should I do?"

I glance up at him and I can see he's taking my question to heart.

"Where's he sleeping?"

"Down the hall, for now. He wants to buy us a house. He said she needs lots of stuff."

"Hmm, I guess he's right. I mean look at Harley." Harley does have a lot of stuff; I know because I buy half of it. "You know; the band is getting some money now. We're doing pretty well. Why don't we all buy a place together? A big house with land." I shake my head, as that would never work.

"Money has never been an issue, Bully, you know that."

We eventually come up with a temporary solution. He or one of the guys will stay with me every night. During the day, I'll play nice with Coen but at night he won't get a chance to make a move. This will work for the interim, but a real solution needs to be made and soon.

We finally leave the bedroom to find an angrily flushed looking Coen. He's not happy with me. Bullet excuses himself to smoke and I sit down with Coen on the couch. I tell him about the guys staying with me at night and he's livid. *That's his child, I'm his wife, etc. etc.*

I try to find a way to compromise. I tell him that if he agrees with the guys sleeping on the couch, I'll agree to go to couple's therapy even though we are *no longer married.*

He relents and adds that I need to go out on at least one date a week with him, alone. He claims that we need to connect, for the baby. I hate how he's already using our daughter and she isn't even born.

So, that's what happens. For a solid month, Coen lives with me in my fully furnished two-bedroom rental. He has a gorgeous mansion. I have a fantastic three-bedroom condominium, but we stay in the rental. We go to therapy twice a week, and every Friday night Coen takes me on a date. The trio and Malice are on rotation with who will stay the night. They don't complain too much as long as I have beer and their favorite snacks. Bullet has pulled back a bit, though. We were together nearly every day until Coen's return, and then he pulled away. I think he's trying to give me some space but I never know with him.

Coen is ridiculously attentive. He makes sure that I'm well fed, that my stress levels stay low, that I've taken all my vitamins, and that I've included extra iron in my daily diet. If not, he runs out and buys me something and then practically forces it down my throat.

By now, my little BB Gun, as I like to call her, has made herself known by stomping all over the remainder of my internal organs. Coen loves it when we lie on the couch and he puts his head on my stomach. I think that's when he's at his happiest. He's positively adorable with the way he loves our mini. He's started reading to her every night before we go to bed and he talks to her all the time. Sometimes she reacts by kicking him and they play this weird game together. He puts his head on part of my tummy and she kicks, then he moves to the other side and she sometimes kicks him there, too. He's going to be an amazing father.

Almost daily, I have to remind myself of what he did. It would be so easy to let him take over and take care of me. Sometimes, I want that. I want to love him like I did before. Sometimes when we are in therapy, I feel that connection to him. He swears he's so sorry that he cheated. He claims he was planning on telling me what happened, but he was scared he'd lose me. I'm not sure if I believe him, but in the end, it doesn't matter.

The truth is simple: I don't trust him now. He betrayed that trust so it's lost. Maybe in time we can regain it, but I doubt he'll be that patient. I often wonder what he's doing when he's not in sight. Is he with someone else? I'm certainly not fulfilling his needs in that capacity, so maybe someone else is. These traitorous thoughts invade my mind constantly, bulldozing over any of the good we've accomplished.

He goes to work every day and I've been quite busy with my case. The courtroom proceedings are concluding and presenting closing arguments has commenced. My hope is that Juanita's case will be dropped. She's a bright girl who deserves a solid future. I have enjoyed getting to know her and her family.

When dressing on Thursday morning, I feel something brewing in the air. All day, I keep my hand on my little BB Gun. I feel this need to keep her close.

Coen, Gunner, and I shared a relatively quiet breakfast this morning. I sent both men off and got my sweat on in the communal exercise room downstairs. I've put on almost ten pounds in the last two months. My doctor, who I saw on Monday, said that weight gain is necessary for pregnancy and that I'm doing a good job keeping healthy. But other than my stomach growing, so are my boobs, my hips, and even my butt. My face has filled out a bit, too. I feel chubby. Coen compliments me daily. He says I'm more beautiful every time he sees me, and he even thinks that the 'fuller' me is incredibly sexy. I think he's just trying to have sex with me.

We're scheduled for court at ten thirty today, and when I get there, I see that poor Juanita is a nervous mess. I do my best to comfort her and her family and they tell me that no matter what today's outcome is, I have impacted their lives permanently and they bless me and my daughter. Though I'm not as religious as I'd like, I'm humbled by their words. With people like them in my life, I feel blessed.

When the verdict is finally delivered, Juanita and I stand hand in hand. I'm confident that the court appointed attorney and I have delivered a strong case against the state but one never knows. Then the judge delivers the verdict; not guilty. Juanita cries tears of joy in my arms and then I'm pulled in from behind as her parents grab me and kiss me over and over again. They can't stop thanking me. I have given them back their world. I have renewed their love of this country and the judicial system. I can't help but smile. If this was my daughter on trial for a crime she didn't commit, I bet I'd act in the same manner.

After ten minutes of gathering my work and speaking with the assistant DA, I walk out of the courtroom. I hadn't realized how late it was. I'm supposed to meet Coen for a late lunch a few blocks away. I grab my phone to call him, part of our mandatory dating agreement, when Juanita joins me on my walk.

"Thank you so much for everything you did for me, Ms. Charlie. When I have my first child, I'm going to name her or him after you."

"You're like a saint, Ms. Charlie and the new house is so cool. They even have a pool, did ya know that?" little Manual asks. He looks so much like his dad, Manual Sr.

"Yeah, little man, I lived there for a few years before I gave you the place, silly."

"Ma, I forgot Osito. Ma, I need him, he'll be scared without me." We all stop to look at the littlest guy, Esteban, who's four and a handful.

"I got it. We'll catch up. Come on." Sr. grabs Esteban and they run back to the courtroom we just vacated.

"Juanita, what are your plans after high school graduation?" She graduates in a few months. She's a bright girl and I hope that she doesn't get trapped in a minimum wage job. I want to help her, even going so far as to talk with Coen about it.

We are walking arm in arm when I feel all the oxygen in the room being vacuumed out. Every hair on my body stands on alert. There's a tussle at the far end of the room, near the exit doors.

Then there's yelling and I see a man carrying some type of gun, it's an AK. Oh my god, it's an assault rifle.

Juanita continues talking and doesn't notice the man cocking the machine as he spies his target to the left of us. Although there's at least a hundred feet between us, I see his eyes narrow and know that the world before me will end.

Then I hear the most go'd awful sounds. First, is the horrid popping; like explosive popcorn or fireworks. It's deafening and reverberates across the room along with the accompanied screams. Without thought, I push Juanita behind me and freeze. I have nothing on me. No weapon to protect myself. People have to go through the metal detector before entering the courthouse.

Seconds extend into an eternity. Everything shuts down and moves in slow motion. I know what is going to happen seconds before it does. And I can do nothing apart from watch in frozen silence.

He swipes the gun across the room and one by one, I watch as people go down. The sound is sickening, but I don't have to wait long for my turn. The impact of the bullets hitting me is so powerful that I fall backwards. It takes a few seconds, or so it feels, for my brain to connect with what has happened. Then pain. So much pain. I think I have been shot twice. I try to look down my body to confirm this horrible stinging and fire that explodes from my middle. Even through my blazer, I can see the blood. My cream camisole is soaking it up and I want to reach down to see if my baby is alright. Maybe she missed the bullets.

I scream in the hopes that she'll hear me and move to let me know she is still with me. But I feel nothing but fire and acid. There's no way she could have survived that. I doubt even I will. My breathing is uneven and with the pounding in my head there is also ringing in my ears. I vaguely hear the moaning and crying surrounding me, plus the continued shooting as the cops show up and the gunman throws his weapon down.

The ringing continues souring my focus and I try to look around. Juanita is a few feet away from me and her eyes are open. There's nothing there, though. She has gone and I sight the blood seeping from a chest wound. It must have been instantaneous. I don't hear the gasping for air that comes from my left, from her. I don't hear the sick rattling of lungs failing, of air vanquishing without meeting its mark.

My legs deaden and I feel a chilled numbness moving north. There are tingles threatening my arms when I realize I have my cell in my hand. Coen is going to break when he learns of this. I need to apologize before it's too late.

I press some numbers with my thumb. When I fell, my arms came up by my head, next to my ears. Though my fingers move, I've now lost the feeling in most of my arms. I hope he can hear me. I think I hear the ringing and then someone answers. When I go to make a sound, nothing comes out. The pressure in my stomach has taken hold of my lungs and captured whatever air I had left.

My eyes feel heavy, though I am fighting to hold them open for a little longer. I need to connect. I need…something. I hear screaming through the phone. The voice sounds so small, so distant. My head is locked to the side watching the little voice scream my name over and over.

A policeman comes over, his weapon still drawn and on alert. He looks at Juanita and shakes his head when he sees her eyes. Then he looks at me and catches my extinguishing gaze. He immediately holsters his weapon and squats down by my side.

"Guys, guys, I've got a live one here. Quick someone get the paramedics." He shouts over his shoulder. Then he looks at my little baby bump covered with blood and god only knows what else. "Shit, she's pregnant." He tries to smile. "Hey there, help is on the way." He tries to reach my hand and sees the phone lying untouched, someone still screaming through it. He looks at it and then picks it up to his ear.

"This is Sergeant John Holden speaking. Were you speaking with a woman moments ago?" He's watching me as he speaks to, I think Coen. I try to focus but everything is starting to get fuzzy. His image swirls and the dizziness welcomes me into darkness.

Chapter 44

I CAN FEEL MY CONSCIOUSNESS SEEP in. The beeping and gurgling noises that can be heard over my head must be what brought me out. There are several voices around me making muffled sounds. I think about connecting them to faces but then I realize that I don't care who is here. I know why they are here and that's enough to make me sick.

The last time I woke in a hospital, I spent time categorizing every injury, taking stock of what still worked and what didn't. I tried to shut out everything before waking and only focused on the now. This time, I don't want to open my eyes. Because the fact that I'm still alive and undoubtedly, my unborn child isn't, makes me wish for death.

I feel a depression on the bed next to my feet and then sobbing. Maybe I'm about to die. No, I wouldn't be that lucky. Instead the heavy pull of sleep welcoming me from the reality of this barren place lulls me away. I gladly go and embrace the short vacation from the perpetual pain.

I come to again when I feel something lifting my eyelids and then intense burning light. I immediately pull back and flinch away.

"Ah, our guest is awake. Mrs. Collins, how are you feeling?" An unfamiliar elder man asks me. I don't respond. I have nothing to say. How dare he ask me how I am? How the hell does he think I am?

With my eyes now fully open, I stare at nothing.

Nothing is here, nothing is happening, nothing is all I feel.

"Oh, thank you Jesus. Love, do you hear me? Charlie?" There's a new shadow hovering nearby. But I'm not here. I am nothing.

"Charlie?" His voice breaks as something warm touches my face. "Doctor, why isn't she talking? What's wrong with her?"

"Mr. Collins, she could be in shock and don't underestimate her concussion. We need to give her time and let her body and mind heal."

They converse further on God only knows what but I have vacated once again. This time, I don't drift into sleep. Sadly, I'm still wide awake. Instead, I drift into my psyche. Let colors and shapes carry me away. Remove the horrid pictures that have begun to cycle through my mind.

I flick back into the present when I hear fighting at the door. There's banging noises and a barrage of voices yelling.

"She's not even your fucking wife, you piece of shit. You fucked that up. Couldn't keep your fucking dick in your pants. I bet you didn't know that, parents Paz. He tore her heart wide fucking open and ripped her to shreds." Then a louder thump. "I should fucking kill you, you fucking son of a bitch."

More banging and grunts, then a nurse or doctor comes to yell at them. I tune out the commotion and surf the freefall of white noise buzzing in my ears pulling me back into the abyss. My eyes still open, the shapes and shadows drift out of focus and I'm gone.

I'm alerted back to the present when crying meets my ears. This time it's closer to me and appears to be coming from my neck area. I think someone is there because there's moisture and the warm body shakes me with each movement.

"You've gotta hold it together, brother. She'd be pissed if she saw you this way."

Then there's chuckling in my ear. "She'd kick my ass anyway, if she saw what I did to Richie's face. Something aint right, man. She's giving up, I can feel it."

"Nah, she's a fighter. You've seen what she's done in the cage. She just needs more time. She'll come back to us and this time we won't let her push us away."

Warmth falls on my face and the colors in my line of sight change, but I don't care enough to identify it. I'm not here. I want to tune the voices out but they're still so close. Why can't they let me go?

"Baby girl, ya gotta pull through. Charlie, do you hear me? Listen baby, I fucked up. I kept pushing you away. I was so fucking wrong. I love you and I want to be with you forever. Whatever you want as long as we're together." The warmth is gone and then I feel pressure on my chest and more sobbing noises. "Please, baby!" The shaking continues.

"Bro, maybe now isn't the time for confessions. She's gotta lot on her plate. We need her to heal."

"She got shot, motherfucker. You have no clue what it's like to hear her on the other line. Then some cop tells me my girl is shot. I'm never waiting again!"

"Visiting hours are over gentleman. Say your goodbyes."

I feel pressure on my face, maybe my lips but I don't feel much.

"I love you, baby girl. I'll come back tomorrow. Wake up for me."

Then I hear additional voices wishing me goodnight and feel more pressure on my head and face. Next the silence greets me. The shadows grow darker and darker until there's nothing left.

I awake again when I feel a tightening on my right side. There's a light flowery scent and I can hear random chatter. "You're awake. Are you hungry?"

I don't make eye contact nor do I respond. She grumbles further and then another voice chimes in. I tune out the first part until I catch the word 'starvation'. I find it deplorably humorous. I couldn't care less if I eat or drink or breathe or die. I feel unequivocally empty.

I stare blankly at the nothingness in the room. The shadows get brighter and new voices and noises come to light. I don't care who's here, I just want everyone to leave. Let me drown in the emptiness.

"Good morning my love, are you ready to join us today? I miss you so much."

"She doesn't want you, Richie. Stay the fuck away from her!"

There's more noises, more arguing but I allow their sounds to numb me, and drag me back under.

I'm alerted back to consciousness when someone snaps their fingers in front of my face. If I cared, I'd think that was rude.

"Charlie, Abba is worried about you. You need to focus." I think I recognize that voice, the perfume, but I don't care. I feel something being shoved against my mouth. I think they're trying to push my lips apart and feed me. I don't think I want food. I don't think I want anything.

"What the fuck is wrong with you? You're only gonna make things worse!"

"You tattooed menace, who are you to judge her own mother? You should leave. Let her *husband* and family deal with this in peace without being attacked every other minute."

More noises. I let it continue to numb me but this time the pull isn't coming as easily. Instead, I feel achiness in my abdomen. The bullet wounds are making themselves known. My barren and shredded womb is calling me to take notice.

"Charlie, it's okay, baby. I'm here. Come back to me and we'll deal with whatever you need. I'll take care of you. Please, baby girl!" Someone says at my side, and then there's pressure on my cheek. I think there's wetness there. Is it mine?

"Don't listen to him, love," comes from the other side of me. "I'm your husband. We can still make this work, Charlie. We're going to make this work. I need you. You know I do."

"Charlie, you need to wake up this minute and take care of your husband. Do you hear me? Quit being so selfish. You always..."

I grab onto the pain. I let it shut out the pandemonium elevating all around me as well as the clamor in my head. The throbbing and stinging centers me. The pain and I connect. It swirls me in its sharpened tendrils and carries me away.

Later, I feel my skin moistened and chilled. There's an unfamiliar humming nearby. I try to focus. I let the pain untangle me, I let the colors sharpen and bring all my thoughts to concentrate on that one sound. It takes work, I have been numb and uncaring for so long that I'm not sure if I'm still capable of connecting again.

I fixate on the shadow closest to me. Slowly, the colors take on shapes and eventually the shapes bring about smaller features. I can see her now. She appears to be in her thirties and has chocolate brown hair and pink scrubs on. I see her.

"Hi there. You feel like joining the land of the living today?" I continue to stare at her. I think I'm supposed to respond but I'm not sure what to say. Land of the living? Is that what they want from me?

"Your eyes are more alert. You have a huge group waiting for you to wake up, sweetie. They have been here ever since they brought you in. A mighty good looking bunch, too. I'd be real quick to get back to that, if I were you."

"Keep them…away." My voice is low and croaks, I'm not even sure if I'm the one who said it.

"What's that, sweetheart?" She pours some water into a cup and then places the straw against my lips. I'm hesitant as I continue to stare at her. "It's okay, sweetie. Nobody's gonna hurt you. Your husband has security right outside the door at all times. You're safe. They caught that shooter. You've got nothing to worry about."

Shooter….

I take a small sip of the proffered drink and wince as it slides down my jagged throat. How long have I been out of it?

"Don't let them…in here. I want…to be alone."

"Sweetie, I don't think that's a good idea."

"My room. No visitors!" The words are stalling in my throat. Catching on the serrated edges and holding them hostage. I have to force them up and I can feel the discomfort again stirring from my stomach.

"Your husband wouldn't…"

"No husband… Annulled. Please. No…no visitors!"

She nods reluctantly. Then continues bathing me and eventually adds the humming, again. I don't recognize the song but I allow it to carry me away. She finishes and asks if there's anything else I need. Food? More water? But I'm no longer responding, swept into the abyss of detachment.

Later, I hear banging on the door. Fighting. Raised voices. My name. They are mad that they cannot visit their favorite plaything. Their favorite toy. I focus on the anger and frustrations and allow it to infuse my bones, to strengthen me.

I cannot stay here.

Here, I am an easy target for their pity. I am an easy target for manipulations. I easily crave their love and affection.

The same nurse cracks open the door and slides in. The voices momentarily grow louder, then shut off with the closed door.

"You've created quite a frenzy out there. Are you sure you want to shut all those folks out?"

"How long have I…been here?" My voice is jaggedly rough again. She pushes the straw back to my lip and I greedily sip. This time the liquid feels delicious slipping down. But with the movement, the soreness in my center reactivates and throbs painfully.

"Four days, sweetie." She purses her lips, probably wondering where I'm going with my questioning.

"How much longer?"

"Depends on you. At this rate, you're gonna be here at least another few days maybe longer."

That won't work. If everyone is this upset today, I can't imagine how they'll be tomorrow. I need to get out of here. I haven't walked in over four days. I doubt they'll let me leave without being able to walk on my own. I have to make the effort.

"Can I get up?"

She smiles, broadcasting her disturbingly white teeth. "Well, look at you. How about we try getting you to sit up before we start walking?" I nod, and then she pushes a button near the bed. It creaks when it comes to life and suddenly I'm slowly being inclined to a seating position. The new pressure on my middle region becomes uncomfortable and I wince. There's a potent burning sensation increasing with every second that passes. I know that if I can't handle this, then I'll never walk, and I'll never get out of here.

"Can I have more pain…medication?"

"Sure thing, sweetie. We need to get food into you, too. I'll be back shortly. You're my only patient, so anything you need is yours." She saunters away. I hear several loud voices when she enters the hallway. I guess they aren't leaving. Why? Don't they want to appease me? I don't understand.

I spend the rest of the day in my room concentrating on the next step. First, remaining seated while eating. Then I had to sit on a nearby chair. After about thirty minutes, the pain harshly kicked in but I didn't relent. I wanted to prove to the nurse that I could handle it. She was so impressed with my progress that she removed the catheter and allowed me to use the restroom by myself.

That was excruciating. There was a lot of blood, reminding me that my baby was no longer with me. I wanted to shut down again but my desire to be free of all these people outweighed anything. Pain, fear, anger. None of it mattered now. I just wanted out. I wouldn't even call it freedom, as this pain will carry with me to my dying day. No, I just want out.

I caught a glimpse of my reflection in the bathroom mirror. In only four days, I looked like a different person. My grey eyes, muddied. My smooth freckled skin, sunken in, and nearly jaundiced. I dared not look lower. I didn't want to see what is left of me. I know it isn't enough, so why bother.

I carefully walked back to the bed and sat on the edge. The pain had caught up with me and taken my breath. The nurse, whose name I never bothered reading, scrutinized me. Looking around the vast room, I notice how much bigger it is than the last room I stayed in. There are flowers and stuffed animals lining the shelves along with balloons and cards. These are things you would send to a new mother, not a lost mother. Why would they send such items? Were they trying to hurt me? Remind me of what had been taken?

"Can I...can I call?" Even speaking was steadily increasing the pain.

"Do you have a cellphone?" Really? I was fucking shot and left unconscious on the fucking floor. What the fuck do you think? I don't like this chick anymore. I must have given her a look because she pulls out an old timey phone and hands me the receiver.

I grab the base and dial. I give her a distasteful look while I wait. I will leave her soon enough, too.

"Allo, qui c'est?"

Hello, who's this?

"Malice." His voice is a godsend. He is my ticket out. I hear him grunt and then the phone gets muffled. It takes a few seconds then he returns.

"Oh, dieu merci, vous êtes d'accord. Ce qui se passe? Pourquoi vont-ils pas nous laisser vous voir?"

Oh, thank god you're okay. What's going on? Why won't they let us see you?

"Détendez-vous. C'était.... moi. Je ne veux pas... voir personne. Envoyer.... à la maison."

Relax. That was...me. I don't want...to see anyone. Send...them home.

"De quoi parlez-vous? Ils sont une mauvaise ici. Ils ont besoin de vous!"

What are you talking about? They are bad here. They need you!

"Je ne ... putain de soins!"

I don't... fucking care!

"Merde. Je sais qu'il ya la douleur, mais ..."

Dammit. I know there's pain but...

"Vous ne savez pas de la merde… avec ce que je vais à travers. Obtenir… débarrasser d'eux!"

You don't know shit…with what I'm going through. Get…rid of them!

"Charlie, peut-être vous avez besoin de penser. Peut être…"

Charlie, maybe you need to think. Maybe…

"Mal, ecoutez ... vous êtes inscrit comme mes proches ... Vous pouvez prendre mes décisions. Non Coen. Non ... mes parents. Vous pouvez venir ... à l'intérieur. Vous pouvez vérifier ... moi sortir."

Mal, listen…you are listed as my next of kin…You can make my decisions. Not Coen. Not…my parents. You can come…inside. You can… check me out.

"Ce qui la baise parlez-vous? Vous avez été perdu pour le monde pendant quatre jours. Vous étiez juste tiré!"

What the fuck are you talking about? You have been lost to the world for four days. You were just shot!

"Je viens de rentrer ... avant de visiter heures ... fin."

Just come back…before visiting hours…end.

The pain is rapidly increasing making speaking difficult. I'm glad that my first real conversation is over the phone and not in person. I don't think I could stand the look on his face right now.

"Que prévoyez-vous?"

What are you planning?

"Ne vous inquiétez.... Dois y aller."

Don't worry. Got…to go.

I hang up. I'm suddenly near exhaustion. My eyelids are fighting to close. I'm not winning the battle against my body. The nurse notices and helps me lay down while tsking at me. What does she know?

As my head hits the pillow, my body immediately responds with growing heavy into the bed. In seconds, my tumultuous mind is put to rest. I bid this moment goodbye and hope that when I wake, I will be stronger and Malice will be here.

I wake to more crying. This time, I'm able to link the smells and sounds to Bullet. How he got in here, who knows? He was never actually a rule follower. He's sitting on the bed next to me and has one arm wrapped around my neck and the other underneath my back. His head is resting against my cheek. I can feel his tears dripping down my face and pooling on the front of my gown. The stubble on his head is scratching me as his shaking continues.

I've never seen Bullet cry. He gets mad, yes. Cry, never.

"You're planning something. I can feel it." He pulls me closer against the broken words. "I won't let you go again. Please, baby girl, please. If you leave, I swear to fucking Christ, I'll find you." Easing up on his grasp, he studies me. "Charlie, do you hear me?"

He cups my face and forces my eyes to face his. But I don't see him. I allow myself to see through him. I don't notice his brilliant fire laden eyes. I remember them, though. They mesmerized me. I hope he finds happiness. He will find love without my interruptions. My presence detrimental to any happiness. I'm a vortex of misery.

"Charlie!" He yells into my face. I feel the spittle fly against me, but I don't flinch or make any outward movements. He needs to leave. I never wanted him or any of them to see me like this. "You're alive! You have to fucking live. Please, baby. Just live. Yell at me. Fight me. Anything…please!"

"What fook you doing here? No visiting. She want quiet." I hear Malice's voice shouting across the room to Bullet. My eyes don't shift, don't focus. I keep the numbness close enough to dull my senses while I allow my thoughts to ground me.

Bullet lets go of me and stands next to the bed. "You spoke with her, didn't you?" Then his voice shifts back to me. "Why are you doing this?" He hovers above me and jerks my shoulders into my pillow a few times. "Wake up, baby! Wake up and tell me what to do!" He's screaming at me and the movement is causing sharp pains to jut up from my injuries. I close my eyes and hope that the dizzying waves of nausea will recede.

"Get off her!" I hear something hit the wall hard, followed by a few more banging noises, grunts and curse words. Then the door opens and Malice yells for Bullet to leave.

"I love you, Charlie! I won't give up. Wherever you go, whatever you do…I'll find you! I fucking love you more than anything in the world. Don't do anything! Please!" The door slams shut and the muffled noises and banging on the other side continue for another minute.

The pain brought me back to the present, to the reality of what needs to be done to end this time.

I need out. I can't think here. I can't think of the little baby girl that I never got to hold. The one that will never bump or swirl in my belly again. The one that I will always wonder whose eyes she had. What color her hair was? Did she smile like Coen? Did she have his temperament or my stubbornness? I wonder if she would have brought her parents together. If we would have ever been able to be a family.

I can't think about if I would have been a good mom. I would have adored my little girl. She would have been the star in my darkened world. She would be the light. Coen once had that light. It dimmed the night he broke my heart. But my daughter, nothing that she would've ever done could dim that light. It would have been blindingly bright.

Every smile would have been hers.

"Qui m'a tiré dessus?"

Who shot me? I whisper after time reenters my space.

"Mason Becker. Il voulait juge McDonough. Il était en jugement et savait qu'il allait."

Mason Becker. He wanted Judge McDonough. He was standing trial and knew he would lose.

"Que de Juanita et sa famille?"

What of Juanita and her family?

"Elle n'a pas fait et la mère a été tiré dans l'épaule."

She didn't make it and the mother was shot in the shoulder.

I knew it. Damn it! She had her entire life ahead of her. She was a kid! Why? I sniffle as the tears slide down my cheeks. This is the pain that comes with living. The aftermath.

"Combien ont été tués?"

How many were killed?

"Six au total. Deux blessés, y compris vous."

Six total. Two injured, including you.

"Et cette Mason? Qu'est-ce de lui?"

And this Mason? What of him?

"Morte."

Dead.

"Il se tué? Flics?"

He killed himself? Cops?

"Non, en prison. Il a été attaqué et tué."

No, in jail. He was attacked and killed.

Hhhmm. That's news to hold onto for a rainy day. Now, I need to focus. I will finish mourning my daughter and Juanita later. First, I need out. Once visiting hours resume, I don't doubt mine will return. As it is, I worry that Bullet is hiding around the corner somewhere. He knows me too well. I do plan something tonight. I plan on getting out.

I spend the next few hours working on getting discharged. The doctor and nurses, along with a psychologist that specializes in loss, come to talk me out of it. They threaten to call Coen repeatedly, saying that he is my husband and he is also the one paying the bills. I threaten them with HIPAA. Don't fuck with a lawyer!

In the end, the doctor signs the release forms. I have to sign double the discharge papers since I'm signing myself out and they're fervently against it. I also get a rundown of how to change my dressing and keep my wounds clean. I even managed to get my prescriptions filled.

With no clothes to change into, I pay one of the nurses for her extra pair of clean scrubs. It's a bit big but goes over the dressing easily. Hospital rules state that I have to be wheeled out of my room, but the location isn't specified. I'm not sure if anybody is still in the parking lot watching, so I decide to have the nurse wheel me to the employee parking lot where Malice picks me up.

By the time we finally drive away from the hospital, it's nearly five in the morning. I tell Malice what needs to be done and where to go and then my eyes slide shut. The night has taken what little strength I had left.

I spend the next seven days inside a hotel in Bangor, Maine, which was a four-hour drive from the hospital, far enough for me and yet quick enough for Malice to get back before anyone realized he was gone. He doesn't know my plans beyond this point. But, as the executor of my estate, he knows I will always be in touch. He bought me a disposable phone for that very reason.

He was reluctant to leave me, but I insisted. I know he thinks of me as family, a little sister of sorts. Perhaps I think of him in the same way. I know I love him enough to make sure he is taken care of. I have it set up so that my estate will pay him monthly. He will remain under my employ and watch over everything until I return. If I return, that is.

Before leaving Boston, I removed as much cash as the many ATMs we hit would allow. I have roughly ten-thousand dollars' cash on hand and the room is under an alias. Malice used the credit card he has under his own alias' name. He also stopped to buy me lots of snacks and water, several t-shirts and sweats, and a backpack from a convenience store. The studio suite I'm staying in has a full kitchen, so when we got in, Malice ran to the local grocery store to pick up some of my favorites. The hotel has complimentary breakfast and an in-house restaurant, but I doubted I would want to move much.

Instead, I spent those seven days mourning so many things. Juanita and the new life I promised her, gone. Coen and the promise of so much. He promised to be faithful, a good father, love me forever, and he swore to never hurt me again. I mourn.

I mourn Loaded Gun and the trio. I helped bring them to where they needed to be. They are on the road to success and the road is vast and beautiful. I have left countless songs in their care and ensured that the label will keep them as long as they are needed. After all, that is why I created the label in the first place, Zap Inc. Records. A palindrome, Zap Inc. is the company that this Paz created to do all of my evil bidding under. Even BedHead is owned by Zap Inc. Nobody ever put two and two together. I know the trio will be in good shape. That's all I ever wanted for any of them.

I mourn Tank, the guy who helped save my life, and even Tornadoes. He represents strength for me. He taught me how to go into the cage and tackle my opponent to the ground. He, too, is better off now. Only steps away from being a UFC champion, he is finally reaching his dreams.

Malice will be fine. I will mourn having him with me daily. But perhaps I was too needy when it came to him. He is free to explore his budding relationship.

And of course, my daughter, and the millions of things that will never come to be. I wish I would have taken those bullets to the chest, as that way she would have survived. Another few months was all I needed and she would have been safe in my arms. For her, I mourn endlessly and eternally.

I spend my last day writing them each a letter that I mail from the hotel. I address how much I love each and every one of them, even cheating Coen. I tell them my future dreams for them, how greatly they have impacted my life, and how I will carry them with me wherever my new journey takes me. Lastly but most importantly, I tell them to let me go. They all need to let me free. I need to move on and so do they.

I leave Bangor and catch a flight towards Atlanta where I have some things stored at a local bank. No identification is needed, as I gave very specific instructions as to how I can access my deposit box. There, I have a backpack filled with false identification papers, credit cards, several weapons, and other such treats. No, I'm not a spy, I'm just prepared. Shit happens, especially in my world.

Goodbye, Charlie. Maybe we will meet again.

Epilogue

Six months later

"JAZZ, I NEED TWO MIC' Lites, two Tequila shots, and one rum and diet with lime," Candy says from the other side of the bar while smacking her bubble gum pink lips.

"Comin' right up, pretty lady," I shout back and get to work popping lids and pouring spirits. I drop the drinks on her tray and grab the next customer waiting at the bar who has been trying to catch my attention. Things are hectic tonight. Halloween is around the corner and I swear it brings all the crazies out to play.

"What can I getcha?" I ask the college aged looking guy who's drooling at my chest. I can't blame him, the uniforms here are the pits. The Whole encourages its employees to dress in a certain manner. For example, I'm wearing the required low cut, super tight tank top paired with a short miniskirt.

"Are you on the menu?" He laughs and looks back at his friend.

"Sorry fellas, if you aint gonna order something *on* the menu then I gotta grab the next customer." I blow some bangs out of my face, as I still haven't gotten used to my new hairstyle. I chopped it all off. The bangs are long, but the rest is shaved on the sides. For the month of October, in honor of breast cancer awareness, a bunch of girls at the bar got our hair dyed pink. It's only the edges of my black bangs, but I like it. I'm only twenty-three, so I might as well do these crazy things while I'm young. Besides, Jasmine Rodriguez, my new name, is a spicy Latina Texan.

I even got several new piercings. I had my septum pierced which now sports a bullring as well as snake bites in my lip. They remind me of the trio. I've also added another tattoo: a date. The date my daughter was taken from me, April 21st, 2016. It resides just over the first bullet wound that struck me.

I've been debating about adding more tats. Maybe a quote from one of the LG songs, but I haven't found the nerve to do so. It still hurts too much to know that they are out there and they miss me. When Loaded Gun won best new Rock and Roll Artists of 2016 at the Video Music Awards last month, I almost died. I felt so proud of them. Then they broke my heart and made a big speech about me, about how I need to come home and how much they love me. I thought I had set them up for success. They needed to let me go. Instead of replacing me in the band as I'd hoped, Gunner took up playing the guitar again. I heard they had a successful tour over the summer and I even went to see them when they went through Houston in July.

I live in a smaller town called Beaumont, which is only a couple hours east of Houston. I've fallen in love with the city. It's close enough to Louisiana that I can still smell those beignets calling, yet Texas enough to indulge in a fine piece of meat. The best of both worlds, if you ask me. The weather has been gorgeous and I'm still close enough to the water, if I ever get homesick, which happens more often then I'd like. But it's a beautiful place to take a leisurely run in the mornings. And I feel safe here.

I haven't fully emerged from my mourning period. Eating is a struggle. Once food tasted like gooey heaven wrapped in bite-size pieces, but now I taste nothing. I can barely identify various food textures let alone flavors. I eat only because I have to. My slimmer figure reflects it. I've dropped several sizes and I wasn't huge to start.

I wait patiently while the duo of dorks drool. Yup, they're done. "You sit on it, sugar. I'll be back." I nod and look further down the bar, where a guy in a black hoodie over a black hat sits and has been waiting patiently. I can't see his face, but I can tell he's a big guy.

"What'll it be?" I lean forward trying to catch a glimpse, but he keeps his head down.

"Patron, Silver," he yells over Disturbed's 'The Light,' his head still locked in place.

"A guy after my own heart," I jest as I walk away and fill his shot. Most people yell for tequila, seldom do they specify. This guy has piqued my interest. Not that I do that. I'm still healing. I don't date. I don't do a whole lot. I do have a lot of girlfriends, though, which is new. I found that befriending guys wasn't an easy road, so I decided to change things up in my new life.

I return with his shot. "That'll be twelve fifty or we can start a tab for ya, if you'd like?" Although his head is down, I see his side smirk. Instead he slides a twenty-dollar bill my way.

"Keep the change, Jazzy was it?" I nod, take the bill, and walk away to fill the till.

I can't help the wide smile that spreads across my face. I have to bite my lip to keep from turning back around. I'd recognize that hand from anywhere. D R U M, is tatted under each knuckle on his right hand. I bet L I F E is tatted just under the knuckles of his left, although I didn't see it tonight to verify.

There's only one man I know who loves his drums enough to tattoo them on his skin. The same man who swore he'd find me wherever I went and follow me in whatever I did.

A bald headed bad ass! Looks like things are about to get interesting!

Don't forget to pick up,
THE GHOST OF ME
For the rest of Charlie's story

Acknowledgments

A SPECIAL THANK YOU GOES OUT to my Beta Readers; Tiffany Allen, Dwan Bloomberg, Penny Elbaz, Laura Floyd, Aimee Garbarino, Marni Hoffman, Sharon Sisselsky, Page Taleton, and Ricki Weiseltheir.

Your input in this crazy harebrained endeavor of mine proved to be invaluable. I can't thank you enough for the time and patience you had with me while I picked your brain. Now you out there in book land have learned priceless information; I may have been a zombie in another life.

To my amazing and talented uncle, Jacob Elbaz, for granting me complete carte blanche on his stunning art. Your digital masterpiece is the perfect canvas for my debut novel. I can't thank you enough!

To Marisa Rose Shor of Cover Me Darlings and her endless supply of creativity. You are a fierce talent. I am in awe of you. Thank you for your patience with me.

To my husband and four children, thank you for enjoying mac n' cheese while mommy had to write because she was on a roll and couldn't quite step foot into reality just yet. "Not again," becoming the new catch phrase in our house. Sad but true. You, my beloved five, are my entire world. Thank you, thank you, thank you!

A special thank you goes out to my mom. After drafting the first six chapters and wondering what the hell to do with these crazy things called words, she encouraged me to keep them words coming.

And to everyone who told me to NOT GIVE UP!!!

There aren't enough words in the English dictionary to show how much I appreciate all of you and how you have aided in bringing my special world to life.

"When I grow up..." doesn't have a time limit.

Thank you to everyone for reminding me of that.

About the Author

NOW IT'S TIME FOR ME to introduce myself to you, the reader. I'm supposed to say something insightful and wow you but to be honest, there isn't much on my plate. Besides, do you really want to know about me and my oddities? How about if we start with this and see where our relationship goes. Think of it as a sweet kiss on the cheek at the end of our first date...I won't go all the way unless I know that we are in a committed relationship.

Never one to follow the rules, I always did things the hard way. Why go to school on your parent's dime, when it's so much more fun to do double duty as student/ parent and graduate in your late twenties? Why have 2.5 kids, when you can have 4? Why be the typical stay at home mom, when you can be the pierced, tatted PTSO President? And the list of conundrums goes on and on.

But it wasn't my story that I found inspiration from; it was every story. Every story that I read over the last two years made an impact. I fell in love with the writings of sexy Alpha Bikers, of the wicked CEO's, the shape shifters, the wild Rockers and yes, even the brawlers. I wanted to bring to life a heroine that encompasses all the strength, the wealth, the deceptiveness as any of those Alphas we readers claim as our BBF (Book Boy Boyfriend for those of you new to this world). And much like our beloved Alphas, Charlie too, is in need of salvation. Her carefully composed and categorized life is about to take a spill. The question is, how far will she bend for those she loves? How far do any of us really change for our loved ones? And more importantly, is it the right move?

www.ingramcontent.com/pod-product-compliance
Lightning Source LLC
Chambersburg PA
CBHW051951240626
47153CB00005B/1709

* 9 7 8 0 6 9 2 8 9 9 8 4 7 *